PET

Catherine Chidgey

PET

Europa
editions

Europa Editions
27 Union Square West, Suite 302
New York NY 10003
www.europaeditions.com
info@europaeditions.com

Library of Congress Cataloging in Publication Data is available
ISBN 978-1-60945-930-7

Chidgey, Catherine
Pet

Art direction by Emanuele Ragnisco
instagram.com/emanueleragnisco

Cover design and illustration by Ginevra Rapisardi

Prepress by Grafica Punto Print – Rome

Printed in Canada

CONTENTS

For my sister Helen,
who remembers

P E T

2014

CHAPTER 1

I know it's Mrs Price, and I know it can't be Mrs Price: that's what I keep thinking. My eyes are playing tricks on me, or the light is, or my memory is. For one thing, this woman looks to be in her thirties, which makes her far too young . . . apart from anything else. And yet she has the same wavy blond hair, the same high cheekbones. Even the voice could be hers.

'Let's get you settled in your chair, Mr Crieve,' she says, leading my father to his recliner. She's just showered him, and his skin is pink and soft, his face freshly shaved. I can smell Old Spice. He leans heavily on her arm as he takes step after slow step across the tiny room. She is stronger than she looks. 'You'll feel better now you've had a shower,' she says, positioning him in front of his chair. 'All nice and clean for your visitors.'

'I'm his daughter,' I say. 'Justine.' Stupidly I hold out my hand, but of course she can't shake it; she is still holding on to my father.

'I know all about you,' she says, and flashes me a smile, her warm brown eyes crinkling at the corners. The same smile I remember. The same eyes.

My daughter Emma, twelve years old, sits on the bed and picks at her nail polish, peeling away shreds of bubblegum pink. Dad eyes her.

'Have you hung up your school uniform?' he says.

'Always,' says Emma, which is true: she never needs reminding to keep her things tidy.

He points a wobbly finger at her. 'This is my daughter Justine,' he says to the woman. 'I bet she's telling fibs. I bet if I checked her room, the uniform would be in a heap. We're always on at her.'

Emma just smiles. 'I made you some gingerbread,' she says, sliding the container onto the bedside table. 'Your favourite.' She has such kindness in her – from her father, I suppose.

'Now feel for the chair with the back of your legs, Mr Crieve,' says the woman. 'Reach for the arms . . . that's right . . . and down we go. Good.'

I sit next to Emma on the bed and watch, feel the familiar guilt rise in my throat – but I can't look after him myself. I can't comb his hair and cut his toenails, dress him and undress him. I can't wash him. Most of all, perhaps, on the bad days I can't keep explaining that he doesn't have to get back to the shop, that nobody has robbed him, that Emma isn't his daughter and I am not his wife returned from the dead. Everyone agrees he is in the best place.

'So handsome,' says the woman, tucking the tips of his collar inside his cardigan – although it's not his cardigan. The laundry is always mixing up his clothes with those of the other residents. 'You look like you're ready to hit the town,' she says. 'Get up to no good.'

'You never know,' he says. 'Maybe I'll sneak out after dark.'

She laughs. 'Naughty man! Off to the casino, is it? Off to the nightclubs, wowing all the girls? You'd better watch out for this one, Justine.'

'I will,' I say. 'I do.'

She nods, pats my hand. 'He's lucky to have you.'

I can't take my eyes off her. Surely Dad sees it too. Surely some part of him remembers. *Sonia*, says a badge pinned to her smart floral tunic. One of those uniforms that's meant to look like normal clothes. The retirement community prides itself on its personal approach, so the residents really feel they've come home. Those in the stand-alone townhouses can even bring a cat or a bird when they move in, if they have an existing cat or bird. No replacement cats or birds can be acquired after the old ones die, though – and Dad isn't in a stand-alone townhouse, he's in a premium room.

'I'll leave you three to it, then,' says Sonia.

I want to talk to her, ask her if she knew Mrs Price – but what can I say? How can I ever explain that story? Though I've had thirty years to think about it, thirty years to go over every detail. The great dark hulk of it always adrift in me.

'Curious Questions in the main lounge at three, don't forget,' she says. 'You need to defend your title.'

'Too right,' says my father.

And then she is gone.

'She's new,' I say.

'Someone new every few months,' he says. 'They don't pay them enough.'

'Doesn't she remind you of anyone?'

'Who?'

'You really don't see it?'

'Who?' says Emma.

'I don't know what you're getting at,' he says, and picks up his newspaper, hands me the real-estate section. I'm always looking for a new place.

'Brick,' he says, tapping a property he's circled. 'Nice and solid. Won't rot.'

He's having a good day, then, and we're supposed to make the most of the good days. I should stay and chat in his premium room, or take him for a walk in the grounds, which really are lovely, with their benches in the shade of oaks and maples and their heady beds of roses. Polite gardeners who nod hello while they clip away at something, train something, keep it all in check.

But I am twelve years old again.

1984

CHAPTER 2

I was lying on my stomach in the late afternoon, running my fingers through the straw-dry grass and unknotting the tousled weeds that grew along our fence line. Down deep, where the sun didn't reach, the stalks were as white as exposed bone. Slaters hurried about in their segmented armour, while a centipede, dislodged from under its dead leaf, looked for a new place to hide. Gently I covered it over again. There at the bottom of our hilly garden you couldn't see the harbour but you could smell it. Arum lilies and hydrangeas grew in great clusters, and the apple tree dropped its sour little windfalls, and nobody could ask me how I was coping. I poked at an empty snail shell, blew on it so it skittered away. Up in the spotless house, curtains drawn, my father listened to his sad records and drank his sad drinks. The sun, still searing just past the end of summer, scraped at my shoulders and neck, and I knew I should go back inside and make my father's dinner while he sat in the darkened living room mumbling *Beth*, *Beth*, *Beth*. I should bring him corned beef with a dob of mustard, just the way he liked it, and potatoes boiled in their skins, and ice cream with tinned peaches, the syrup pooling at the bottom of the plate. I should let him tell me I was his best girl, and how lucky was he? And then I should scour the kitchen sink until it gleamed, and polish the taps that showed me my own face all misshapen and wrong, and iron the tea towels with their pictures of birds and maps and castles, folding them into squares to fit on the tea-towel shelf – but not yet. Just a bit longer with the weeds and the dirt, the empty shells and the dead leaves and the frantic hiss of cicadas. The sunburnt grass as light as nothing.

A twinge in my temple. I sat up, sat back on my heels, steadied myself. I was fine. Fine. But was it the sun? My head felt high and hollow, and I could taste burnt sugar, and no, it wasn't the sun but my own body about to turn on me again. Hadn't I grown out of it? Hadn't the pills worked? I looked at my hands, and they were strange hands, and the garden was a strange garden, the arum lilies looming at me like birds with skinny yellow beaks, the sky hazy, covered with plastic, and I could hear my mother's voice though I knew it was not real: *I'm home*. And here it came, the seizure, thundering through the hot air, knocking me to the ground.

When I opened my eyes I was lying on the couch, facing the deep-buttoned back. I blinked. Slowly the threads of pale blue and dark blue and white joined into their upholstered pattern: an old-fashioned lady sitting on a swing in a flouncy dress, her waist pulled in tight, her feet the tiniest slippered nubs. Ribbons trailing in the breeze. Cherubs. Butterflies.

I touched my fingers to the bump on my temple.

'Oh, love,' said my father.

'I was in the garden,' I said. 'Wasn't I?'

'You're fine, everything's fine,' he said.

'How did I get inside?'

'I helped you. Here, drink this.'

'I don't remember.'

The water swishing the taste of blood across my tongue.

Once, when I was little, I'd held a stolen coin in my mouth so no one would take it from me: that was the taste.

'I thought the pills had worked,' I said. 'I thought I'd grown out of it.'

'We'll go back to Dr Kothari. I imagine it's trial and error.'

'What does that mean?'

'Well, we might have to try the pills again.'

'No. They make my mouth dry and give me the shakes. Can't we just see how it goes?'

'Maybe he can give us something different to try, until we get it right.'

'It *was* right, though. I thought I didn't need the pills any more.'

'I'm sorry, love.' He poured himself another drink.

In a small voice I said, 'What if it happens at school?'

'Mrs Price will look after you.'

'They'll think I'm a freak.'

'Mrs Price won't let them.'

I was silent for a moment. Then I said, 'Can we see how it goes?'

He sighed, nodded. 'One more seizure, though, and it's back to Dr Kothari. You could hurt yourself, love, and we can't have that. We just can't.'

I don't recall much about the rest of that day – I usually suffered memory loss from a seizure and sometimes couldn't account for hours of time – but one detail has stayed with me through the years: watching *The Love Boat* while I lay with my head on my father's lap. As the opening song played, Captain Stubing looked through his binoculars, and Isaac the bartender put fruit on the rim of a glass, and Julie the cruise director beamed in front of the Sydney Harbour Bridge because she was supposed to be marrying an Australian, though he sounded nothing like an Australian and would in fact leave her at the altar because he was dying and loved her too much. And Vicki, the captain's daughter, who had the same haircut as I did, stood on the deck in her sailor suit with all the blue ocean behind her. Vicki, who lived on the ship and got to visit Puerto Vallarta and Acapulco and Mazatlán, and what would that be like, to live in so many different places but also no place at all?

'Where are they?' I said.

'What?' said my father.

'When they're sailing, which country are they in?'

'Hmm,' he said.

'And what if someone dies on board? What happens then?'

'No one dies on *The Love Boat*.'

'But in real life.'

'A captain can bury people at sea,' he said. 'He can marry people, and he can bury people.'

'You can't dig a hole in water,' I said. I felt too heavy to move.

'It's an expression.'

I knew that Vicki was actually much older; if you watched the credits at the end of the programme, and squinted to read the year in tiny Roman numerals, you could tell that New Zealand was years behind and we were watching the past.

And my father stroked my ear as the passengers filed on board, the sound of his hand the sound of the ocean.

CHAPTER 3

In the morning I could still feel the remains of the seizure: mud in my head, mud in my legs. My father said I could stay home if I liked, but I wanted to go to school because Mrs Price had promised us a surprise – a surprise and a test, though not one we could study for. I made sure I had my special pen. My mother had bought it for me when she took the ferry to the South Island, just before she was diagnosed. I could keep it as a souvenir, she'd said, and she showed me the tiny white ship inside that slid back and forth when you tilted it, gliding into the green of the Sounds, gliding into the open ocean. I tried not to use it too much, because I didn't want the ink to run out, but I always wrote my tests with it. I thought it brought me luck. The talismans we cling to.

'What do you think the surprise is?' I whispered to my best friend Amy as we took our places at our desks.

'Maybe something to eat?' said Amy. 'Some more of her Russian fudge?'

Mrs Price had brought a batch to class in the first week of term. If we were good, she'd said, there'd be more treats, because good things happened to good people. And every boy and girl had sat up straight then, and nodded, and listened, and spoken when it was their turn to speak, not just because of the good things in their future, the treats, but because they wanted to please her. She was new to town and new to St Michael's that year, and younger than our parents, and prettier than our mothers, who wore fawn slacks and plastic rain bonnets. She made us feel special just by the way she looked at us, as if we had something important to say and she couldn't wait to hear it. Often she'd rest a hand on our shoulders like an old friend, then lean in and listen. Laugh when we wanted her to laugh. Offer kind words before we knew we needed them. Tell us how bright we were, what original thinkers. If we came to school with a new haircut we really weren't sure about, she'd put her hands on her hips and say, 'Look out, David Bowie!' or 'Christie Brinkley, eat your heart out!' When she sent home a note asking if one or two fathers could come on Saturday to fix up the wobbly desks and chairs, a dozen men showed up, hammers and drills at the ready. The story was that her husband and daughter had died in a car accident, though nobody quite knew when or how, or whether she had been in the car at the time, and nobody liked to ask. Each morning she arrived at school in a white Corvette with the steering wheel on the wrong side, the American side, and it had no back seat and no boot, so where on earth did she put her groceries? But perhaps she ordered takeaways like people on TV; perhaps she ate in French restaurants where candlelight caught in gigantic mirrors. Glass bangles clicked at her wrists, and she wore her wavy blond hair with a deep fringe like Rebecca De Mornay in *Risky Business* – not that we'd been allowed to see the film, because it wasn't suitable. Around her neck a gold crucifix with a tiny gold figure of Jesus, all ribs and thorns.

I lifted the lid of my desk and put away my exercise books. At the start of term I'd covered them with leftover wallpaper from home: the stripes from my bedroom for Religion, Maths, Social Studies and Science, the bunches of fuchsias from the dining room for Language and Reading. My mother had chosen the patterns when she first got sick, pinning the samples to the wall and scrutinising them at different times of day, in different lights. She wanted the house to be perfect, she'd said. I hadn't understood.

I double-checked that I had my special pen in my Care Bears pencil case.

'What's that?' said Melissa Knight, who sat on the other side of me.

I showed it to her, tilting it to make the ship move.

'Can I have a go?'

I hesitated, then handed it over. 'Careful,' I said. 'It's very valuable.'

Melissa had long caramel-coloured hair and pierced ears and a spa pool, and I could never be her, though Amy and I practised her walk and her laugh. One lunchtime, too, we folded down the tops of our tunics and knotted our blouses above our belly buttons like Melissa did. When Paula de Vries saw us she whispered something in Melissa's ear, but Melissa didn't even care, because she wasn't mean the way some pretty girls with pierced ears could be mean.

Mrs Price was standing at the front of the classroom, watching us, waiting for us all to settle down. Melissa gave me back the pen.

'Today, people,' said Mrs Price – she called us people instead of children, which made us feel responsible – 'we're learning about the eye.'

She asked Melissa to hand out a cyclostyled diagram, because Melissa was one of her pets. It wasn't fair, but what could anyone do? The tingly smell of the purple ink rose from the newsprint sheets, and we followed with our fingers as Mrs Price pointed out the cornea, the sclera, the retina, the optic nerve, and then we wrote the names in our neatest handwriting and added arrows to show the right spots on the drawings that didn't look much like eyes. I forced myself to concentrate; I was still groggy from the seizure.

'Of course,' said Mrs Price, as if she knew what we were thinking, 'the best way to learn is to see the thing for ourselves, isn't it?'

She smiled her special smile and walked to the back of the classroom, and there on the activity tables, hidden under a cloth so as not to ruin the surprise, were rows of scissors and scalpels and sharp little tools like the dental nurse used in our mouths. She took the lid off an ice-cream container, and Karl Parai said, 'Strawberry ripple!' in his deep new voice that had arrived over summer, but Mrs Price laughed and said no, definitely not strawberry ripple, and inside the container sat a pile of eyes. Cows' eyes. Enough for one between two.

'Mr Parry was kind enough to supply these,' she said, 'so make sure you thank him next time you're in his shop.'

Leanne Parry beamed; she had kept the surprise to herself, the secret, and now Mrs Price was singling her out for it. Mr Parry was the local butcher who gave every child a slice of luncheon sausage whenever they went with their parents to buy their meat. 'You look like you could do with some fattening up,' he'd say, winking as he weighed chops or sharpened his big silver knife. He gave out pencils sometimes, too: metallic green, with *Parry's Meats High Street* running down the side, but I'd never used my one – never even sharpened it – because it was too nice. Then I'd lost it.

'All right, people, find a partner,' said Mrs Price, and Amy grabbed my hand and held on tight, too tight.

'I don't think I want to do this,' she whispered, but already Mrs Price was handing out the eyes with a soup spoon and the pairs of children were taking their places at the dissecting trays. I had the feeling I had seen this moment before: the trays, the rows of glittering tools. The dead eyes looking in all directions. My own hand reaching for something sharp. Strange thoughts often followed a seizure; I tried to blink them away.

'First of all,' said Mrs Price, 'let's trim off what we don't need – all the scraggy bits from around the edges, yes? Use your scissors to snip them free, or your scalpel. These are the remains of the eyelid, and the muscles that move the eye.'

I offered the scissors to Amy, but she shook her head.

'Don't be afraid to handle it firmly,' said Mrs Price, walking around the tables. 'You'd be surprised how tough it is. Good, Melissa. *Good*, Leanne.' She rested a hand on Leanne's shoulder and watched as she neatly removed the trailing pieces of flesh.

Picking up our specimen, I began to cut. I still felt so heavy in my limbs.

'Careful to leave the optic nerve,' said Mrs Price. 'The little stump at the back. Your cow can't see without it.'

The eye was slippery under my fingers, like the grapes Amy and I peeled when we played Slaves. I thought I could make out some eyelashes. I pushed the scraps to the edge of the tray.

'Now, look at the cornea. Can everyone find the cornea? You'll see that it's cloudy blue – this is what happens in death. In life it's clear, like a plastic bag filled with water, to let the light through.'

'Death?' said Amy. 'Death?' She pushed her thick black plait over her shoulder as if it might touch something dreadful.

'Duh,' said Karl, and he waggled his cow's eye at her and made a mooing sound.

Mrs Price showed us how to snip right around the eyeball to cut it in half, though we mustn't push the scissors in too deep because that would damage the lens. I had worried I might feel disgusted, might even have another seizure, but it was no different from chopping up chicken for a casserole or touching the muscular foot of a snail, and the jelly inside the eye no worse than egg white. And how easily it all came apart, one hemisphere detaching from the other, a severed world. Mrs Price pointed out the blind spot, where the optic nerve attached to the back of the eye and there were no light receptors. We couldn't see anything at that point, she said, but our brains filled in the gaps for us without our even noticing, and wasn't that amazing? Wasn't God amazing?

Amy was leaning in now, poking the lens with the probe.

'Make sure you're taking note of all this, people,' said Mrs Price. 'Make sure you're remembering. It's important.'

Next we cut out the cornea and studied the pupil, which she told us meant *orphan* – a child looked after by an adult, taught by an adult – but it also meant *little doll*, because of the tiny reflections of ourselves we saw in another person's eyes. I checked: and yes, there I was in Amy's pupils, a shadow girl caught in the curve of black.

'Do you see that the pupil is just a hole?' said Mrs Price. 'We think it's something solid, that black dot, don't we, but in reality there's nothing there.'

Next to me Melissa had turned pale, all the blood gone from her lips and cheeks. When she started to gag I leapt away, and the vomit just missed my foot. The puddle glistened on the floorboards between us, full of bad and bitter things.

'Oh sweetheart,' said Mrs Price. 'Come away. Come and sit down.' She led Melissa to the front of the classroom and settled her in the story chair, brought her a glass of water.

'I'm really sorry,' said Melissa.

'Nonsense,' said Mrs Price, stroking her hair. 'God made some of us more sensitive than others, and that's a beautiful thing – yes? Never apologise for it.'

Melissa nodded, her face as white and lovely as a saint's, while the rest of us watched and wished we were sitting in the story chair, and that Mrs Price was stroking our hair and talking to us in her kind and quiet voice, and if only we'd thought to vomit.

'Hey Justine,' whispered Karl, and when I turned to him he lunged for my chest, shoved his hand inside my blouse. Something slithered down my skin, a cool wet mass that came to rest at the waistband of my tunic. I knew he wanted me to scream.

'Is that a cow's eye?' I said.

He was laughing too hard to answer.

I untucked my blouse and the thing plopped to the floor like some kind of clot, some awful part of me expelled from my body.

'You're such a moron, Karl,' said Amy, but I didn't think she meant it, because we had both agreed he looked like a Māori John Travolta, and we'd written his name in biro on our shoulders and thighs where nobody could see. I tucked myself in again and returned to my work, picking up my probe and starting to ease the retina away from the blind spot behind it.

'All right, people, I need a volunteer,' said Mrs Price. 'Who's going to clean this up for us?' She waved at the vomit.

No one raised their hand.

'You know we're a team,' she said. 'A family. We help one another.'

Silence.

'Do I need to choose someone myself?'

'I'll do it,' said a voice next to me.

And there was the smile we all lived for, spilling across Mrs Price's beautiful face.

'Amy! Thank you, my darling. Go and see Mr Armstrong for a cloth and bucket.'

At lunchtime we went to the adventure playground where everything was immense, like the contents of a giant's garden: huge tractor tyres set in concrete, and a row of stormwater pipes we could crawl right inside, and great wooden spools that had once held steel cable, and a climbing rope that stretched higher than was safe, surely, and that burned our hands and legs when we shinnied back down to the ground. Some of the younger girls were playing elastics, jumping in and out of the long stretchy band they hooked around their ankles, then knees, then thighs. *England, Ireland, Scotland, Wales*, they chanted. *Inside, outside, puppy-dogs' tails.* Tangling and untangling themselves. Over on the field, other children gathered up handfuls of dry grass clippings and built them into hand-high walls. *This is the living room. This is the bedroom. Here's the kitchen. That's the front door.* The bossier ones assigned roles: *I'm the mum and you're the baby. I'm the big sister and you're the grandma. You're the dad and I'm a robber. You have to do what I say.* Amy and I climbed into the stormwater pipes and leaned back against the cool interior. We opened our lunchboxes, and I gave Amy one of my cheese and Vegemite sandwiches, and she gave me one of her pork dumplings. Mostly she brought sandwiches or a filled roll, like the rest of us – she'd told her mother not to give her foreign things – but now and then Mrs Fong insisted on using up the leftovers. I loved those days; we always swapped. We could hear Melissa and Paula talking on top of the pipes, where they were trying to get a suntan.

'Oh my gosh,' Paula was saying, 'are you okay? Maybe you should go to the sick bay. Make sure it's nothing serious.'

'It was the eyes, that's all,' said Melissa. 'When we opened them up. The smell of them.'

'I didn't think they smelled of anything,' said Paula.

'What? It was in my hair and clothes, on my skin . . . you couldn't get away from it.'

'I really don't remember that.'

'Let's talk about something else.'

'Do you remember a smell?' I whispered, and Amy shook her head. Maybe Melissa's brain was sending her a false message, the way mine did when a seizure was coming and I swore I could taste burnt sugar – but I didn't want to think about the seizures. They couldn't be starting up again. They couldn't.

'She called me her darling,' said Amy.

Even now I can see her hugging her knees to her chest. Though I wish I couldn't.

'What?' I said.

'Mrs Price. She called me her darling. First time ever.'

We would have done anything for her.

After lunch Mrs Price said, 'I hope you were paying attention this morning, people. We're going to do a little test now – just a little check to see if you remember the new words we learned. Amy, would you pass these around, please?'

And everyone knew why she chose Amy: Amy had cleaned up the vomit. And I thought that perhaps I should have volunteered to clean it up myself, because who knew what privileges might now come Amy's way? But when she gave a sheet to Karl Parai he sniffed the place where her hand had been and said he could smell sick, and the whole class laughed even though Mrs Price said it wasn't funny.

'So all you need to do is label the parts of the eye,' she said. 'It shouldn't take long – five minutes at the most.'

I looked in my pencil case for my special pen, but I couldn't find it. Not in my pencil case, not in my desk, not on the floor. Nowhere.

'Off you go,' said Mrs Price, and everyone started to write. Everyone except me. I raised my hand. My arm twice as heavy as it should have been.

'Yes, Justine?'

'I've lost my pen.'

Titters from around the classroom.

'Don't you have a spare? Or a pencil?'

'It's my special pen.'

More titters.

'Are you being smart, Justine?'

'No, Mrs Price.'

'Do you have another pen?'

'Yes.'

'Then use that.'

I stared at the diagram of the eye, the empty lines waiting for their labels. I couldn't remember a single answer. Mud in my head, my hands, my arms, my legs. Next to me Amy was filling in the last gap and sitting back. I could have turned my head to read the answers – I could have, I could have, and Amy wouldn't have minded – but I was no cheat. Outside the classroom window the sunflowers swayed on thick green stems, and bees heavy with heat circled the dark centres. And still I couldn't remember, and Mrs Price was saying, 'Just one more minute,' and there was not enough time. I wrote my name at the top of the page. Underlined it. At the front of the room the Virgin Mary gazed out from her picture frame, her heart full of roses and fire.

'All right, people, you'll be marking your neighbour's work, so pass your tests to the left, please,' said Mrs Price.

Melissa handed hers to me, and I handed my own to Amy. Karl made to pass his out the open window.

'Obviously,' said Mrs Price, 'if you're on the end of a row, you stand up and take your test to the person at the start. I shouldn't have to tell you these things. You're not little children any more.' But she wasn't angry with us the way our other teachers used to get angry with us. It was like we were sharing a joke, like we were part of a special club.

Karl grinned at me as he passed. Black hair flopping over his forehead. Eyes flecked with gold.

'All right, what's the first answer?' said Mrs Price, and the class said, 'Cornea.'

'Correct,' she said, and I ticked Melissa's work. 'And the second?'

'Sclera,' everyone except me said. Another tick. Out of the corner of my eye I could see Amy putting big crosses on my empty test, racing ahead to the last gap, because it was clear I hadn't written a thing.

'Excellent,' Mrs Price was saying. 'I'm very pleased with you, class.'

When they'd finished she got everyone to call out the marks so she could enter them into her blue book, which meant it was a real test, though she hadn't told us so. Most people scored five out of five; there were a few fours and one three.

'And Justine?' said Mrs Price.

'Nothing,' said Amy.

'What do you mean, nothing?'

'Nothing. Zero. She didn't write anything.'

'Oh dear,' said Mrs Price.

'Well, she wrote her name at the top,' said Melissa, leaning across to peer at the page. She patted my arm. 'You got that right.'

Everyone laughed.

'All right, thank you,' said Mrs Price. 'There's no need to make fun of someone when they fail.'

'I wasn't making fun,' said Melissa, but Mrs Price held up her hand and said, 'Let's move on,' and Melissa was no longer part of the special club, which was the worst feeling ever.

'I wasn't making fun,' Melissa whispered to me as she returned my test.

I nodded and shoved it deep inside my desk, underneath the exercise books that looked like bits of home, the little walls of a dismantled house. I took a deep breath in and held it. Dr Kothari had said that moments of high emotion could trigger a seizure; I wasn't going to let myself cry.

When the bell rang I could hardly wait to escape. I put away my books, lifted my chair on top of my desk and headed for the door with Amy, but Mrs Price said, 'Justine? May I see you for a moment?'

And hadn't I longed for that? Hadn't I dreamed of Mrs Price asking me to run an errand for her, or help her in the classroom after school? Every day her favourites – her pets – stayed behind and clapped the blackboard dusters together, closed the top windows with the long, long cords which they looped around hooks so nobody choked themselves. They polished the brass candlesticks on the altar to Mary and picked fresh flowers from the convent garden to put in her cut-glass vase. The really lucky ones got to go to the shops at lunchtime to collect things for Mrs Price: her dry cleaning, her prescriptions, her tins of diet milkshake powder that made you feel full. She'd give them money from her wallet – and sometimes even the wallet itself – and if there was any change they were allowed to stop at the dairy for sweets: paper bags crammed with chewy milk bottles and jet planes and spearmint leaves and Eskimos, or little boxes of sugary white sticks with a red dot on one end to make them look like lit cigarettes. Elegantly the pets held these between their fingers, strolling through the playground past less favoured children, flicking away imaginary ash.

'I need to see you too, Melissa,' said Mrs Price. 'Leanne, you can clean the blackboard dusters outside, please. No one else today.' She waited until the others had left the classroom and then she said, 'Melissa, I think you owe Justine an apology.'

'Sorry, Justine,' said Melissa.

'Why are you apologising to the floor?'

Melissa raised her eyes to me. 'Sorry, Justine.'

'For?' said Mrs Price.

'For, um, hurting your feelings?'

'For making fun of you,' said Mrs Price.

'For making fun of you,' said Melissa.

'And I know it was wrong, and I promise not to do it again.'

'And I know it was wrong, and I promise not to do it again.'

'Justine, do you accept Melissa's apology?'

Melissa looked like she wanted to cry. It was horrible – and yet I paused before I answered. Watched her fidget with her pretty hairband, the collar of her blouse. 'I suppose so,' I said at last.

'All right then,' said Mrs Price. 'Melissa, you can go, but you'll need to do some serious thinking about your behaviour. About the kind of person you want to be. Yes?'

'Yes. Thank you,' said Melissa, her face burning red. She all but ran from the classroom.

Mrs Price waited until she'd gone and then motioned for me to sit down in the story chair. I'd never sat there before. 'What happened this afternoon, my darling?' she said, settling herself on the edge of her desk. 'With the test?'

'Am I in trouble?' I said.

'Trouble? No – I'm just a bit worried. From what I've seen so far, you're one of the brightest in the class. What happened?'

'I . . . I had a seizure yesterday,' I said.

'Oh,' she said. 'I didn't realise.'

'Sometimes I feel strange afterwards . . . sleepy and, and heavy . . . not myself. Like my body isn't mine and my memory isn't mine.'

'My poor darling,' she said. 'I'm glad you've told me. You know you can tell me anything, yes?'

I nodded.

Leanne burst back in with the blackboard dusters, her hands powdery with chalk.

'Finished!' she said. 'Is there anything else?'

'Just pop them on the ledge, thanks, Leanne,' said Mrs Price.

'Sure! Any other jobs?' It was the first time she'd been asked to help, and I could see the hunger shining in her eyes.

'Not today, thanks.'

'Okay.' Leanne didn't move.

'I need to talk to Justine now.'

'Oh, okay. Thank you. Thanks.'

'We thought I'd grown out of the seizures,' I said when Leanne had left. I felt very small, sitting there in the story chair, Mrs Price looking down at me from above. The light was behind her, and her hair glowed buttery soft; I wanted to reach up and touch it.

'What was all that about the pen?' she said.

'I couldn't find it. I know it was in my pencil case this morning – I showed it to Melissa.' My voice began to shake.

'But you had another one. I don't understand.'

I studied my hand. The mole on the first knuckle, the

branching veins. The hangnail that hurt when I pressed it. I pressed it. 'My mother gave it to me,' I said. 'As a souvenir.'

'Oh yes?' said Mrs Price, and waited.

'My mother . . .' I began. The scar on my thumb from when I'd picked up broken glass before I knew better. The half-moons rising from my nail beds. The hangnail that hurt. I pressed it again.

'Your mother?' she said.

'She died last year.'

'Oh my love. Oh my sweetheart.' She was crouching next to the story chair, putting her arm around me. I could smell her perfume: jasmine and honeysuckle, or something like it. 'They should have told me,' she said. 'All these things I don't know about you. All these important things.' She squeezed my shoulder, and we sat there for a moment. She didn't say that everything happens for a reason, and she didn't say that time heals – I knew it couldn't, because the more of it that passed, the further away from me my mother slipped. The corridor outside the classroom was quiet now, the school grounds empty, though I could see one of the nuns in the convent garden behind the adventure playground: Sister Bronislava, just visible through the gap in the cypress hedge, cutting a head of lettuce. Mrs Price said, 'You're a very strong person, Justine, I can tell. You don't even know what's inside you.'

'I want my pen back,' I said. I knew I sounded like a baby, but it was true.

'Of course you do, my darling.' She paused. 'You said you showed it to Melissa this morning?'

'Yes, before school.'

'Hmm,' she said. 'You're not friends with Melissa, are you?'

'Not really.'

'But you'd like to be?'

I nodded.

'Girls like Melissa . . .' she said. '*Everyone* wants to be their friend. They don't have to try.' She patted me on the knee. 'Now, this mark of yours. This zero. It won't do.'

'No, Mrs Price. I'm sorry.' I had disappointed her, I could tell.

She opened her blue book, tapped her finger on the zero next to my name – and then she took a bottle of Twink, whited out the zero and wrote a five in its place. 'There,' she said. 'All fixed.'

'But . . . is that allowed?' I said, and she laughed.

'My classroom, my pupils,' she said. 'My rules.'

'Thank you.'

She waved a hand. 'I know you'll earn it.'

'I will. I will,' I said.

'You do look sleepy, though. Shall I give you a lift home? You're not far from me, I think.'

'I help Dad in the shop after school on Fridays.'

'Which shop is that, my darling?' She was taking a little brown bottle from her handbag and swallowing a pill, then hitching the bag over her shoulder, ready to go.

'Passing Time Antiques.'

Dad was talking to a customer, examining a figurine she wanted to sell: a little girl dressed as a shepherdess.

'She was my mother's,' the woman was saying. 'She always sat on the mantelpiece. We were never allowed to touch her.'

My father tented the figurine under a thick dark cloth he kept behind the counter and shone his black light over the piece, looking for damage invisible to the naked eye. 'Here, you see?' he said, pointing to the back of the shepherdess's head. 'A repair. She must have taken a knock.'

'Not that I remember,' said the woman. 'We've always been so careful.'

'Maybe someone dropped her and didn't own up. She's not worth much in this condition, I'm afraid.'

Those were the words he used whenever he had to deliver bad news to a customer: I'm afraid. *I'm afraid this is a reproduction. I'm afraid nobody wants these now. I'm afraid this is of little value. I'm afraid this is beyond repair.* He seemed genuinely sad for the woman – but then, he'd seemed sad most of the time since my mother had died. 'Come here, love,' he'd say to me when he was drinking. 'You're not going anywhere, are you?' And I'd tell him no, I wasn't going anywhere. He'd tuck my hair behind my ears and call me his best girl, and ask why my mother had to leave, which was a question I couldn't answer, but that didn't stop him asking. He was sorry, he said, for being such a mess, and he knew he was the parent and I was the child and not the other way round, and soon, he promised, he'd pull himself together and get on with life, because there was nothing else for it, just nothing else. Then, in the morning, he'd shower and shave, gulp two coffees and head for the shop, almost back to normal, as far as most people could tell.

Mrs Price was looking around, peering in chests of drawers, touching the hair of a porcelain doll and making its glass eyes close. Another customer – a man about my father's age, wearing a navy-blue suit and a big showy wristwatch – sidled over to her and said, 'You seem like a lady with excellent taste. Do you reckon I should blow six hundred bucks on that?' He pointed to a stag's head mounted on the wall.

'For yourself?' she said.

'Yeah,' he said. 'For the dining room. A conversation piece, you know?'

'Hmm,' she said, reaching up to feel the stag's dusty fur as if to assess its quality. 'That depends on what sort of conversation you want to have.'

'Well, how about, *Will you have a drink with me?*' His eyes were all over her, darting from her lips to her legs to her chest.

She laughed. 'That's a strange thing to ask someone who's already in your dining room.'

'Sense of humour,' he said. 'Like it.'

'To be honest,' she whispered, 'I think it's a steal.'

'Yeah? I mean it's small change to me, right, six hundred, but I was planning on making a lowball offer. You see how faded that is?' He pointed to the price tag. 'Been here for ages.'

'Not much call for stags round here, maybe.'

'Three-fifty tops, I reckon,' he went on. 'Maybe that's an insult, but do I look like I care? Thrill of the chase, etcetera.'

'Cheeky,' she said.

'Oh I can be. I can be.' He was smirking, sliding a business card from his wallet. 'Maybe you can help me get it up,' he said. 'The stag.'

'Maybe I can,' she said. 'I'll check with my husband.' And she turned away, rolling her eyes at me across the shop.

'Hey, wait on,' said the man, the hand with the big showy watch reaching out to grab her elbow. 'You didn't say anything about a husband.'

'Sure I did. Just now.'

'Yeah, but before that.'

She shrugged, shook him off.

He paused, then said, 'Not a deal breaker, as far as I'm concerned.'

She laughed again, but it sounded different this time. 'I hope you and the stag have many happy years together,' she said.

His eyes narrowed. 'You know,' he hissed, 'it's bitches like you that give women a bad name.'

And he left.

'Are you all right?' I said, rushing over.

'Absolutely fine,' she said. 'But thank you, my darling. It's sweet of you to look out for me.'

'He shouldn't have called you that.'

'He showed his true colours. They always do, one way or another.'

'Who?'

'Men, my darling!'

'Oh.' I supposed she must have had to deal with that sort of thing all the time. But she'd enjoyed it, hadn't she? Teasing him in that clever way?

'So many beautiful things,' she said, opening an Edwardian lady's travelling case. She ran her fingers over the silver-topped bottles, the sky-blue silk lining.

'It has a secret compartment,' I said. 'See, there's a little button here, and when you press it—' The mirror in the lid lifted away, revealing a narrow storage space.

'For money?' she said.

'Or love letters.'

The woman with the shepherdess was wrapping her up in a pillowcase and saying, 'No no, it's not your fault, we should have realised,' and my father was saying, 'If there's ever anything else . . .'

On her way out of the shop the woman paused in front of a similar figurine – an undamaged milkmaid. She turned it upside-down to check the price, stared at it for a moment. Placed it gently back on the shelf.

'Hi darling,' said Dad, kissing me on the forehead. 'Who's this?'

'Mrs Price,' I said. 'She gave me a lift.'

'Ah, the famous Mrs Price.' He held out his hand. 'Everything all right?' He looked worried.

'Everything's fine,' she said. 'Justine was just a bit tired. And please, call me Angela.'

'Neil.'

His fingers were black with silver polish; they usually were. All these years later, decades after he had to let the shop go, I can still see the stuff caught in the whorls of his skin. I was embarrassed, but Mrs Price didn't seem to mind. As his eyes flicked up and down her body, she smiled a lingering half-smile. The air around her felt charged. Something was happening, and I was no part of it.

'It's kind of you to drop her off,' he said.

'My pleasure.' She stroked one of the crystal spears hanging from a Victorian lustre vase, and it tinkled against the others. 'My grandmother had a pair of these,' she said. 'She called them her earthquake vases because you could see them trembling at the slightest movement, even if you couldn't feel anything.'

'An early warning system?' said Dad.

'Yes!' She laughed. The spear was still swinging, scattering little bits of rainbow across the wall. How beautiful she looked, standing there in her cork-wedge sandals and her batik skirt, smoky sunglasses hooked in the V of her top. She began to fiddle with the tiny crucifix around her neck, the chain so fine it almost disappeared against the gold of her skin. 'I was very sorry to hear about Justine's mother,' she said. 'About your wife.'

My father nodded, back to his solemn self. 'Thank you.' There was nothing else to say.

CHAPTER 4

Amy and I were walking her cocker spaniel on the cliffs above the rocky beach – we went there most weekends, to let Bonnie have a good run around. Stunted, prickly shrubs flanked our way, blown into the shape of the slopes by the relentless wind, and clusters of feathery fennel swished and bobbed. Bonnie darted through the flax bushes that shook their hooked black seed pods like beaks. We knew never to stray far from the track, and certainly never to get anywhere near the edge; it was a long way down to the shore, where the kelp made shifting shadows in the water. Old gun emplacements and observation posts dotted that part of the coastline, looking out to the harbour's mouth for an enemy that never came. Sometimes we climbed inside them to feel the strange hush of the thick concrete walls, to run our fingers over the steel beams clotted with rust. A few times we'd seen Mrs Price jogging along the cliff track in her lime-green leggings, her candyfloss-pink crop-top, bright as some sleek tropical fish. That day we'd timed our walk for when we thought she might be there, and we were both keeping an eye out for her, wanting to be the first to say hello.

'Tell me what her car was like again,' said Amy.

'Black seats,' I said. 'Boiling hot when I first climbed in – I burned my legs.'

'What else?' Amy threw Bonnie's old chewed tennis ball, and the dog brought it straight back. Above us the seagulls glided on the wind, their bellies flashing white.

'A tape deck that played music when she pressed the button,' I said.

'What was the song?'

'The one about getting physical and hearing your body talk.'

Amy giggled, threw the ball into the wind again. 'What else, though?'

'A Saint Christopher medal stuck to the dashboard. And she looked in the mirror before we left school and put on some fresh lipstick. Pink, with little sparkles in it.'

'But what was the main thing about the car? What was the thing you did wrong?'

Amy knew already; she'd made me repeat the story a dozen times that week.

'I went to get in the wrong side, because it's an American car.'

'And what did Mrs Price say?'

'She said, *Do you want to get me arrested?*'

We laughed, but I could see myself in the driver's seat: smoky sunglasses shading my eyes, my lips shimmering as I sang along to the getting physical song and made up words for all the ones I didn't know.

I threw Bonnie's tennis ball, and she shot off after it. The wind lifted our light cotton skirts, and we had to keep holding them down for modesty's sake, though I liked the push and gush of it. I snatched at a fennel frond, crushed it in my palm to release the thick aniseed scent, while somewhere below us the waves destroyed themselves on the rocks.

'Not even Melissa's had a ride in that car,' said Amy.

'It was just because I wasn't feeling well,' I said.

'No. You're the new pet.'

'Don't be stupid.'

But Amy had been keeping watch, keeping count. 'She let you clean the blackboard on Wednesday, and you've read the morning prayer twice.'

Bonnie dropped the tennis ball at my feet and nudged my shoe, then looked up at me, waiting.

'I haven't really thought about it,' I said. A lie.

'Are you blind?' said Amy.

Bonnie nosed the ball closer to me, and I flung it ahead of us, all my weight behind it. I was aiming along the track, but the wind seized it and it veered towards the cliffs, bounced once, bounced twice, then disappeared over the edge. The dog streaked after it, her paws churning up the grass, and I heard Amy yell, 'No! Bonnie, no!' while I just stood there. Every gull in the sky began to shriek, as if they could see something terrible coming, something unstoppable. And on Bonnie ran, heading straight for the edge, and I shut my eyes while the gulls wheeled and screamed, and it was all my fault, my own stupid fault, and what would we tell our parents? Amy would hate me now, she would hate me forever, and I could never make it right – and then I heard her sobbing, 'Good girl. Good girl,' and I opened my eyes and saw her burying her face in Bonnie's neck. And of course she hadn't leapt to her death: of course pure dumb instinct had stopped her. Though Mum and Dad had warned me to keep close to the track at all times, I ran for Amy and Bonnie, and the three of us pressed ourselves low to the ground and gazed over the edge, tracing the path of a loosened stone as it tumbled down to the rocks, down to the waiting water.

I still dream about that sometimes.

Amy didn't speak to me on the way home. She clipped Bonnie's leash to her collar and strode off down the track, and I had to rush to keep up.

'It wasn't on purpose,' I said. 'Amy? I'd never do anything like that on purpose. You know I love Bonnie. I love her so much, she's like my own dog. Dad won't let me have a pet because I'll only get attached. Amy? Amy?' I was gabbling, I knew, but she gave no indication she even heard me. On she marched, her mouth a hard line.

'I'm sorry. I'm so sorry,' I kept saying. 'Will you just look at me? You can have my Care Bears pencil case if you like. You've always wanted one. *Please*, Amy!'

Whenever Bonnie stopped to sniff at something, Amy yanked on her leash. I was supposed to be staying at her house that night: what if she didn't speak to me the whole time? What would her parents think?

We were at the corner of their street when the idea came to me. She was still hurrying on ahead, but I grabbed at her hand, and when she tried to shake me off I said, 'I'll tell you something else about Mrs Price's car.'

She paused for a moment, shot me a sideways look. 'Like what?'

'It has a cigarette lighter, underneath the tape deck.'

'So?' she said. 'My dad's car has one of those.'

'Oh,' I said. 'Well, but I bet he doesn't let you smoke.'

'What?'

'She told me not to tell anyone.'

'Not to tell anyone what?'

Bonnie was whining, nudging Amy's foot for the lost tennis ball.

'After she put on her pink lipstick,' I said, 'she lit a cigarette. One of those menthol ones.' I was making it up as I went, but it felt true – Mrs Price wouldn't smoke just any cigarettes. 'Then she asked me if I wanted a try,' I said. That felt true too.

'She did not!' said Amy, but I knew I had her.

'She passed it to me, and I took a puff and blew it out like they do on TV.' I mimed this for Amy, my mouth a softly puckered O. 'It tasted pepperminty. Her lipstick was on it, but I didn't mind. I flicked the ash out the window and gave it back to her, and she said I mustn't tell anyone. So you can't either, okay?'

'Okay,' said Amy. 'Wow. Okay.'

When we got back to her house, Mrs Fong had made my

favourite: sweet and sour chicken with jasmine rice, which she served in dishes patterned with blue dragons. Around the edges translucent dots formed snowflakes and stars. Mrs Fong said that some people thought they were rice grains set in the clay, but really they were holes filled with glaze, and if you held a dish up to the window the light shone through. She kept them for special guests.

She asked me to say grace, and we all held hands like a family. Amy had told me they'd only become Catholics to fit in, and to get her and her little brother David into St Michael's, but it had stuck: they knew all the proper words at Mass – even at Benediction – and Father Lynch said they were a beautiful example of the reach of God's love right into other religions. They still had a shelf in their living room where they displayed family photos of dead people and burned incense by the statues of Chinese gods – the Goddess of Mercy was my favourite, with her gleaming white robes and her white crown. But they also had a table with a plastic Mary and Jesus who looked like they were made of icing, and on the wall a life-size photo of the Pope, with a crumbling sprig of cypress from last year's Palm Sunday tucked behind one corner and a little holy-water font from the Christian supplies shop underneath.

Mrs Fong said, 'Please, start while it's hot,' and Mr Fong and Amy and David picked up their chopsticks and began eating.

A pair of chopsticks sat next to my plate too. I tried to balance them between my fingers, but they kept sliding across each other, falling apart like pick-up sticks. When I did manage to grasp a piece of chicken, it plopped into my lap as soon as I lifted it.

'I forgot your fork!' said Mrs Fong when she noticed me struggling. 'Oh my goodness, you'll starve – you'll disappear! Amy, get Justine a fork, please.'

'I don't know what's so hard about it,' said Amy. 'David's been using chopsticks since he was three.'

'Don't be rude to your guest,' said her mother.

'Mrs Price can use chopsticks,' said Amy. 'She showed us, with two pencils.'

'She's very sophisticated,' I said. 'I think she's lived overseas.'

'Mum was *born* overseas,' said Amy. 'Dad went and got her from Hong Kong.'

'Mrs Price, Mrs Price,' said Amy's mother. 'All I ever hear these days.'

Bonnie lay in her basket, watching me with her big dark eyes. Amy had begged and begged her parents to let her have a dog, until finally, for her birthday, they took her to the SPCA to choose one. 'I saved her life,' Amy liked to tell me. 'She'll love me forever.'

Over dinner Mr Fong asked me about Dad's shop. The Fongs were in business too – they owned the fruit and vegetable place on High Street, where they stacked oranges and apples and grapefruit into impossible pyramids, arranged carrots and parsnips into the most exacting zigzagged stacks. Sometimes they tried things like star fruit and kumquats, but these were too exotic for most of their customers and didn't sell, not even on special when they needed to get rid of them. On a shelf near the back, a few imported items gathered dust: star anise, soya sauce and oyster sauce, prawn crackers, sesame oil, jasmine-flower tea made from real jasmine buds dried into little white knots. There were signs that said *Please Do Not Squeeze The Produce*, and a curved mirror like the back of a soup spoon that let the Fongs see into every corner of the shop. I think it's a hamburger place now; I've only been back once, and it was hard to tell what had been where. I hadn't wanted to linger.

'Say I want a dining table,' Mr Fong was saying to me, patting theirs with the flat of his hand. 'Why would I buy old instead of new?'

'Not old,' said Mrs Fong. 'Antique.'

Their house had mostly new furniture, though some of it was

meant to look Victorian. In the corner of the living room stood a black lacquered chest – the hundred-eye chest, they called it. The rows of tiny drawers were covered in Chinese writing; Amy kept her felt pens and scissors and dolls' clothes and glue and glitter in them, and her board games in the lower, larger cupboards. I had always wanted to have a proper look inside.

'An antique table doesn't cost much more than a new one,' I said. 'And it'll be better quality – solid wood. And not the same as everyone else's. Though yours is very nice,' I added.

'So used costs more than new?' said Mr Fong.

'Not used,' said Mrs Fong. 'Antique.'

'And used,' he said. 'And dearer.'

'But not like used cars. Used clothes.'

'Hmm,' he said. 'Where does he find it all? These used things?'

'Auctions,' I said. 'The For Sale page in the paper. Often people come to him when they have something to sell.'

'When someone has died,' he said.

I hadn't really considered that.

We still had all of my mother's belongings – her books and her shoes, her clothes, her sewing machine, her hairbrush.

'I don't know,' I said.

'When someone dies,' said Mr Fong, 'people often get rid of things. Try to make a bit of money.'

My mother's hairdryer with the big plastic hood. My mother's bicycle with the wicker basket on the front.

My father reading the death notices in the paper, circling certain ones.

'I don't . . .' I began. 'I'm not . . .'

Mrs Fong said something to her husband in Chinese, and he glanced at me, nodded. He didn't ask me anything more about where Dad found the things for the shop.

'How are you coping at home?' said Mrs Fong. 'You and your father.' I knew what she meant, though she was careful not to mention my mother directly.

'We're fine, thank you,' I said, and ate my sweet and sour chicken. Mrs Fong squeezed my hand, served me seconds and then thirds, and I ate those too.

'You're always welcome here, Justine,' she said. 'Isn't she, Eric?'

'Always welcome,' said Mr Fong. 'Any time.'

I still think about that.

After dinner Amy and I played Guess Who? and Operation. I couldn't seem to hold my hand steady and kept setting off the buzzer when I tried to tweezer out the Operation man's organs.

'You lose,' Amy said every time. 'You're the big fat loser.'

Later we went upstairs to have a bath and get into our pyjamas – we still bathed together at her house. Dad thought we were getting a bit old for it, though he wouldn't say why.

We lathered ourselves with her Scrubby Puppy: a plastic dog with foam rollers for feet, and a hole inside that held a cake of soap. The water turned milky with suds and we couldn't see ourselves below the waist, and we might have been mermaids swimming in a milky sea – that's what we pretended, what we sometimes still pretended.

'You've got bosoms,' said Amy.

'Not really,' I said.

'You have. Those are bosoms. You'll need to get a bra.'

She turned around so I could do her back, and I pushed her thick black hair out of the way, then rubbed the rollers over her spine and shoulder blades not because she was dirty but because it felt nice.

'Do they hurt?' she said. 'The bosoms?'

'No,' I said, but I thought of my mother after her operation. The thick dressings taped in place. The scars. I dipped the plastic dog in the water and rolled it back and forth over Amy. She had three little moles in a row just above her waist; I wondered if she knew. I said, 'Where do you even find a bra?'

'James Smith's. You have to strip naked and they grab them and measure them and then they hook you into one.'

'How do you know that?'

She shrugged her soapy shoulders.

'My turn,' I said. I handed her the dog and we both turned around. She began to work on my back.

'Who's the prettiest in the class?' she said.

This was one of our favourite games: ranking the girls. One of us asked the questions – 'Who's the prettiest? Who's the second prettiest?' – and then the other counted to three, and we both had to give our answer at the same time.

'One, two, three,' I counted, and we said, 'Melissa.'

She always took the top spot, and then usually Selena Kothari, the doctor's daughter, and then Rachel Jensen or Paula de Vries, once we'd discussed how they were doing their hair or whether they had sexy legs. We picked out their faults, too, which could affect their value depending on our moods – a big behind, hairy arms, fat earlobes, a crooked tooth, a flushed neck when we had to run around the block for PE. Mostly we ranked each other fourth, and fourth was believable; fourth was fair. That day, though, Amy asked, 'Who's the fourth prettiest?' and I counted to three and said, 'You are,' and at the same time she said, 'Katrina Howell.' I wasn't the fifth prettiest either, or the sixth or seventh, and after that we were well into ugly. Leanne Parry, the butcher's daughter, who smelled like the cold sausages and heels of salami she brought in her lunchbox. Vanessa Kaminski, who was fat.

'What about me?' I said to Amy when we reached double digits.

'What about you?' She scrubbed the dog hard over the bumps at the base of my neck.

'Ouch! Be careful.'

'Who's the eleventh prettiest?' she said.

'One, two, three . . . Janine Fenton,' I said.

'Janine Fenton,' she said.

'Amy, what about me?'

'Oh, I must have forgotten you.' She perched the dog on the cliff of my shoulder, then pushed it so it toppled forwards into the water. I watched it floating upside-down, the white innards starting to turn to mush.

'I wasn't aiming for the edge, you know,' I said. 'With the tennis ball.'

'It looked like you were.'

'Amy, what sort of person do you think I am?'

She didn't answer.

'Anyway, she never would have jumped.'

Silence. Then I felt the water shift behind me, and heard the low strangulations of the drain. Amy had pulled out the plug and climbed from the bath.

It took me a long time to fall asleep that night. Mrs Fong came and kissed us both on the cheek and warned us not to talk too late – but Amy didn't seem to want to chat. From my mattress on the floor I could see underneath her bed: a balled-up sock, a splayed book. Further away, in the dusty darkness, something that looked like a pen. I reached out and grasped it, drawing it to me slowly, silently – but it wasn't my missing pen; of course not. I'd looked everywhere for it at home, at school and at the shop. It had simply vanished. The orange streetlight shone through a crack in the curtains, even when I closed my eyes. It was hot and still, and Amy had pushed her blankets to the end of her bed where they towered at her feet like a wave about to break. Her dolls watched me from the shelf: Barbie, who had knees you could bend, and Skipper, her little sister, with her freckles and her flat chest. When we played dolls, neither of us wanted to be Skipper.

After a while I heard Mr and Mrs Fong climbing the stairs in their slippers. The sound of water running; the scrape and jangle of coat hangers as clothes were put away in the wardrobe in the next room. Then the house fell silent.

'Amy?' I whispered.

Nothing.

'Amy?'

I reached out a shadowy finger, prodded her shadowy back.

'What?' She sounded annoyed.

'Are you asleep?'

'Yes.'

The iron roof ticked as it started to cool.

'Amy?'

A grunt.

'Have I done something wrong?'

She sighed, rolled over, but I couldn't make out her face. 'It's kind of embarrassing, the way you suck up to Mrs Price,' she said.

'What? I do not!'

'Well, if you can't see it . . .'

'How do I suck up?'

'Um, riding in her car?'

'I didn't *ask* for that. She offered.'

'Exactly. You're the new pet. Melissa's out, you're in.' An edge in her voice that I hadn't heard before.

'As if.'

'Remember last month? Paula was her favourite at the start of term, and then something changed and it was Melissa. Now it's your turn.'

I did remember that. Nobody knew what Paula had done – Mrs Price simply stopped asking her to empty the pencil sharpener, or to spread the newspaper on the activity tables, or to go to the stationery cupboard and find a new box of chalk. Paula pretended she didn't care, but we saw the way she watched Melissa taking over her jobs – Melissa and the other pets. There were three or four of them at any one time, usually the pretty girls, the handsome boys, who already had lots of friends and didn't need extra success. Sometimes, though, she'd choose an unpopular child – and straight away, that child's luck started to change. I saw it happen with Leanne after her father donated the cows' eyes for us to dissect: first Mrs Price asked her to clean the blackboard dusters, and then to close the windows and sweep the floor, and then to tidy the craft drawers cluttered with broken scissors and dried-out pots of glue and scraps of cartridge paper too small to be useful. The other girls began to sit with Leanne at lunchtime, and draw hearts on her pencil case, and Melissa even did a sketch of a horse for her, which was her speciality; we all thought she would be a famous artist one day. And then Mrs Price changed her mind and chose a new pet, and we all went back to ignoring Leanne, who kept the horse picture Blu-Tacked to the underside of her desk lid nonetheless.

'You even sound different around her,' Amy said. 'Your voice goes all high and whispery.'

'I like her,' I said. 'What's wrong with that?'

'Yeah, but you sound like you're five years old.' Amy let out a single hard laugh.

'Maybe you're jealous.'

'Pfft.'

'You are, aren't you?'

'Oh my God. I don't care about cleaning the blackboard dusters. I'm embarrassed for you.'

'Jealous. Jealous.'

'Shut up.'

'You shut up.'

'Girls!' Mrs Fong knocked on the wall. 'That's enough chitter-chatter. Off to sleep now, please.'

At church the next morning Mrs Price arrived just ahead of us; we saw a young man holding the heavy glass door open for her, saying, 'After you. Please, I insist.' She floated in past him, brushing against his chest, murmuring her thanks as he beamed in her wake.

'Can we sit next to her, Mum?' Amy whispered. 'Can we?'

But the Fongs sat where they usually sat, and Mrs Price found a spot over the other side, slipping in next to the Kaminskis. Mrs Kaminski nodded at her and must have said something about her silk scarf, because Mrs Price unwound it from her neck and held it to the cheek of Mrs Kaminski, who closed her eyes for a moment with a look of bliss on her face. That was how Mrs Price made us feel when we were close to her – adults as well as children. Drifting in a state of bliss, eyes closed.

Amy didn't go to Communion: when our row stood and began to make their way up the aisle, she stayed in her seat, arms crossed. Mrs Fong nudged her, but she shook her head. It was because she had sinned, I decided. She had said horrible things to me the night before, and now she was in a state of sin and not a state of grace, and she knew it. Mrs Fong glared, cocked her head towards Father Lynch.

'I had toast,' Amy whispered. 'Right before we left.'

You couldn't receive Holy Communion if you had eaten in the last hour; you couldn't allow the body of Christ to slosh around in your stomach with the cornflakes and the bacon.

But I knew she was lying.

CHAPTER 5

The following Friday morning, when Mrs Price said she'd need the overhead projector, Melissa started to stand up from her desk.

'Let me see,' said Mrs Price, running her finger through the air, past all the other pupils, past Melissa, until she stopped and pointed at me. 'Justine. Will you get it for me, please?'

'Told you,' hissed Amy, and Melissa shot us a look as she sat back down.

The projector was stored on its trolley in the stationery cupboard when not in use, so I wheeled it to the front of the classroom, plugged it in and switched it on, then nudged it until the block of light fitted on the screen.

'Perfect. Thank you, Justine,' said Mrs Price, and I could feel tingles in the back of my neck and all across my scalp, and maybe it was true: maybe I was the new pet.

We were studying the Aborigines, and learning what Australia was like before it was discovered, because it was important to know about people who were different from us. Mrs Price was wearing a white peasant blouse with a beaded belt, the fringed ends tapping at her thighs. Whenever she looked down or blinked we could see her silver eye shadow, her eyelids flashing like fish – sometimes they still flash through my dreams – and she was Debbie Harry, she was Olivia Newton-John, she was Agnetha. She put up a transparency of Australia and began to draw on it with a red marker to show how the Aborigines wandered from place to place. They were Stone Age people, she said, among the most primitive on earth, who didn't grow crops, didn't settle on farms, didn't keep herds of animals, but kept moving around to find food and shelter. They took with them very few possessions, and they built no proper homes, only campsites. Imagine, she said: if you were lucky you might sleep in a hollowed-out tree trunk, or a hut made of bark. The shadow of her hand swooped across the map as she spoke, passing as a thundercloud over the vast empty stretches of desert. We wrote down the things she told us, pausing to white out our mistakes with Twink, though often we could still see them showing through our sticky corrections. Imagine you have no soft bed, Mrs Price went on, no TV, no books, no toys, no shoes. Only animal skins for clothes – when you wear clothes at all. Your father might walk hundreds of miles to trade stone axes, boomerangs, ochre, pearl shells. You daub mud on your body to keep away the mosquitoes, and you eat snakes and lizards and witchetty grubs. By now we were giggling, wrinkling our noses.

'I bet Amy eats creepy crawlies,' said Karl.

Melissa laughed, and so did I.

'That'll do, Karl,' said Mrs Price.

'Chicken feet, octopus, rotten eggs . . .' he said.

'Yes, thank you, Karl.' But wasn't there the trace of a smile on her lips?

When I stole a look at Amy, her face was expressionless. She was pretending to write down what Mrs Price had said about the Aborigines, but really she was drawing a picture of a snake, its long forked tongue flicking all the way over to the next page of her exercise book.

The next transparency showed a girl called Millingi. Mrs Price had been reading us a book about her, and we knew that Millingi's mother was dead, and that her father, the headman of their tribe, had taken two extra wives, but one of them couldn't have children and had thrown herself off a cliff.

In the picture Millingi was dabbling her fingers in a stream, perhaps about to drink some water – taking care not to drink her own reflection, because that would spell her early death. She was kneeling down and holding her arm across her body, but we could tell she was naked. Soon it would be her turn to marry. She'd been promised to Goomera at birth, so she could not choose her husband: this was the tradition where she lived, said Mrs Price, though it might seem strange to us. She picked up her blue marker, took off the lid. When Millingi and the other Aborigine girls were preparing for marriage, she said – when they were learning the wisdom known only to women – they glued live butterflies to their bodies and danced a special dance to the music of didgeridoos and possum-skin drums. She began to draw these butterflies on the transparency, covering Millingi's arms and legs and body until she was clothed in tiny wings.

'But how does she sit down?' said Paula.

This was a good question, and we all waited for Mrs Price to tell us the answer.

'The same as any of us, I expect,' she said.

'But won't she squash the butterflies?' said Selena.

Mrs Price looked at the picture, put her head on one side. We loved it when she did that, because it meant she was really thinking about what we'd asked. 'Perhaps she doesn't sit down,' she said. 'Perhaps she just keeps dancing.'

Yes, we thought, that made sense; that sounded right. Covered in butterflies, imagining your husband, wouldn't you dance and dance and dance for love?

At lunchtime I went to the stormwater pipes as usual. Paula, Selena and Melissa had already draped themselves across the top, their long hair rippling down the hot concrete flank. As I started to climb inside, Melissa said, 'Can you do a cartwheel with roundoff?'

I realised she was talking to me. 'I think so,' I said. 'I mean, sure.'

'Go on then,' said Paula.

The three of them sat up and watched as I put down my lunchbox, tucked my tunic into my knickers. Then I walked to the grass in front of the pipes, raised my arms and began a cartwheel, twisting my hips halfway through so I landed with my feet neatly together.

'That was pretty good,' said Melissa.

'Thanks,' I said.

They lay down again, fanned out their hair.

Inside the pipes, Amy was eating her lunch: Mrs Fong's spring rolls. She glanced up at me. Carried on eating.

'Cheese and lettuce sandwich?' I said.

She took one and held out a spring roll to me. 'Told you you're the new pet.'

'I don't know why she likes me,' I said.

'But she does. *And* you want her to.'

'I suppose.'

'You do. I can tell.'

I took a bite of spring roll.

'Mum said we shouldn't worry about what other people think,' said Amy. 'We should only worry about what's inside us.'

'I don't know what's inside me.'

'Neither do I.'

'Anyway, you want her to like you too.'

'Yeah.'

Above us we could hear Melissa talking about Karl. He'd drawn her a picture of a spaceman – he was good at drawing spacemen – and dubbed her home on the back of his bike. She'd drawn him a picture of a horse.

'So is he your boyfriend now?' said Selena.

'I think that's how it works,' said Melissa.

Amy pretended to vomit, so I did too. Then I said yes when

she asked if I wanted to play knucklebones, even though I could never get past threesies and she always won.

After lunch Mr Chisholm, the headmaster, came to read us a story. He visited our classroom once a fortnight or so, and we loved him and we were scared of him; he was the one who strapped us for bad behaviour, and sometimes he drew blood. The top of his head was bare and smooth and went pink in the summertime, and he wore little narrow glasses that he polished clean with a checked handkerchief. He'd trained to be a priest, and even though he had left the seminary – and there was no shame in changing your mind, children, no shame in letting God show you the right path – he had never married. When he was a boy, he'd told us, he'd been in the Napier earthquake and had seen a woman in a white dress trapped in a destroyed building, buried up to her waist in debris. She was calling and calling for someone to come and help her, but the whole place was on fire and nobody could get close enough. His mother told him not to look as she hurried him away, but he glanced back over his shoulder all the same, and the woman in the white dress had raised her arms, and she was on fire, her clothing was on fire, and he decided she was an angel of fire and her burning white sleeves were wings. He could be dramatic like that.

Thinking about it now, I don't know why he shared such a dreadful memory with us.

He sat down in the story chair, his finger marking a page in the *Just So Stories*, and said, 'In a silver casket in a chapel in a cathedral in Italy, there is an ancient cloth.'

Mrs Price was nodding, playing with the tiny crucifix she always wore.

'It is hand-woven linen, this cloth, over four metres long,' he went on. 'It has scorch marks and water marks from a fire four hundred years ago, when molten silver dripped on it. And it holds an image: the front and back of a sunken-eyed man laid out for burial.' He uncrossed his legs, leaned forward in the story chair. 'I've seen it with my own eyes,' he said. 'I waited sixteen hours to see it, along with three million others – the entire population of New Zealand. Why did I do that, children? Why did I travel to the other side of the world to see a piece of fabric?'

No one knew; no one spoke.

'Because it's not just a piece of fabric,' he said. 'It's the burial cloth of Jesus. The Shroud of Christ. I'll pass round a picture, so you can see him for yourselves.'

He handed a postcard to Mrs Price, who handed it to Katrina Howell in the front row. I craned my neck and tried to see.

Gregory Walsh put up his hand.

'Yes, Gregory?'

'Did the whole country go?' he said.

'I beg your pardon?'

'You said the entire population of New Zealand.'

Mr Chisholm blinked behind his narrow glasses. 'They came from all over the world, Gregory,' he said. 'The pilgrims. I was just giving you an idea of the size of the crowds.'

'Because I don't think Mum and Dad went,' said Gregory.

'No,' said Mr Chisholm, sharing a glance with Mrs Price. 'No.' He paused, looked around the room in that dramatic way he had, and we fell silent once more.

They'd done tests on the cloth, he said; they'd taken ultra-violet photographs that showed more than could ever be seen with the human eye. The blood was real blood, not paint or ink or dye. The wounds were real wounds – punctures on the man's brow, scourging on his back, rivulets of blood running from his wrists, feet and side. They'd even found pollen from plants that bloom in Jerusalem at Easter time – flowers as well as thorns. And they'd made out the presence of coins on the eyelids, placed there to hold them shut after death in case the dead person was looking for someone to take with him to the grave.

I jumped when Amy tapped me on the hand. She giggled and leaned into my face, staring right at me, her eyes huge.

You had to stand back from the cloth, said Mr Chisholm – too close, and the markings broke up into meaningless blotches. When you looked at it from a distance, the figure took shape: the body of the crucified man, his serene face. Nobody knew how the image had been formed – it did not sit on the surface of the cloth, but within it. The flax fibres themselves had darkened, and the colour could not be dissolved or bleached away. Some people, he said – some scientists – believed that a powerful burst of light had produced it, a flash of radiant energy springing from the body itself. He burst open his fingers as he spoke, and Mrs Price shuddered her shoulders, gazed around at us. Think about that, children, he said. Think about what it might mean. The Shroud was evidence of Christ's death, yes – but perhaps it also showed his return to life. A snapshot of the resurrection.

Amy passed Mr Chisholm's postcard to me, and I saw the face of the dead man, or perhaps the resurrected man: white eyes, gaunt cheeks, a broken nose. I turned it over and read the message written on the back. *Dear Mum, I queued for nine hours but it was worth it. Don't forget the maidenhair. Love, Dennis.* I passed it along to Melissa, who looked as if she didn't even want to touch it.

Then Mr Chisholm opened the *Just So Stories* and read us 'How the Rhinoceros Got His Skin'. Hiding behind my pencil case, I painted Amy's nails white with Twink, and she painted mine, but she brushed it on too thickly and it curdled. I told her it looked pretty anyway. Then we laid our heads on our arms, and Amy and I mouthed *olive juice* at each other because it looked like *I love you* but wasn't. Karl drew a picture of a space-man, and Melissa drew a picture of a horse. And the rhino took off his skin and left it on the beach, and when he put it back on with the cake crumbs inside he couldn't stop scratching and wriggling, and forever after he was not comfortable in it.

Amy and I usually walked to town together after school on Fridays, she to her parents' fruit and vegetable shop and I to Passing Time Antiques. She was waiting for me that day, but Mrs Price asked me to clean the blackboard for her – to wash it off with a wet sponge, and to wipe all the dust from the chalk ledge too. She chose Melissa to close the windows, which wasn't as good a job because it didn't take very long – the window-closer got only a couple of minutes with Mrs Price.

'I'll ring you later, okay?' I said to Amy.

'Okay,' she said, but she lingered for a moment, watching as I shifted all the pieces of chalk out of the way. Then she was gone.

While Melissa pulled the windows shut and looped their long, long cords around their hooks so nobody choked themselves, I took the blackboard dusters outside and banged them together. Melissa had left by the time I came back in, and Mrs Price was sitting at her desk, marking our projects about Victorian England with her red pen. I went to get a bucket of water from Mr Armstrong, the caretaker, so I could wash the blackboard. It sloshed over the sides as I made my way down the polished corridor that we weren't supposed to skid along in our socks, though at the end of each term the nuns waxed it and then let us tie rags to our feet and slide over its toffee-coloured boards. Up above the rows of coat hooks, in a carved niche outside the Primer One room, the plaster figure of Jesus held up his second and third fingers in blessing. The statue was made in several different sections and the hands could swivel; every so often a child climbed up there and turned the blessing hand backwards so it looked like Jesus was giving us all the fingers. Usually a teacher noticed before too long.

'What would I do without you?' said Mrs Price as I balanced

on a chair to reach the top of the blackboard with the sponge. 'By the way, my darling' – she twisted around in her seat – 'did you find your special pen? Was it in your schoolbag, maybe?'

'No,' I said, rinsing the sponge and squeezing it out again.

'Oh, I'm sorry.'

'Thanks.'

'I don't suppose any other pen will do.'

'Not really.'

'I understand. I'm sorry.'

From above I could see her writing comments on Dominic Foster's project: *Neater printing, please* and *Keep your work tidy, Dominic!* She gave him a B-minus, though I didn't think his work looked untidy – and then, when she marked Karl's, which really was messy, she wrote *Excellent!* and *Outstanding!* He got an A-plus.

When I finished the blackboard Mrs Price said she needed me to shake out the square of carpet under her desk. Together we pulled it free, and I lugged it out to the grass; it was heavier than it looked. The hessian backing scratched at my arms, and the grey wool smelled of dust. I could see a flattened area in the middle, where Mrs Price's feet had crushed the pile, and a single strand of blond hair caught the afternoon light. I plucked it off and slipped it into my breast pocket, then banged the carpet against the grass over and over, the dust rising around me.

She was swallowing one of her pills from the little brown bottle when I came inside. 'Oh my goodness, you're filthy!' she said. 'All over your uniform. Your father will be furious with me.'

'He won't mind,' I said.

She started brushing at my tunic. 'You're just trying to make me feel better.'

'Really, he won't.'

'Really? Really and truly?' She stood back, ran her eyes over me.

'Mrs Price?' I said.

'Mmm?'

'Do you believe what Mr Chisholm said? About the Shroud. The burst of light from the body.'

'The snapshot of the resurrection,' she said.

'Yes.'

'To be honest with you, Justine, I'm not sure. I know I *want* to believe it.'

'Me too,' I said.

'It's a beautiful thought, isn't it – that a person who has died can come back to life in a brilliant burst of energy. Like a flash of lightning, or a firework.'

I nodded.

She took my chin in her hand, turned my face towards the window – and then she licked her thumb and rubbed at a smudge on my cheek.

'Do tell your father I'm sorry,' she said. 'And give him my best.'

Months and months later, after everything went wrong, I found the single blond hair still coiled in the bottom of my breast pocket. It had knotted itself into the seam's loose threads; not even washing had dislodged it.

2014

CHAPTER 6

The next time Emma and I visit Dad there's no sign of Sonia the caregiver. We borrow a wheelchair and take him to the café across the road; it's in a hardware store, the tables set up next to the garden supplies section. Pottles of seedling courgettes and tomatoes sit next to concrete statues of geese, and sacks of mulch are stacked along the wall like sandbags against some unnamed disaster. I order a single-shot flat white for Dad and wait for him to remark on the standard of coffee at the retirement community and the fact that the portions of sugar in the little paper packets never equal a proper teaspoon.

At the table opposite us, a toddler grabs for the crayons inside a miniature watering can and starts to scribble on the paper placemats provided for children.

Emma smiles at him, and he holds up the picture to show her. 'Wow,' she says. 'Really good.'

He hands her a crayon, and she leans over and colours in a bit of pirate ship.

'Sorry,' I say to his mother, but she waves her hand.

'Who are they?' says Dad.

'Just some nice people,' I say.

'Do we know them?'

'No.'

'They could be anybody, then.'

'Sorry,' I say again to the mother, who carries on chatting with her friend.

At one point the little boy wanders away, plopping himself down next to the seedlings and shoving a handful of soil in his mouth. Why isn't his mother watching him?

Emma dashes over and lifts him away. 'Yucky,' she says. 'Not nice.' She holds a serviette to his mouth for him to spit out the dirt. When she returns him to his table, his mother barely glances in his direction.

Maybe she's exhausted.

Maybe she's letting him test his boundaries.

When Emma was little, I couldn't shake the feeling I would lose her. She used to complain about how tightly I held her hand when we were crossing the street or making our way through the supermarket. Once, I remember, when just the two of us went on a bush walk, she wanted to play hide and seek. I hid first, crouching down in a patch of ferns, easily visible in my yellow windbreaker. I knew she saw me straight away, but she preserved the illusion for as long as possible, calling out to me, her voice a question – *Mummy? Mummy?* – skirting around my hiding place as if she had no idea where I'd gone. Then it was her turn to hide, and I covered my eyes with my hands. I could smell the forest floor on them, the black earth from beneath the ferns, sporey and dank. I heard Emma's footsteps snapping twigs, crunching dead leaves. After that, silence. I made myself finish counting, *eighteen, nineteen, twenty,* and then I began to look. Nothing. Not a trace of her. I checked behind every tree, parted the undergrowth and called her name. Peered down the steep bank that dropped away to the stream below. Nothing, nothing.

'Emma!' I yelled. 'Emma!' Not a question but a plea. 'Come out, darling – I'm worried.'

Around me the bush was silent: even the stream, even the birds.

'Emma! It's not funny any more!'

Could someone have taken her? Could she have fallen?

Then, from a long way back up the track, I heard her laugh. The sound flitted down to me like the notes of an unseen bird, and I dashed towards it and finally saw her curled up in the scrub, her green jersey and brown hair all but invisible.

I thought: how did she move so far from me so quickly?

And I thought: I don't deserve her.

At the café Dad is examining his flat white, which has a smiley-face design in the foam. 'The things they can do these days,' he says.

'Is that a new shirt?' I ask, though I am the one who buys all his clothes.

'This?' he says, peering down at his chest. 'No, I've had this for ages.'

I know, if I check inside the collar, that the label will show someone else's name.

Emma waves at a girl walking past – a classmate from school. Her father is manoeuvring a trolley piled with paving stones.

'Who's that?' says Dad.

'The prettiest girl in my class.'

'You shouldn't say things like that,' I tell her.

'But she *is* the prettiest.'

'Still, you shouldn't say things like that.'

'It's just a game we play, Mum.'

'Everyone is pretty,' I say.

'Shannon Ricci isn't.'

'Everyone is pretty in their own way.'

'Shannon has hairy arms.'

'I never liked hairy women,' says Dad. 'The first girl I slept with had hair bursting out everywhere. Upstairs, downstairs.'

'That's probably enough about that,' I say.

'Like on her feet?' says Emma. 'She had hairy *feet*?'

'All over the place,' says Dad. 'Lena Saad. They were Lebanese.'

'Dad.'

'I suppose I can't say that now. I suppose it's racist. But she was very, *very* hairy.'

He takes a packet of sugar and turns it end to end, trying to find the way in.

'Here,' Emma says, and tears it open for him.

'It's very nice to get out and about,' he says. 'Have a proper coffee. They use instant where I live – I suppose they make hundreds of cups a day, but still.' He stirs in the sugar, breaking apart the face made of foam. When he takes a sip, he grimaces.

'Another one?' says Emma, already tearing open a second packet.

'They're never the full teaspoon,' he says. 'They say they are, but they're not.'

I first noticed his symptoms around six years ago. He'd turn up wearing odd socks, or two different shoes, and then he started getting lost when he drove to our place, and had to ring me for directions. He forgot certain words – wallet, tissue, stereo, lawnmower. He forgot our cat's name and called her The Meow. One evening he rang me after dinner and sounded so upset I thought something awful must have happened.

'I can't open the new ice cream,' he said.

'What do mean, you can't open it?'

'I can't get the . . . the flat thing off the top.'

'The lid?'

'Yes, the lid, the jolly lid.'

'There's a tab under the rim,' I said. 'Slip your thumb underneath it and pull it away. Then the lid should lift right off.'

'What was all that about?' said Dom when I hung up.

'I'm not sure,' I said.

Dad's GP referred him to the geriatric clinic, and when I picked him up for the appointment I checked he was properly dressed.

'What's the matter with you?' he said as I tried to peer at his socks.

'Nothing. Nothing.'

For the first few minutes in the car we chatted about this and that, and he seemed perfectly all right.

Then he said, 'Where are we going?'

'The hospital,' I said. 'The geriatric clinic.'

'Geriatric!'

'The older persons' clinic,' I corrected myself.

'I'm sixty-eight!'

'You're seventy, Dad. Anyway, they just want to do some tests.'

'What kind of tests?'

'I'm not sure. I imagine they'll ask you about your memory.'

'I don't like the sound of that.' He stared out the window. After a few moments he said, 'Where are we going?'

In the waiting room a woman my age sat with her elderly mother. She caught my eye as we took a seat, and we both murmured a hello. There was hardly anything to the mother: a little wisp of a person, her legs thin as wrists in their baggy tan pantyhose. She kept plucking at her ragged cardigan, pulling at loose ends, unravelling stitch after stitch. Eventually the daughter said, 'Mum, you'll have nothing left,' then glanced over at me again. 'Sorry. She won't wear anything else.'

Dad picked up the newspaper and turned straight to the death notices. Old habits.

When it was our turn, the doctor said I was welcome to sit in on the consultation, as long as I let Dad answer the questions.

'Of course,' I said.

She looked like she'd just come from the gym: black leggings, a high ponytail and an oversize sweatshirt. Around her neck, a greenstone pendant carved into a fish hook.

'No cheating allowed,' said Dad, holding up a finger to me by way of warning. 'We'll pretend you're not here.'

Above his head, on the pale green wall, a framed print of horses galloping through the surf. Next to it, a button labelled *DURESS*. I sat on my hands.

'All right, Mr Crieve,' said the doctor, her voice neutral, her pen poised to note down his scores. 'I'm going to start by asking questions that require concentration and memory. Some questions are more difficult than others, and some will be asked more than once.'

He had no trouble telling her the date, including the month and year.

'And what is the season?' she asked.

'Winter.'

'What day of the week is it?'

'Tuesday. Isn't it?' He paused; she'd already noted his score. 'Or are we at Wednesday already?' Looking at me for a clue – but I kept my eyes on the horses in the surf. It was Friday.

'What city and country are we in?'

'Auckland, New Zealand,' he scoffed.

'What is the name of this place?'

'I just told you.'

'I mean where we are right now.' She pointed her finger at the linoleum floor, then stopped herself.

'Well, the . . . the hospital,' he said.

'And what level of the building are we on?'

'Why does that matter?'

She noted something down.

'I am going to name three objects. After I have said them I want you to repeat them back to me. Remember what they are, because I will ask you to name them again in a few minutes: apple, table, penny.'

'Apple, table, penny,' he said. 'This is ridiculous. Apple, table, penny.'

Next he had to count backwards in sevens from one hundred.

'Ninety-three,' he said. 'Eighty- . . . eighty-six. Sixty-nine . . .' He looked at me. I looked at the horses in the surf. 'Sixty-one?'

'All right,' said the doctor in her neutral voice, scoring him. Now I am going to spell a word forwards, and I want you to spell it backwards. The word is *world*. W-O-R-L-D. Please spell it in reverse order.'

'D. R.' He stopped. 'No, that's not right.' I could feel his eyes on me, imploring. I slid my gaze across to the *DURESS* button. 'Ah . . . D. O. L. . . . No, sorry. Sorry.'

The doctor wrote something down.

'And what are the three objects I asked you to remember a few moments ago, Mr Crieve?'

He opened his mouth. Closed it again. Shook his head.

Another note on her score sheet.

'What is this called?' She held up a watch.

'Wristwatch,' he said.

'What is this called?' She held up a pencil.

'Pen. Pencil! Pencil!'

She asked him to repeat *No ifs, ands or buts*.

'No ifs, ands or buts,' he said.

She asked him to read and obey a written command, and he closed his eyes. She asked him to write a sentence, and he wrote *What am I doing here?* She asked him to take a piece of paper in his right hand, fold it in half with both hands and put it in his lap. She asked him to draw a clock face, including all the numbers, and showing eleven o'clock.

I could see his distress when he got something wrong, sense it welling in the small room with its wipe-clean bed and its model of a normal brain, its *DURESS* button. The jumbled clock face. The world backwards.

In the café, Emma takes out a mirror from her little shoulder-bag and examines her reflection. Frowns. Smears on a bit of lip gloss.

'It's very nice to get out and about,' Dad says again. 'They use instant coffee where I live.' He takes another sip. 'All the same, I'm very happy where I am.'

1984

CHAPTER 7

Over the next week, Mrs Price began to give me more and more jobs to do, and I said yes every time. In the stationery cupboard I cranked the handle of the cyclostyle machine to print copies of our handouts and tests – she made me promise not to read the test questions, because that wouldn't be fair to the other children, and I didn't, I didn't. I picked pansies and asters and sprigs of alyssum from the convent garden for Mary's altar, and I cleaned the tank that housed Susan, the axolotl. Mrs Price had brought her to class at the start of the year and said we could keep her as a pet, and back then we had crowded around her, jostling to see this strange creature. Axolotls – Mexican walking fish – are not fish at all but a type of salamander, Mrs Price told us, but while other salamanders transform into land-dwellers as they mature, axolotls keep their feathery gills and stay forever in the water: they never grow up. And although to begin with we had rushed to Susan's tank every morning to peer in at her, soon she was no longer a novelty – we had tired of her. By now her tank was overdue for a clean, and I scooped her gently into a Tupperware container – Mrs Price explained that axolotls are mostly cartilage rather than bone, and very delicate, very easy to hurt. As I changed the water and scraped the film from the inside of the glass, Susan watched me with her golden eyes, fanning her fringed gills, splaying her oddly human fingers. I lifted out the large flat pebbles, the plastic treasure chest and the clay flowerpot she liked to hide inside, and I scrubbed them clean with a toothbrush, wiped the leaves of the fake plants. Then I returned her to the tank and fed her a worm, which she snatched at and swallowed in one bite.

I was an hour late to the shop that day, and Dad was angry.

'I thought something terrible had happened,' he said. 'You can't just not turn up.'

'I was with Mrs Price,' I said. 'Helping her. I wasn't doing anything dangerous.'

'Yes, but how was I supposed to know that? Why didn't you ring me?'

'I didn't have any coins.' A lie: I'd been so engrossed in helping Mrs Price, I hadn't even thought of ringing him.

I disappeared out the back to sort and clean the new stock, washing the dirt from jardinières, rinsing cut crystal until every facet shone.

He wandered out a bit later with some blank price tags and started attaching them to the items I'd finished with.

'A hundred and fifty dollars?' I said, holding up a Royal Doulton teapot.

'You have to understand,' he said, 'that you're all I have.' He took the teapot from me, wrote *$175* on the tag.

'I do understand,' I said. I pointed to a sterling cruet set. 'Two hundred dollars?'

'More.' He still sounded cross.

'Shall I make you schnitzel for dinner?'

He sighed and handed me a ten-dollar note. Tucked my hair behind my ear. 'Straight there and straight back.'

Mr Parry's butcher shop was just around the corner, a few shops down from the Fongs' fruit and vegetable place, and I waved to Mrs Fong as I passed. She was stacking oranges out the front, unwrapping them from their layers of purple tissue and placing each one with its tiny green star at the top, while Amy served at the counter. 'What are they meant to be?' I heard a customer ask as he eyed a small pile of avocados. Next door was the newsagent's, with its oversized magazine covers in wire cages – *Scoop! Inside Monaco's palace* and *What it's like to be called a Rapist* and *Amazing things to make with pegs* – then the drycleaner's – *LEATHER & FUR, DRAPERY & CURTAIN, WEDDING GOWN.* Then came the butcher's, tiled in red and white, an awning shading the big front window where all the meat lay on display: coils of sausages, mountains of mince and chops in stainless-steel trays edged with plastic parsley. The specials painted on the glass in thick white letters. Haunches hanging from hooks.

'Nice to see you, Justine,' said Mr Parry.

I used to go there all the time with Mum, but Dad and I hadn't shopped there in a while; it was easier to get everything we needed at the new supermarket. Fruit and vegetables as well as meat.

'You look like you could do with some fattening up,' he said. He winked and passed me a slice of luncheon sausage, and I said thank you and ate it and felt like a child. 'And how are you coping these days?'

'Fine, thanks,' I replied. The meat had left a film of fat in my mouth and on my fingers. I fixed my gaze on the scales as he tore a length of paper from a thick roll and wrapped the schnitzel. He didn't ask me anything else.

It was around this same time that the stealing started, though at first we didn't know it was stealing. Karl's R2-D2 eraser went missing, and Leanne Parry's stripy scarf that she'd knitted herself, and Vanessa Kaminski's bell-shaped umbrella that you could lower right down over your head and shoulders because it was see-through. Jason Asofua lost his bottle of Twink, and Jason Moretti said it was a stupid thing for someone to take because it was all dried up anyway. I lost the cotton-wool bumblebee I kept pinned inside my desk, hanging down from the old inkwell hole; the dental nurse had made it for me, and it twitched on its length of floss whenever I lifted the lid. Amy had pretended she wasn't jealous when I brought it back to class, but I saw the way she watched as I flicked it to make it spin and dance for her. Besides, she had her own prize brought back from the dental clinic: a pool of mercury, caught in an empty needle case, breaking apart into silvery dots and then reforming itself over and over. Everyone coveted that, but it never went missing.

When I lost my bee I pulled out all my books, looked on the floor around my desk, even checked inside my pencil case – but like the ferry pen my mother had given me, the soft little creature with its gauze wings and its ink-dot eyes had vanished. Paula lost her Sleepwalker Smurf, which was the rarest of all the Smurfs we had collected and the one everybody wanted: we'd made our parents buy their petrol at BP stations because they were the only ones selling the plastic figurines. It would turn up, we told Paula, but she sobbed no, no, it was gone for good, and not just lost: *stolen*. Didn't things go astray all the time, though? Weren't people always losing this and that? Weren't we careless children? Then Mrs Price lost something too: her frosted-pink lipstick, taken from her handbag in broad daylight, she said. She was deeply saddened we had a thief in our midst; she thought St Michael's had taught us better values than that. We were all friends, and what sort of person stole from their friends? We were a team – a *family*. Did they really think they could get away with it? She didn't want to involve Mr Chisholm, but she would speak to him if she had to. We listened to her with lowered eyes, every one of us feeling guilty, because as far as Mrs Price knew, every one of us *could* have been guilty.

'Told you there was a thief,' said Paula, pleased to be right, even though being right wouldn't bring back Sleepwalker Smurf. Her father had tried to find her another one, driving to BP stations all over town, but they weren't selling them any more. Certainly, though, because of her tears, nobody thought Paula was the culprit – except how did we know the tears were real? We were all looking at one another askance, all keeping a close eye on our belongings. Katrina Howell accused Selena Kothari of hiding her own pack of marker pens at home and then announcing them stolen just to place herself in the clear, but Katrina had no proof of this, and maybe her accusation was in itself suspicious.

Then one morning when we were waiting in class for Mrs Price, I heard Rachel Jensen whisper to Jason Asofua that the only person who hadn't lost anything was Amy.

'I don't think that's true,' I said.

'What's not true?' said Jason Daly, so Jason Asofua whispered it to him.

'Really?' he said. He whispered it to Jacqui Novak.

By now they were all staring at Amy.

'What?' she said.

'Everyone but you has had something stolen,' said Rachel Jensen.

The children in the row in front of us turned to look too.

'What about Dominic?' said Amy.

'Two of my Matchbox cars are missing,' he said.

'Well, Brendon, then.'

'I've lost my harmonica.'

'See?' said Rachel.

'That doesn't mean anything,' said Amy.

Jason Moretti said, 'My mum told me your dad gave her the wrong change one day. She has to count it every time now.'

'My dad—' began Amy, but Natalie O'Carroll cut across her.

'They shove the rotten fruit to the bottom of the bag and then put better stuff on top,' she said. 'It's not the Kiwi way. You don't notice till you get it home, and then it's too late.'

Karl pulled his beautiful eyes into slits and said, 'You want apple? Nice juicy? You buy cheap cheap.'

Everyone started to laugh, and after a moment Amy joined in too, so she can't have been upset – that's what I told myself. We were all still laughing when Mrs Price walked in. Rising to our feet, we said, 'Good *mor*ning, Mrs Price, and God *bless* you, Mrs Price.'

'What's so funny?' she said.

I blushed; I didn't know why.

'Justine?'

I glanced at Amy, who was staring out the window. 'Karl was just pulling faces,' I said.

Mrs Price motioned for us to sit down. 'He should be careful,' she smiled. 'One day the wind will change.'

At lunchtime I headed for the adventure playground, but Amy wasn't in the stormwater pipes. Karl and some of the other boys were hurling stones up into the branches of the walnut tree, and Melissa and Paula darted about, snatching at any walnuts the boys managed to dislodge and depositing them in a pile.

'Hey Justine!' Karl yelled as I walked past. I thought he was mad with me for telling Mrs Price he'd been pulling faces, but he said, 'Do you want a go?' and gave me his stone.

It was warm from his hand, smooth as an egg in my palm. I peered up at the tree, looking into the brilliant green leaves that seemed filled with light, filled with the sun.

'Go on,' said Karl. 'Do some damage.' He sounded like a film star.

'Yeah, do some damage,' said Melissa.

I thought of the tennis ball I'd thrown to Bonnie up on the cliffs; the way the wind had pulled it over the edge and down to the razor rocks below. Bonnie streaking after it, stopping just in time. I tested the weight of the stone in my hand, then reached back my arm and threw, putting all my weight behind it. Two walnuts pattered down. I picked up the stone and tried again, and knocked another walnut free.

'She's better than you,' said Jason Moretti, shoving Karl's shoulder.

'Shut up,' said Karl – but he was looking at me with a half-smile, his head tilted back like he was making his mind up about something. The gold flecks in his eyes sparked in the sunlight. My skin felt like it was covered with butterflies, hundreds of tiny wings beating. Then, as Jason Moretti and Jason Asofua started flinging their stones at the branches once more, Sister Bronislava came rushing over. 'Children, children!' she called, her black veil swooping behind her. 'This is very dangerous! You will hurt someone!'

She was tiny and dark-eyed and Polish, one of the last few nuns living in the convent, and she jumped at loud noises, because in Poland, in the war, she'd seen her whole family shot right in front of her. That was the story we'd heard, at least, the story we whispered among ourselves, and it had to be true: those with older brothers and sisters said that one lunchtime, when she was patrolling the adventure playground for dangerous behaviour, a car had backfired and she had dashed behind the big tractor tyres to crouch for cover. The sisters didn't teach proper classes any more, though they still kept an eye on us when we were playing, and came to take us for singing and folk dancing, and private elocution if you wanted to sound like you came from somewhere else, somewhere better. Sister Bronislava had been our teacher in the primers, back when we started school, and I had clung to her when my mother left me there on my first day; I had buried my face in her long black skirts, and she'd stroked my head for a moment or two, and let me fiddle with the black rosary beads she wore at her waist. Then she'd said, 'So. Enough tears, I think,' and it was time to sit down at my desk. At Mass on Easter Sunday she gave us each a hard-boiled egg painted with flowers and birds; we were supposed to eat them, but I hadn't wanted to crack the beautiful shell of mine, and it went bad.

The boys left their stones where they fell and said, 'Sorry, Sister.'

She picked them up and said, 'You could split your heads open. Knock out teeth, eyes. Kill yourselves.'

'Yes, Sister,' they said.

'And what are you doing here, Justine?' she said. 'This is not like you.'

'No, Sister,' I said. 'Sorry, Sister.' I didn't want to surrender my stone, the stone Karl had given me, but she was waiting with her hand out. I passed it to her.

And now that I think about it, couldn't we simply have found other stones after she'd gone? But we didn't.

The boys began taking the walnuts from the pile and stamping on them, crushing the shells and picking out the flesh. Jason Asofua offered one to Melissa, but she shook her head and said, 'A single walnut has twenty-six calories.'

'Justine?' said Karl. He was holding out two perfect halves on his palm. They were pale gold and lustrous, entirely different from the dusty brown pieces that rattled around in a packet in the pantry at home. I bit into one, and the thin skin gave way to the sweet and buttery kernel. Karl ate the other. If I close my eyes, I can still taste it.

I stayed with the group for the rest of lunchtime, and we played Mother May I, but only as a joke, because we were too old for it by then. Paula was Mother first, making us take half-steps and baby steps so it seemed we'd never reach her. I kept forgetting to say Mother May I and had to go back to the start while all the others crept closer and closer to Paula. She let Melissa win, because she always let Melissa win, because Melissa was beautiful. Melissa let Karl win – *Karl, take seven giant steps* – because she wanted him to tag her. When the bell rang I saw Amy emerge from inside a tractor tyre in the adventure playground and walk back to class alone. And I saw Mrs Price watching us from the staffroom window.

CHAPTER 8

W e'd finished learning about the Aborigines by then and had moved on to Animals Between the Tides, filling the pages of our Science books with drawings of rock crabs and cushion stars, periwinkles and black nerita, Neptune's necklace and chitons and sea anemones. That week, before the weather turned too cold, we went on a class trip to the rocky shore below the cliffs. Sister Bronislava came too, and a few mothers, so they could keep an eye on us and make sure we didn't slip and cut ourselves on the rocks or get swept out to sea. I was hoping I might be able to sit next to Karl on the bus, but Melissa got there first, so I sat with Amy. Melissa's mother took the seat at the front, next to Mrs Price; she had the same caramel-coloured hair and green eyes as Melissa, and the same pretty tilt to her nose, but she was very overweight. Her thigh, encased in tight navy-blue slacks, bulged well past the edge of the seat, and through her clingy shirt I could make out the lines of her bra cutting into the fat on her back.

'That's Melissa in a few years,' Amy whispered in my ear.

I'd been thinking the same thing, but I whispered back, 'Don't be mean.' Melissa was my friend now; I'd even been to her house and sat in her spa pool, and she'd sprayed me with her Charlie perfume and shown me the drawer where her big sister kept her tampons and sanitary pads. We'd ganged up on her little sister when she wouldn't leave us alone, pestering us to play hairdressers: *You're too ugly*, we'd told her. *You have nits.*

Mrs Knight had made us hamburgers and chips for dinner, frying the chips in a proper deep fryer. For herself she made gazpacho, which was what the Weight Watchers cookbook called cold tomato soup, and she measured out a third of a cup of cottage cheese and spread it right to the edges of one slice of brown toast. Melissa left two chips and a small piece of hamburger uneaten; she told me it was a good habit to get into.

At the beach the air was hazy, the sky blurring into the grey horizon, and the breeze smelled of wet driftwood and kelp.

'Can anyone tell me what happened just out there?' Mrs Price asked, pointing to the narrow mouth of the harbour. 'A terrible, terrible thing,' she prompted when nobody answered. 'Only sixteen years ago.'

Mrs Jensen raised her hand. 'The *Wahine*?' she said.

'Correct!' said Mrs Price, and Mrs Jensen glanced around the group, looking pleased with herself. 'The *Wahine* ferry sank in a violent storm, and fifty-one people died. Our worst modern maritime tragedy.'

As she told us about the disaster, we looked out across the water and imagined we could see the listing ship. How could it have happened in the harbour, so close to home? The captain lost his bearings in the terrible conditions, she said, and reversed straight into Barrett's Reef while trying to avoid it. After the ship capsized, some of the people drowned, but others died from exposure, or from injuries received during the rush to evacuate. In the water, survivors linked arms but were forced to let go of their neighbours when they succumbed. And while rescuers waited on shore on this side of the harbour, many survivors were swept to the eastern side only to be dashed to pieces on the rocks. That was where almost all of the bodies washed up.

'Is this entirely suitable?' Mrs Knight murmured to Mrs Moretti.

'Look at them lapping it up, though,' said Mrs Asofua – and

it was true. As usual, we were hanging on Mrs Price's every word.

'My sister had sent me a birthday parcel,' said Mrs Jensen. 'It must've been on the *Wahine*, because it never reached me.' She tsked. 'A beautiful moss-stitch cardigan, it was, with mother-of-pearl buttons. Took her weeks.'

We scrambled over the rocks with our activity sheets, looking for all the things Mrs Price wanted us to find, ticking them off one by one, then sketching them in their correct positions on a cross-section of a rockpool.

'Maybe we'll find the tennis ball,' I said to Amy, but she snorted.

'That's long gone.'

'We're in the right place, though. You never know.'

'It's probably in Australia by now.'

'What's probably in Australia?' said Mrs Price.

She did that sometimes – listened to conversations, joined in those she found interesting. Amy beamed at me.

'I walk my dog up there on the weekends,' she said all in a rush. 'Well, you know that, don't you. Justine threw her tennis ball over the cliffs a while ago. She thought we might find it down here, but I told her there's no way.'

Mrs Price nodded. 'Look at the high-tide line. The water would take it, for sure.'

'Told you so,' said Amy.

'I didn't throw the ball on purpose,' I said. 'We were sticking to the track but the wind caught it. It was just an accident.'

'It can get very windy,' said Mrs Price.

As if by way of proof, a sudden gust snatched Gregory Walsh's activity sheet from his hand; he chased it along the beach but could not catch it, and Mrs Price told him no, she didn't have any spares and he should have been more careful. Gregory was not one of her pets. Paula trod on a dead seagull and screamed and screamed, so Mrs Moretti took off Paula's sneaker and washed it in the water while Paula stood there on one leg. Those of us downwind of the dead bird caught the stench of the thing then, and how had we not noticed it before, when it had been there all along? We held our noses, pretended we were going to be sick, and everyone else rushed away from it, but I wanted to see. I poked its sandy breast with a stick, lifted one of its wings, which still seemed to open just as a wing should even though the feathers were ragged, lacy against the light. 'Come away from there, Justine,' said Sister Bronislava, but Mrs Price said, 'She's all right. Look as long as you like, my darling.' She nodded at me, and I knew that she understood. I thought: she has lost someone too.

After we'd finished our activity sheets and tucked them safely away in our bags Mrs Price assigned us new names: Mussel, Sea Lettuce, Cat's Eye, Rock Oyster, Phytoplankton, Zooplankton, and so on. Then we had to sort ourselves into food chains, holding hands with those we thought we might eat and those we thought might eat us.

'No more than five to a chain,' called Mrs Price as we searched for our predators and our prey.

I was Seagull, and I held hands with Melissa, who was Starfish, and she held hands with Gregory, who was Cat's Eye, and he held hands with Amy, who was Microalgae.

This was how nature worked, said Mrs Price: everyone had their part to play, everyone formed a link in the chain, and if a single link was missing then the whole thing collapsed. She pointed to Amy and the other Algae and Planktons. 'You are the producers,' she said. 'You make food from sunlight, from the very air. Isn't that a kind of miracle, people? Then a consumer, who can't make its own food' – she pointed to the Sea Urchins, the Limpets, the Periwinkles, the Snails – 'a consumer comes along and eats you. You become part of its body. But then *another* consumer comes along' – the Starfish, the Mussels, the Oysters – 'and eats the consumer that ate you, and so on up the food chain until we reach' – she pointed to me, flourished her hand – 'the terminal predator.'

'So she's safe?' said Melissa.

'She's safe,' said Mrs Price.

'That's not fair.'

'It's nature, my darling. If you're at the bottom of the food chain you can't do anything about it, and if you're at the top, well, you can't do anything about that either. It's what you're born to.'

Mrs Knight murmured something to Mrs Moretti again, who looked over at us and nodded her head.

We broke for lunch then, taking out our sandwiches and our filled rolls, and finding somewhere dry to sit. I'd been hoping Amy might have some of Mrs Fong's leftovers to swap, but she'd brought her usual sandwiches too. The rocks held the heat of the autumn sun, and we closed our eyes and listened to the waves and the high cries of the gulls. I could feel the cliffs behind me, pushing back against the sea, and when I looked up at their jagged silhouette I lost my bearings for a moment, and the whole world seemed to tilt. I slammed my palms to the rock to hold myself steady before I registered that the clouds were moving, not my body, not the immense cliffs.

Mrs Price sat nearby, sipping one of her diet milkshakes from a plastic shaker, though she was the perfect size and shape.

'I tried those,' said Mrs Knight. 'I've never been so ravenous.'

'They're not for everyone,' Mrs Price agreed.

'The cost, apart from anything else! It's a lot of money for not very much at all, isn't it?'

Mrs Price smiled, took another sip.

'And I mean, look at you. Well, maybe I should give them another try. Do you feel full?'

'Honestly, I do,' said Mrs Price. 'But I suppose I talk myself into it.'

I closed my eyes and dozed again, and when I sat up she

was picking her way from group to group, offering us chunks of coconut ice that she had made herself. 'The secret,' she was saying to Mrs Jensen, 'is an egg white, lightly beaten.'

'An egg white!' said Mrs Jensen. 'Well I never!'

I ate my piece in one go, shattering the pink and white layers between my teeth and swallowing hard. I could have grabbed the tin and wolfed down the whole batch: the milky-sweet mouthful reminded me of something I couldn't quite name, something like hunger. But Mrs Price was manoeuvring past me now, and as she stepped across the rocks to the next group of children, Melissa's mother stretched out a leg and tripped her up. It wasn't on purpose – later Mrs Price herself insisted that it was just a silly accident, just a case of bad timing – but she scraped her shin when she stumbled, and it started to bleed.

'Oh my goodness!' said Mrs Knight. 'I am so sorry! What can I do? Tell me what to do!'

Mrs Price was still holding the tin of coconut ice, though all the pieces had slid to one end. She shook them back into place. 'It's nothing,' she said.

But no, Mrs Knight could see that she was bleeding, and there would be a first-aid kit on the bus, wouldn't there, because they had to carry one by law, as far as she knew, and she'd go and ask the driver.

Mrs Price glanced down at her shin, at the line of blood creeping towards her ankle. We were all looking at it as if it couldn't be real.

'Come, sit down,' said Sister Bronislava, and then, without being asked, I was taking a clean handkerchief from my pocket and kneeling at Mrs Price's feet and pressing on the wound the way you're supposed to.

'Good girl, Justine,' said Mrs Price, though I felt her flinch.

The rest of the class finished their lunch, and two of the mothers lit cigarettes. Jacqui Novak scratched hopscotch squares in a patch of damp sand while Jason Daly and Karl flicked seaweed at each other. Jason Moretti found a pāua shell, whole and perfect, all the colours of the sea and sky caught in its iridescent scoop. Everyone was jealous. Jason Daly said he'd actually seen it first but hadn't been quick enough to grab it, and Vanessa Kaminski said maybe they should share it, but Jason Moretti said you couldn't share a shell, could you. His mother agreed.

'Here we are!' said Mrs Knight, waving the first-aid kit, a little out of breath. She knelt down next to me and opened the lid. 'Excuse me, Justine.'

'Thank you, Mrs Knight,' said Sister Bronislava, holding her hand out for the kit the way she'd held her hand out for the stones we'd thrown at the walnut tree.

'Oh,' said Mrs Knight. 'Right you are.' And we understood her disappointment: she'd wanted to help Mrs Price, earn her gratitude. Be near her.

As soon as Sister Bronislava bathed the cut we saw that it was just a nick.

'I told you it was nothing,' said Mrs Price. 'Such a fuss.'

'These things often look worse than they are,' said Mrs Knight.

All the same, because there were no plasters, Sister Bronislava had to use a huge dressing, as if something much worse had happened.

'Have another piece, Justine,' said Mrs Price, nodding at the tin of coconut ice.

I made it last longer this time, pressing it to the roof of my mouth and sucking instead of biting. I could have lived on it.

'Can you still smell dead seagull?' said Paula to nobody in particular.

I sucked and sucked.

Mrs Knight was saying that it just wasn't on, the complete absence of plasters, and the children's safety had been compromised, and she'd take it up with the bus company.

When nobody was watching I folded the bloody patches to the inside of my handkerchief and slipped it back in my pocket.

By the time we'd packed up to leave, the sky had cleared to a deep hot blue. 'Look,' said Sister Bronislava. 'You can see the South Island.' We squinted into the bright distance and said we could see it, though we might have been looking at a faint cloud on the horizon, some sort of optical illusion; we couldn't be sure. Then Dominic Foster pointed out the ferry, the tiny white ship sailing south, and we waved and called, though it was too far away for anyone on board to notice us there on the shore.

'Where's my pāua shell?' said Jason Moretti.

Nobody knew. We lifted up bags, shook out jackets, but it had vanished.

'Someone's taken it,' he said, casting his eye over us.

'What a thing to say, Jason!' said his mother. 'I do apologise, Mrs Price.'

'Not at all. I can see he's upset.'

'It was right here,' he said. Before anyone could stop him, he'd grabbed Jason Daly's bag and upended it: lunchbox, drink bottle, activity sheet, pens, but no pāua shell.

'Jason! Jason!' said his mother. 'What's got into you? Where's my lovely boy?'

'I *know* someone's taken it!' he said.

'Well now,' she said, scanning the rocks and sand as if the shell might still materialise, 'you have to remember where we are. Things don't stay put on the beach. They drift away, they're buried . . .'

'Let's all look for another pāua shell for Jason on the way back to the bus,' said Mrs Price. 'All right, people?' She had such a knack for fixing things, for making everyone feel better.

Nobody found a pāua, but Amy offered him a whelk, which he declined.

'Take it home for your dinner, eh Amy?' said Karl.

She tossed it in the sea.

I found a dead crab I thought he might like, but he didn't want that either, and nor did he want Selena's fan shell. In the end he accepted a sea urchin from Leanne Parry, though he said it wasn't as good as the pāua.

'Thank you, Leanne,' said his mother. 'That's very kind of you. Isn't it, Jason.'

'Yeah,' he said.

'So we're all friends again,' said Mrs Price.

I was going to throw my crab away, but Karl said, 'Can I see?'

I handed it to him, and he pounced it along my arm, pretending to nip me.

'Ugh,' said Melissa.

He sat next to me on the bus. Still fiddling with the crab, he said, 'I know. I know what we'll do.' His whole body shook with laughter, and he leaned in close to my ear and whispered, 'We'll put it in Susan's tank. It'll freak her out.' His lips brushed my earlobe as he spoke, and I found myself saying, 'Okay.'

Before school the next morning, when everyone was still playing outside, Karl held back the tank cover, and I dropped in the crab. I aimed it behind the clay flowerpot so it couldn't easily be seen. Down it sank, pincers swaying, as if the water had brought it back to life. Susan didn't notice it at first, but after a moment she swam over and peered at it with her golden eyes, her gills curled forwards. Then she bit it, shook it, bit it again. We laughed and laughed.

CHAPTER 9

When the lunchtime bell rang that day, Mrs Price said, 'Justine, do you have a moment?'

Amy looked at me, and I looked at Amy, and we knew what was coming. 'See you later,' she murmured, and headed outside.

Mrs Price said, 'I need someone to pick up a few things from the chemist – would you mind?' She gave me her wallet and a list: *green-apple shampoo, Haliborange tablets, prescription*, it read in her pretty handwriting. 'And something sweet for yourself,' she added, smiling at me.

Sister Bronislava was patrolling the playground, and she stopped me at the front gate and asked where I was going.

'To the chemist, for Mrs Price,' I said, beaming at her, showing her the list and the wallet by way of proof.

'So you're the new one,' she said, and I nodded: yes, yes, I was the new one!

Sister Bronislava didn't smile. 'Off you go, then,' she said. 'Be careful.'

I carried the wallet tucked under my arm like a grown-up. I felt the women I passed looking at me, wondering why I was out of school alone, and then they noticed the wallet and decided I wasn't doing anything wrong – I wasn't one of *those* girls – but rather, I was a girl entrusted with responsibility, a mature and reliable girl.

'Hello, Justine,' said Mr Buchanan, the chemist. 'Haven't seen you in a while.'

The last time I'd been there was when my mother was sick, I realised. She and I had collected her pain medicine, and when she'd said she didn't want to become dependent on it, he'd told her there was no such risk: the pain and not the patient took the drug, in essence. I thought of her pain as a person when he said that; a bony figure who shared her bed. In more recent years, I have sensed that figure – or something like it – in my father's premium room. It lurks behind the shower curtain, folds itself away inside the recliner.

'How are you coping?' Mr Buchanan asked me.

'Fine, thank you,' I said. 'I have a list from Mrs Price.'

'Ah,' he said, and fetched the items for me.

I opened her wallet. Inside, where a photo should be, a card read *I am a Catholic. In case of emergency, please contact a priest. If I am in danger of imminent death, please read the back of this card to me.*

As Mr Buchanan dropped her prescription into a paper bag – a little brown bottle of pills – he said, 'Would you let her know that I won't be able to get these for her any more?'

I thought that was strange, but I didn't say anything.

'And how's the head these days?' he asked. 'Are the seizures staying away?'

'Yes,' I lied.

'Excellent,' he said. 'Looks like you're one of the lucky ones who grow out of them.'

And I did feel lucky. I did.

I was hardly through the school gate before my classmates were mobbing me, asking if I'd bought anything at the dairy. I produced my box of candy cigarettes, and they stretched out their hands.

'Justine! Justine!' they called, jostling to get closer to me.

I took a candy cigarette for myself, and then I gave the rest to my favourites – my pets, including Amy. We began to take deep puffs.

'Thank you, my darling,' said Mrs Price when I delivered her things to her. 'That saves me a lot of bother.' She opened the bottle of pills and shook one into her hand – and I realised I'd seen them before. Same size and shape, same colour.

I hesitated. 'Mr Buchanan says that he won't be able to get those for you any more.'

'What?'

'That's what he told me to tell you.'

'Did he say why?'

'No.' For a second her face changed; I saw her eyes glitter with rage. 'I'm really sorry,' I said. I thought I was going to cry.

'Oh – no, my darling. It's not your fault.' She covered my hand with hers, gave me a sad little smile.

'I might be able to get you some, though,' I said.

Straight after lunch Sister Bronislava came to take us for singing. As she entered the classroom we stood and said, 'Good after*noon*, Sister Bronislava, and God *bless* you, Sister Bronislava.' Because of her fear of loud noises, we knew to sit down quietly and not to scrape our chairs or bang the lids of our desks.

She handed out the songbooks, and we started with 'Dance to Your Daddy', and Mrs Price sat with us and sang along, smiling and nudging and catching our eyes like a best friend. Then she said she'd leave us in Sister Bronislava's capable hands, and we worked our way through 'When Irish Eyes Are Smiling' and 'The Pearly Adriatic', 'The Zulu Warrior' and 'The Leaving of Liverpool'. My favourite was the one about Marianina the fairy: the poppies whispered to her to teach them how to bend, and the ocean waves longed for her to turn them into foam. Two seats down from me Karl was singing in his deep new voice about the clouds: *Marianina, come again, we have tried to dance in vain, come and turn us into rain.* He must have noticed me looking at him because he looked back at me – *Come, oh come, and turn us into rain* – and I was weightless, I was flying. A moment later he passed me a note via Amy: *Want to see something funny?* I nodded, and when we finished the song he opened his desk and fired his cap gun half a dozen times behind the lid.

Sister Bronislava froze, and her songbook dropped to the floor. Eyes wide and white, she hurtled past the blackboard, knocking over Mrs Price's chair and scrabbling at the door to the stationery cupboard. Then she shut herself inside.

Nobody knew what to do. We could hear her taking ragged gasps. Karl was looking at me and laughing, wanting me to laugh too. I could smell gunpowder. Paula was pressing her hands to her temples and muttering, 'Oh this is bad, this is bad, we're in so much trouble.' The smoke from the cap gun curled away into nothing.

'Should we get Mrs Price?' said Jason Moretti.

'No!' said Karl.

I couldn't meet his eye.

Then Dominic went to the stationery cupboard and knocked gently on the door. 'Sister?' he called. 'It's Dom. Everything's all right. Everything's fine. I'm going to come in now, okay? It's just me, Dom.'

He kept talking in his softest voice as he opened the door and stepped inside. We heard Sister Bronislava whimpering and Dom saying, 'You're okay, you're safe, nobody will hurt you,' and he sounded just like our parents when we had a bad dream.

When he led her out of the cupboard by the hand we could see that she was crying, and adults did not cry unless something was very, very wrong.

'I'm going to take Sister back to the convent now,' said Dom, still using his soft voice. 'Can someone help me?'

Karl chewed his lip, stared at the floor.

'Aren't we going to sing "Jamaica Farewell"?' said Brendon

Fitzgerald, who liked to do a Caribbean accent, though we all thought he sounded Welsh.

'Shut up, Brendon,' said Amy.

'I'll help,' I said, and I took Sister Bronislava's arm, and together Dom and I guided her along the corridor and down the steps and across the adventure playground. The climbing rope swung in the breeze, as if someone had just jumped off. Over by his shed, Mr Armstrong the caretaker was tipping some dead leaves and broken branches into the steel drum he used for burning rubbish. Sister Bronislava was quiet now, but I could feel her trembling.

We let ourselves in the door at the back of the convent. The kitchen smelled of Sunlight liquid and mutton, and flypaper fluttered from the ceiling. On the oilcloth-covered table a little vase of pansies sat next to salt and pepper shakers in the shape of Māori warriors, and in the sink a plastic drainer held tea leaves and egg shells. And there beside the humming fridge, its cord coiled neatly around its handle, the sisters' electric knife. Father Lynch had given it to them for Mother's Day the previous year, and had told everyone about it in his Mother's Day sermon. Although the sisters had no real children, he said, they showed us all a mother's love in the many ways they cared for us, and it was right to let them know we appreciated them. They could use the knife for slicing bread and various meats, he explained, as well as for cutting the crusts off the stacks of club sandwiches they made for parish events. It would save them an enormous amount of time.

Dom was still murmuring to Sister Bronislava: 'Just along here now, Sister. Good. Good. You're doing well. Not much further.' Beyond the kitchen lay a series of rooms panelled in dark wood: the dining room, with its water-into-wine wall hanging Sister Marguerite had quilted, and the parlour, reserved for guests, with its statues of Mary and Jesus standing about as if waiting to be offered a seat. In the lounge a dozen mismatched armchairs were set along all four walls, with nothing in the middle of the room. Over in the corner, by the piano, a harp jutted into the empty space like the prow of a ship. A lei of paper flowers hung from it, made by the Island ladies for Polynesian Week.

We couldn't see anyone else around, so we decided to take Sister Bronislava to her bedroom. She was still as white as a Communion host. When we reached the staircase, Dom said, 'Are you all right to go up, Sister?' and she nodded, but she wouldn't let go of us.

Three abreast, we climbed the stairs. A stained-glass window on the landing – the letters *IHS* emitting red and yellow rays – cast lozenges of light on our feet as we passed. I used to think it meant I Have Suffered, until my mother told me it was secret code for the name Jesus.

I had never seen the upstairs of the convent before; I didn't know what to expect. Sister Bronislava's room was at the end of the long hallway and looked out over the cypress hedge to the adventure playground. There was pale grey carpet patterned with flowers, and a single bed covered in a pink candlewick bedspread. One wooden chair, a small chest of drawers. A small mirror, too small to see yourself properly. Nothing else.

'Here we are now, Sister,' said Dom. 'Let's sit you down on the bed. You'll feel better after a little rest.'

'You're very kind,' she said. 'Bless you. Bless you.' And she kissed his hand.

'Can I get you a glass of water? Something to eat?'

She shook her head. 'Oh, it was all such a long time ago,' she said. 'Forty years. The other side of the world.'

I waited for her to say more. I wanted to know how her family had died – I wanted the *details* – but she waved a hand and said, 'These stories are not for children.'

No pictures in the room, I realised – just a crucifix hanging above the bed. No dressing table. No photos.

'Where are all your belongings?' I blurted out.

Sister Bronislava unlaced her ugly black shoes and slipped them off, then smiled at us. 'Thank you for helping me. I am all right now.'

On the way back to class I said, 'How did you know what to do? All those things to say?'

Dom shrugged. 'I have little brothers and sisters.'

'How many in your family again?'

'Nine. I'm number three.'

'Nine! You're so lucky.'

'It's all right. I don't like it when they mess up my coin collection. And my sisters gang up on me.'

I knew Claire in the year below us and remembered the two older girls from before they left St Michael's: tall, skinny, good at netball. They all wore badges on their uniforms: pairs of tiny gold feet, the soles facing up. When I'd asked Claire why, she'd said because they were a Catholic thing, but also because they were the only jewellery Mr Chisholm allowed.

'I wish I had brothers and sisters,' I said. 'Mum lost lots of babies before me.'

'Oh.' He nodded, though neither of us really knew what *lost* meant.

'I have two cousins in Australia,' I went on, 'but I never see them.'

'You might still get brothers and . . .' He stopped. 'Sorry. That was stupid. Sorry.'

'It's okay. I guess Dad could get married again.'

I hadn't even thought about that until I said it, and as soon as the words were out of my mouth I wanted to take them back.

Mr Armstrong emerged from his shed and threw some more rubbish on the fire. The flames whooshed high.

'Is this what we've taught you at St Michael's?' Mrs Price

was saying when we returned. 'Do you think this is acceptable behaviour? Christian behaviour?' The cap gun sat on her desk, and she prodded it as she spoke.

Karl stood at the front of the classroom, his head hanging. 'No, Mrs Price,' he said.

'We do not taunt those who have suffered. We do not throw their sorrows in their faces.'

'No, Mrs Price.'

'I don't even know what to say to you. I'm at a loss.' She picked up the cap gun and strode to the door. 'Wait here.'

We all knew what that meant – and sure enough, a few moments later she returned with Mr Chisholm. Mr Chisholm and the strap.

Melissa started to cry and turned her head to look out the window. Amy closed her eyes. But I watched.

'Which hand do you write with?' said Mr Chisholm.

'My left,' said Karl.

'Hold out the other one, then. We're not cruel, you see. We're not unnecessarily cruel.'

Karl held out his right hand. Mrs Price was sitting in the story chair, far enough away that the strap wouldn't catch her. She crossed her legs, rested her elbows on the wooden arms.

'How many shots did you fire?' said Mr Chisholm.

'Um . . . six?' said Karl.

'All right, six it is.'

We heard the strap suck the air like a gasp and then smack against Karl's palm. I'd thought he would take it without flinching – he always seemed so fearless – but at the first blow his face contorted and tears began to roll down his cheeks.

'What a baby!' said Jason Asofua. 'What a sook!'

The headmaster paused. 'I beg your pardon?'

'Nothing, Mr Chisholm,' said Jason.

'Would you like a turn next?'

Jason shook his head.

The light from the windows glinted off Mr Chisholm's narrow glasses and we could not see his eyes. He raised the strap again, flicking it back like a whip and then hurling it down on Karl's hand. *Two*, I counted in my head.

At the third blow, Karl snatched his hand away.

'Come along now,' said Mr Chisholm. 'I'm sure you want this over with just as much as I do. Yes, there we are. Good man.'

Three. Four.

Karl was sobbing now, his shoulders and chest shaking.

'Nearly there,' said Mr Chisholm.

Five.

'You can do it, Karl,' said Mrs Price from the story chair.

He held out his hand again.

Six.

'Good, so that's that,' said Mr Chisholm. 'You can go back to your desk now.'

Amy pulled out Karl's chair for him. He was cradling his right hand in his left, and I could make out a line of blood gathering in the crease of his palm.

'Enter it in the log book, please, Mrs Price,' said Mr Chisholm, and Mrs Price wrote down what Karl had done and the day he'd done it, and the punishment he'd received, because those were the rules.

After school I cleared away Dad's whisky glass from the night before and returned the almost empty bottle to the sideboard, tidied the newspaper with the death notices circled. Down the hallway, in the sunless white bathroom, my mother's unused medication sat in the mirrored cabinet. I knew I should go and sort through it, all the rattling pills that hadn't helped much in the end, and I knew I should do it before Dad came home from the shop. Still, I paused to make three pieces of cheese on toast with Vegemite – I was starving, I told myself.

Then I dusted and vacuumed the living room, which didn't really need it, and then I started on the windows. *Keep the place nice for your dad* – that's what my mother had told me – and I thought that if I kept it clean enough, somehow he'd clean his life up too. Stop drinking. Turn back into his old self. When I stood on a step ladder to reach the top of the living-room windowpane, I saw a tiny bit of the harbour: our ocean view, Mum used to joke. Perhaps I didn't need to plunder the mirrored cabinet after all; I hadn't promised Mrs Price anything, had I? I sprayed window cleaner on the ranchslider and wiped it off with a rag torn from my old pyjamas. Elephants and bunnies – how babyish. At the bottom of the glass the security sticker was starting to peel away in the ruthless afternoon sun. **BURGLAR BEWARE!** it read. *ARTICLES OF VALUE ON THESE PREMISES ARE INVISIBLY MARKED FOR* **INSTANT POLICE IDENTIFICATION!**

A man had come to the door one day when Mum was sick, selling the security kits. 'You look like the kind of lady who wants to keep her family safe,' he'd said to her.

'What's this about?' she'd said. 'We don't have a lot of time.'

She was standing there in her dressing gown – embroidered with butterflies – and ratty old slippers that she insisted were more comfortable than the ones Dad and I had bought her. It was clear she had nowhere to be. Her hair, which had grown in grey and coarse after the treatment, was sticking out at crazy angles. I hung back at the end of the hallway, hoping the man wouldn't notice me and connect me with this person who looked nothing like a mother.

I'm not proud of that. Though there are worse things I've done.

He showed her the kit. For just twenty dollars, he said, she'd get an invisible marker and three stickers—

'Twenty dollars?' she interrupted. 'For a pen? That's far too dear.'

'You get the stickers as well,' said the man, 'and the stickers glow in the dark, so potential offenders can see them even at night. You write your personal code on all your valuables, and then if they're ever stolen, the police can identify them.'

'How do they do that?'

'They check them with a special light.'

'Like a black light?'

'Yes, exactly.'

'But they'd have to be found for that to happen.'

'Sure, of course,' said the man. 'The thing is, the stickers act as a powerful deterrent, so you're highly unlikely to be robbed in the first place. The pen's a safety net, if you will.'

Mum wrote our details on everything in the house after that: the TV, the telephone, the lamps and vases, the coffee table, the vacuum cleaner, her sewing machine, the record player, the records themselves. When she wasn't sleeping, or staring into the drugged distance, she seemed possessed by a nervous energy, moving from room to room and looking for things she hadn't yet labelled. Dad said we should just let her do it; she was taking a lot of medication and wasn't thinking straight.

'If it makes her happy—' he began.

I didn't really know how to talk to her by that stage; she kept coming out with strange remarks that she'd repeat over and over, and sometimes it seemed she was chatting to people I couldn't see. Not that I believe in ghosts.

'Doesn't it feel wrong to be back?' she'd say. 'Doesn't the ground feel like water?' For a while she kept asking me where Alex was – her brother, who had died of meningitis in his teens – and then she started saying, 'I'm home. I'm home.'

Then, late one night – it must have been 2 or 3 A.M. – I heard Dad talking to her in the living room, pleading with her to put away the invisible marker and go to bed.

'I'm not a child, Neil,' she snapped. 'Don't tell me what to do.'

'You need your rest, love.'

'I'll get plenty of rest soon enough.'

'Don't say that.'

'Can't you stop pretending?'

A month later, she died.

We were never burgled, so maybe the stickers worked.

I finished wiping the last trickles of window cleaner from the ranchslider, and then I went to the garage. Dad worked on bits and pieces for the shop out there – dining chairs that needed new webbing, chests of drawers with broken veneer. He could fix almost anything: heat marks, water marks, sun damage, rot. I loved that about him. I opened a cupboard and pushed the bottles of linseed oil and turps out of the way – and two bottles of whisky. They were turning up all over the house by then, but I knew better than to say anything or to shift them. It was just for the time being, he told me once when he was drinking. Soon, very soon, he'd stop, because he wouldn't need it any more. I closed the cupboard, checked the drawers under the tool bench that were cluttered with sandpaper and fine steel wool and blocks of wax. It didn't take me long to find what I was looking for: a black light.

Back in the house, I closed the living-room curtains, making sure to overlap them where they met, and then I shut the door to the hall. Almost completely dark.

I turned on the black light.

I don't know what I expected to see – I suppose I just wanted evidence of the things my mother had touched, the things she had chosen to safeguard. And yes, there was the code the salesman had told her to use, inked in her neat hand across the base of the TV: our phone number, followed by 83 for the year. There it was on the base of the record player, too, and on the underside of the coffee table, fluorescing an eerie violet-white as I shone the beam across the wood. I thought of Sister Bronislava's empty bedroom. My lost pen with the ferry that slid between the Sounds and the open ocean. Things mattered, they *mattered*: they reminded us who we were. I started to wriggle out from under the table, and as the beam shifted I noticed something else. Words. Whole sentences, in fact. Lying on my back, I passed the black light over them line by line.

And how long is the winter? You must support her head. See how it lolls on its little stalk. When he tossed the coin we watched it flutter above us like a silver moth. Who is the man at the door? Alex, Alex, give it back. It's my turn now. Tails. Heads. Tails. Far too dear. I can hear the baby's heartbeat. I'm home. How hungry are you? I'm home.

The handwriting was my mother's, but there was a looseness to the letters, an urgency. I checked the TV and the record player again and found other sentences. There were some on the back of the heater too, and underneath the standard lamp, and when I pulled the heavy art-nouveau sideboard away from the wall I discovered more.

I think it's too green to burn. You could never make yourself. Too green and too wet. Only God could make you. And that's why you are His, you belong to Him. They have pierced my hands and feet; they have numbered all my bones. Bake until a knife comes out clean. Elizabeth Celine Crieve. Elizabeth Celine Crieve. Look: nothing but smoke.

Everywhere I shone the black light, I found more writing. On the bottom of the old steamer trunk, and on the back of the Venetian mirror that hung above the fireplace, and behind the bookshelves, and on the books too. I checked the dining room, the kitchen, the bedrooms, the bathroom, the hall; my mother had not missed a single room. She'd even written along the skirting boards behind the curtains, though it dissolved where the daylight could reach it: those sentences finished halfway through. The ink had also vanished from certain spots on things we handled a lot: the bottoms of vases that I picked up to dust, balancing them on my palm as I wiped them clean; the

corners of the record covers of my father's sad records; the rec-
ipe book I pulled from the shelves several times a week, looking
for dishes that Dad might like, new dishes that my mother had
never made. He and I had been rubbing the ink away little by
little in the months since she had died, I realised. How could
we have known of these erasures? Yet still I wanted every lost
letter back. I recognised some phrases – snatches of hymns and
prayers, or things she often used to say, or her own name written out in full. Others I could not decode: they were memories,
I supposed, or pieces of them. Memories and fears.

*Will it hurt? Will I know who I am? Hold on tight to the
chains, legs back, legs forward to kick the sky. When beggars die,
there are no comets seen. I wanted the one with the eyes that
closed when you laid her down, but they bought me the cheaper
one with the fixed eyes. Father Maguire says we are born perfect
but inevitably we sin. Aren't you a clever girl. How cool it was on
the deck as we sailed through the Sounds. I clung to the rail and
could not trust my legs. Wellington far behind me. The air full of
water. Who is there? Who is there?*

My father would be home soon. I hid the black light under
my bed, behind the skirt of my Holly Hobbie bedspread. Then,
as if someone could hear me, I crept to the bathroom. Her pale
blue dressing gown swung on its hook as I opened the door.

In the mirrored cabinet I looked older: for the first time I
could see my mother in my reflection. Her cushiony upper lip,
her dark blue eyes. Her dead-straight reddish hair. I trailed my
fingers down the side of my face, over my collarbone and chest.
Amy was right: I needed a bra – and I needed someone to take
me to James Smith's to get one. What did you even ask for in
such a shop?

I opened the cabinet. My mother's medication was clustered
on the top shelf, above Dad's brush and comb and his Old
Spice. No one would know, I told myself. No one would miss
it. The brown glass bottles clinked as I sorted through them

to find the one I wanted: morphine sulphate. I buried it at the bottom of my schoolbag, ready for the next day. Ready to give to Mrs Price.

Rachel Jensen was crying as she took her place at her desk after the morning break: her Ronald McDonald doll had been stolen.

'It was right there in my bag,' she said. 'Hanging right there.'

Other children had lost things too – a koala keyring, a four-coloured biro, a pair of PE shorts, a packet of raisins from inside a lunchbox. We didn't know who we could trust.

'This is very serious, people,' said Mrs Price. 'It's clear that the thief has no intention of stopping. I must ask you all not to leave anything valuable – anything that the thief might deem valuable – in your bags.'

'You should check Amy's bag!' said Rachel. 'She still hasn't lost a thing!'

'Is that true, Amy?'

Amy nodded.

Without a word Mrs Price went out to the corridor.

'Don't worry,' I whispered.

'I'm *not* worried,' said Amy, glaring at me.

'Sorry, Rachel, no luck,' said Mrs Price when she returned.

'She must have stashed it somewhere then,' said Rachel. 'Dirty thief.'

Just then Brendon called from the back of the room. 'Mrs Price! It's Susan – she's hurt!'

Mrs Price ran to the axolotl tank and looked inside. 'She's cut her leg on something sharp,' she said. She bent down to peer behind the clay flowerpot. 'People,' she said, 'why is there a dead crab in Susan's tank?'

Karl glanced at me and waggled his eyebrows.

'Who put this here?' said Mrs Price, her voice rising.

She lifted the cover from the tank, reached in and grabbed

the crab. '*Who put this here?*' she asked again, brandishing it at us, droplets of water flying. 'Look how sharp it is! *Look!* You all know that Susan can injure herself very easily! You all know we don't put anything sharp in her tank!'

I had never seen her so angry. I sank down in my seat.

'I've had just about enough of the sneakiness in this class,' she went on. 'The stealing. The cruelty.' She ran her eyes over us, looking from face to face. 'We are supposed to be a family!'

'Justine found a crab at the rocky shore,' said Rachel.

'She did,' said Jason Moretti. 'She tried to give it to me, but it wasn't nearly as good as my pāua.'

'Justine, did you put this in Susan's tank?' said Mrs Price.

The air in the room felt like water. I couldn't breathe.

'I did,' said Karl.

Everyone turned to look at him.

'I see,' said Mrs Price. 'Why on earth would you do that?'

Karl shrugged. 'I never thought it would hurt her.'

'Do I need to get Mr Chisholm again, Karl? For the second time in as many days?'

Another shrug.

Mrs Price regarded him in silence. He stared down at his right hand, which was puffy and bruised where the strap had hit him.

'I am going to give you another chance, Karl,' Mrs Price said at last. 'Come here.' She scooped Susan out of the tank with the Tupperware container and handed her to him. 'Take her to the activity tables. Gather round, people,' she said, waving us over. 'We might as well learn something from this.' From the shelf she took one of the dissection kits we'd used for the cows' eyes. 'Put her on the tray,' she said. 'And gently! You don't want to hurt her more.'

We could all see Susan's injured leg now, cut halfway through, the foot almost detached.

'No way a dead crab could do that,' muttered Amy.

I didn't think the crab looked sharp enough to have caused such a bad wound either – but I supposed Mrs Price knew about these things, because she was the teacher. She slid the scalpel from the dissection kit and gave it to Karl. 'Cut it off,' she said.

He stared at her. 'What?'

'Cut the foot off. It's what a vet would do.'

'But I'm not a vet. I mean . . .'

'You'll be doing her a kindness. Trust me.'

Susan's feathery gills were fluttering, and she began to squirm towards the edge of the tray.

'Oh no you don't,' said Mrs Price, nudging her back into place. 'Quickly now, Karl. She won't like breathing air for too long.'

He looked wildly around the table at us. When he caught my eye, I nodded at him.

'Do I cut it right through?' he said to Mrs Price.

'Right through. Trust me, she won't even feel it.'

Some of the girls covered their eyes, but Mrs Price said, 'Everyone watching, please. This is a useful lesson.'

Karl held Susan down on the tray, and then he began to cut. At the first touch of the blade, she jolted under his swollen right hand.

'I think she's feeling it,' said Paula.

'Shh! Let him concentrate,' said Mrs Price.

Four strokes of the scalpel and it was done.

Mrs Price returned Susan to her tank. 'There now,' she murmured as she lowered her into the water. 'That'll feel better.'

After school I stayed behind to help, as usual – I didn't even need to be asked. Melissa, Selena and Rachel, who were the other pets at that point, contented themselves with the lesser jobs; everyone knew that I was the favourite of the favourites, the top pet.

'I thought I might have a little party,' said Mrs Price as we tidied the classroom for her. 'You're all such a help to me – I thought it might be nice to give you a bit of a treat.'

She handed us each an invitation with a picture of Wonder Woman holding up her bullet-proof bracelets, the Lasso of Truth looped to her hip. 'My place, Saturday afternoon. Yes?'

Yes, yes, yes, we said.

After the others had left I fetched my bag from the corridor and reached inside. For one panicky moment I thought the pills might have been stolen – but there at the bottom was the little glass bottle, cool as sea water.

'For you,' I said, giving it to Mrs Price. My stomach felt like Christmas morning.

'What's this?' Then, when she read the label, she smiled her beautiful smile just for me. 'Aren't you a sweetheart,' she said. And she slipped the bottle into her handbag.

One other thing that remains with me from that day: as I turned to leave I saw Susan's foot in Mrs Price's rubbish bin, white and perfect, like a baby's.

CHAPTER 10

The day we buried my mother, Lorraine Downes was crowned Miss Universe. Dad and I watched the TV broadcast the following night, sitting side by side on the couch while our plates of macaroni cheese cooled and congealed on our laps. Outside, the wind whipped the weatherboards and the rain clattered on the roof. She was so beautiful, Lorraine Downes, with her soft blond waves and her wide smile – the most beautiful woman in the universe, and she came from New Zealand. We already knew she'd won, but we pretended all the same: Venezuela had a decent chance, we said. Ireland could well take it out. When Gambia won Miss Amity, we agreed it was the kiss of death – and as soon as we'd spoken the word we caught ourselves, glanced at each other, then back at the Parade of Nations. Dad took a sip of his drink.

We'd watched the pageant every year, he and I, always scoring the contestants according to our own impossible standards – it was our little game, just between the two of us. The year my mother died we were even pickier, scanning each contestant for flaws: Aruba had bulky thighs, Gibraltar was fat, Argentina had wonky teeth and far too much makeup, Honduras's eyes were too close together. Bahamas could hardly walk for the weight of her national costume: a spiky yellow sunburst that looked homemade. Why was Finland dressed in animal pelts with a dead fox on her head? Was

Uruguay meant to be a matador? We yelled our scores at the TV: four out of ten! Four point five!

Lorraine Downes wore a white dress with oversized kōwhai flowers trailing from one shoulder.

'That's a bit of a stretch,' said Dad.

'But what's our national costume anyway?' I said.

'Hmm,' he said.

We were especially brutal in the swimsuit parade, noting thick waists and problem ankles, chests too small and chests too large. I'd learned what to look for. Three point five! Three! The host reminded us that the initial swimsuit judging had already been completed under competitive conditions, with each candidate wearing the same style suit. That was fair, we remarked – they wouldn't have been able to hide behind zigzags and ruffles. Dad poured himself another drink. A fresh burst of rain rattled down.

Soon enough they'd chosen the twelve semi-finalists and displayed their preliminary scores for the seven million of us watching around the world. When USA scored the highest we shouted, 'Rigged! Rigged!' She was so fake. We gave her a two. They whisked the sixty-eight losers off stage in an ad break before the personal interviews, and we cringed a little when we heard Lorraine's accent: was that what we sounded like? Venezuela made the mistake of asking for an interpreter and then not really using him; she wanted to succeed in all her ambitions, she said, but she might as well have said nothing at all; she might as well have kept her mouth shut.

'Three!' I yelled.

'Three point five,' yelled Dad, 'but only because of the legs!' He drank his drink.

Finland talked about her American penpal, and the host said if any young men were watching and wanted a penpal who looked like her, they should send him ten dollars and he'd see what he could do. USA said she wanted to be a dentist and she would design a horseshoe-shaped office with all the chairs looking inwards to a garden filled with small animals she could care for, like rabbits. 'Fake!' we shouted. 'Fake!' We gave her a one point five.

We scrutinised the judging panel; they'd go for someone leggy and tanned, we thought, with long hair and lots of teeth. Perhaps someone like Lorraine, we murmured . . . but still we pretended we didn't know the outcome. We put aside our uneaten meals, and Dad filled his glass once more. The semi-finalists began to pick their way down a wide flight of stairs in new swimsuits: purple lycra that looked dark at the crotch, as if their bodies had leaked. It was just the lighting, we decided, but shouldn't somebody have noticed? Didn't they have rehearsals and checks and so on to make sure nothing went wrong? An unseen woman announced how much each contestant weighed, and Lorraine was not the lightest.

Then Dad said, 'Did you hear that?'

'Hear what?' I said. 'The rain?'

He turned down the TV. 'The bell.'

We'd given Mum a bell to keep by her bed when she was sick: a pretty thing that Dad had brought home from the shop. It was made of cranberry glass, with a clear glass clapper inside, and for months we'd been listening out for it, rushing to see what she needed. Could we bring her a few bites to eat? Wash her face? Fetch her some more ice chips so she could hold them in her poor sore mouth?

'I didn't hear anything,' I said.

Dad held up a finger and listened, then drained his drink in one swallow. He disappeared in the direction of their bedroom while I kept watching the silent contestants descend the stairs in their dark-crotched swimsuits and take their places on the stage. Lorraine Downes stood on the end of the row with her right knee bent, her right heel lifted.

When Dad didn't return, I followed him down the hall and found him sitting on the bare bed, his face in his hands. The curtains thrashed at the open window, and the bell lay on its side, spattered with rain.

'I thought . . .' he said. 'I thought . . .'

'It was just the wind.' I pulled the sash window shut and righted the bell, wiping it dry on my jersey. He winced as the little glass clapper chimed. The bedroom was freezing cold.

'It would have been a wedding present originally,' he said. 'Rare to find them still intact these days.'

And yes, I'd worried it would break every time Mum rang for us, the glassy notes carrying the length of the house; it seemed such a fragile thing to make such a noise.

'What do I do with it now?' he said.

'Take it back to the shop?'

He stared at me. 'I can't *sell* it.'

'No,' I said. 'No, sorry . . .'

'I can't sell it, and I can't keep looking at it.'

'I don't know, Dad.'

She was so light towards the end, so small; she seemed to disappear into the mattress, her body hardly making a bump under the blankets.

I can't remember what happened to the bell.

In the living room Dad poured a fresh drink, and I turned the TV back up. We were just in time to see the five finalists announced; USA grabbed at Lorraine Downes's hand like they were friends.

'Fake,' I said.

Dad drank.

In silence we listened to the prizes the winner would receive: ninety thousand dollars, a personal-appearance contract, first-class flights, jewellery, shoes, tanning lotions and oils, a speed-boat, a camera, makeup, perfume, a mink coat, a convertible, evening gowns, a home computer with a special help key. Then a singer called El Puma took each of the finalists by the hand and sang right into their faces about being guilty of not giving them the love that they wanted.

'Look at USA,' I said. 'She thinks she's already won.'

Dad drank.

'Six for England?' I said. 'Do you think? She has pretty eyes, but I don't like that nose.'

He drank.

El Puma pulled Lorraine in close. 'I'm guilty, my love,' he sang at her while she smiled and smiled.

'Nine point five?' I said. 'For Lorraine?' Her slender arms, her slender waist. One hundred and twenty-four pounds. I wondered how much I weighed.

USA cut in while El Puma was still singing to Ireland, which must have been planned but looked pushy all the same.

'That's got to count against her,' I said.

And then Miss Universe 1982 was taking the stage, and she looked like Wonder Woman, and she climbed the stairs to sit on a throne of silver. The host announced that their computer had tabulated the judges' results, and these had been reviewed by representatives of an international accounting firm, and then it was time, it was coming, and I crossed my fingers for Lorraine as if I didn't already know. One by one the runners-up were escorted off the stage by men dressed as soldiers of some description, and it was down to USA and New Zealand, and when the host said the first runner-up was USA the camera zoomed in on Lorraine. She started to cry, and I started to cry, and she walked across the stage and waved to the crowd, waved to the seven million watching her, and I wanted to see her every expression, but the credits were skimming across her, covering her up, and everything was over far too soon.

'We won,' I said to Dad.

'Yeah.'

The other contestants were mobbing Lorraine on her throne, and she had to hold her crown in place while they kissed her and mauled her and then tried to wipe the kisses away.

'Night then,' I said.

'Night.'

He poured himself another drink.

CHAPTER 11

Amy rang me on the Saturday to see if I wanted to walk Bonnie along the cliffs after lunch.

'I can't, sorry,' I said. 'I've got a school thing.'

'What school thing?'

'With Mrs Price.'

'I haven't heard about that.'

'Yeah, it's just a few of us.'

'Oh.'

'Yeah.'

'Okay, well . . . see you at church tomorrow?'

'Maybe.'

In fact, I was going to church less and less. Dad had all but stopped after Mum died, and most Sundays I preferred to burrow down in my bed and read books. When Father Lynch remarked that he hadn't seen me at Mass in a while, I said I'd been going to the afternoon service at the hospital chapel because it reminded me of my mother. How easily the lie came to me.

I knew that things were changing between Amy and me, and I felt bad about it – I did. Part of me wanted to just go to her house and play Guess Who? and Operation and rank our classmates from prettiest to ugliest: that would be easy, comfortable. I wanted to argue about who got to be Barbie and who got to be Skipper, who got to be the Slavedriver and who the Slave; I missed our games, even though Amy could take things too far. *Slave, peel me a grape! Yes, master. Stupid slave! Pick out the seeds! But don't wreck the grape! Yes, master. Slave, dance for me! On one leg! But first, bring me a butterfly! Yes, master.* And I had no nice clothes to wear to Mrs Price's – nothing like the jumpsuits and Levi's and ruffle-fronted blouses that Melissa and Selena and Rachel had. I searched to the back of my wardrobe and to the bottom of every drawer and found only little-girl things: appliquéd animals, duck-shaped buttons, sturdy pinafores and dungarees. The one top I liked wouldn't do up across the chest any more, and I could hardly wear my school uniform.

Folded between two T-shirts was the handkerchief I'd pressed to Mrs Price's leg a few days earlier. The blood dried to dead-leaf brown. Who would keep such a thing?

When Dad was in the shower I stole into his room. He and Mum had matching antique armoires – too big for the house, really, but Mum had fallen in love with them at an auction, and he'd bought them for her. Neither of us had opened Mum's since we'd chosen her burial clothes; Father Lynch said we'd know when the time was right. I turned the tasselled key, and the door swung back, and there were all her things just as she had left them. Her sundress with the cherries. Her lace-collared blouse like Princess Diana's. The velvet skirt that was too tight at the waist but that she couldn't bring herself to give away to the St Vincent de Paul. That's your fault, she'd said, laughing, jabbing her finger at me. I could hear her. I could *smell* her. I trailed my hand across the clothes, and they swung on their hangers. She would know what to ask for at James Smith's.

The shower water was still running, but I didn't have much time. I pulled out piece after piece, holding each one up against myself to gauge the size: too baggy, too long, too low-cut. I was almost ready to give up when I found them: her blue-gold taffeta harem pants and the matching jacket with the padded shoulders. If I cinched it in with a wide belt and rolled up the cuffs to show the gold lining, I thought I could get away with it.

I was shifting all the hangers back into place when something caught my eye on the floor of the armoire. The invisible marker. The lid was on the wrong end, as if someone had just been using it, but the tip was dried out. I pushed the clothes aside and looked at the back wall. Big and blank and hidden away in the dark. I could hear Dad singing to himself under the shower. Hurrying to my room, I stuffed the taffeta outfit into my school-bag and retrieved the black light from under my bed. Then Dad turned off the shower and slid open the cubicle door.

I never showed him all the writing I found. I told myself that it would only upset him to see just how delirious she was at the end. But also – I thought that all those lines and fragments of lines were messages from my mother just for me. Some kind of code that would tell me how to be like her.

I shone the black light inside the armoire – and yes, there on the back wall, my mother's luminous hand.

She said I'm scared and I said no you're not. Look at the pave-ment in front of you, not at the wheels. Who are you? The petals of my father's best Rosa Mundi. White splashed with crimson or vice versa. Are there any more bids? Her nose bled and bled and it was my fault and she said it was my fault. Named for Fair Rosamund, the mistress of the King, though I didn't know what a mistress was. Elizabeth Celine Crieve. Beautiful burl walnut, ladies and gents. You don't see these every day. Elizabeth Celine Crieve. Come away from the edge. Going once. Going twice. You've no one to blame but yourself. Who are you? Oh my little girl. Oh my own darling one.

As soon as I heard the bathroom door open, I shoved the black light inside the armoire, turned the key and rushed to sit on the bed.

'Hello, you,' said Dad. He smelled of Old Spice and Imperial Leather soap.

'Hi,' I said. 'I just thought I'd let you know, I don't need a ride to Mrs Price's.'

'Is Mrs Fong taking you?'

'Amy's not going. No, I'll bike there.'

'Is she all right? Amy?'

'She wasn't invited.'

'That's not very nice.'

'It's just for the ones who help Mrs Price. A bit of a treat.'

'You could stop by Amy's afterwards, maybe.'

And I could have: I easily could have.

'Dad,' I said, 'it's not my fault Mrs Price chose me and not her. If I go to her place she'll want to play the same games we've played for years, like we're still little kids. She needs to grow up.'

He studied me for a moment. Then he said, 'Well, I don't mind dropping you off. It'd be nice to know where you're going to be.'

'She's my teacher. I think it's safe.'

He sighed. 'Okay, okay.'

'I'll be back for dinner,' I said, and kissed his cheek. Old Spice, Imperial Leather soap. Whisky.

Once I was down on the flat I took the slightly longer way to Mrs Price's so I could stop at the toilets in the park. My mother had told me never to go inside them alone, though she hadn't explained why. I shut myself in a cubicle and hung my school-bag from the hook on the back of the splintered door. There were phone numbers written on the walls, and names inside hearts, and *Nicky is a slag* and *Michelle has crabs*, and drawings I couldn't decipher but knew were obscene. I pulled off my Aran jersey and my corduroys, trying not to let the fabric touch the wet concrete floor. Then I put on the blue-gold taffeta.

'Justine, my darling, come in! Don't you look incredible! The others are through here – follow me.'

Mrs Price's perfume drifted behind her as she walked – jasmine, and sweet warm wafts of something like honeysuckle.

She'd pulled her blond waves into a high ponytail, and she wasn't wearing any makeup. Her eyes looked different without it: smaller, flatter somehow. The house was much more modern than our old villa, with textured ceilings that sparkled when tiny bits of glitter caught the light, and amber lightshades suspended at different heights. Melissa, Selena and Rachel sat in the sunken living room, sipping from tall glasses. Through the windows I could see the back yard: paving stones winding their way across a neat lawn, white wrought-iron chairs at a white wrought-iron table, and a large rock garden that bristled with cactuses and succulents. Mrs Price took my hand and led me down the steps into the carpeted conversation pit.

'What's your poison?' she said. 'Traffic Light? Spider? Fanta with a cherry?'

'Spider, please,' I said, and she disappeared to the kitchen.

'I love your outfit,' said Melissa, fingering the flared hip of my mother's harem pants. 'You look so different.'

And they looked different too: teased hair, a dusting of eye shadow, a hint of lip gloss.

They'd all taken their shoes off, I noticed, so I slipped mine off as well. The taffeta rustled with my every move, and I could feel my narrow shoulders slipping about underneath the jutting pads of the jacket. Plates of brandy snaps and chocolate crackles and Russian fudge sat on the coffee table, and there were orange halves spiky with toothpicks stuck through cheese and grapes. I took a seat, the blush-pink carpet lush as grass at my back, the latest *Australian Women's Weekly* lying open next to me. It was bigger and glossier than the New Zealand magazine, and more expensive. I remembered my mother laughing about it with a friend: they actually published it monthly now, she'd snorted, but they could hardly call it *that*.

'Here we are,' said Mrs Price, handing me my drink. The glass was a tall, narrow trumpet with an opal sheen, and the vanilla ice cream was fizzing on top of the Coke. There was a straw made of glass, too, with a little glass spoon on the bottom for stirring. It was so fine, so thin, I thought it might snap in my mouth.

Selena sucked the cream from a brandy-snap tube, and Rachel hissed at her not to be so vulgar.

'No rules here, my darlings,' said Mrs Price, putting on a record: Duran Duran, which our parents thought was nonsense. 'Now, tell me all your secrets.'

We laughed, glanced at one another.

'Like what?' said Rachel.

'Like anything. Which boys do you like?'

'Karl,' said the three of them in unison.

'Karl,' I said, nodding.

'He's very handsome, isn't he?' said Mrs Price. 'Those eyes. That hair. But are you going to share him? Cut him in four pieces?'

We laughed again.

'Jason Moretti has gorgeous eyes too,' said Selena.

'He knows it, though,' said Melissa. 'You want one who doesn't know it.'

'What about Brendon?' said Rachel. 'Nice eyes and nice smile.'

'Maybe,' said Selena.

'Dom's nice too,' I said.

'Dominic Foster!' said Melissa. 'He's so freckly and skinny.' She wrinkled her nose.

'You can tell that his mum knitted his school jersey,' said Rachel. 'It's not even a proper one.'

'What else?' said Mrs Price. 'What other secrets do you have?'

Selena said that she hated her piano lessons and wanted to give up, but her parents had just spent a thousand dollars on a piano. Melissa said that once, in the middle of the night, she'd caught her mother eating chunks of butter right off the block.

'We all are so much more complicated than we appear,' said Mrs Price. She slid a grape off a toothpick with her teeth.

'I hate my legs,' said Melissa.

'Your legs, my darling?'

'Ugh, look at them. I'm so hairy.'

'That's not really a secret,' said Selena.

'Sweetheart, it's the down of a peach!' said Mrs Price, running her hand over Melissa's shin. 'You're perfect. You're all perfect.'

And in that moment, cushioned in her blush-pink sunken living room, we believed her.

'And what about the stealing?' she said. 'Who do we think is the thief?'

'I *know* it's Amy,' said Rachel.

'Oh?' said Mrs Price. 'How do you know that?'

'I already told you – she's the only one who hasn't had anything stolen.'

'Yeah, but she doesn't really have any good stuff,' said Selena.

'She doesn't, it's true,' said Melissa. 'Only the mercury from the dental nurse.'

'That's why she's stealing everybody else's stuff!' said Rachel. 'She's such a liar. She should just kill herself.'

'Justine, what do you think?' said Mrs Price.

I stirred my drink. The ice cream had melted away into the Coke and the whole thing looked like silty water. 'I need a bra,' I blurted. 'I think you get them at James Smith's, but I don't know what to ask for.'

Rachel started to giggle, and Mrs Price shot her a look.

'You do get them at James Smith's, my darling,' she said. 'That's exactly right. I'll take you there after school one day, yes? Thursday?' She patted my knee and smiled.

'So has Mr Price gone out for the afternoon?' said Selena, who clearly didn't know about the car accident that had killed him and their daughter.

Mrs Price turned to her, still smiling. 'There's no Mr Price.'

'Oh,' said Selena. 'I just thought . . .'

'No,' Mrs Price said smoothly. There was a silence, and then, as the next song started, she jumped to her feet. 'This one's my favourite!' she said, and began dancing to 'Hungry Like the Wolf'.

And we jumped up too, and we copied what she did with her body, and we let ourselves go and danced and danced, clawing the air and snarling and baring our teeth like wolves.

When the song finished we flopped to the soft pink carpet again to catch our breath.

'My dad won't let us listen to them,' said Rachel. 'He says they're all a bunch of poofs.'

I thought Mrs Price might tell her off for using such a word – we'd never use it at school – but then I remembered: no rules here.

'How silly,' said Mrs Price. 'It's just hair and makeup.'

'And women's blouses,' said Rachel.

Mrs Price sat up. 'Does your father mind *you* wearing makeup?'

Rachel pressed her lips together as if to hide them. 'A little bit's okay, I think,' she said, and I knew she'd put on the lip gloss after her father had dropped her off.

'Let's have some fun,' said Mrs Price. 'Come on.' She gestured to us to follow her.

I thought it was the most beautiful bedroom I'd ever seen; the kind of room Lorraine Downes would sleep in. Heavy satin curtains held back by gold ropes, and a queen-size bed with a dark pink velour headboard to match the fitted dark pink bedspread, and gold scatter cushions everywhere. In the corner, a piece of exercise equipment I recognised from the ads in my mother's magazines: the Speedslimmer, designed to beat ugly tummies and attack all your troublespots. Mrs Price lifted a lid on her dressing table, and the whole thing opened like a cocktail cabinet to display rows and rows of makeup. 'Who's first?' she said.

She made up each one of us in turn, applying blusher to give us cheekbones, brushing on eye shadow as fine as pollen. We closed our eyes and felt her touching our delicate lids, turning them fuchsia, tangerine, peacock green, electric blue, and then she stroked the mascara wand through our eyelashes, and we tried to hold very still. The lipstick came last: her frosted pink, as pink as coconut ice. When we looked in her mirror, we did not recognise ourselves.

'What about you?' I said to her reflection. 'Shall we make you up too?'

She laughed, clapped her hands. Took a seat on the velvet stool.

We didn't really know what we were doing, but she taught us all the tricks. Lighter shadow on the lid itself, darker shadow in the socket, something shimmery on the browbone. Silver in the inner corners to open up the eyes. Blend, blend, blend. Concealer to cover up every flaw. Blusher to the hollows of the cheeks, all the way to the temples. Don't be afraid of going too far. An extra dot of gloss in the centre of the bottom lip to give it pout. We took down her ponytail and teased and sprayed her hair, pinning it up this way and that, parting it on one side then the other to see what suited her best, just as we did with our dolls.

'But where are you going?' we said. 'What are we making you up for? A nightclub? A movie? A romantic dinner?'

'A Duran Duran concert,' she said, though they had never been to New Zealand, because we were too far away from everywhere else.

'And what will you wear?' we said, and she opened her wardrobe and said, 'You choose.'

It was a small room in its own right, and it looked like a shop; some of the clothes still had price tags attached. Perhaps a batwing blouse with a wide belt and jellybean-yellow tights? Or a brocade bolero with a polka-dot dress? Or striped legwarmers over jeans? Or something sexy and slouchy and off-the-shoulder?

'You have so many pretty things,' we said, and she said, 'When I was a child, I had nothing. Nothing.'

In the end we chose a strapless gold gown with a choker of fake pearls – faux, she said, not fake – and a wide-brimmed black hat. Black stilettos, the heels as skinny as our pinky fingers, and a gold clutch purse. We laid it all out on the bed and unhooked the tiny gold crucifix from her neck – the chain felt as fine as hair – and when she stripped off her clothes we pretended to look away. She asked us to help her with the zip of her dress and the clasp of her choker, and then there she stood, as beautiful as a model, as beautiful as the lady from the Speedslimmer ad.

'Speaking of hairy legs,' she said, and showed us her stubble. We could hardly see it – tiny dots of pepper on her golden-brown skin – but we could feel it all right.

'Simon Le Bon wouldn't like that, would he, girls?' she said, and winked at us. Off to the bathroom we went.

Hitching up her gown, she sat on the edge of the bath while we soaped her legs and ran the razor over them. We'd never used one, and we were terrified and thrilled. She closed her eyes and let out a long, delicious breath. Before we left for home, she made us wash our faces – our little secret, she said.

Dad was asleep on the couch when I got back, and I couldn't wake him, so I put a blanket over him and ate dinner on my own. Then I took the black light from my mother's armoire and returned it to the garage.

Even with everything that happened afterwards, in unguarded moments I still find myself longing for that day. It shimmers in my memory: the sparkling ceilings, the opalescent glasses we drank from like grown-ups, the shine of our eyelids and cheeks and lips, my mother's blue-gold taffeta – and Mrs Price herself, her teased blond hair all aglow in the diffuse light from the bathroom window; Mrs Price in her golden gown with her silky golden legs.

CHAPTER 12

I heard you went to her house,' Amy said on Monday morning. 'Paula told me.'

'It was nothing much,' I said.

'That's not how Paula described it.'

'How does Paula know? She wasn't there.'

'Melissa told her. Do you know what Mum said?'

'Of course I don't.'

'She said it's not fair of Mrs Price to invite some people and not others.'

I sighed. 'What do you want me to do, Amy? Say no to these things?'

'Yes, actually.'

Mrs Price's Corvette pulled into the school then, and for one crazy moment I thought: who is driving the car? A ghost? Then my brain registered that Mrs Price was behind the wheel, only the wheel was on the left.

'Anyway, I've got a penpal,' said Amy. 'I got her from the *Woman's Weekly*. Her name's Vigga, and she lives in Denmark.'

'Great,' I said.

'Her interests are dancing, gymnastics, music and tennis. I'm probably going to visit her in the May holidays. It's spring over there in May.'

I didn't believe her, about visiting Denmark, but she was jutting her chin and daring me to say so.

'Lucky you.'

At lunchtime Mrs Price took all the girls in our class to the back room of the church. The Nit Nurse was waiting there for us – that was what we'd called her ever since the primers, when she came to check our hair for lice – but today she was showing us the periods film. She set up the projector while Mrs Price waved the boys away from the window.

'Well now, that's strange,' said Mrs Price, putting her hands on her hips. 'The curtains are missing.'

We all turned to look – and yes, the window was bare, just the empty runners left hanging from the track like beads on an abacus. Perhaps someone had taken them down for washing? Perhaps the school was replacing them? They were quite old and faded, after all. Mrs Price asked us to help her check the storage cupboards. 'You remember them, girls, don't you?' she said. 'Thickly woven cream fabric, with threads of orange and brown.'

But there was no sign of the curtains anywhere. We wouldn't be able to see the film properly without them – the day was far too bright, and besides, the boys kept sneaking back to peer around the edges of the window. Eventually Mrs Price found an old altar cloth and hung it over the curtain track. Pinpoints of light broke through the worn spots in the brocade. Running along the bottom, picked out in gold thread, the words *Holy Holy Holy*.

We'd already had a talk about periods the year before, though it hadn't explained much: we might notice we smelled a bit; we might need to pay extra attention to personal cleanliness. Rumour had it that Leanne's had already started, but she wasn't giving anything away, and when Paula had tried to look under the toilet cubicle door to find out, Leanne had trod on her fingers. The film showed a mother telling her daughter that her body was about to change – that she'd notice her breasts developing, and hair appearing under her arms and between her legs. Once a month a lining would grow inside her, and she'd release an egg – like a chicken? whispered Selena – and if her body didn't need the egg and the lining for a baby, it would shed them as blood.

So you see, said the Nit Nurse, there was no cause for alarm. Our bodies knew exactly what to do and would do it entirely of their own accord.

We weren't sure we liked the sound of that.

She asked if we had any questions.

'Does it hurt?' said Amy. 'The blood?'

It wasn't like cutting a finger, said the Nit Nurse. Our bodies were designed to bleed in this way – so no, it didn't hurt.

Katrina said it hurt her mother, who had to take pills every month for the pain.

For most people it was painless, said the Nit Nurse.

Vanessa said her sister cried because it hurt so much.

Well, she was one of the rare unlucky ones, said the Nit Nurse, because for most people it was painless.

Natalie said her cousin went to A&E once because she was in agony and couldn't walk.

Well, that was the exception that proved the rule, said the Nit Nurse.

We looked at one another.

The boys were waiting for us when we came out of the church.

'What was it about?' they said. 'Was it rude? Did it have people with no clothes on?'

We wouldn't tell them; we were ashamed to tell them. We walked along in silence, and we knew it was coming for us. Blood was coming.

'You guys are no fun,' said Jason Moretti.

'Yeah,' said Karl. 'You're boring.' He snatched up a handful of dead leaves and threw them at Melissa. She flicked them out of her hair and kept walking.

Our silence only made them more boisterous, and they leapt around us, pulling faces and trying to get our attention. Jason

Asofua turned his eyelids inside out in that disgusting way he had. Finally Amy grabbed some dead leaves, threw them at Karl, and ran off. The boys roared after her, chasing her back towards the classrooms, and she zigzagged about, just out of reach. Then at the edge of the field, Karl managed to catch at the tail of her untucked blouse.

'Ambush!' he yelled, and the other boys piled on, tackling her to the ground and stuffing leaves down her back and up the skirt of her tunic. I wasn't sure if she was screaming or laughing, but soon enough she had wriggled free and was racing for the classrooms, her short plait half undone.

When I stepped into the corridor I saw the boys clustered down the far end, by the Primer One room. Brendon and Gregory were holding a desk steady, and Jason Asofua was holding two chairs stacked on top of it while Karl kept watch. Amy stood on tiptoes on the uppermost chair, stretching to reach the statue of Jesus in his niche. Grasping his plaster hand, she swivelled it round the wrong way so that he was giving the fingers. The boys cheered, and she grinned, took a wobbly little bow on her wobbly pedestal. I thought: she will fall. She will fall and hurt herself. I started to run.

'Amy!' I called. 'Amy, what are you doing?'

'Is someone coming?' said Karl.

'You're not safe up there,' I said.

'Shut up, Mum,' said Amy, and the boys guffawed.

'Shut up, Mum, shut up, Mum,' chanted Gregory.

'Come on. The bell's about to ring.' I reached my hand up to her, but she shoved it away. The chair teetered.

'Hey,' said Gregory, lifting her tunic with his index finger, 'I can see your flied lice.'

'I can see your egg foo young,' said Brendon, lifting her tunic from the other side.

She smacked at their hands. She was starting to blush, the colour creeping up her neck.

'Come on, Amy,' I said.

'Leave me alone,' she snarled.

Just then the bell rang, and all the boys disappeared. Even Karl. 'Sorry,' he called over his shoulder. 'You're on your own.'

She climbed awkwardly down to the desk and then to the floor and pushed past me, dragging the furniture back into the Primer One room before any adults came.

The funny thing is, no one noticed Jesus's hand – not a single teacher. It stayed like that, casting an insult down on us all instead of a blessing.

On the Thursday afternoon, just as she'd promised, Mrs Price took me to James Smith's. The other girls looked on as I hopped into the Corvette – I made sure I remembered to get in the right side this time – and I gave them a queenly wave as we drove off. Mrs Price looked like a movie star in her smoky sunglasses.

'Just kick it out of the way if it's annoying you,' she said, nodding towards her handbag that was sliding around at my feet. 'A completely impractical vehicle, I know.'

Plastic torsos, twisting at their waists and dressed in plain bras and lacy bras, sat on the lingerie department counters. Racks of underwear hung all around us, and full-sized mannequins modelled winceyette nighties for winter.

'Good afternoon, ladies,' said the saleswoman. 'How may I help you?'

She must have been in her late fifties, with dyed black hair scraped into a thin little bun, and cheeks chalky with pressed powder. A tape measure hung around her neck.

'We're looking for a bra for Justine,' said Mrs Price. 'A first bra.'

'Of course, madam,' said the saleswoman, smiling the way just about everyone smiled when they met her. 'If you and your daughter would like to come to the fitting room—'

Mrs Price didn't correct her, and neither did I.

The saleswoman whisked the velvet curtain closed and told me to undress. 'Just on the top, dear,' she said as I began to step out of my tunic. 'We don't need to see everything.'

There was a mirror fixed to the back wall and a hinged one on the right, so I could view myself from different angles. The saleswoman stood back, regarding my breasts, my shoulders, my ribcage. 'Not a moment too soon,' she said. 'A timely fit is crucial to proper development.' She slid the tape measure from her neck and passed it around my ribs; it felt cool against my skin, like smooth green leaves. 'Breathe out, please,' she said, and pulled it tight. She measured me around my breasts next, and said she'd bring us some bras to try. Did we have any colour preference?

'White, I think,' said Mrs Price.

The woman nodded her approval and slipped around the side of the curtain, careful not to let anyone see inside.

Mrs Price put her handbag on the floor and sat down on the little bench. 'Excited?' she said.

I nodded. I wasn't sure if I should cover my chest, but she didn't seem bothered. She was looking at me in the mirror, her head on one side.

The saleswoman brought back half a dozen white bras and hung them up. 'Straps first,' she said, undoing one made of T-shirt material and holding it up for me. I poked my arms through, and she positioned the cups to sit underneath my breasts before hooking it closed again. 'Lean forward,' she said. 'Let yourself fall into it. Good girl.' Then her hands were inside the cups, scooping me into place.

I caught my breath with the shock of it, but in the mirror Mrs Price's face was calm, and I knew that this was all quite normal; this was simply something women did.

The saleswoman checked the fit, sliding a finger under the lower edge, looking for bulges and pressure points. A poor fit could cause gland problems, she said. Problems with the pectoral muscles and the posture; deformation of the shoulder girdle. Permanent dents. She lengthened and shortened straps, tutting at every bra I tried; none of them passed the test. The second lot were no good either.

'Miss Fawkes?' said a voice on the other side of the curtain. 'Do you know where the new Triumph Amourettes are?'

'Would you excuse me a moment, please, ladies?' said the saleswoman. She slipped out again.

'Is it me?' I said to Mrs Price. 'Is something wrong with me?'

But no, she said, no no, sometimes it just took a little while to find the right one. 'Would you like me to have a hunt?' she asked. 'See what I can see?'

'Yes please.'

While she was gone I flicked through the bras that didn't fit. I had really liked the one with the tiny white bow at the front. Maybe if I just tried it on again . . . but as I pulled it from the hanger, I knocked three others to the floor, and when I bent to pick them up I noticed Mrs Price's handbag. Sitting right there. Unzipped.

Before I could think better of it I was peering inside.

I suppose I should say I'm not proud of that either.

The soft panels of patchwork leather – some snakeskin, some alligator, some tooled with crazy patterns – seemed to collapse at my touch. I pulled the bag open wide: a couple of lipsticks, a comb, her wallet. Some scuffed receipts. A crumpled handkerchief, two tampons. A notebook with a tiny red pencil pushed through its spiral binding. The brown glass bottle containing my mother's pills. In the zipped side pocket, a mirror, and in the wallet, where a photo should be, the card that said what to do if she was in danger of imminent death. I pulled it out, turned it over: *Oh my God, I am heartily sorry for having offended Thee. I detest all my sins . . .*

Then I saw something else at the bottom of the bag, half hidden in the folds of the satin lining. I lifted it out. Stared at it.

A pen.

A tiny white ship caught in its plastic casing, sailing past the mole on my knuckle, down towards my thumb.

The curtain swished, and Miss Fawkes let herself back into the cubicle with a new selection of bras.

'Have you been on the ferry?' she said, nodding towards the pen.

'No,' I said, tilting it upside-down. 'My mother went on it.' I watched the little ship gliding slowly north again.

'Are you all right, dear?' said Miss Fawkes. 'I'll see where your lovely mother's got to, shall I?'

But Mrs Price's feet appeared just then on the other side of the curtain, and I heard her voice saying, 'Justine? Is it this cubicle?'

I shoved the pen back in the handbag and the handbag back under the bench, then opened the curtain to let Mrs Price in.

'I found a couple of others,' she said.

As I tried the bras on, I watched her in the mirror. At one point I thought she might be looking at her handbag, noting its slightly different position, but I wasn't sure.

Miss Fawkes narrowed it down to two bras. She asked me which one was more comfortable, but I couldn't decide. I had no sense of my body. My head felt high and hollow, the way it did before a seizure, though no seizure came.

'I'll give you a bit of time, shall I?' said Miss Fawkes, and left us alone.

'What do you think?' said Mrs Price.

'I don't know.'

Did she look at her bag again?

'The satin one's more grown up, but it might show through clothes,' she said. 'Let's try it under your blouse.'

I took off the cotton bra and put my arms through the straps of the satin one. Mrs Price did up the clasp for me, her fingers like moths at my back. 'Lean forward,' she said, so I leaned forward – and as I glanced down at the bag, my skin went cold. There on the top, quite visible, lay the ferry pen. And Mrs Price was walking around to stand in front of me, and she was looking me in the eye, and I thought she must know that I'd searched through her things, that I'd found the pen. I tried to think of something to say – but then she smiled and slipped her hands inside the cups, shifting me, putting me in the right place.

I must have flinched, because she said, 'Sorry. I'm cursed with cold hands.'

She passed me my blouse, and I fumbled with the buttons; they were too small, too slippery. I didn't care what the bra looked like. I didn't care which one we chose. I wanted to escape the cubicle, with its walls so close and its mirrors that caught me at every angle.

'Does it show through too much, do you think?' said Mrs Price. 'Well, maybe that's not a disaster.'

'I'll get this one,' I said, though it felt so tight I could hardly breathe.

On the way to the car, I saw Dominic Foster's older sisters sitting in the window of the doughnut shop. They waved at me, their high-school blazers glittering with the badges shaped like tiny gold feet.

Dad was waiting for us when we got back to the house; he'd shut the shop early, and he came rushing down the front steps and over to the car as I was climbing out. 'Thank you so much for this, Angela,' he said. 'Can I offer you a cup of coffee? A sherry?'

'A sherry would be just the thing, actually,' she said. 'Only a thimble, mind.'

She stayed for over an hour, talking and laughing with my father, telling him what an excellent pupil I was, what a fine young woman I would become. When he offered her a second sherry she said, 'That would be very naughty,' and he said, 'You don't have far to go.' She was already holding out her glass.

'I love your couch,' she said, running her hand over the blue-and-white fabric: the old-fashioned lady on her swing, surrounded by cherubs and butterflies.

'Mum chose it,' I said.

'Yes, it's a very feminine piece.' She smiled at my father, and he smiled back as if they were sharing some private joke.

'But what's this?' she said, picking up the newspaper folded open to the death notices, a handful of them circled. 'Are you in the market for a wealthy widow?'

'How did you know?' he said.

'Just something about you. Too well-mannered. Too charming.'

He laughed. 'Well, you're not far from the truth – with the death notices, I mean. I buy pieces from estate sales for the shop.'

'Ghoulish.'

Dad grimaced. 'Is it?'

'I'm teasing.'

And really, I should have left them to it – left them to their adult conversation with its shades of meaning and suggestion. But on I sat, looking from one to the other as they seemed to forget I was there.

'Well!' said Dad when she'd finally gone. 'Isn't she a breath of fresh air?' I thought he might keep on drinking the sherry, but he put the bottle away.

We ate dinner in front of *The Love Boat*. That night Vicki, the captain's daughter, was trying to dress older to catch the eye of a boy, and a psychic researcher who had booked the honeymoon suite wanted to summon a ghost – a drowned bride who had stayed in the same cabin. Vicki ended up admitting her real age, and the psychic researcher found out his wife had made the ghost story up: she herself was the pale face at the window, staring through her lace veil. All evening I thought of the car ride home with Mrs Price, the handbag on the floor at my feet. How it had slid towards me as we turned to the right, nudging against my shoe like a dog before sliding back towards Mrs Price. I imagined the little ferry inside the pen, inside the satiny dark, sliding back and forth too. Heading for the misty Sounds, the arms of green bush reaching into the water to welcome the passengers ashore. Heading for the open ocean, no land in sight.

2014

Chapter 13

A few weeks pass before I see Sonia at the retirement community again. I'm beginning to think I've made her up, until one weekday afternoon I find her there, rubbing moisturiser into Dad's lower legs.

'Hello again,' she says. 'Look who's here, Mr Crieve.'

For a moment he seems not to know me – Emma isn't with me this time – and then he smiles. 'Hello, love.'

I set about tidying that week's newspapers into a pile. Most are unread.

'What are you doing with those?' he says.

'I'll put them in our recycling bin.'

'I think I was keeping them for a reason. I read something about you.'

'No, nothing about me. I'm not newsworthy.'

'Where are my scissors?'

He often gets stuck on this idea: that I'm in the papers, that he needs to cut out the stories.

'All done, Mr Crieve,' says Sonia. 'I'll let you catch up with Justine.'

'She's been in the paper, you know,' he says.

'You must be very proud of her.' She winks at me and peels off her blue gloves, balling one neatly inside the other before dropping them in the bin. I know that I should play along with her – that this is best-practice dementia care – but I can't bring myself to pretend.

'See you,' she says.

'See you,' says Dad.

I sit on the bed – the premium room is too small for any chairs other than the recliner – and I smooth the rumples from the polycotton duvet cover. 'She seems lovely,' I say.

'Who?'

'Sonia. The caregiver.'

'Oh, she won't last. None of them last.'

Next to the bed his wedding photo hangs crooked, knocked on its nail when Sonia shut the door behind her. There they are cutting the cake, the two of them, younger than I am now, Mum in her cap of silk flowers, Dad with a carnation pinned to his lapel. Together they hold the knife, about to cut into the sugary latticework of the bottom tier. The plastic columns holding everything up have blurred into the weave of his suit; it looks like the cake is floating in mid-air, drifting away from them as they hold still for the camera. All the silver horseshoes pressed into the sides; all the daffodils and jonquils crammed into the little vase on top. I right the photograph. The call bell is looped behind it, the red button at the end of the cord within easy reach of the bed.

'Don't press it!' says Dad.

'No, I won't press it,' I say.

'It's only for emergencies! You mustn't press it!'

Some distress is normal, the doctor has told me. The best thing to do is deflect.

'Emma found an egg-shaped pebble in the garden,' I say. 'She's decided it's a snake's egg, and she's trying to hatch it. Really she's too old for that kind of thing.'

'A snake's egg?' he says.

'That's what she thinks. Dom told her not to get her hopes up, but she's made it a nest of grass in an old chocolate box. Keeps it on a hot-water bottle in her room. We probably should have nipped it in the bud.'

'I wouldn't let a thing like that in the house,' he says. 'Sounds like a very bad idea.'

'It's just a stone, Dad. It's not a real snake's egg.'

'But you never know, do you? That's the problem.'

I gather up the newspapers, kiss him on the cheek. He stares at the bundle in my hands.

'Did I want something?' he says. 'Was there something in there?'

On the way home I pick Emma up from netball practice.

'I could have walked,' she sighs.

'You're still too young.'

'You walked all over the place at my age.'

'They were different times.'

'Different how?'

'Simpler.' I don't want to tell her the terrible things that can happen to children when they're just walking along, walking home. 'How was netball?' I say.

'Jordan Butler bit Destiny Nguyen.'

'What?'

'Destiny kept obstructing her, so Jordan bit her on the arm. Lopini Tupou said she must have her period and that's why she went crazy.'

'I hope she was disciplined.'

'She had to apologise to Destiny.'

'That's it?'

'Jordan struggles with conduct disorder.'

'So she can get away with whatever? No consequences?'

'It's not like she's got rabies or anything.' Emma takes a sip of water from her bottle.

'They would have given her the strap in my day,' I say.

'They would not.'

'Absolutely. Right across the bare skin.'

She shakes her head and says, 'That never happened. I don't believe you.' But she keeps quizzing me on the details: who held the strap? Was there blood? Could other people watch?

I wish I'd never said anything.

The blood in the creases of Karl's palm.

The leather sucking the air like a gasp.

When we're almost home, Emma says, 'Is it true your period makes you go crazy?'

'No, darling. You might feel a bit down around that time – a bit sensitive. That's all.'

'Does it hurt?'

'No,' I say, keeping my eyes on the road. 'Not really. Not much.'

I sleep uneasily that night. At one point our cat Blizzard pads up the duvet and stands over me, batting my face until I stroke her. Scratching me if I stop. 'Go see Daddy now,' I whisper when my arms grow tired, shoving her over to Dom's side of the bed because I know he's a softie, but he grunts and hides under the covers and says, 'You created the monster, not me.'

A little later I wake unable to breathe, and my fingers fly to my throat to prise away the phantom that has me in its grasp – and I feel the soft weight of Blizzard lying on my chest. Nothing else. Nobody else.

1984

CHAPTER 14

Amy placed half a dozen pears on the dish of the scales that hung from their shop's ceiling. When the needle settled she tipped them into a paper bag and then, with one deft movement, flipped the bag and twisted the corners. She'd tried to teach me the manoeuvre once, but I'd sent the fruit flying.

'It's okay, never mind,' Mrs Fong had said. 'Takes many years to learn.'

Amy gave the customer his change and took off her apron.

'We'll be back by three,' she told her mother, choosing two apples from the top of a perfect stack.

'Remember to keep to the track,' said Mrs Fong.

'Yes, Mum,' said Amy, drawing out the words, rolling her eyes. 'Can Justine stay tonight?'

'Not tonight.'

'But it's the holidays!'

'Not tonight.'

Amy and I had patched things up, more or less, but her parents seemed cooler towards me. I didn't really want to stay at their place.

We made our way through the back of the shop, passing the concrete tubs where Mrs Fong washed the root vegetables, and the table where Amy bundled up spring onions and parsley, and the calendar showing scenes from Hong Kong, and the banana-ripening room that smelled sweet and warm. Bonnie almost knocked us down when we untied her, licking our hands and faces. Then we headed to the cliffs.

It was a cold day, nearly winter, and the wind cut into our cheeks up there on the exposed track. I made sure to throw the new tennis ball well away from the edge.

'So are you going to tell anyone about Mrs Price?' said Amy.

I glanced over my shoulder, as if she might be jogging along behind us, listening in – but we were quite alone. I shook my head. 'There must be some other reason she had it in her bag.'

'Like what? What other reason?'

'Maybe it fell in there and she didn't notice.'

'That's stupid.' Amy hurled her apple core towards the cliffs, but it stopped just short; straight away a gull swooped down and snatched it. I was still eating mine, gnawing away every last bit until only the stalk remained.

'Yuk,' she said, watching me. 'You know the seeds grow inside you, right? They sprout in your stomach and send their roots down through your guts, and the branches come out your eyes and mouth.'

'That's stupid too.'

She shrugged. 'It's what I heard. Anyway, why didn't you just ask her about the pen?'

'I don't know. I was scared.'

'Scared of what?'

'She might not like me any more.'

'Why do you care so much if she likes you?'

I threw the ball for Bonnie.

'Justine, you know what you saw.'

'I *think* so.'

'You *know*.'

'It's just a pen. It doesn't really matter. Maybe she picked it up by accident. Maybe someone else put it there and she doesn't even know. Anyway, you want her to like you too.'

Amy was silent.

'You want her to like you too,' I repeated.

'Yeah,' she said.

We walked into the wind, our hair blown straight back behind us while the water in the harbour churned and turned, grey-white, white-grey, the colour of the gulls. Our eyes were watering, and our faces stung, and we struggled to remain upright; at every step the wind threatened to lift us off our feet, push us off the track and towards the edge, where we never dared to stray. It clattered the leaves of the flax bushes, rushed into the old gun emplacements, the abandoned observation posts, stirring up the grit and the rubbish and sighing at the empty horizon.

'I thought you were going to visit your penpal in the holidays,' I said. 'Vigga, from the *Woman's Weekly*. In Denmark, wasn't it?'

'Oh, she's busy with a gymnastics tournament. She's probably going to represent her country. I'll go in August instead.'

'You'll have to show me her letters.'

'Mm. They're kind of private.'

'Hello, you two!' called a familiar voice. Mrs Price, dressed head to toe in aqua-blue lycra, with a sweat band around her forehead, jogged up to us. She looked like the instructors on *Aerobics Oz Style*, ready for the high-impact segment. 'Isn't it wild up here today!' she said, panting, still jogging on the spot. 'Don't you love it?' She held two fingers to her opposite wrist, feeling for her pulse.

Bonnie whined and pawed at her tennis ball, pressed herself against Mrs Price so she had to stop jogging.

'Bonnie!' said Amy, tugging on her collar. 'I'm so sorry.'

'It's fine – she only wants to play,' said Mrs Price. 'Don't you, eh? Oh, you remind me of my lovely old girl. Yes you do. Yes you do.' She fondled the dog's ears, then flung the ball for her, further than either of us could have managed. 'Better get going,' she said, waving at us over her shoulder. 'Got to keep the heart rate up.'

We watched her disappear around the corner.

'Even Bonnie likes her,' I said.

'What are you going to do, though?' said Amy. 'About your pen.'

'Look for more proof, I suppose,' I said.

Back at her house we played marbles with her little brother David, until he lost his favourite marble to Amy and shoved it in his mouth rather than surrender it to her. After that she and I played a game of Cluedo, which her father had just bought for her. When Amy won she pretended to stab me with the tiny plastic dagger, but the blade kept bending against my ribs and I refused to die. Then her parents arrived back, and she tidied the game away into the hundred-eye chest, and I went home.

When the new term started I decided to keep a closer watch on my classmates, checking the corridor every ten minutes at lunchtime in case anyone was picking through our jacket pockets and schoolbags. I peered in the classroom windows, too, cupping my hands around my eyes to see inside. And after school, when Mrs Price left me alone for a moment, I searched her handbag: no pen.

One morning Father Lynch came to talk to our class. He was very forward-thinking – we knew that because he'd told us so himself. He'd had no trouble dropping the word *men* from the Mass when the Pope announced it had to go from *This is the cup of my blood. It will be shed for you and for all men so that sins may be forgiven.* I'd heard Mrs Jensen muttering about it to Mrs Moretti after church one Sunday; extreme feminists had pushed through the change, she said. Sometimes I heard them whisper the old wording in church when Father got to that bit.

That morning he came to tell us about Santiago, which he had just visited with a group of other priests. The name sounded like one of the ports where the Love Boat docked, and I wondered if priests were allowed to play shuffleboard and drink cocktails beside the clover-shaped pool – if they were allowed to wear swimming togs, even. Father had green eyes with long dark lashes, and very thick brown hair on his head and on the backs of his hands; perhaps his chest was like that too.

I needed to stop thinking about Father Lynch's chest.

Did we know how lucky we were? he asked us. Did we know how free? The people in Santiago, in Chile, lived under military rule, many in muddy shantytowns with no running water and no proper electricity. Could we imagine not being able to turn on a tap? Or a light? Some Catholics there spoke out against the government, and they were sent to prison or simply disappeared. Some were tortured. Some executed.

We opened our Religion books to a fresh page and copied down the words Mrs Price wrote on the blackboard: *Chile, shantytowns, government, tortured, executed*. Then we each wrote three reasons we were lucky to live in New Zealand. Gregory said the All Blacks, and Mrs Price said he was missing the point.

After that Father showed us a film about a man in Chile who dressed as a clown and printed forbidden leaflets. When he was arrested he did not deny his illegal activities, and they strapped him to a metal bed and gave him electric shocks. They whipped him all over his body; they covered his face with a cloth and poured water over it so he couldn't breathe. With his clown's makeup all streaky, he leaned against the bars of his prison cell and began to sing: *We will all be free one day, free to laugh and free to play, free to choose and go our way, yes we will all be free.* He knew they would kill him, but he sang his song anyway. Then they took him from his cell and stood him in front of a brick wall. Then they shot him.

We watched with our hands over our mouths. Halfway through the film Katrina Howell asked to leave the room, but Mrs Price directed her back to her seat and said it was important we understood what was happening in the world. We were old enough to know the kinds of risks brave Catholics were taking.

'Is he a *Catholic* clown?' asked Gregory.

'Shh,' said Father.

'Why don't the words match their lips?' asked Vanessa.

'Shhhh!' said Father.

At the end, when the Catholic clown lay dead and full of bullet holes, the rest of the prisoners started clattering their tin mugs across their bars and singing: *We will all be free one day* . . .

Father turned on the lights and motioned for Paula and Katrina to open the curtains. 'He could have saved himself,' he said. 'If he hadn't sung the song, they wouldn't have shot him. Why did he sing the song?'

No one spoke.

'Come on, people,' said Mrs Price. 'What do you think?'

We knew there was a certain answer they were waiting for, the two of them standing at the front of the classroom with their splendid hair, but we had no idea what it was.

'He had a lovely singing voice?' said Brendon at last.

'That wasn't his voice,' said Vanessa. 'The words didn't match his lips.'

'He did have a lovely singing voice,' said Father, ignoring Vanessa. He ran a hand through his thick brown hair, glanced at Mrs Price.

'Well, how was he using his voice?' she said.

My head was starting to feel strange.

'How do you think the other prisoners felt when they heard him singing?' Mrs Price persisted.

'Hopeful?' said Melissa.

'Thank you!' said Mrs Price, and she smiled at Father, who talked for a few minutes about the value of hope, and solidarity, and sacrifice.

Then we all had to write a letter in our Religion books from the clown to his family, saying goodbye, explaining why we were going to let ourselves be shot. It wouldn't be marked; it was just a useful exercise for us to think about such a situation. Melissa was scribbling away to my right. When she saw me looking, she curled her arm around her work the way she did when we had a test.

Dear Mum and Dad, I began. My head was definitely feeling strange: hollowed out, not quite part of my body. Amy glanced at what I'd written and wrote the same thing in her exercise book: *Dear Mum and Dad*.

'Now what?' she whispered.

I shrugged: don't ask me. My hands were feeling strange too, and I watched myself write, and the hands were not my own; the words were not my own. *I am sorry to be leaving you in this way. I know you will be sad but it is my only choice. Remember me.*

Amy copied me word for word.

When the bell rang, everyone rushed for their lunchboxes to get their morning snacks, then streamed towards the adventure playground.

I lagged behind. I thought I heard my mother: *I'm home. Justine? I'm home.*

My head high and hollow, my hands not my hands. The sky all hazy, covered with plastic.

I could taste burnt sugar.

The freckled face hovered above me. 'Hello,' it said.

'Hello.'

'Are you feeling better?'

'Where am I?'

'The sick bay.'

A green vinyl bed beneath me. On the shelves, rolled bandages. An antiseptic smell.

'You had a seizure,' said the face.

'Where?'

'Just outside the classroom.'

I swallowed. 'Did I . . . did I do anything embarrassing?'

The face moved a little further away from me, and I saw it was Dom Foster's.

'No,' he said. 'You just fell over and shook a bit.'

I groaned. 'And everyone saw?'

'Well . . .' he said, and I knew that the whole class, probably the whole school, had witnessed my body betraying me.

'Is your tongue okay?' said Dom.

I checked. Nodded.

'That's good.'

'Who brought me here?'

'I did. And Mrs Price asked me to stay with you.'

'Thanks.'

He shrugged. 'My little brother has epilepsy.'

'Oh?'

'He has to wear a helmet.'

'I'm not wearing a helmet.'

'You'd look nice.'

'Shut up.'

'I should tell Mrs Price you're awake.'

While he was gone I sat up. I must have cut my knee, because someone had put a plaster on it. My eyes felt heavy as marbles. Slowly I walked to the door. Mr Chisholm's office was opposite the sick bay, and I could see him pinning a poster to the wall above his desk: an enlargement of the face on the Shroud.

'Ah, Justine!' he said. 'Back in the land of the living, I see – you poor old thing. Care for a toffee?' He came out to the hallway and offered me a sweet from the tin he kept on his desk.

Mrs Price appeared then too. 'How are you feeling, my darling? Shall I ring your dad? Would you like to go home?'

'I'm okay,' I said, taking a toffee but leaving the wrapper on. In fact, I would have loved to climb into my bed with its soft flannelette sheets and its Holly Hobbie bedspread and its view of the apple tree, but I wasn't going to be the weird girl who was sent home because she had something wrong with her.

Everyone looked at me when I returned to my desk. I could hear them whispering, their voices like distant traffic, distant waves.

The rest of the morning blurred into nothing, until the lunchtime bell. In the corridor children were pulling on scarves and hats: the June day was dry but had turned very cold, the kind of cold that chapped your lips and cheeks.

'I can't find my gloves,' said Amy.

Nobody paid any attention, and I was still too groggy to respond.

Amy searched her bag again, then dashed back into the classroom. 'Mrs Price! Mrs Price, someone's stolen my gloves!'

'Right, that's it,' I heard Mrs Price say, and she marched into the chilly corridor. 'Nobody is going anywhere until I've checked your bags and pockets. Form a line, please.'

Unsmiling, she worked her way from pupil to pupil. Those at the back of the line shifted about uneasily as the numbers dwindled, checking over their shoulders to see if Mr Chisholm would appear. When she reached me, I held out my bag, and she gave me a quick little smile. She removed my lunchbox, my library books – and then her expression changed. Hardened.

Reaching deep inside the bag, she pulled out Amy's red woollen gloves.

Everyone gasped.

'Are these yours, Justine?' she said.

I couldn't speak. I shook my head. *Had* I taken them? Most of the morning was hazy . . . Perhaps I'd slipped them into my bag for some legitimate reason. Though I couldn't think what.

Mrs Price was saying something. I forced myself to focus on her words.

'. . . explain yourself,' she said. 'Well, now's your chance.'

She was looking at me, waiting, but I had no language. Hadn't I been here before? Standing in this same spot, accused of something? The seizure, I told myself – the seizure was jumbling my thoughts.

'I've seen her hanging round the corridor at lunchtime,' said Paula.

'*And* she was in the sick bay for ages,' said Selena.

Then Amy spoke.

'I must have dropped the gloves in there by accident this morning,' she said. 'Our bags hang side by side – I was in a rush – that must be it.'

'Are you sure about that, Amy?' said Mrs Price.

She nodded.

'Justine?'

I nodded too.

Mrs Price scrutinised the two of us. Then she said, 'All right, people, show's over. Off you go to lunch.'

'Is that really what happened?' I whispered to Amy once everyone had drifted away.

'I don't know,' she said. 'Is it?'

I must have gone straight to bed when I got home, and fallen into a deep sleep. Voices woke me a couple of hours later: Mrs Price and my father, talking in the living room. I pulled on my dressing gown and crept down the hall.

'There was something else,' she was saying. 'It's a delicate matter . . . We have a thief in the class.'

'A thief!' said my father. 'Justine's not mentioned it.'

'Well,' said Mrs Price. 'Well,' she said again, 'I thought I found a stolen item in her bag today.'

'*What?*'

'Don't worry, don't worry – I was wrong. But I just thought you should know that things are a bit . . . fraught in the classroom at the moment. In case that contributed to the seizure.'

'Thanks,' Dad said. 'It's very good of you to come by. Not many teachers would bother.'

'Justine's a special girl,' she said. 'I absolutely adore her. And it's lovely to see you again too, of course.'

'And you,' said Dad.

He started when I entered the room. 'Ah, there's my girl. Feeling better?'

'I think so,' I said. The ceiling glassy. A voice in my ear.

'And look who's here. Angela was worried about you – isn't that nice?'

Mrs Price smiled her beautiful smile and patted the couch next to her, the blue-and-white fabric with the lady on her swing, and I went and sat down. She put her arm around my shoulders and said, 'What are we going to do with you, my darling? Hmm?'

And I admit that I lapped it up. I was special. I was adored.

'You know,' she said, 'I was just admiring how spick and span your place is. Your dad said that's all your doing. We were wondering if you might like a little cleaning job at my house . . . ?'

'A job?'

'Yes.' She laughed. 'I'd pay you. We thought you might like a bit of pocket money, and I could do with the help.'

'Yes please,' I said.

And so she handed me a key: the key to her house.

CHAPTER 15

D r Kothari checked my blood pressure and heart rate and asked me to step on the scales.

'Everything all right at school?' he said.

I nodded.

'Selena can't stop talking about your teacher. Mrs Price this, Mrs Price that.'

'Justine's the same,' said Dad. I saw a smile flicker over his face.

Dr Kothari fiddled with the weights on the scales. On the corner of his desk, a family photo: Selena and her pretty sister dressed in matching blouses. 'Honestly, you'd think she could walk on water,' he said. 'Girls that age!'

'Should we be worried?' said Dad. 'About the seizures, I mean. Only we thought she'd grown out of them.'

I knew he was concerned for me, but I couldn't help feeling I'd done something wrong.

'Things sometimes worsen during puberty,' said Dr Kothari, writing a prescription for a new kind of pill that shouldn't have so many side effects. 'The rise in hormonal levels can wreak havoc. They can even trigger seizures in people who've never had them before.'

I had known Dr Kothari since I was little. I'd sat in his consulting room with my mother when she'd told him she thought she could feel something in her breast; it was probably nothing, she'd said, but she'd decided to be sensible and have it checked all the same.

That was hormones too, wasn't it?

I wanted to ask him, but already he was handing the prescription to Dad and standing up from his chair to see us out.

Afterwards we stopped in at Mr Parry's to get a bit of ham for our sandwiches.

'Neil!' he said to my father, who hadn't been there in months. 'How *are* you?'

'Fine, fine,' said Dad. 'A couple of hundred grams of the shaved ham, please.'

Mr Parry caught my eye, winked at me. 'You look like you could do with some fattening up,' he said, already handing me a slice of luncheon sausage.

'No thank you,' I said.

The next day I started my cleaning job at Mrs Price's. There was no answer when I knocked at the front door, so I went around the back and found her weeding the beds of cactuses and succulents in the rock garden, her hands sheathed in thick gloves.

'Come in, my darling, come in,' she said, and led me inside.

She asked me to tackle the kitchen first, though I didn't think it looked very dirty.

'I've fallen into some bad habits, I'm afraid,' she said, and pointed out the cooking spatters around the hobs, the grime baked to the inside of the oven. There were grubby fingerprints on the fridge door and the light switches, and fly dirt on the ceiling. The more I looked, the more I saw.

She leaned against the door frame for a while and chatted, sipping a diet milkshake from her plastic shaker. At one point she said, 'You know, Justine, you remind me of myself when I was your age. The same curiosity about the world. The same fearlessness.'

'I'm not fearless,' I said.

'Ah,' she said, 'but you look it. That's more than half the battle.' She smiled. 'What scares you, my darling?'

I dipped my sponge in the soapy water and rubbed at the marks on the electric kettle. 'Losing someone,' I said. 'Someone else.'

She nodded. 'I understand that too.'

After a while she went to do some marking. She'd be in her study if I needed her, she said.

In the laundry I tipped out the dirty water – it was almost black as it disappeared down the drain – and then I headed back to the kitchen to make a start on the floor. As I passed the sunken living room I saw Mrs Price's handbag on the edge of the conversation pit. I glanced down the hall: the study door was closed.

The bag contained the same notebook with the same tiny red pencil, the same wallet and comb. My mother's pills, pattering softly inside their bottle as I shifted them aside. A gamey scent rose from the leather, the patches of snakeskin and alligator skin bumpy under my fingertips. In the distance a dog barked and barked, raising some kind of warning. And there in the zipped pocket, tucked away with the little mirror, the ferry pen.

'Justine?' said Mrs Price. 'What are you doing?'

I whirled around, the pen in my fist. How long had she been standing there, watching me? 'I'm sorry, I'm sorry!' I blurted. I felt a little dizzy: probably the new pills.

She gave a puzzled smile and motioned for me to join her in the soft pink conversation pit.

'What's going on, sweetheart?' she said.

And out it all came, my blubbering confession: finding the pen in her bag when we were at James Smith's, telling Amy about it, looking for it again in the classroom and not finding it and wondering if I'd imagined it, then finding it again just now.

'But I don't understand,' said Mrs Price. 'What's so special about this particular pen?'

I blinked. 'It's the one my mother gave me,' I said. 'The one that was stolen.'

She drew in a deep breath, closed her eyes for a second. 'Oh my darling,' she said. 'Have you been worrying? Oh my poor love.' She moved closer to me, put her hand on my knee. 'Do you know where I went for my summer holiday, Justine?'

'No,' I said in a small voice.

'Christchurch,' she said. 'And do you know how I got to the South Island?'

'No.'

'I took the ferry, darling. And I picked up some postcards in the gift shop, and I didn't have anything to write with, so I bought a pen there too. Do you see?'

I nodded.

'From memory they had hundreds of the things. Thousands. They must be all over the country. Come here.'

She opened her arms to me, and I laid my head against her chest and sobbed.

'There now, my darling. Shh. There now. Shh, shhhh.'

'I'm so sorry,' I said. 'I'm horrible, horrible.'

She stroked my hair. 'Don't say that. It hurts me to hear you say that.' She sat back, wiped my face with her fingertips. 'Will you do something for me?'

'Yes,' I whispered.

'I want you to keep the pen. Will you do that?'

'Yes.'

'Good girl. I know it's not the same one – not the one from your mother – but perhaps it can still be special. Yes?'

'Yes.'

The next day, and every day after, I kept it with me so I would not lose it again, slipping it into my tunic pocket every morning, and then, after school, transferring it to the clothes I wore at home.

'I knew it would turn up,' Amy said when I showed her. 'Where was it?'

'At the bottom of a bag,' I said.

Which wasn't a lie.

'Now, people,' Mrs Price called from the back of the class-room, and we all turned around. She was glowing with excite-ment. She could hardly contain herself. 'I'm sure you remember what happened to Susan,' she said. 'What happened to her foot. Well, come and see.'

As we all pushed back our chairs and stood up, Karl remained at his desk.

'Are you okay?' I said.

'I don't want to see that thing ever again,' he muttered.

'Karl,' called Mrs Price. 'You too. Everyone must see. It's quite miraculous.'

We hadn't looked very closely at Susan in weeks – we hadn't wanted to – but Mrs Price was standing aside now and beam-ing at us, waving us over to the tank. Susan was swimming out of her flowerpot, her gills quivering as she moved through the water. She watched us with her little golden eyes.

'Well?' said Mrs Price.

Vanessa was the first to notice. 'Her foot's grown back!' she said, pointing.

We all clamoured to see then – and yes, somehow, the sev-ered foot really had reappeared. All five tiny fingers present and perfect. Not even a scar.

'That's not Susan,' said Jason Moretti.

'Yeah, it must be a different one,' said Jason Asofua. 'She must've swapped it.'

'What's that, Jason?' said Mrs Price.

'It's a different one,' he said again. 'You swapped it.'

'Now why would I do that, people?' she said. 'Why would I try to trick you?'

Nobody knew.

'The thing about axolotls,' she said, 'is that they can regen-erate. It's true: you are looking at one of God's miracles. I could cut off Susan's foot a hundred times, and it would grow back. I could crush her spine, sever it through, take out an entire section, and she would replace it, heal without a scar. I could even cut away part of her heart, and in a few weeks it would be back to normal, no sign of any damage.'

I stole a look at Karl, who had pushed his way through to the front now and was smiling his broadest smile, nudging the person next to him and saying, 'See? See?'

In fact, Mrs Price went on, making the most of the learning opportunity, the ancient Aztecs first recognised the axolotl's astonishing powers of transformation. They believed that Xolotl, the dog-headed god of lightning and fire, guided souls to the underworld and also guarded the sun on its nightly journey through the world of the dead. When the other gods decided to sacrifice themselves to the sun, Xolotl wept until his eyes fell from his head – and he escaped the sacrifice by transforming into a salamander: an axolotl. She flourished her hand at the tank.

I bent down, placed my finger against the glass wall. Susan walked across the flat stones to me, moving perfectly on her perfect new foot. Susan, with her eyes like the sun. Susan, who would never grow up. She nudged the glass, decided my finger was not food, and moved away again. On the other side of the tank, Jason Daly was creeping his hand along Karl's shoulder and saying something about zombies. Karl shrugged him away and looked at me through the silvery water, his face serious by then. I wanted him to wink, to smile – to acknowledge the erasure of our crime. But perhaps he wasn't looking at me at all.

Sometimes I find myself thinking of Susan even now – of the way she regrew, of the way Mrs Price staged that miracle just for us. And although I know she must be long dead, sometimes I imagine that she is still regenerating. Resurrecting all the damaged and amputated parts of herself, and living forever.

CHAPTER 16

M ore and more things were going missing; something new disappeared every day. When Brendon's Rubik's Cube was stolen, his mother came to see Mrs Price. I heard them talking as I cleaned the blackboard dusters outside the classroom window: *expensive item . . . gift from his beloved aunt . . . unacceptable . . .*

'People, this cannot continue,' Mrs Price told us the next day. 'I've spoken to Mr Chisholm, who says that he is quite prepared to bring in the police.'

The whole class began to murmur: the police! We squirmed in our seats as if we were guilty of something.

Mrs Price wanted us to search our hearts, she said. Search our consciences. If the thief came to her and confessed, and returned all the missing items, there would be no questions asked. No punishment. However, she said, holding up her hand, if by Monday nobody had owned up, she would ask each of us to name the person we thought was responsible.

That week we were all so kind to one another, sharing bottles of Twink and pairs of scissors without complaint, standing aside at the drinking fountain to let someone else go first. We laughed at one another's jokes whether they were funny or not; we planned birthday parties aloud, including anyone within earshot – and anyone we deemed risky – on our guest lists. But we were also on guard, making sure we were never in the classroom or corridor alone. Making sure we never so much as admired a friend's new PE sneakers or highlighter pen. Rachel and Paula were still whispering about Amy, and the suspicion around her was spreading; I could tell, and so could she. *Dirty thief*, our classmates called in her wake. *Liar. I wish you were dead. Why don't you kill yourself?* Mrs Price heard them but never intervened. I didn't know what to think; I just knew I had to be careful. I said no when Amy invited me round to play on the Wednesday.

'Okay. Doesn't matter,' she said, and leaned in close as if to tell me a secret. 'Guess what?' she whispered. 'I heard that breast cancer's genetic.' She poked me in the chest as she said *genetic.*

I knew what the word meant; I remembered the charts we'd drawn when Mrs Price was teaching us about Our Traits. The generations of gingerbread people colour-coded for tallness, brown eyes, right-handedness.

Amy laughed. 'Your face!' she said. And then, in a louder voice, poking my chest again: 'What've you got down there, anyway? All the stolen stuff?'

At lunchtime I went straight to the school library. Sister Bronislava was on the desk, and she nodded at me as I passed. Down the back, Dom was reshelving the returns. I pretended to look at Junior Fiction before drifting across to Science and flicking through books on rocks and minerals, books on horses and electricity and stars. There was one on New Zealand trees, and even one that played the songs of different New Zealand birds when you pressed a row of buttons. I couldn't see anything helpful.

I must have seemed lost, because after a while Sister Bronislava came over. 'What are you looking for, Justine?' she said.

Dom was just two shelves away.

'I was wondering if you have any books on breast cancer,' I said as quietly as possible.

She knew about my mother; she'd given me a prayer card to Mary when she'd died: Our Lady of Sorrows robed in gold, eyes downcast while angels placed a golden crown on her head and a white bird spread its wings across her heart.

'I think that is not something you want to read about,' she said.

'But are there any books?'

'No,' she said, 'we do not have such books. What do you need to know?'

'Someone told me it's genetic.'

'I think that person was trying to scare you. Finding your weak point.'

'Is it true? Is it genetic?'

I could see her considering her words. 'Sometimes diseases run in families and sometimes they don't,' she said. 'These things, these bad things that come to us – we can't control them. What happened to your mother . . . Justine, you're twelve years old. When you're a grown-up there will be all kinds of treatments we can't even imagine. All kinds of cures. We mustn't let the past poison us. We must trust in the future God has in mind.' She returned to the issues desk.

Dom's trolley was empty by then, and he came to put away all the books I'd pulled from the shelves.

'I love this one,' he said, opening the birdsong book. He pressed the buttons and we listened to the kingfisher, the silvereye, the tūī, the bellbird.

When I went to Mrs Price's after school that week to clean, she asked me to dust the whole house – a proper going-over, she said, not just a flick round the edges the way she usually did. She needed to slip out to the supermarket, so she'd leave me to it, all right?

I started down the dark end of the L-shaped hall, wiping along the skirting boards and across the mirror that hung next to the bathroom, standing on a high stool to reach the amber lightshade, then opening doors to clean along the tops. One door – the spare bedroom at the end of the hall – was locked, so I just did above the door frame. Things were dirtier than they looked; my cloth came away fuzzed in grey. In the master bedroom I lifted the telephone from the bedside table and wiped underneath it, then wiped the phone itself, digging into each hole on the dial, rubbing away the prints on the receiver. I tackled the Speedslimmer next, cleaning its gangly steel body and its rubber footrests, careful not to get the cloth caught in the high-tension springs. Rounds of crocheted lace left behind patterns on the dressing table: snowflakes made of dust. I opened the lid to the makeup compartment and ran a finger over the eye shadows in their little boxes, the lipsticks in their golden tubes. Then I opened a drawer.

It was so full that the contents puffed up over the edges, all but forcing themselves into my hands. I picked up a coffee-coloured bra with the price tag still attached and held it to my chest, then a teal bra trimmed in black with a matching camisole, then a boned corset in bridal white. Mrs Price hadn't been gone very long; I had enough time. I pulled off my school uniform and my plain white bra, then slipped inside the teal set. I shivered: it felt like slipping inside a flower. I found the matching knickers and put them on too – just a tiny triangle of teal at the front, and the rest made of see-through black lace. The pieces were too big for me, but not by much. If I stood a certain way – waist twisted, shoulders back, bottom out – I could pass. 'Now, people,' I said to the dressing-table mirror, 'who wants a piece of coconut ice?' I walked towards my reflection, swaying my hips, and I walked away from it, watching over my shoulder. I climbed onto the Speedslimmer and grasped the handle, gliding the seat along the runners, attacking my troublespots. I lay back on the gold scatter cushions and didn't know what to do with myself. Out in the rock garden the cactuses looked fuzzily green in the afternoon sun, and on the ceiling above me the tiny grains of glitter sparked like the flecks of gold in Karl's eyes.

I made sure to put everything back in the drawer the way I'd found it, and then I returned to my dusting. When Mrs Price came home I was just finishing the dining room.

'Help me bring in the rest of the groceries, would you, my darling?' she said.

In the bags I saw vegetables and grapes, a bottle of wine, a whole fresh chicken, and expensive chocolates and cheeses.

'The place looks so much better,' she said. 'You're a wonder.'

'I couldn't do the room at the end of the hall,' I said. 'The spare bedroom? It was locked.'

'Oh yes, I should have mentioned it,' she said. 'You don't need to bother about that one.'

She took a twenty-dollar note from her wallet and handed it to me.

'This is far too much,' I said.

But she insisted.

When I got home, Dad was making sausage casserole with mashed potatoes – my favourite. He hadn't cooked properly in months. He'd laid the table with the windmill tablecloth and the nice china we kept in the sideboard, and he'd even polished our serviette rings. Mine was solid silver, from 1872: one hundred years before I was born. He'd given it to me when I was christened, and it was engraved with a J so elaborately barbed I used to think it was a fish hook.

'I wanted to tell you something, love,' he said, and my scalp began to prickle. Hadn't we sat at this very table, hadn't he and Mum said those same words, when the cancer came back? I waited as he wiped his mouth and took a sip of water, wiped his mouth again.

'I wanted to tell you,' he said, 'that I'm seeing Angela tomorrow. Mrs Price.'

Some dark space in me opened up and sucked at my ribs, my throat.

'Is it about the stealing?' I said.

'What? The stealing?'

'Things going missing from the classroom. It's not me, you know.'

He smiled. 'No, it's not about anything like that. She's . . . she's invited me round to dinner. What do you think?'

'Dinner?' I said.

'Yes.'

I straightened the tablecloth where it had rucked up next to my plate, smoothing down the latticed windmill blades, the clumps of tulips. Splashed against the Dutch sky, an old gravy stain that had never come out. Already my mind was swooping ahead. We'd go clothes shopping together. Go on holiday together. She'd paint my nails for me, come to the hairdresser's with me. *Something a bit older for her this time*, she'd say, pointing to a picture in a magazine as we sipped on our diet milkshakes that made us feel full.

'Justine?' said Dad.

'I think it's wonderful,' I said. 'And I think Mum would approve.' I really believed that. I told myself I really believed it.

He exhaled. 'Let's not tell anyone yet, all right?' he said. 'Anyway, it's just dinner. We don't know what'll come of it.'

I nodded. Maybe a trip to Australia for all of us, so she could meet his brother Philip. Maybe even a bridesmaid's dress. My mother would approve. She would, she would.

'Are you missing anything?' he said.

'Like what?'

'I mean from the classroom. Has anything been taken?'

'No,' I said. I saw no reason to mention the stolen pen. To all intents and purposes, I had it back.

Amy rang when we were finishing off the dishes – Dad was twirling the tea towel into a whip and flicking it at my legs like he used to. Bit by bit, I thought, he was coming back to me.

'Who are you?' he said into the receiver. 'What business do you have with my daughter?' His stupid old game, but Amy always played along. 'I'm a jewel thief, and she's my rich customer,' she'd say, or 'I'm her secret twin who's been missing for years,' or 'I'm a private detective, and I need to ask her some questions.'

'A Miss Fong for you,' said Dad, handing me the phone. 'Sounds shifty.' He carried the good china through to the living room to put it away in the sideboard.

'I'm on the upstairs extension,' said Amy, keeping her voice low. 'I was trying you all afternoon. Where were you?'

'At my cleaning job,' I said.

'Oh right,' she said. 'That.'

She never would be happy for me, I thought. 'What do you want?'

'Mrs Price is the thief,' she whispered.

'What did you say?'

'Mrs Price came into the shop today—'

'Can you talk a bit louder?'

'My parents will go crazy if they hear me.'

'You're sounding kind of crazy yourself,' I said. 'Must be genetic.'

'She bought some pumpkin and potatoes. Some kūmara. Some grapes.'

'Okay, and?'

'I was watching her in the curved mirror. She was over by the shelves with all the imported stuff. She stole a jar of jasmine-flower tea.'

'What do you mean?' I said, glancing through to the living room to see if Dad was in earshot.

'I mean, she stole a jar of jasmine-flower tea. Slipped it into her handbag when she thought nobody was looking.'

'I don't believe you.'

'I saw her.'

'Those mirrors twist things.'

'Justine, I *saw* her.'

'No,' I said.

'No?'

'No. I unpacked the groceries myself.' Careful not to say too much in case Dad overheard.

'Well, it was in her handbag. Did you unpack that?'

'Of course not.'

'There you are then.'

'What did your parents do when you told them?' I still didn't believe her.

'I didn't tell them,' said Amy.

'What?'

'She saw me looking at her. After she slipped it into her bag, she looked up at the mirror and saw me watching. And she kind of nodded at me, like – I don't know, like it was our secret.'

I twisted and untwisted the phone cord. 'It all sounds pretty strange.'

'It *was* strange. I didn't know what to do.'

'Strange as in not real.'

'You don't believe me? Why would I make this up?'

'I have no idea. I better go.'

'I went after her,' she said quickly. 'I followed her outside, and I just asked her, point blank, to show me inside her bag.'

'Oh my God.'

'She said no, so I told her I'd seen her take the tea and I knew she was the one stealing our things at school, too.'

'Jesus, Amy!'

'She grabbed my arm and dug in her nails and called me a little bitch. Then she said I should watch myself, because there'd be serious consequences if I spouted that shit to anyone else.'

'So did you tell your parents *that*, then?'

A pause. 'No.'

'Because it never happened.'

'Because I thought . . . I thought they might be mad with me for making waves at school. They worked so hard to get us accepted.'

'Honestly, it doesn't even sound like something Mrs Price would say. I better go.'

'Tell her parents what?' said Dad when he came back to the kitchen.

'Someone's picking on her at school.'

'Oh that's rough. I hope you're sticking up for her.'

'Sure,' I said.

My tongue felt too big for my mouth. A side effect of my new pills.

Amy tried to talk to me about it in class the next day, but I wouldn't listen.

'Just look for it next time you're there,' she whispered. 'One of our jars of jasmine-flower tea. Please?'

At lunchtime I sat with Melissa and Selena, and we watched the boys wrestling on the giant wooden spools, pushing one another off the edge. Rachel was doing some errands for Mrs Price, and she smiled a triumphant smile at me as she left the school grounds, but I didn't care: I was working in Mrs Price's *house*. My father was *seeing* her. How long before I could tell everyone the news?

I was happy for him – I was happy for both of us. That afternoon in the shop, instead of asking me to work out the back – washing the china and glassware he'd bought, ironing the creases from ancient tablecloths and nightdresses – he let me serve at the counter. I took people's money, swathing their purchases in layers of tissue paper while he priced some new items.

'What do you think this is worth?' he asked me, holding up a carriage clock. 'Five hundred dollars?'

'More,' I said, and he laughed and wrote $550 on the tag.

Yes, I was happy for him, but all the same, after he'd left for dinner with her on the Friday evening, I took the black light and climbed into my mother's armoire. This was a game I'd started: I'd think of a question, then close my eyes and shine the light on a random spot. Whatever words it caught were my mother's answer.

'Do you approve of Mrs Price?' I said.

I shut my eyes, aimed the black light.

Who are you? said my mother.

Dad was humming to himself when he came home, and the next morning he made me pancakes for breakfast, just like he used to before Mum got sick.

'People,' said Mrs Price on Monday, 'I'm disappointed to report that nobody has owned up to the stealing. I have my own thoughts about it, but I need to hear yours.'

She asked Katrina to hand out blank slips of paper, one each. Rachel scowled; Katrina had been given more and more jobs lately.

'You are all to write down the name of the person you suspect,' said Mrs Price. 'Fold your pieces of paper in half when you're finished, and I'll collect them.'

My classmates picked up their pens, stared at the little slips. It felt like a test. I took the ferry pen from my tunic pocket. Through the window I could see the clouds skidding across the smoke-grey sky, the climbing rope thrashing in the wind. Beyond the rippling hedge, the convent with its quiet polished rooms.

Mrs Price was watching us, beautiful Mrs Price, perched on the edge of her desk in her Brooke Shields jeans. The gold crucifix glinting at her throat. 'I'm asking for total honesty,' she said. 'Don't be afraid.'

Everyone else was writing down a name already. I stared at

the mole on my knuckle, turned my slip of paper over as if I might find something on the back to help me, some kind of clue or advice. Nothing. I glanced at Melissa's desk, but she cupped her hand over her paper as she wrote. Amy was sitting up straight in her chair, fiddling with the end of her plait, her slip folded and waiting. Mrs Price moved through the rows of pupils, collecting the secret names, her perfume drifting behind her: jasmine and honeysuckle, the ghosts of summery flowers, and something darker too.

The pen felt unwieldy in my hand – thick and sticky – but she was almost at my desk, and I had to give her a name, I had to help her.

I wrote: *Amy*.

I suppose there was no going back after that.

CHAPTER 17

Mrs Price didn't say anything about the names or the stealing for a few days. We had no idea what to make of it. Was she discussing the matter with Mr Chisholm? Had they already alerted the police?

When I went to her house on the Thursday, she asked me to clean the bathroom. I scrubbed the faint greasy ring from around the bath, picked out the hair from the drain. Inside the medicine cabinet I found a bottle that looked like my mother's pills, only someone else's name was on the label, and I didn't recognise it. I touched the handle of the razor we'd used to shave her legs. A powdery drop of rust on the blade.

She was in the study, preparing our lessons. 'Help yourself to some milk or cordial if you're thirsty,' she called. 'Or there's Ribena in the pantry. And shortbread in the tin.'

'Can I bring you anything?' I asked on my way to the kitchen.

'Aren't you a sweetheart. No, I'll soldier on – but thank you.'

I poured myself a glass of milk and took two pieces of short-bread. Next to the electric kettle sat the canisters of tea, coffee and sugar. I listened for any footsteps in the hall, then eased the lid from the tea: just ordinary teabags inside. I found nothing in the cupboards, either – only crockery and glasses, and a cake mixer and baking trays, and the cleaning products under the sink. Everything as it should be. Still listening for footsteps, I searched the pantry, shifting tins of beetroot and salmon and diet milkshake powder to check at the very back. I tried not to make any noise that might give me away, but I knew I had to work quickly. At one point I knocked a tin of spaghetti to the floor.

'Everything okay?' called Mrs Price.

'Fine thanks,' I called back. 'Nothing broken.'

'Did you find the shortbread?'

'Yes, it's delicious – thank you.'

I had to climb on a stool to reach the top shelf of the pantry, but could see only jars of preserves and a few dog-eared sachets of soup. I could hear Mrs Price approaching, and my head felt dizzy, my feet unsteady on the small stool. 'Maybe I will have a bit of shortbread,' she was saying. 'One tiny piece. You're a terrible influence, Justine!'

In the cramped space my breaths turned quick and shallow. I knew I should climb down; I knew she was coming. But there, at the very back of the top shelf, behind a glass mould shaped like a fish: a jar of jasmine-flower tea. The buds dried into little white knots.

I leapt from the stool and shoved it back under the kitchen table, then grabbed the shortbread tin and offered it to Mrs Price as she stepped through the door.

'Twist my arm, then,' she said.

Leaning back against the edge of the sink, trying to blink away the dizziness, I drained my glass of milk in two gulps.

'You must be working too hard,' she said. 'You're quite red in the face.'

'Scrubbing the bath,' I said.

'Am I that filthy?'

She laughed as I tried to stammer an apology; she was only joking, she said. I mustn't take everything to heart.

That night on *The Love Boat* Captain Stubing reunited with an old flame who wanted to cram a whole lifetime into her few days on board. When the captain said he'd devote himself to it, she asked who'd steer the ship.

'What ship?' said the captain, embracing her.

'That seems irresponsible,' said Dad.

'Well?' Amy asked the next morning as we hung up our bags. 'Did you look?'

'Did I look for what?'

'You know what I'm talking about!' she hissed. 'The tea!'

'It doesn't prove anything,' I said.

'I knew it!' said Amy. 'Now what happens?'

'Nothing. You didn't even tell your parents. I bet you'll get in trouble if you tell them now.'

She hadn't thought of that.

'Anyway,' I went on, 'she's probably had it for months. Probably bought it ages ago, didn't like the taste and put it at the back of the pantry.'

But something inside me was fizzing. What if Amy spoke up? What if Dad and I lost Mrs Price? Except Amy was wrong; she had to be wrong. I could hardly sit still in class, and when Sister Bronislava came to take us for singing I tapped my fingers and feet in time to the songs just to counter the rush of my blood. I wanted to jump out of my skin. *I am bound for California by way of stormy Cape Horn*, I sang, though I couldn't hear my own voice. Amy and Karl in my left ear, Melissa in my right. *And I will write to thee a letter, love, when I am homeward bound . . .*

When the bell rang for lunch I bolted for the adventure playground and hauled myself up the climbing rope, ignoring the sting in my palms. I'd never made it to the top before. I could see right across the cold school grounds: the breeze-block back of the church, the bare walnut tree, the convent garden with its vegetable patch and its flower beds, its fibreglass grotto to Mary. All the classroom windows taped with rumpled paintings and chains of paper people holding hands.

'Good work, Crieve,' called Karl. 'What are you, like a spy? An assassin?'

I shinnied down faster than I should have, the rope on fire between my palms and knees. My body was taking over, making its own decisions. Karl and the three Jasons were wrestling one another on the big wooden spools while other boys – lesser boys – cheered them on from below, calling for blood. I clambered up onto the spools and grabbed Jason Daly's jersey from behind, hauling him to the ground in one easy move. The boys below whooped and whistled, and I grabbed Jason Asofua and dispatched him as well. Jason Moretti hung on for longer, his fingers digging into my upper arms, his nostrils flared . . . but over the edge he went. Then Karl and I circled each other, crouching low, his gold-flecked eyes locked on mine. The noise of the playground receded and I couldn't feel the cold, and when the wind blew Karl's hair over his forehead and he shook it away I knew he was looking at me differently, seeing me in a new light. We pounced at the same time, gripping each other's shoulders, straining to push each other away. I could feel his every fingertip.

'Looks like you chose the wrong guy to mess with,' he said, so I laughed in his face like a spy, like an assassin. He shoved at me hard, and I began to tilt backwards into nothing but air, but I was still holding on to his shoulders, and he stumbled then righted himself, pulling me back up too. We planted our feet and pushed with all our might, gaining ground and losing ground each in turn. Somewhere in the distance boys were shouting at us, and girls now too, but they reached us only as snatches of static. Then we heard a different voice: 'People! People! What do you think you're doing?'

Mrs Price was running across the adventure playground, and the crowd below us had disappeared. 'What on earth is going on?' she called. 'Get down from there at once.'

We let go of each other and jumped to the ground. It seemed a long way – too far, too high – and the impact cracked through my shins.

'Are you animals?' she demanded, looking first at Karl and then at me. 'Well?'

We shook our heads: no, we weren't animals. We were just playing. It was just a game.

'What would your father say if he knew you were carrying on like this, Justine?'

'I don't know,' I said.

'What would Mr *Chisholm* say? Justine? Karl?'

We didn't know that either.

'He'd get out the strap,' she said. 'For the pair of you. Wouldn't he.'

We nodded.

'I'll have to give this some thought,' she said. 'Off you go.'

All afternoon we wondered what was coming. When she stood up from her chair and said she had an announcement to make, we looked across Amy's desk at each other. This was it. She was going to summon Mr Chisholm.

'People,' she said, 'I've had a chance to check the names you wrote down for me on Monday.'

The entire classroom fell silent. Not a single thing had gone missing that week; somehow we thought the problem had gone away.

'There were a few different class members mentioned,' she went on, 'but one of you came up again and again, and this accords with my own investigations.' She gazed around the room in that way she had, taking us all in. 'I have decided to name this person,' she said. 'Not so we can take some kind of nasty revenge. Not so we can mount an attack. No. Jesus teaches us forgiveness. He teaches us that as good Catholics we must turn the other cheek. So I have decided to give her a chance to put things right.'

The thief was a girl, then. I bit the inside of my lip.

'Amy,' she said, her voice gentle. 'What's the reason for your behaviour? Is everything all right at home?'

We all turned to stare at Amy.

'Told you so,' said Rachel. 'She should just kill herself.'

'Let's give Amy a chance to speak,' said Mrs Price.

And Amy did the worst thing possible: she started to cry.

'Yes,' said Mrs Price, nodding. 'It's a terrible feeling to be found out, isn't it?' She'd come over to Amy's desk and was rubbing her back. 'But the beautiful thing, my darling, is that you can undo it. You can ask for forgiveness.'

'Do we get our stuff back, though?' said Paula.

'Obviously that would be part of asking for forgiveness,' said Mrs Price.

'I don't have your crappy stuff!' snarled Amy. 'I don't have it because I didn't take it!'

I can still see her face, all twisted and furious.

Mrs Price stepped back, sighed. 'You're not ready,' she said. 'I understand. People, we're going to give Amy some time. She needs to come to this in her own way. Let's all of us remember her in our prayers tonight – she's part of our family.'

There wasn't much of the afternoon left, and when the bell rang, Amy ran for the corridor without saying goodbye.

'Karl and Justine, will you stay behind, please?' said Mrs Price. 'No one else today, thank you.'

'I can do the windows,' said Katrina, but Mrs Price repeated: no one else today.

Karl emptied the rubbish bin and closed the windows while I cleaned the blackboard and the dusters.

And that was our punishment, which was no punishment at all.

He walked beside me on the way home, wheeling his bike up the hill. 'I thought we were in for it,' he said. 'What happened?'

I shrugged. 'That's just the way she is.' As if I'd known her for years.

'Maybe she was too busy with Amy,' he said. 'But I would've won.'

'What?'

'In the playground. I was just about to push you off.'

'Pfft,' I said, shoving into his side.

He shoved back, laughing as mud spattered up the back of my leg.

'What do you think about Amy?' I said.

'She's your friend. What do you think?'

'I don't know. I guess she's been . . . different lately.'

'So have you.'

I kept walking, looking at the ground so he wouldn't see me blushing.

'Anyway,' he said, 'just about everyone wrote down her name. And Mrs Price thinks it's her too.'

'She must have proof,' I said. 'She couldn't just say that, could she?'

'Yeah, she'll have proof,' he said. 'That's what it sounded like.'

We walked along in silence for a little way. I didn't want to believe it, but it seemed to be true: Amy was the thief. I felt as if she had died.

'Hey,' said Karl, catching my hand and pulling me towards him. I could smell the sea. Soft rain was starting to fall, and the tiniest of droplets shone in his black hair. 'Can I ask you something?'

I swallowed. Nodded.

He said, 'Do you think Melissa likes me?'

CHAPTER 18

Mrs Fong didn't ask how I was when I rang Amy that evening. 'I'll get her,' was all she said.

'Yeah?' said Amy when she picked up the receiver.

'I thought . . . I thought I'd see how you were doing,' I said.

'How do you think?'

'Um, not very good.'

'Well, don't worry,' she said, 'you can *pray* for me.'

'I walked home with Karl today,' I said.

'So?'

'He held my hand.'

'He did not.'

But I could tell she was interested. I could tell she was jealous.

'Karl likes Melissa,' she said.

'Do you think?'

'Duh! It's so obvious!' she said. 'Oh my God – you thought he liked you.'

She couldn't stop laughing, so I said, 'Dad's gone to the movies with Mrs Price.'

'*What?*'

'And he had dinner at her house last week.'

'Why didn't you tell me?'

'I'm telling you now.'

For a moment both of us just listened to the crackle on the line. Then I said, 'Amy, did you steal all those things?'

She hung up.

The next week, Melissa passed me a note in class. I started to unfold it, but she jabbed me with her elbow and whispered, 'It's for Karl.' I handed it to Amy, who handed it to Karl; he grinned when he read it, wrote something in reply, drew what looked like a spaceman, then returned it to Amy. And so it went for the next few days: muffled laughs, fleeting glances, while Amy and I sat in the middle and passed the messages back and forth.

On Thursday, when I went to Mrs Price's to clean, she asked me to do the vacuuming. I started in the study, then shut the door for her so she could get on with her work. At the end of the hall I tried the door to the spare bedroom, but it was locked.

When I'd finished, she came out to pay me.

'Sit down for a minute,' she said, gesturing to the kitchen table. 'Would you like some banana cake?'

She cut me a slice and watched as I ate it. She didn't have a piece herself but ran her finger along the knife blade and licked off the icing.

'So tell me,' she said, 'do you think Amy is going to own up?'

I shook my head; I'd tried to swallow too large a bite of cake.

'It's very sad,' she said. 'Has she mentioned anything about it?'

'Not really. Just that she didn't take the things.'

'Very sad,' she said again. 'I know it must be hard for you. And I know it must be hard seeing Melissa so friendly with Karl.'

She knew everything about us, Mrs Price. She saw everything. I squirmed.

'It's all right, my darling,' she said. 'Shall I tell you the trick with boys?'

I nodded.

'The trick is to let them think they're in control. Don't show how strong you really are. Don't wrestle with them, for instance.' She smiled. 'Be a bit mysterious.'

'Okay,' I said, though I didn't quite understand what she meant.

'I can see why you're drawn to Karl,' she went on. 'He's very handsome, of course – but there was the business with Susan, too, wasn't there.' She was still smiling. 'The business with the crab in her tank. He covered up for you.'

I opened my mouth, but nothing came out.

'It's a noble thing, to take the punishment for someone else,' she said. 'A beautiful thing.' She reached over and touched my arm. 'I have to ask you, Justine – are you involved in any way with the stealing?'

I flinched, as if she'd burned me. 'No!' I said. 'Not at all!'

'Okay, my darling. Okay. Someone wrote down your name, you see. I had to ask.'

I didn't let myself cry until I was biking away from her house, but then the tears came, and I could hardly see where I was going. When I reached St Michael's I turned in the gate, rode to the adventure playground and crawled inside the stormwater pipes. I could smell smoke: Mr Armstrong was burning rubbish. In the distance I saw fiery little scraps blowing from the steel drum and extinguishing themselves mid-air. I lay down and wept, the concrete cold against my side even through my jersey and jacket.

'Are you all right?' said a voice.

At the end of the pipes, a pair of legs in thick woollen trousers. Mr Armstrong peered in. 'Justine, isn't it?'

'Hello.'

'What are you doing here so late, love?'

'I was on my way home. I just stopped in.'

'To cry?'

'Yeah.'

'You'll freeze out here.'

'Yeah.'

'Come on.' He reached in an arm and helped me out of the pipes.

In his shed he cleared some papers off an old dining chair and offered me a seat.

'What *is* all this?' I said. Around the chair lay a mess of paper: handwritten pages, typed pages, thick manila folders, cyclostyled newsprint, crayon drawings, finger paintings.

'When the teachers have a clear-out, they bring me their rubbish to burn,' he said, and then, as I noticed the gallery of children's paintings hanging on the corrugated-iron walls: 'Some of them are just too nice.' Above the window, one of Melissa's horse pictures; further along, one of Karl's spacemen. Coiled in a corner, a lumpy snake – far too real, for a moment, until I remembered making one myself in the primers, stuffing an old pantyhose leg with scrunched-up newspaper, then daubing on scales. Mr Armstrong took a crisply ironed handkerchief from his pocket and handed it to me. 'Dry your eyes – that's better. Is there trouble at home?'

'No,' I said. 'It's here.'

'You're in Mrs Price's class, aren't you?'

'Yes.'

He nodded. 'Look after yourself, love,' he said. Then, lifting one of the stacks of paper, he went back outside to the incinerator and fed the fire.

I could smell the smoke all the way home up the hill – in my hair, on my clothes and my skin. In fact, the smell grew stronger as I rode up our driveway – and no, I wasn't imagining it: smoke was rising from behind our house. I threw down my bike and ran around to the back garden.

It took me a minute to make out my father through the haze of the bonfire. My eyes stung, and I blinked, blinked again, and there he was in front of the apple tree. For one feverish moment I thought he was lifting a body onto the flames, until I drew closer and saw it was an overcoat. My mother's overcoat.

'Dad! What are you doing?'

Next to him, a pile of Mum's clothes.

He dropped the overcoat onto the fire and picked up the next garment: the velvet skirt that was too tight in the waist.

'Dad!' I shouted again. Hadn't he heard me? I grabbed his hand, snatched back the skirt.

'It's long overdue,' he said. 'We should have done this months ago.'

He picked up the sundress with the cherries, and I snatched that back too, but I was too late to save the things he'd already thrown on the flames. I could see bits and pieces of them – the cuff of a striped blouse, the rubbed sole of a slipper. The blue-gold sheen of the shot-taffeta harem pants. A sleeve lifted, filled with air, filled with fire, and fell.

'Weren't you even going to ask me?' I said.

'Justine, you've never so much as looked at the things in almost a year.'

I pushed past him and gathered up the remaining clothes in my arms. He didn't try to stop me, at least. Inside, I returned my mother's blue satin dressing gown to the hook on the bathroom door and hung the other items in her armoire. Then I locked it and hid the key in my old doll's cradle.

He didn't say anything when he came in – he just kissed me on the forehead. Not a trace of whisky on his breath.

Dad was seeing Mrs Price again on the Saturday. He'd bought a new shirt, and he ironed it in the kitchen, the smell of the hot fresh cotton mingling with the Old Spice he'd patted on his cheeks. After he'd gone I went out to the garden and raked through the ashes of the bonfire. Picked out a pair of metal buttons dull as dead eyes.

He'd left me some money for fish and chips, and I biked down to the takeaway place in the dark, my light casting its fluttery beam across the cracked pavement. While I waited for my order I flicked through a *New Zealand Woman's Weekly*, taking in the shapes and poses of the models in their Stylish Outfits for Rainy Days. Britain's Young Slimmer of 1983 said she lost over four stone because her husband told her he didn't like fat women. A royal biographer revealed that the Queen had to maintain her size-12 figure as her clothes were planned a year in advance. In the advice column I read a letter from a schoolgirl who had kissed her much older neighbour. *It feels like I have millions of butterflies in my stomach. My mother has told me I'm not to be alone with him. Am I too young for this?* The reply was curt and clear: *The 'butterflies' you describe sound like the awakenings of sexual attraction. Your very innocence might lead you into deep trouble, so heed the voice of experience.*

I tucked the warm parcel of food down the front of my jacket and pretended it was a baby, and when I got home I ate it in front of *Fame*, which Dad couldn't stomach. That night a rebellious student saved the principal from choking on an apple, and a food fight as well as a dance routine broke out in the cafeteria, and a substitute English teacher who was really a singer sang in an empty theatre even though she said she wasn't supposed to because of nodes on her vocal cords which she made up. I pushed the metal buttons around in my palm, trying to remember the garment they'd come from. A jacket? A cardigan? I could no longer recall. When *Fame* finished I unlocked my mother's armoire and slipped the buttons inside the pocket of her houndstooth trousers. The house was utterly silent; Dad wouldn't be home till late. I went out to the garage and found the black light, then returned to the armoire and climbed inside.

'Am I too young for this?' I said.

I closed my eyes and aimed the black light at the wall of the armoire to find my mother's answer.

Going once. Going twice, she said.

After that I moved from room to room, reading the invisible writing – or what was left of it. More words had faded since I'd last looked, and there was nothing I could do, no way to stop them from vanishing. *Far too dear . . . the baby's heartbeat . . . numbered all my bones . . . a knife comes out clean . . . kick the sky . . .* In the hall, our family photographs watched me as I passed: Mum and Dad in Venice, before they'd even thought about me; Mum and Dad on their wedding day, her veil foaming over her shoulders; Mum and Dad cutting their wedding cake. Me as a chubby baby on a picnic blanket; me on my first day at St Michael's; me making my First Communion, a blood blister on my thumb, my hair rucked up under my own stiff little veil. A studio portrait of the three of us against a brownish sunset. Mum in a bikini.

I had never thought to check the photos. I lifted down the wedding portrait, turned out the hall light and shone the black light across the back of the frame – and my mother's white words shone back up at me, seeming to float in the dark.

Hail, Queen of Heav'n, the ocean Star,
Guide of the wand'rer here below.

A hymn to Mary, scattered across the photographs, a line here, half a line there.

Thrown on life's surge, we claim thy care,
Save us from peril and from woe.
Mother of Christ, Star of the sea,
Pray for the wand'rer, pray for me.

I still don't know why – maybe it was the hymn – but I went to the pocket of my school tunic and pulled out the ferry pen Mrs Price had given me. Under the black light, the little white ship glowed . . . and on the plastic that encased it, so did the invisible ink. Someone had marked it. My mother had marked it. My skin turned cold, and my head swam. Could I make out a J, followed by a U? It was too faded to tell. The white streaks hung over the water like mist, like foam.

2014

Chapter 19

The manager of the retirement community welcomes everyone to their St Patrick's Day celebrations. She hopes we'll enjoy the Irish dancing, kindly presented at no cost by the pupils of Fancy Footwork. To all the children hunting for the pot of chocolate coins, she wishes the luck of the Irish. We mustn't forget the pony rides starting at 3 P.M. in the front garden; for the protection of all concerned, parents are required to sign a permission slip if their children want to participate. And, she says, making an expansive gesture that takes in the entire streamered lounge, we should help ourselves to as much green sponge cake as we like!

Emma drags me over to the reception desk to sign up for the pony rides, pressing the pen into my hand. *I agree that Pony Parties NZ are not liable for the injury or death of a participant or spectator arising from the inherent risk of livestock activities . . .* She's always bringing home permission slips like this, her teachers absolving themselves of all responsibility in the case of disaster on a trip to the zoo or at swimming sports day. As I sign, I think of the film Father Lynch showed my class about the imprisoned clown shot by firing squad. They'd never show something like that nowadays. Not to children. Still, we like the local Catholic school – small classes, a zero-tolerance approach to bullying, which is why we chose it. Emma has taken to it like a natural. I remember one day when she was quite little, maybe six, she started telling me that Jesus died to save us all.

'People didn't love God enough,' she said, 'so he had to sac-rifice his son.'

'That's a big word,' I said. 'Sacrifice.'

'Yes,' she said, 'and I know what it means. And Jesus is God's son and actually also God.'

'Some people believe that,' I said.

'No, but it's true,' she said. 'We learned it at school. And God sent Jesus to suffer and die for us.'

'Well, some people believe that, and other people believe other things.'

'Mum,' she said, taking my hand, 'don't worry. It has a happy ending.'

She'll probably grow out of it – we did. We married in a garden rather than a church. Dom's mother lent me her aqua-marine earrings for something blue; they weren't at all to my taste, but I thanked her and wore them anyway.

'You know you can always come back,' she said to me on the morning of the wedding.

'We're Aucklanders now,' I said.

'I meant you can always come back to your faith.'

Of Dom's siblings, only his younger brother Peter still goes to church these days. Which is a terrible strike rate. But his mother worships every week without fail, and goes to confes-sion once a month. We've no idea what she admits to, but in private we like to make things up.

Emma shoots off now to search for chocolate coins behind cushions and pot plants. Caregivers circulate, painting sham-rocks on the faces of the residents. I can't see Sonia, and I'm relieved; I told Dom I was going to ask her if she was related to Mrs Price, but on the way here in the car I lost my nerve. Emma had decided to come with me, and I can't bring it up in front of her, can I? We've been so careful to shield her from all that.

'Who are you?' says Dad.

'I'm Justine,' I say. 'Your daughter. That's Emma over there, looking for the treasure. She's your granddaughter.'

'What is this?'

'A bit of a party. For St Patrick's Day.'

A caregiver sits down beside him and dips her brush in green paint. 'Top of the morning to you!' she says. It's 2.30 in the afternoon. Steadying her hand on Dad's cheek, she begins to paint a shamrock, but finishes only one heart-shaped leaf before he smacks her away.

'I'm so sorry,' I say. 'He's tired.'

'I'm not tired,' he says.

'It's all right, Mr Crieve. Maybe later,' says the caregiver, moving on to the next resident.

'What is this?' says Dad.

'A little party for St Patrick's Day.'

'Who are you?'

'I'm Justine. I'm your daughter.'

The dancers take the floor then, thundering in from the foyer in their short dresses and their tightly curled wigs. Under the makeup and the bouncing hair, they must be about ten years old. Dad's scratching the green heart on his cheek, frowning at the colour that comes away on his fingertips.

'I'll get that for you,' I say, licking the corner of a serviette and wiping the paint away.

Then I see her – Sonia – over by the tea and coffee trolley, laughing with another family. Pecking the cheek of an elderly man who's wearing a *Kiss me, I'm Irish* sweatshirt. Letting them touch her shoulder, her hand. Just as if Mrs Price were back. And even after all this time, even after everything that happened, I catch myself thinking: leave her alone. She's mine.

1984

CHAPTER 20

When I found the invisible ink on the ferry pen, I threw the thing to the back of a drawer. I didn't want to see it or touch it: I didn't want to believe what my mother's faded handwriting was telling me. Still, I couldn't stop thinking about those ghostly marks. I needed someone to explain them, to absolve Mrs Price. In the past I would have gone straight to Amy, but we were hardly talking – and anyway, she would only have crowed that she was right about Mrs Price, and insist on exposing her when I really wasn't sure. I no longer ate my lunch with Amy in the stormwater pipes, choosing instead to sit with Melissa and her friends. I couldn't tell them, though – they'd never speak to me again if I suggested that Mrs Price, our beautiful Mrs Price, had lied to me. I couldn't tell Karl, either – I'd been avoiding him, ashamed of my stupid, unrequited crush. And I certainly couldn't tell my father; he was so happy now. No more whisky bottles hidden around the house. No more sitting in the dark, listening to sad records.

But was Mrs Price treating me differently? Had she cooled towards me? Did she know, somehow, what I thought I had discovered? The following week she asked Brendon and Jacqui to stay behind instead of me – new pets. Perhaps, though, she was just trying to downplay the fact she was seeing my father, because they didn't want anyone to know yet.

In the end I decided Mr Chisholm was the best person to help me, so at lunchtime on Wednesday I went to his office.

'Come in, please,' he said, smiling, motioning to a vinyl chair underneath the poster of the Shroud face. 'How can I help, Justine?' He was punching holes in a pile of typed pages and transferring them to a ring binder.

'It's about Mrs Price,' I said.

'Oh yes?'

'I had a pen – a special pen.' I cleared my throat. 'I thought I'd lost it, but then I saw it in her bag.'

He stopped punching holes, peered at me. 'What were you doing looking in her bag?'

'I wasn't!' I said. 'I wasn't. I just saw it in there. And then I asked her about it, and she said it wasn't my pen, it was a pen that looked like my pen that she bought at the same place' – I was making little sense, I knew – 'and she gave it to me, but I realised because of the markings on it that it *is* my pen after all. I think.'

'What exactly are you getting at, Justine?'

'I . . . well, she had my pen.'

'You're telling me that Mrs Price picked up a pen that belongs to you, and then when you made her aware of her mistake she gave it back?'

'Well,' I said again, 'well, she told me it *wasn't* my pen but I could have it anyway.'

'That sounds very generous of her.' He took off his little narrow glasses and polished them on his checked handkerchief.

'Yes,' I said. 'But I'm pretty sure it is my pen.'

Mr Chisholm opened the back of the hole punch and emptied all the confetti into the rubbish bin, then started punching holes again.

'And you *have* the pen,' he said. 'I'm sorry, Justine, but I'm finding it difficult to see the problem here. At any rate, a pen is just a thing, and we are far too invested in things. Remember the story of the man who had no shoes who was feeling sorry for himself until he saw a man who had no feet.'

'Yes,' I said.

'Yes,' he said.

A pause.

'Thank you, Mr Chisholm.'

'Any time, Justine.'

By the time Thursday came, I wasn't sure what to think. At Mrs Price's, she asked me to wash all the windows. I scrubbed the frames inside the house with an old toothbrush, wiping away mould and fly dirt and dead moths, then cleaned the glass. She gave me a long-handled brush for the outside, and I worked my way around the house, the water trickling down my arms and inside my sleeves. At the back, the curtains in the spare bedroom were drawn, though a tiny chink showed near the top. I cast about for something to stand on – something light enough for me to carry so Mrs Price wouldn't hear me dragging it. The rubbish bin, over by the laundry door. Silently I shifted it to below the window and climbed on the thin metal lid. I thought it might collapse beneath me; I could feel it flexing under my feet, and I tried to spread my weight as evenly as possible. Then I put my eye to the gap.

It was hard to make out much – a single bed with shapes on it that might have been toys or cushions; a shelf crammed with items I couldn't distinguish in the gloom. I heard the study window opening and Mrs Price calling: 'Justine? There's a hot cocoa in the kitchen. Are you there? Justine?'

That same feeling of dizziness I'd been having since I started on the new pills. I jumped down and darted along to her window to stop her from leaning out. 'Thanks!' I said, giving her a wave, then rushing to return the bin to its usual spot.

She smiled at me as we drank our drinks, her brown eyes crinkling at the corners. 'You know,' she said, 'I'm becoming very fond of your father.'

'I know.'

'I hope that's all right . . . ? I want you to be happy, my darling – that's very important to me.'

I nodded, though I wasn't sure what I was agreeing to. My arms ached from washing the windows.

She dug the sugar spoon deep into the bowl and lifted it out, letting the sandy grains trickle into a tiny white hillock. 'I think we get on so well – your father and I – because we share a similar history.' She glanced up at me, then back to the sugar. 'I had a daughter, you see. A husband and a daughter, but they both died. I keep a few of their things locked away in the spare room – I can't bring myself to look at them, I suppose, but I don't want to get rid of them either. Perhaps you can understand.'

Yes, I nodded, yes of course I understood. 'I'm so sorry,' I said. She'd never spoken of the car accident that had killed her family, and I was ashamed of myself for trying to pry through the curtains. These things were private.

'Well,' she said, gesturing to the clean kitchen window. 'Doesn't everything look so much sharper?'

On Friday, at Passing Time, Dad asked me to tighten the clasp on a delicate Georgian bracelet – an easy job, but his fingers were too big and he couldn't see what he was doing. It was the prettiest thing, made up of seven little gold hands with cuffs of flared gold lace. Each hand wore a tiny ring set with gemstones of different colours.

He draped it over my wrist when I'd finished, and we both admired it.

'What do you think?' he said. 'Do you like it?' His way of checking if he should put something aside for me for Christmas or my birthday.

'I love it,' I said. 'I *love* it.'

'I knew you would. But you haven't even noticed the best part. Look at the stones.'

'What about the stones?'

'Well, what are they?'

'A sapphire . . . a diamond . . . is that a topaz? They're very small.'

'The value's not in the carat weight,' he said. 'It's in the meaning. Look again. Start with the diamond.'

He pointed to each stone in turn and I named them. 'Diamond . . . emerald . . . amethyst . . . ruby . . . emerald . . . sapphire . . . topaz.'

'So what's the meaning?' he said. 'What's the code?'

'D . . . E . . . A . . . R . . . E . . . S . . . T,' I said, smiling. 'Dearest.'

'Dearest,' he said. 'A message from the lover to the beloved.' I knew he liked teaching me about the antiques trade. I had an eye for it, he'd told me once.

'Dad,' I said, 'you know the black light?'

'Mm.' He didn't attach a price tag to the bracelet, and he didn't put it in the display cabinet. Instead, he shut it away in the safe under the counter.

'If something shows up,' I said, 'and it's not a repair, and it's not invisible ink, what else could it be?'

'Traces of blood can fluoresce,' he said. 'Traces of urine. Even sweat.'

'So you might see that – traces of sweat – on something handled a lot?'

'It's possible.'

That was it, then. The marks on the pen weren't my mother's ink but Mrs Price's fingerprints – or my own. Nothing more.

At home I retrieved the pen from the back of the drawer, and from then on I carried it with me again, slipping it into the pocket of whatever I was wearing, until I hardly had to think about it.

CHAPTER 21

Mrs Price said, 'I made some biscuits for the occasion.' She peeled the tin foil from the plate and showed us: thin slices of shortbread cut into little crowns and decorated with silver balls.

'Perfect,' said Dad, kissing her on the cheek, and I knew that he loved her.

'Still looking for your wealthy widow, I see,' she said, picking up the newspaper and scanning the circled death notices. 'Lilian sounds promising. Only one child, by the sound of it. So much easier to swoop in and help yourself.'

'You're awful,' he said, and she waggled the newspaper in his face.

'Am I the one stalking the newly bereaved? Hm? Hmm?'

'It's a service,' he laughed.

'You keep telling yourself what you need to hear.'

We settled on the couch, the three of us, and I turned on the TV.

The sound of a helicopter, city lights seen from above – and there, waving from a dark hilltop as the camera circled her, Lorraine Downes in a strapless white evening dress, her Miss Universe sash and her twinkling crown.

'What have they done to her beautiful hair?' said Dad. 'She looks like Princess Anne.'

'She *sounds* like Princess Anne,' said Mrs Price.

We laughed, because it was true: Lorraine's voice had changed over the course of the year, her New Zealand vowels faceted into something tighter, sharper, more careful. 'Arriving by boat down there on the Miami River,' she enunciated, her long shimmery earrings trembling, 'are eighty-one beautiful young women, headed for the magnificent new Miami Convention Centre, where my successor will be chosen.'

I helped myself to a crown biscuit, the silver balls shattering like shot between my teeth.

'Good?' said Mrs Price.

'Good,' I mumbled.

Dad took one as well, demolishing it in a single bite.

'We might have to keep you on,' he said.

Three days earlier, he and I had visited Mum's grave to mark her one-year anniversary.

He'd touched me on the shoulder, lightly, lightly. 'You know it's not as if I've forgotten her, love.'

'I know.'

Somewhere in the distance, bells sounded: wind chimes on a grave.

I poked our supermarket flowers into the vase. Out of the bunched cellophane they looked small, meagre. We both touched her headstone, the way people do, as if she might be able to feel us.

'I didn't go looking,' he said, and I wasn't sure if he was talking to me or Mum. 'It just happened. She has a way of making you feel like you matter . . . you know? And it's still early days.'

Mum had never watched Miss Universe with us. 'Such a load of nonsense,' she'd said as we yelled out our scores. 'None of it's real, Justine. You need to understand that.'

'Shh,' we said, peering around her at the screen.

'Ugh, I can't be in the same room as you.'

'Shhhh!'

But Mrs Price joined right in with the game, gleefully

pointing out squinty eyes and big noses, weak chins, protruding ears, rounded shoulders, scrawny chests. Look at England's eyebrows! And France's mole! What was Portugal even doing there? Was that really the best the Cayman Islands could scrape together? Didn't we think there was something of the chihuahua about Malta? She gave a series of little yaps.

I looked at Dad, and he looked at me, and we both started to laugh.

She was crueller than we ever were. No mercy for Thailand's lisp, nor for Guatemala's crooked mouth. No mercy when Lorraine Downes stepped irrelevantly from a spa pool and then popped up in a cigar factory. She raised an eyebrow at Dad when Poland and USA staggered under the weight of a slippery python at the zoo and said, 'I bet they're popular with the boys.' Venezuela looked like a prostitute, Germany like a Nazi. Nothing escaped Mrs Price.

I have never laughed so hard.

I knew that Dad loved her, and I knew that I loved her too.

CHAPTER 22

Melissa had invited every girl in the class to her thirteenth birthday, even the unpopular ones like Leanne and Vanessa: every girl except Amy. As we arrived, she showed us her presents, which she'd displayed on Mrs Knight's sewing table in the rumpus room: a manicure set in a pink zipped purse, a pair of tasselled cowboy boots, a 24-pack of coloured felt-tips, a velvet dressing gown, a Cabbage Patch doll with its own birth certificate and adoption papers. 'I had to swear an Oath of Adoption,' she said, pointing to the paperwork. *In front of another person, raise your right hand and say: 'I promise to love my Cabbage Patch Kid™ with all my heart. I promise to be a good and kind parent. I will always remember how special my Cabbage Patch Kid™ is to me.'* She'd signed her name as the adopting parent, and her mother had signed as witness. 'And these are my big present,' she said, turning her head so we could admire her earrings, though we'd already noticed them and wanted them the moment we arrived. They were real sapphires, she said, because sapphires went with her eyes, did we see? Yes, we nodded, yes, they were the exact same dark blue, and her parents must have spent a fortune.

'I can't wear them to school, though,' she sighed. 'So stupid.'

We all agreed: it was stupid and unfair not to let us wear jewellery. Did they *want* us to look ugly?

'You're allowed to wear those gold badges,' I said. 'The little feet.'

Everyone turned to look at me. What badges? What little feet?

I told them about the badges Dom's sisters wore, and Paula nodded: she knew the ones.

'They're real baby feet,' she said. 'So cute. I've seen them at the Christian supplies shop.'

'How can they be real?' said Selena.

Paula shrugged. 'That's what the lady at the counter said.'

We filled our plates with the food Mrs Knight brought down to the rumpus room – sausage rolls, Cheezels, lamingtons, cream horns, saveloys, chocolate crackles, fairy bread – and ate more than we could possibly have room for, and then we filled our plates again. Even Melissa gorged herself, her tongue stained bright red with raspberry fizzy. 'Oh my God,' she said, holding her stomach and turning side on, 'I look like I'm having a baby.'

Then Mrs Knight came back downstairs to start the games, and Melissa's little sister Tanya was allowed to join in even though Melissa didn't want her to. Rachel won Pass the Parcel – a strawberry lip gloss we all coveted, but she wouldn't let us try it because of germs – and Mrs Knight let Leanne win the colouring book for Statues despite the fact that Paula said she definitely saw her move her elbow and it wasn't fair.

Melissa saved the Chocolate Game till last. We sat in a circle on the floor, a king-size bar of Caramello on a dinner plate in the middle. Next to it, a knife and fork, a pair of dice and a pile of winter clothes: a scarf, a hat, some gloves and ski goggles so we could disguise ourselves. We began to roll the dice. Whenever someone rolled a double, she had to scramble into the clothes and eat as much chocolate as possible using only the knife and fork.

'You don't mind chocolate germs, then,' Natalie said when it was Rachel's turn to grab the cutlery and shovel chunks of Caramello down her throat. Rachel ignored her, stabbing the tip of the knife into the bar to break off an entire row.

We were all impatient for a turn, impatient to guzzle as much as we could before our time ran out. Mentally I ranked the other girls as they stuffed themselves: ugly, ugly, ugly. As soon as I rolled a double, I snatched the winter clothes off Paula.

'Hey!' she said. 'You scratched me!'

'Gently now, girls,' said Mrs Knight.

I didn't care. My gloved fingers fumbled with the knife and fork, and then I was away, hacking off three squares, four squares, crouching down low to the dinner plate like a dog.

When we'd finished, Selena said, 'So who's the winner?'

'There's no winner,' said Melissa.

'But what about a prize?' said Selena.

'The chocolate's the prize,' said Mrs Knight.

'But the chocolate's all gone.'

'Yeah,' said Melissa. 'You had your prize when you ate it. You ate the prize.'

'Okay, okay,' said Selena. '*God.* Just asking.'

'I didn't even have any!' wailed Tanya. '*And* I didn't win anything!'

'Mum, can you get rid of her now?' said Melissa, and Mrs Knight took Tanya back upstairs, and we lay on the floor and quizzed Melissa about Karl. How many times had he dubbed her home on his bike? What did he write in his notes in class? Had he tried to hold her hand? Had he tried to kiss her?

There had been petting, said Melissa. *Heavy* petting.

What was petting?

You know, she said, fiddling with her sapphire earrings.

No, we said.

When a boy tried to touch you, she said.

Touch you where?

You know, she said.

No, we said.

Your bum cheek, she said. That was petting.

And heavy petting?

Your boob.

We digested that.

'Well, my dad's been seeing Mrs Price,' I said, and a dozen faces turned away from Melissa to look at me.

'What do you mean, seeing?' said Paula.

'Going out with,' I said.

'Like on dates?' said Leanne.

'Yes. They've been to the movies and to dinner, and she watched Miss Universe at our house. He's taking her out again tonight, in fact.'

Who could trump that?

Later I went upstairs to use the bathroom, and Tanya was waiting for me when I came out.

'What are you guys talking about?' she said.

'Nothing much,' I said.

'Boys?'

'No.'

'You are. You're talking about boys.' She blocked my way so I couldn't go back down to the rumpus room. I stepped to the side, and so did she, and back and forth we went at the top of the staircase.

'What's the problem, Tanya?' I said.

'Have you got a boyfriend?'

'No.'

'I bet you want one, though. So you can kiss him.'

'No.' I tried to push past her again, but she wouldn't let me. She laughed, flicked her long, caramel-coloured ponytail over her shoulder – so I grabbed it. Yanked it, hard. I could feel the skin stretching away from her skull at the roots. Her head snapping to the side.

'Mum!' she screamed. 'Mum!'

When Mrs Knight appeared, Tanya ran to her and said, 'She pulled my hair! It really hurt!'

'Oh I'm sure that's not true,' said Mrs Knight.

'She *pulled* my *hair*!' said Tanya. 'On purpose!'

'No no,' said her mother. 'Justine would never do something like that.'

But I saw the way she was looking at me. I can still see it.

At lunchtime on Monday the girls all flocked to me for the details of the date. Did Mrs Price wear a strapless ballgown like Princess Caroline of Monaco? Did they feed each other oysters?

I wasn't there, I said – but my friends were hungry for information.

'She wore her hair up,' I invented. 'He gave her a single white rose and they danced a slow dance to a lone violin.'

I knew Amy was listening inside the stormwater pipes. When I mentioned the violin, she snorted.

Katrina bent down and peered at her. 'Oh my God, she's been there the whole time. Weirdo. Eavesdropping weirdo.'

'Ugh,' said Paula. 'Some people should get their own lives.'

'Look at her hiding in there like a rat,' said Natalie.

'Like a big yellow shit,' said Rachel.

Everyone laughed.

Sister Bronislava walked past just then, scanning the playground for dangerous behaviour.

'Everything all right, girls?' she said.

'Yes thank you, Sister.' We weren't hanging upside-down; we hadn't climbed too high. We weren't about to break a bone or choke.

When the bell rang, though, she came over to me again and took me by the elbow. Her grip was surprisingly firm for someone so small. 'Justine,' she said in a quiet voice as the others disappeared back to the classroom, 'I don't like what I'm seeing.'

'What are you seeing, Sister?' I said, but I knew.

'The way you are treating your old friend.'

'She's been stealing from us!' I said.

'Are you sure about that?'

'Everyone's sure.'

'Are you?'

I pulled free of her grip.

'Justine, you are making a mistake.'

'I have to go,' I said. I needed to get back to Mrs Price.

Amy wrinkled her nose when the girls in my class began to show up wearing tiny gold feet pinned to their uniforms.

'You know what they are, right?' she said.

'What?' I said.

'Dead baby feet.'

'Don't be dumb.'

'It's true. They're from a ten-week-old dead baby that was never born.'

'How does that even work? How did they get the feet if it was never born?'

'I don't know, but it's true.'

I'd been planning on asking Dad if I could get one of the badges too, but I changed my mind.

CHAPTER 23

On the first day back after the August holidays we waited in the chilly pews for our turn to confess. Mrs Price had brought us over to the church that morning in place of our weekly Religion lesson; we'd feel so clean afterwards, she told us, so free and light that we'd practically float.

She went first, by way of example, and I could hear her voice through the closed door, though I couldn't make out any words – just a peal of laughter now and then. I didn't know anyone who laughed in confession. When she emerged she nodded to Jason Asofua, who was next in line, then knelt to say her penance.

One by one we entered the dark confessional to tell Father Lynch our sins. I studied the statue of St Michael while I waited: great white wings folded at his back, one sandaled foot bearing down on the head of a coiled serpent. His breastplate shone as he lifted his golden spear, about to plunge it into the mouth of the scaly creature at his feet. And the serpent's jaw was open wide, all its teeth on show, its forked red tongue. It stared up at the archangel – begging for mercy? Or willing him on?

Slowly our numbers dwindled until Amy and I were the last two left waiting in the freezing church. I pushed my fingers under my thighs to try to warm them. Mrs Price sat at the far end of our pew, hands folded in her lap, eyes closed.

'I miss you,' whispered Amy. She was staring at the floor.

I didn't know what to say. 'How's Bonnie?' I whispered back. Our voices turning to mist as the words left our mouths.

'She's okay. We got her a squeaky rugby ball. She misses you too.'

'Give her a pat from me.'

'Give her one yourself. Come and walk her on Sunday.'

And how easy it would have been to say yes. To go to Amy's on the weekend and to get out all the old games from the hundred-eye chest while Mrs Fong made sweet and sour chicken and the Goddess of Mercy watched from her shelf and the Pope gazed down from his life-size photo on the wall. We'd rank the girls in our class from prettiest to ugliest, placing each other fourth, because fourth was believable; fourth was fair. And then we'd walk along the cliff track with Bonnie, throwing the ball for her so she could bring it straight back, her whole body hectic with joy.

'What are you going to confess?' I whispered.

She shrugged. 'The usual. Said a bad word, was rude to Mum, wouldn't share with my little brother.'

'Nothing else?'

'I don't have anything else! *She's* the thief!' Behind her hand she pointed to Mrs Price – then she dropped her voice still further. 'I'm going to turn her in. I told her that, too, and she just laughed, but she's scared. It'll all come out. You should have a good look in her house. That's where she's stashed everything, for sure.'

'I have looked,' I said, a hot hate flaring in my chest.

'Well, look again. But either way, I'm telling on her, and she knows it.' She paused. 'I know you accused me. When she asked us about the thief – I know you wrote my name.'

'No I didn't.' My tongue too big for my mouth.

She snorted. 'You can't stop pretending, can you? Anyway, I wrote you.'

'What?'

'I wrote your name. So we're even.' She turned to look at me, smiling the faintest of smiles. 'What are *you* going to confess?'

'How was Denmark?' I hissed.

'What?'

'Weren't you going to visit your penpal in the holidays? Or was she busy with gymnastics again?'

Mrs Price was sidling along the pew to us, I realised. 'I shouldn't have to ask you to be quiet,' she whispered, holding a finger to her lips.

Then Jason Daly came out of the confessional and it was Amy's turn, and Mrs Price and I sat in silence while Jason murmured his penance. Amy can't have been in there for much longer than a minute. When she came out, she left the church straight away. No penance.

Mrs Price sighed. 'She'll never own up, will she? Well, at least she's stopped stealing from us.'

And I admit it: I loved the way she spoke to me like an adult.

And I would have done anything to stop Amy ruining things for her.

That hot hate in my chest, impossible to smother, impossible as a seizure.

In the confessional I could just make out the silhouette of Father Lynch on the other side of the screen, sitting there with his green eyes and his lovely hair, waiting for me to reveal all my sins. I couldn't come up with much for him: said a bad word, was rude to Dad, wouldn't share with my best friend. As I was speaking, I thought I could hear someone just outside the confessional: soft footsteps on the floorboards, perhaps an ear brushing the door. The sense of a held breath. Father was waiting for me to confess more, I knew.

I said, 'Is it true you can't tell anyone what I say in confession?'

'It's true,' he said. 'You can speak freely – unburden yourself of whatever's troubling you. You're quite safe.'

'Even if I tell you about a crime someone's committed?'

'Even then.'

'Even a murder?' I didn't know why I said that. I wondered if he recognised my voice.

'I'm just the mediator,' he said. 'You're not really confessing to me – you're confessing to God. I can't pass on a single word you say – not even to save my own life, or the life of another.'

But the stealing had stopped, hadn't it? So there was no need to talk about it.

'Once there was a king,' he went on, 'who was certain his wife was seeing other men. He went to her priest and demanded to know what she said in confession, but the priest refused to tell him, even when the king had him tortured. In the end the priest was thrown into the river and drowned. That priest was St John of Nepomuk.'

'The king must have known a saint would never tell,' I said.

'Well, he wasn't a saint at that stage,' said Father. 'He became a saint *because* he didn't tell.'

'And was she?' I said.

'Was who what?'

'Was the queen seeing other men?'

'Well, no,' said Father. 'No, she was entirely innocent, but that's not the point of the story.' He paused. 'Is something pricking your conscience?'

I shook my head, remembered he couldn't see me and said, 'I was just curious.'

And then, as I began my Act of Contrition, I swore I could hear footsteps padding away. Mrs Price had gone by the time I emerged.

Outside, the cold air stung my nostrils. Someone was giggling nearby, and I headed around to the side porch of the church to see. That part of the building was hidden from view, butting up against the high fence that marked the boundary with the property next door. Two years earlier we'd dug a hole in the narrow strip of grass there and buried the chicks we'd hatched in our classroom; they'd lived only a few days because we hadn't looked after them properly. I couldn't remember their names. We'd made a grave marker from ice-block sticks, but it was long gone.

I recognised the giggling as I drew nearer: Melissa. She was sitting in the porch with Karl, both of them huddled together on his jacket. He was flicking a lighter, trying to coax a flame, while she held a half-smoked cigarette between her lips.

'What are you doing?' I said, and they jumped.

'Oh my God, Justine!' said Melissa. She'd shoved the cigarette under Karl's jacket, but she brought it out again. 'Do you want a turn?'

'Where did you get it?'

'Here,' she said, casting her hand around at the chippie packets, chewing-gum wrappers, dead leaves and cigarette butts that the wind had blown into a high-tide line.

'But you don't even know whose mouth it's been in,' I said, and they both laughed.

'You don't even know whose *mouth* it's been in,' mimicked Karl.

'Go on,' said Melissa, holding it out to me. 'Dare you.'

'No thanks,' I said, and walked along the narrow strip of grass to the big open field. Tiny bird bones somewhere beneath my feet. Tiny skulls, tiny beaks.

Dom was down by the walnut tree, crouched to the ground, digging his fingers into the dirt. As I watched he lifted something from the sparse grass: a disc of ice. Usually they smashed any frozen puddles they could find, the boys, but this one had survived in the shade of the tree. It was the size of a dinner plate, and he held it above his head the way Father Lynch held up the host in Mass, looking through its wavy lens to the sky. After a few moments he lowered it to look at the school buildings, the adventure playground, the convent hedge, his own hand – and, finally, at me. I could just make out his face through the ice, hazy and strange, like a face in a dream. His fingertips bright red with the cold.

'Who are you?' he said, holding the frozen disc right in front of his eyes now.

'Who do you think?' I said.

'Hard to tell. Are you even human?'

'What else would I be?'

'A fish. A ghost.'

'A ghost fish.'

'Maybe.'

'A walking fish.'

'Hmm.'

We stood face to face, just the ice between us. It was beginning to melt where he held it at the edges. I could see the spatter of his freckles, his wispy brown hair, his pale eyebrows. I placed my index finger against the glassy cold, and he leaned in close and pressed his lips to the ice on the other side, and then, before I could say anything, he pulled away.

The school grounds were empty of children, but in the distance I saw Mrs Price walking back to the classroom. Dom turned the piece of ice towards her, and together we watched through it as her body flexed and stretched into impossible shapes. My finger tingled.

'What do you think of her?' I said.

'She's manipulative.'

'What does that mean?'

He shrugged. 'Dad said it to Mum when I told them about the slips of paper. How we had to write down who we thought was stealing. He said it was a shocking way to treat children, and he wanted to complain to Mr Chisholm.'

'We're not children, we're seniors.'

'And next year we'll be turds.'

'What?'

'That's what they call third formers. My sister told me.'

'Oh.' I kicked at a dead leaf. 'What did your mum say? About complaining to Mr Chisholm?'

'That we had six more Fosters to get through St Michael's and we shouldn't make things difficult.'

'I didn't tell my dad about it,' I said.

'He's seeing her, right?'

'Sort of.' I dug my hands into my tunic pockets to try to warm them. 'I'm her cleaner,' I said. 'I go to her house once a week.'

'Every Thursday,' he said.

'How do you know that?'

'I know about you.'

Mrs Price had disappeared into the classroom by then, and Dom leaned the ice against the trunk of the walnut tree, pulled the cuffs of his home-knitted jersey over his fingers.

'Who did you write?' I asked, and he smiled.

'Nobody. I handed back a blank slip.'

I'd never thought of doing that.

The next few times I was alone in her house, I checked to see if the spare room was unlocked. And closed my eyes in relief when the door handle refused to give.

Chapter 24

I t was only just light outside. Rain was pelting down on the iron roof, and I wanted to stay in bed, but it was a school day – and I needed to go to the toilet. Pushing back the blankets, I made my way to the bathroom, unwilling yet to open my eyes properly. I took in the hallway in blinks, trailing my hand along the wall so I didn't trip.

The steam was the first thing I saw, rushing out of the bathroom when I opened the door, warm against my sleep-creased face. As it thinned, I made out a figure at the vanity, turning to look at me over her shoulder, though this seemed to take many seconds. She wore a satin dressing gown: pale blue, embroidered with butterflies. My mother's dressing gown. And she was turning, she was turning, and I was not yet awake, and the steam billowed around her, and surely she was my mother, standing there at the vanity just the way she used to, and she was turning to tell me she needed more time, I had to give her a little more time. In the mirror, her fogged reflection.

'Hello?' I said, and still she was turning, and as she turned she said my name.

'Justine. Justine, I'm so sorry.'

Mrs Price. Not my mother but Mrs Price, wearing my mother's dressing gown. The floor seemed to tilt beneath me.

'It's all yours, my darling,' she said. She brushed past me into the hall, her wet hair darkening the pale blue satin over her shoulders, dripping down her back. She smelled of my soap. The dressing gown unbelted, gaping apart. A glimpse of breast.

Then she disappeared into my parents' bedroom.

I stood there for a moment, staring into the empty hallway. I could hear the rumble of my father's voice, his only-just-awake voice, and Mrs Price's lighter notes. A muffled laugh.

I pulled down my pyjamas and sat on the toilet – and there, on the inside seam of my pants, a blotch of blood. Blood in the white toilet bowl, too, and blood on the paper when I wiped. It must have come in the night, my body setting things in motion while I slept. I wasn't sure what to do, and my mother wasn't there to tell me. Turning on the shower, I stripped off my pyjamas and climbed inside. I moved the dial to hot, then hotter, tried to disappear in the steam. My shampoo bottle sat on the shower floor, not on the ledge. The soap was still wet. I watched the blood trickle down my leg, dark as Ribena syrup.

They were both waiting for me in the kitchen when I came down for breakfast. My father was making porridge, and Mrs Price, dressed in her own clothes, was smearing butter on a piece of toast.

'There you are,' said Dad, as if he'd lost me, as if I'd only just returned from a long trip.

'I got my period,' I said, and his face froze.

'What?' he said.

'Oh, my clever darling,' said Mrs Price, putting her arm around me. 'Isn't that wonderful news, Neil?'

'Yeah.' His face still frozen. The porridge bubbling away. 'What do we do now?'

'Let me take care of everything.' She squeezed my shoulder. 'You know, when it happened to me, nobody told me what was going on. I thought I was dying.'

'I'm fine,' I said. 'I found some things of Mum's in the bathroom.'

'Of course,' said Mrs Price. 'Of course. Well, if you need any help . . .'

'What are you doing here?' I said.

She and Dad looked startled. Yes, they said, they realised it must be a bit of a surprise. They hadn't planned it; they'd just had a very late night and decided it was safer for her to stay rather than Dad dropping her home when he'd had a couple of glasses of wine. And as a matter of fact, they said, exchanging glances, they had some wonderful news of their own. Mrs Price nodded at Dad: you tell her.

'Well,' he said, taking the porridge off the heat so it didn't burn, 'we're getting married.'

'Married,' I said.

'Yes,' he said.

'It's only been four months.'

'I know it must seem fast, love . . .'

'When?'

'In December, we're thinking, when the weather's nicer. Right after school finishes.'

'That's only two months away.'

'It'll be pretty low-key. Afterwards we'll all have Christmas together, and then we thought you could stay with the Knights while we go on our honeymoon. We thought you might like that.'

'Where will you go?'

'Nowhere very far away. Maybe Lake Taupō. And you'll get to see Uncle Philip – he's coming over to be best man.'

'Will you be bridesmaid?' said Mrs Price. 'Please say yes.'

'Yes,' I said.

And wasn't this what I'd wanted? Hadn't I already imagined the bridesmaid's dress, and myself inside it?

Of course, word spread. Plenty of people had seen the two of them out on dates by then, and Dad even started going to church again on Sunday mornings, the three of us sitting to-gether like a real family.

'It must be nice to see your father so happy,' said Mrs Knight when I stayed at Melissa's one weekend. 'And so soon after your poor mother . . . well. I'm sure it's for the best.'

'Lucky pig,' said Melissa. 'Lucky cow. Are you on a diet?'

'No,' I said.

She pinched my waist. 'You'll have to go on a diet.'

'Why?'

'It's what you do. She'll be on one, for sure. She'll be living on her diet milkshakes and nothing else. Or maybe she wants you to be a bit fat.'

'Why would she want me to be a bit fat?'

Melissa rolled her eyes. 'So she'll look better! Don't you know anything?'

'*Am* I a bit fat?' Weight gain was one of the common side-effects of my new pills.

She stood back, looked me up and down. 'You're borderline. You'll need to be careful.'

'This is Mrs Price we're talking about,' I said. 'She calls me her darling. She wants me to look beautiful.'

'Lucky pig. Lucky cow.' Melissa pinched her own waist. 'Where will you live after the wedding?'

'In our house,' I said, frowning. 'Where we've always lived.'

She flicked her hand as if flicking away our entire property. 'Of course not,' she said. 'But maybe you'll get an attic bedroom with Austrian blinds. Maybe your own bathroom!'

'Dad,' I said, 'where will we live after the wedding?'

'Here,' he said. 'For the next little while, at least.'

'What do you mean, the next little while?'

'Well, it might be nice for us to make a fresh start in a new place. And we might need somewhere bigger.'

'This was big enough for you, me and Mum.'

'Mm,' he said. 'Angela might like to live somewhere different eventually, though.'

I couldn't bear to think of leaving behind the walls and

skirting boards my mother had written on – all her invisible messages – but when I tried to find them the next day, before Dad came home from the shop, they'd disappeared. The only words the black light still illuminated were the ones in the darkest places: shut away inside seldom-opened drawers or behind the clothes in my mother's armoire. Hidden on the backs of the photographs in the hall.

Virgin most pure, Star of the sea,
Pray for the sinner, pray for me.

I took the fabric samples for the bridesmaid's dress to school to see what my friends – my new friends – thought. They clustered around me, holding up the swatches of chiffon to their own bodies, imagining their own dresses of pale pink, dusky pink, maroon.

'I'm getting a flower crown,' I said. 'And a proper manicure, and pantyhose, and high heels.'

'It's not *your* wedding, you know,' said Rachel.

We all ignored her.

'You should get your colours done,' said Natalie. 'My mother had her colours done, and she's never looked back. You'd be an autumn or a spring, wouldn't you?'

'I . . . I don't know,' I said.

'Well, you're not a summer or a winter. You're probably an autumn. Do you suit brown and pumpkin? Does mustard bring out your best?'

'Mustard?'

'Are you porcelain or ivory?' she demanded.

'I don't know,' I said again. 'Is there a difference?'

She tsked. 'It's all about undertone.' She was draping the pieces of chiffon around my neck one by one. 'Not the maroon,' she said. 'See how it has a downward drag on her face?'

The other girls nodded, heads tilted, assessing me. By that stage every one of them was wearing the tiny gold feet, like they were in a secret club.

'Now look at the dusky pink. The light goes on inside her. She comes alive. We want to lift the jawline and hide dark circles.' She grabbed my hand and examined my palm. 'Mm,' she said. 'You must never confuse a golden cast with a sallow cast.'

'Maybe they'll have a baby,' said Paula. 'Do you think?'

It hadn't occurred to me. Was that what Dad had meant by needing a bigger place?

'Maybe she's already having one,' whispered Katrina. 'You have to get married quickly if you're having a baby.'

We all laughed without really knowing why.

Later, in class, I scrutinised Mrs Price's stomach. It seemed as flat as ever.

And very soon after that, late one Sunday morning, I had another seizure. I'd wanted to get some fresh air, according to Dad, and had headed out to the cliff track, but I didn't remember that. I didn't remember leaving the house, and I didn't remember walking along the stony path above the sea, the wind knocking itself into my mouth in great salty gasps. How far did I go? Did anyone see me? And if so, did anyone try to help? I didn't remember if I saw Amy up there, and I didn't remember if we'd talked, if we'd argued. I must have stumbled home when I came to. I could just about recall lurching through the door, and Dad picking me up and laying me on my bed and telling me to rest – and then, in the afternoon, Mr Fong phoned our house.

'No, she's not here,' I could hear Dad saying. 'We haven't seen her for weeks ... Well, I'm sure she can't be far away ... Yes ... Yes, of course I will.'

'Who was that?' I said. My head still groggy, my limbs waterlogged. My tongue too big for my mouth.

'Amy's dad. She's a bit late coming home from walking the dog. You didn't see her up there, did you?'

I gave a slow blink. 'I didn't see her.'

She wasn't at school the next morning either. Mrs Price stood in the corridor outside our classroom, talking quietly with Mr Chisholm as we filed in. After we'd taken our seats, he came in too, and we stood and began to say, 'Good *mor*ning, Mr Chisholm, and God *bless* you . . .'

He motioned for us to sit down. Mrs Price wrung her hands beside him, her face white as milk. The class fell silent.

'Children,' he said, 'I'm afraid I have some dreadful news. There is no easy way to tell you this – Amy has had a terrible accident, a terrible fall, which she did not survive.'

A gasp rippled through the room. Next to me, Melissa's hand flew to her mouth. I looked at the picture of Mary that hung behind Mrs Price, her heart full of roses and fire, and something pricked and burned in me. A great rushing in my ears. I was dizzy, dizzy, teetering on an edge. For a moment I thought: I can take Amy's homework round to her. But no, no – that was impossible. *A terrible accident. She did not survive.*

Mrs Price stifled a sob, and Mr Chisholm placed his hand on her shoulder.

If an adult was crying, it must be true.

Amy must be dead.

'Where did she fall?' asked Karl.

Melissa glared at him, but Mr Chisholm nodded: of course we wanted to know how it happened; she was our friend and we wanted to know. 'I understand she was walking her dog up on the cliffs,' he said. 'She must have strayed too close to the edge.'

I was shaking my head, I realised. 'No,' I was saying. 'She knew – we *both* knew – never to go near the edge.'

Mr Chisholm spread his hands. 'Perhaps a sudden gust . . . a slippery patch of mud . . .'

I thought of the day we'd lost Bonnie's tennis ball, when it was snatched by the wind. The shrieking of the gulls as she shot off after it. Amy and I peering over the edge of the cliffs, tracing the path of the loosened stone that bounced all the way down to the rocks.

'I know this will have come as a shock,' Mr Chisholm went on. 'We must try to help one another through this tragic time. Father Lynch is waiting for us over at the church, where we'll say the rosary for Amy.'

And what else was there to do but pray? We got on our knees, our whole class, our whole school; we bowed our heads and closed our eyes, and we said the words. After a time they stopped making sense, and somewhere in the murmuring of two hundred voices I thought I heard Amy whispering to me as she had whispered that day when we waited to confess: *I miss you. I miss you. I wrote you.* I opened my eyes, looked around. Next to me I could see a tiny barbed twig caught in the sleeve of Dom's jersey. Just in front of me, Sister Bronislava fed her rosary beads through her fingers, her small thin body curling in on itself as she spoke the Our Father, and Mrs Price rested her head on her clasped hands.

After the wedding, would I call her Angela?

What had happened to Bonnie?

How did nuns keep their veils on?

With Amy gone, nobody could tell on Mrs Price, could they?

Horrible. I was a horrible person for wondering about such things when Amy was lying dead . . . well, where? Where was she lying? In the funeral home they'd taken my mother to, with its non-denominational stained glass and its vases of silk gladioli?

And then, another thought: if I'd been walking with her, she wouldn't have fallen.

Or we both would have fallen.

'We should probably let the police know you were up there,' Dad said that afternoon. 'They might want to ask if you remember anything.'

'But I don't,' I said. 'Nothing.'

'Nothing at all?' he said. 'When you came home you told me that's where you had the seizure.'

'I don't remember,' I said. Then I started to cry.

'All right, love,' he said. 'It's all right. The seizures aren't your fault.'

The day we found out was Guy Fawkes Day. I watched the neighbours' fireworks burst open in the night sky while ours sat untouched in their foil bag. The smell of gunpowder when I opened the window.

'Those poor people,' said Dad. 'I can't imagine losing a child.' He stopped himself, glanced at Mrs Price. 'Oh my God, Angela, I'm so sorry.'

'It's fine,' she said. 'Really.'

I'd tried to find out more about the daughter and husband she'd lost, but nobody knew anything beyond the bare facts: that they'd both died in a car accident in Auckland. I'd asked Dad if he'd seen inside the locked room in her house, where she kept their things, and he'd said I mustn't pester her about it; some topics were too painful to discuss, and we had to let people nurse their own sorrows however they chose.

She was painting my nails the dusky pink we'd chosen for the wedding – testing what it looked like so there were no surprises on the big day. Every now and then she brushed a bit on my skin by mistake, then paused to scrape it off with her own nails.

'I'm not very good at this, am I?' she said. 'Don't worry, the makeup artist will do a much better job.'

But I thought my hands looked beautiful, and I couldn't stop admiring them.

'Are you all right to come for the dress fitting, my darling?' said Mrs Price. She knew it was awful timing, only a day after we'd found out about Amy, but the wedding was in just over a month and the dressmaker couldn't rebook. Perhaps it would take my mind off things.

She drove me to the fitting that afternoon and watched as I pulled the dusky pink chiffon over my head. It felt so soft and cool, like wearing water, and I twirled back and forth and did not think about how long it might take to fall from a cliff, and whether you would strike anything on the way down, and whether you would feel anything at the point of impact. Mrs Price's own dress hung shrouded in a white cotton bag, ready for her to take home. I wasn't allowed to see it.

'Terrible thing, that young girl at the beach,' the dressmaker said as she chalked my hem. 'I've been saying for years that they should have a rail.'

'She was one of ours,' said Mrs Price. 'Part of the St Michael's family. I taught her, and she was Justine's close friend.'

'No!' said the dressmaker. 'But how dreadful for you! Oh dear, I shouldn't have mentioned it.'

'We're doing our best to soldier on.'

'Of course you are. Of course.' For a moment or two she continued marking the hem with her slip of blue chalk. Then she said, 'Did she suffer much? Do we know?'

'Let's talk about something else,' Mrs Price said in a pleasant voice.

Afterwards, in the car, she apologised to me on the dressmaker's behalf. I'd never seen her so angry. 'People are idiots,' she said. 'They're nosey, and they're idiots.'

I remembered the curiosity when my mother was sick: acquaintances we hardly even knew asking all kinds of personal questions about her disease, her death. How far had it spread? Would her hair grow back? How long did she have? Was she in a lot of pain? Did she still recognise us at the end?

'I just need to make a quick stop,' Mrs Price said. We were a long way from home, in a neighbourhood I didn't know. She parked outside a row of shops and ducked into the chemist, emerging a short time later clutching a paper bag. I could hear the pills pattering inside their glass bottle.

'For my nerves,' she explained, though I hadn't asked. 'This business with Amy . . . it's bringing everything back to the surface. I know you're struggling too, my darling.'

On Saturday morning I was having breakfast when the phone rang. Dad answered, and I found myself thinking it would be Amy, asking me to come and walk Bonnie with her. I waited for him to launch into his old routine: who are you? What business do you have with my daughter? Then I realised it couldn't be Amy; of course it couldn't be Amy.

'Dominic Foster,' said Dad, handing me the receiver.

I shooed him out of the kitchen, and he raised his eyebrows. 'Boyfriend?' he mouthed.

'Go away!' I mouthed back.

He can't have gone far; he returned to the kitchen as soon as I hung up. 'Well?' he said.

'Can I go round to the Fosters' this afternoon?'

'Aren't they the ones with the two dozen children?'

'Dad.'

He held up his hands: sorry, sorry. 'It's nice you have another friend. Really.'

Mrs Foster gave me a hug when I arrived and said that though it was hard for us to understand, God had his reasons for calling Amy back to him. 'You'll be all right,' she told me. 'He doesn't give us any burdens we can't carry.' She smelled of pastry and had wet hands and a tiny shred of grated cheese in her hair.

Dom was in the sunroom – a narrow space off the bedroom he shared with two of his brothers. It had been an outside porch once, and you could still see the wooden weatherboards, their mint-green paint chalky to the touch. A desk sat in front of the wall of windows and a couch was jammed into one corner, crowded with old kapok cushions – the kind that had to be punched back into shape after you sat on them. Dom had his coin collection spread out on the desk, and an empty album of little transparent pockets.

'Should I group them by country?' he said. 'Or size? Or value? Or age?'

'Value?' I said.

'But face value, or bullion value, or numismatic value?'

'Hmm,' I said. I had no idea what he was talking about. I took a seat next to him and fiddled with a magnifying glass. 'Do you think . . .' I began. 'Do you think we'll be able to see her at the funeral?'

'Maybe,' he said. 'Sometimes they have the lid off, don't they?'

'At my grandmother's funeral they did.'

My first dead body. Dad had kissed her on her powdered forehead, but I'd hung back. She was both herself and not her-self: a copy carved from soap.

'What about when your mum died?'

I shook my head. 'She wanted the lid on. Dad said she was very clear about that.' The cheap veneer masquerading as solid oak. The wreath of yellow carnations because we couldn't get daffodils and jonquils. 'I want spring flowers,' she'd said, and we'd said yes, yes, we'd get spring flowers for her, though it wasn't spring, wasn't anywhere near spring. The promises we make.

Dom held out a coin to me. 'An Israeli agora,' he said. 'My uncle sent it to me from America.'

I studied it under the magnifying glass. I couldn't read the writing, but the picture showed three sheaves of wheat like the design on one of Father Lynch's robes. 'So light,' I said. 'It can't be worth very much.'

'Aluminium. And see the wavy edge? That's so people can find it when they're rummaging in their wallets. And so blind people can tell it apart from other coins and won't pay too much at the shops.'

'What could you buy with it?'

He tilted his head, looked up into the corner of the room. 'Two or three apples, I suppose.'

'What if I don't like apples?'

'Everyone likes apples.'

'But say I don't.'

'A sausage roll, then.'

'Do they have them over there?'

'I'm not sure.'

A white cat leapt onto the desk and started batting at the coins, sending three or four of them to the floor. Calmly Dom picked them up, and the cat pushed them to the floor again.

'Shall I shift her?' I said.

Dom scratched her under the chin. 'She'll get sick of it soon.'

And sure enough, after one more shove the cat lost interest in the coins and settled herself on the open album. Dom didn't seem to mind that either.

At one point a small boy tore into the sunroom, screaming: 'She's going to get me, she's going to get me!' He was wearing a padded helmet, and dived between Dom and me and under the desk. Dom's sister Claire lunged after the boy and dragged him out by his feet. 'You will pay!' she yelled. 'In blood!'

'Help me, help me,' he begged, grabbing at our ankles, but Claire prised his fingers away and carried him upside-down from the room. 'She's a witch!' he yelled. 'Say the magic words!'

I could hear other sisters cackling in the hall: 'Tie him up and drop him in the cauldron. I'll pick the parsley and you chop the onions.'

'Is it always like this?' I said.

'Sorry,' said Dom.

'Is he the one with epilepsy?'

'Peter – yes.'

'Won't they hurt him?'

'He has the helmet.'

'But I mean . . .'

'He loves it. Really.'

I could hear Peter screaming. Or laughing. Or screaming.

'What's this one?' I said, picking up a copper coin that showed three skinny, roaring lions.

'From Guernsey,' he said. 'Twenty pence.' He turned it over. 'Look, that's a milk can.'

I peered at it under the magnifying glass. All the little dents and scratches. 'Why would you put a milk can on a coin?'

'I think they have lots of cows there. And this one's two pence, from the Isle of Man. One of my favourites.' A bird in flight, its wings spread wide above the island.

I sat next to Dom and studied the collection. There was an Irish coin with a harp on one side and a hare on the other; another with a harp and a twisting fish. One cent from the Bahamas, cast in bronze, with a starfish on the front; a thick pound coin with words in Latin running around the milled edge. Three Japanese coins with holes in the middle. An American silver dollar from 1921 that said *PEACE* at the bottom – that one was rare, Dom told me, because when the value of the silver had risen higher than the face value of the coins, people started melting them down.

'This one needs a clean,' I said, picking up a little Canadian five-cent piece blighted with green dots. Under the magnifying glass they looked like the ruffled patches of lichen that grew on our roof. Dad scraped them off with a putty knife every year; Mum and I used to joke that when he clambered around on the corrugated iron, it sounded like a monster bird had landed on the house.

'You never clean coins,' said Dom. 'That makes them almost worthless. Collectors want to see the build-up of the years.'

'But ones that haven't been used at all are the most valuable?'

'Yes,' he said. 'Yes, uncirculated coins are worth a lot.'

'So collectors want to see they've been used but also want them not to be used.'

'Hmm,' he said.

'What about that one?' I pointed to a large dark coin worn almost smooth.

'A Victorian penny. You can't even read the year any more.' He turned it over, handed it to me. 'Look, that's Queen Victoria. Or used to be.' Her silky profile featureless, rubbed flat.

'I think it's my favourite,' I said.

'Keep it.'

'Oh, no, I couldn't. That's not what I meant.'

He shrugged. 'Keep it.'

I tilted it to the light, followed the faint line of the nose, the neck, the hair caught in a bun.

I said, 'She has a locked room at the end of her hall.'

'What?' said Dom. 'Who does?'

'Mrs Price. A spare bedroom. I've never seen inside.'

'What do you think's in there?'

'Amy thought . . . Amy thought she was the one taking our things.'

It sounded crazy even as the words left my mouth, and I felt the blood burning my cheeks.

But Dom was nodding, and then he said what I knew he'd say: 'You have to get in there.'

'I do not.'

'So why did you tell me about it?'

'No reason. I shouldn't have said anything.'

'You did, though.'

'Forget it. Pretend I didn't.'

Later, after what happened with Mrs Price, I started carrying the penny with me in place of the ferry pen. Each morning I slipped it into my pocket, and throughout the day, whenever I recalled the things I wanted to forget, I'd feel for it to check I hadn't lost it. I'd rub the queen's copper face, trying to discern the shape of her, at the same time knowing I was wearing her away. And at night I kept the penny beside my bed, even after we moved to Auckland for a fresh start. When I couldn't sleep, I'd turn on my bedside light and look at the colour of it, and remind myself of the colour of Dom's freckles.

CHAPTER 25

It wasn't until the funeral that I heard about the note. Our class filed in as a group, and I had to sit at the end of a pew, next to Melissa and Karl. They put their arms around each other, and when she wasn't sobbing, Melissa rested her head on Karl's shoulder. All around me my classmates were murmuring in their church voices.

'I heard they could hardly recognise her,' said Rachel.

'Completely mangled, I heard,' said Paula. 'Every bone broken.'

'There must have been so much blood.'

'Gallons of it, Leanne said.'

'She should know.'

'Why?'

'Her dad's a butcher. She'd know about these things.'

'Poor Amy,' said Rachel.

'We were right there where it happened, on our rocky shore trip.'

'I know. I know.'

'I miss her.'

'I miss her too.'

'They'll have to give us our stuff back, right? The Fongs?'

'I'd say so. It'd be very rude to keep it.'

'Mm. Very rude.'

'Mm.'

'What did the note say, exactly?'

'Mum didn't know.'

I turned around, the blood thudding in my throat. 'What note?'

They looked startled, caught out.

'What *note*?' I said again.

'A jogger found Amy's dog the next day,' whispered Rachel. 'It had a note tied to its collar.'

'What do you mean, a note?'

'A note from Amy. You know.'

'So awful,' said Paula.

'It was an accident,' I said. 'Mr Chisholm told us. A gust of wind. A patch of mud.' But even as I spoke, I knew it didn't make sense. Amy and I never walked near the edge – our parents had told us not to so many times. The wind or the mud couldn't have carried her that far. I imagined her tying the note to Bonnie's collar. Fondling her ears, telling her to stay. Leaving the track and heading for the point where the ground dropped away – and then taking one more step. A loose stone following her fall, bouncing off the rocks.

And the music was starting, and they were bringing in the coffin – bringing in Amy, just as they'd brought in my mother. Carrying her down the same aisle, placing her in the same spot in front of the altar while Father Lynch waited in his same black vestments. Someone was putting the words to the hymn on the overhead projector and adjusting the focus until they were sharp: 'Only a Shadow'. I couldn't sing; I just moved my mouth. I had thought I'd be able to see Amy one last time – I'd pictured myself laying a hand on her blunt black fringe, perhaps tucking a flower against her cheek – but the coffin was closed. *They could hardly recognise her. Every bone broken.*

As Father Lynch began the Mass I studied the wood of the pew in front and saw all kinds of patterns in the grain. Clouds and puddles, pieces of map, ripples in water, fingerprints, eyes. A woman I didn't know read a poem about death being nothing at all. 'I have only slipped away to the next room,' she said.

It sounded like a haunting. Then Father Lynch read from the Bible: were we unaware that we who were baptised into Christ Jesus were baptised into his death? We were indeed buried with him through baptism into death, so that, just as Christ was raised from the dead by the glory of the Father, we too might live in newness of life. Although Amy was no longer with us in physical form, he said, she would live on in the memories of her we would carry in our hearts. We must take comfort in the fact of God's infinite mercy. He did not turn away the sinner, no matter how grave the sin. The church, he said, had revised its position on this matter in recent times.

Though he was choosing his words carefully, I realised he meant suicide: the sin of suicide.

And what memories of Amy would I carry in my heart? Sharing our lunches in the cool curve of the stormwater pipes? Staying the night at her house, lacing my legs around hers in the bath? Or completely failing to defend her, to save her?

When I went up to Communion I slid my hand along the flank of the coffin. The gleaming wood felt cool, cold. I tried to catch Mrs Fong's eye on the way back to my seat, but she was staring straight ahead, glassy and unblinking. The Communion wafer sat on my tongue like paper, and I couldn't chew it, could hardly swallow it. I looked up at the statue of St Michael: the serpent's head pressed beneath the archangel's holy sandal, its mouth open to receive his golden spear. In the crying room at the back of the church, mothers jostled their babies on their laps, tried to distract them from screaming. The glass was supposed to be soundproof, but I thought I could make out their high cries.

That evening, at our house, I asked Mrs Price about the note.

'I don't think we need—' my father began, but she touched the back of his hand and said, 'Neil, you know these things have a habit of coming out.'

He sighed, nodded.

She said, 'Amy did leave a note, my darling, attached to her dog's collar.'

I started to cry. 'What did it say?'

'I don't know, sweetheart. That's between Amy and her parents. Now then, now now. We mustn't blame ourselves. We knew she was troubled – the stealing was evidence of that – but how could we have foreseen what she would do?'

I asked everyone in my class what they thought, waiting for them to say that it was nobody's fault, to produce some logical reason I hadn't considered – but they didn't. Instead, there were sidelong glances in my direction. There were whisperings. Amy's friends should have looked after her better; they should have known how unhappy she was. A true friend would have known.

'You care too much about what other people think,' said Dom. 'Just ignore them.'

'Of course I care!' I said. 'Don't you?'

'Not really. Anyway, it's their fault as well.'

'As well?'

'All of us.' He took my hand, and I let him. 'Have you seen inside the locked room yet?' he said.

I shook my head. 'I tried when she was out, but no luck so far.'

'What do you mean, you tried?'

'Well, I checked to see if she'd left it unlocked.'

'That's it?'

'Dom, Amy took the things.'

'Did she?'

He was starting to annoy me. 'What else am I supposed to do? It's *locked*.'

But I knew: I knew.

'Find the key, of course.'

I never caught sight of my mother after she died, the way some people say they catch sight of the dead – perhaps because she was sick for such a long time, there was no question in my mind that she really was gone. Some days, though, I'd glimpse Amy across the adventure playground, or in the throng of children passing through the gate at home time, or crouching behind the tank at the back of the classroom, peering through the water at Susan's miraculous new foot. Oh, there's Amy, I'd think – I must try to talk to her – and then my brain would realise that my eyes were playing tricks on me.

Mrs Price took down our posters about the rocky shore and gave them to Mr Armstrong to burn. Nobody mentioned the stealing, the accusations – certainly, nobody mentioned the slips of paper Mrs Price had handed out. Her public naming of Amy as the thief. Somehow we all knew we should keep quiet.

In class we were studying Māori Myths and Legends. Mrs Price sat in the story chair and read to us about Māui and his brothers – how, long ago, their days were very short because the sun used to rush across the sky. Tired of living most of their lives in darkness, they travelled to the red-hot pit where the sun slept and caught him in a snare. Māui struck him with his sacred jawbone, and after that, beaten and tired, the great ball of fire moved more slowly, and the days were longer. We painted pictures of the sun thrashing against the flax ropes, the sun bloody and defeated, crawling across the sky. Outside, too, the days were lengthening, growing warmer.

Less than a month until the wedding.

When Mrs Price asked me to stay behind one day not long after the funeral, I thought she was going to give me one of my old jobs – but Amy's parents had requested the things from her desk, she said: would I deliver them round to their house? Since I knew her family best.

'David could take them home, couldn't he?' I said.

She shook her head. The Fongs had moved Amy's little brother to a new school.

Together we cleared out her exercise books and her Bible, her scratch 'n' sniff stickers that smelled like fake berries, her Blu-Tack snail, her coloured pencils worn down to the wood. Her stack of shimmery fifty-cent pieces that nobody had ever stolen. Her little pool of mercury, caught in a plastic needle case, forever breaking apart and restoring itself. Two library books, now overdue – boarding-school stories about eccentric French teachers and midnight feasts and firm friends.

'Please do give the Fongs my best,' said Mrs Price.

Nobody seemed to be at home when I parked my bike and walked up the driveway. The lawns – normally clipped as close as a billiard table – needed attention, and the letterbox was choking on junk mail. Cobwebs around the front door, mud on the welcome mat. I knocked, waited, my schoolbag heavy on my shoulders. No movement inside the house. Then, the softest of footfalls – brocade slippers on carpet.

'Yes?' said Mrs Fong when she opened the door.

'I've brought Amy's things,' I said.

'Oh yes?' Her voice slow, drugged.

'Her books and things, from school. You wanted them.' I pulled them out of my bag. Tried to unsquash the Blu-Tack snail.

'We wanted them, yes. Her things.' But she didn't take them from me.

'Who's that?' called Mr Fong, and then he was at the front door too, holding Bonnie by the collar.

'It's Justine,' said Mrs Fong. 'She's brought Amy's things from school.'

I'm embarrassed to admit it now, but I'd thought they might invite me in. Ask me to stay for a meal. I could help with the dishes afterwards – dry the blue-dragon china with the snowflakes and stars that shone when you held them to the light.

'Put them there,' said Mr Fong, gesturing to the hall table just inside the door. Neither of them moved out of the way; I had to lean inside, stretching my arms across the threshold, so that the mercury scattered into tiny silver beads. Bonnie strained towards me, whining, but Mr Fong held her back. The house didn't smell of Mrs Fong's cooking. It smelled of other people's casseroles, thawed, reheated. It smelled of withered flowers that needed throwing out. It smelled of dust. In the living room I could see the shelf with the incense and the photos and the Chinese statues, the Goddess of Mercy watching the front door. On the wall, the life-size picture of the Pope. The brown sprig of cypress saved from Palm Sunday had slipped almost completely behind the frame; only the tip showed now, like an earwig.

I cleared my throat. 'I was just wondering,' I said, 'about the note. Amy's note.'

'What were you wondering?' said Mr Fong.

'Well,' I cleared my throat again, 'I was wondering what she said. If she gave a reason.'

'You're very concerned about Amy all of a sudden.'

I felt myself blushing and I began to stammer. 'I . . . I was . . . she was always . . .'

They both just stood there, watching me flounder.

'Thank you for bringing her things,' Mr Fong said at last. He began to close the door.

'Oh, Mrs Price sends her best,' I said, and his eyes flashed.

'You tell that woman she is not welcome in our shop. Do you hear?'

'Mrs Price?' I said. What had Amy told them?

'Yes. Her.'

I nodded. 'I'm sorry.'

'You should be. You should be sorry.'

I wanted to ask him what I should be sorry for, and how

I could fix things, but he was jabbing his finger at me and I thought I should leave.

'I'm sorry,' I said again – but he had already shut the door.

After that I biked around to Mrs Price's house to do my cleaning. She was out, so I let myself in with my key and made a start on the dishes in the kitchen. There were knives smeared with butter and honey, prickly with crumbs; coffee mugs edged with lipstick. I scraped the debris from a stack of dinner plates into the bin: bacon rind and gristle and sucked bones, bruised coleslaw, a desiccated wedge of tomato, the smashed shell of a boiled egg. On the windowsill, an abandoned cup of cocoa, its silky skin growing soft white mould. In the fridge I found the plastic shaker, still half-filled with a strawberry diet milkshake. I took a sip, and it tasted good – sweet and juicy and thick, like strawberry bubblegum.

On the kitchen table, a cruise brochure.

The photo on the front showed the ship cutting its way through endless blue and, in the blue sky above, a white sea-bird, its wings filled with sunlight. With my dishwater-wet pinky finger I lifted the brochure open. Inside, people lay on deserted beaches, smiled at platters of fruit in their deluxe rooms. They sat in sumptuous restaurants where crystalware glinted like ice and chefs displayed extravagant buffets; they looked into each other's eyes as waiters set fire to food. They danced on the deck, the sun huge and red on the horizon; they pulled on snorkel masks; they gambled. Entertainers entertained them: cancan girls, a man working a puppet dressed like himself.

I closed it again, left it as I found it.

No sign of Mrs Price.

I returned the shaker to the fridge; there was an aftertaste in my mouth. Something bitter. Something artificial.

At the end of the hall, the door to the spare bedroom still would not give. Where would someone keep a key? Not on the hook by the back door, not in the drawer under the phone. Not on top of the fridge. Not in the art glass bowl that looked like it was melting. Not in any of the desk drawers crammed with staples and clips and hole punches and scissors. I went outside, to the back of the house, and tried to peer in the window again – but the curtains had been shut tight.

Mrs Price was letting herself in the front door when I came back inside.

'Afternoon tea?' she said, dumping her handbag and keys on the hall table.

She put the kettle on and looked at the dishes soaking in the steaming sink. 'You're a wonder, Justine, honestly. I'd be overrun with rats without you.'

'It's not that bad,' I said.

'Well, I hope your father knows what he's in for.' She laughed, and her tiny gold crucifix jostled at the base of her neck. 'Would you like to try this?' She reached up to the top shelf of the pantry and produced the jar of jasmine-flower tea.

I swallowed. 'The Fongs sell that in their shop,' I said.

'Do they,' she said, looking me right in the eye.

'Is that where you got it?'

'I can't remember. Why?'

'I was just wondering.'

'I don't know – I've had it for ages. Keeps forever. How were they?' She hadn't taken her eyes from me.

I swallowed again. 'They said you can't come back. To the shop. They said I should tell you.'

Calmly she spooned the dried jasmine buds into the teapot. 'That's understandable – they're grieving, and I must remind them of what they've lost. I imagine you do too.'

I thought of Mr Fong, jabbing his finger at me. *You should be sorry.*

'Oh no,' she said, snatching up the cruise brochure and pressing it to her chest. 'Did you see this?'

'I couldn't really help it.'

'My silly fault! It was meant to be a surprise.'

'For Dad?'

'For *you*.'

'I don't understand.'

She smiled, lowered her voice, though we were quite alone. 'We're going on a cruise for our honeymoon.'

'Dad said you wouldn't be going very far away. Lake Taupō, he said.'

'That's part of the surprise! You might as well know, my darling, since it was my idea – we want you to come with us. But let's keep it our secret, yes?'

'Okay.'

'Aren't you excited?'

'I'm . . . it's a big surprise.'

'We'll have so much fun, the three of us.'

And maybe she'd meant me to see the brochure.

And maybe not.

We drank our jasmine-flower tea, and I picked at the label on the jar that was pasted over the original label: *Jasmine tea is the tea and jasmine flowers to fight, scenting system. Its aroma fresh spirit lasting, colour yellow and bright, soft and soft leaves at the end of tender.* I didn't like the taste – musty, dusty – but it seemed childish to say so.

'Right, I'm off to get some exercise,' she said. 'I have a wedding dress I need to fit into.'

She shut herself in her bedroom, and in a moment I heard the creak and scrape of the Speedslimmer. I went to the hall table and lifted her keys, careful not to let them jangle, then crept to the spare room. Softly I tried each one in the lock. None fitted.

At school Mrs Price had stopped asking me to help her in the classroom – it wouldn't be fair to everyone else, she said. How desperate they were for her attention, shooting their hands into the air whenever she asked a question, whether they knew the right answer or not. And even then – even *then* – I couldn't help myself. I had to tell them about the cruise.

'There's a waiter who carries drinks on his head,' I said. 'There's a casino where you can win millions of dollars. I'm getting a bikini that ties in bows at the sides.'

'But where will you sleep?' said Melissa.

'On the ship,' I said.

'But in the same room as them?'

'Better take your ear plugs as well as your bikini,' said Karl, and they both gave a sly laugh.

At lunchtimes I started going to the library. I didn't care what I read, and after a few visits Sister Bronislava stopped asking me what I was looking for. If Dom was working there, he brought me books he thought I might like: *I Can Learn About Weather*; *Come to France*; *Animals That Burrow*. We listened to the bird-song book, too, imagining ourselves deep in the bush where fantails and riflemen called from the dark branches above us. Other days I just pulled the *Britannica Junior* from the shelf and started reading: Peel, Dr Robert; Pegasus; Peking, China. Flint glass; Flintlock; Flip-flop. The more I read, the more I realised how little I knew. And there were only two more weeks of primary school, and in class a feeling of anticipation filled the air, something pressing at our eardrums, fizzing against our skin. The holidays were coming, high school was coming, and we wouldn't learn anything more at St Michael's. Instead, we made Christmas decorations: paper chains from *Woman's Weeklies*, strips of recipes spliced to autumn fashion spreads and advice to the lovelorn, all linked in rustling loops. We broke the spines of *Reader's Digests* and folded them into many-faceted stars; we built nativity scenes inside shoeboxes, lined the mangers with torn tissues for our Plasticine babies. The nuns waxed the corridor, and we tied rags to our feet and skidded from one end to the other, sailing past every classroom that had once been ours, all the way down to the primers. The statue of Jesus watching us, obscene fingers raised.

The wedding was only two weeks away as well, of course, and almost every day after school Mrs Price had to take care of something: sampling cake, paying the last deposit to the travel agent, finalising the flowers. She rushed from errand to errand; there was not enough time, she said.

I felt it too. Soon she and my father would be married, and she would sleep in my mother's bed, hang her clothes in my mother's armoire. I wanted it and I didn't want it and I had no idea how to stop it. How to hold back the days, snare the sun.

Then the stealing started again.

CHAPTER 26

No helpers today, thank you, people,' Mrs Price said when the school bell rang. She was off on one of her wedding errands – picking up the shoes she'd had customised to match her dress.

I parked my bike around the back of her house and let myself in. It wasn't my usual cleaning day, but I couldn't wait until then: I had to find the key to the locked room. I had to know what was inside. My classmates were openly accusing me of taking their coloured pencils and their Care Bears, their walkie talkies, their knucklebones. Rachel had lost the strawberry lip gloss she'd won at Melissa's party; she narrowed her eyes at me and said she'd seen how jealous I was. Yes, said everyone, yes, I was jealous. I'd been best friends with Amy, they said, and obviously we'd worked as a team to take all their things – but at least Amy had shown she felt guilty.

Dom snorted when they came out with that. 'Amy wasn't guilty,' he said, 'she was bullied.'

'He's in on it too!' they cried, pointing their fingers, clamouring like gulls.

I lifted Mrs Price's cutlery tray out of the cutlery drawer but found only crumbs underneath. I pulled every book from the book shelves, ran my hands along the tops of the swagged pelmets. I unfolded the towels and sheets in the linen cupboard, then returned them to their same wonky stacks. I even looked in the garden for fake rocks that were hollow inside – I'd seen them advertised in junk-mail catalogues, alongside decorative hourglasses and tiny crystal animals. I felt like a thief.

In the medicine cabinet in the bathroom I found the bottle of pills she'd collected from the chemist on the other side of town when we went for my dress fitting. Someone else's name on the label. I slipped the bottle into my pocket. A step over the edge. A stone bouncing off rocks.

Four o'clock. Depending on traffic, I had perhaps another fifteen minutes. There were simply too many hiding places, too many secret nooks I hadn't even considered. Returning to the living room, I lay on my back in the conversation pit and checked the bottom of the coffee table – nothing but unvarnished wood. As I lay there, though, I remembered finding my mother's writing underneath our own coffee table. The words of the hymn came to me: *Hail, Queen of Heav'n, the ocean Star . . .* The whole song scattered across the backs of our family photos for some urgent and delirious reason.

There were no photos in Mrs Price's hall, nothing but a mirror to cast light into the dark end of the L-shaped passage. It hung next to the bathroom – and opposite the spare bedroom. Again I caught my mother in my reflection; her upper lip, her eyes. *Save us from peril and from woe.* I lifted the mirror from its hook, turned it around – and there, swinging from a nail in the top corner, was a key. And then I heard a key sliding into a lock, and for a split second I thought my imagination had conjured the sound, plucked it straight from the knot of my desire to find that sharp-toothed little thing. But then I heard the key *turning* in the lock, the front-door lock, and I flung the mirror back on its hook and darted into the laundry just as Mrs Price stepped inside.

She went to the kitchen first – unloading shopping, as far as I could tell by the clink of jars and tins, the soft suck of the fridge. I held my breath as she passed by the laundry, closed my eyes as she paused in the hall. I heard the faint scuffing of wood against wallpaper – was she nudging the crooked mirror straight? – and then she went to her bedroom. A zip opened with a long, lazy buzz: the cover protecting her wedding dress, I supposed. She would be holding the gown up to herself, perhaps even slipping it on, seeing how it looked with her wedding shoes. Millimetre by millimetre I turned the handle of the laundry door and let myself outside. Retrieved my bike from the back of the house and silently wheeled it out to the street, then jumped on and pedalled up the hill for all I was worth.

Dad was making apricot chicken that night – Mrs Price had taught him how. I sat at the kitchen table and peeled cloves of garlic for him while he chopped the onions and tried not to cry.

'Only a week and a half to go,' I said.

'Can you believe it?' He was grinning from ear to ear.

'Not really. It's happening so fast.'

He put down his knife. 'You love her though, don't you? You love her as much as I do. I could tell that from the very start, back when you brought her into the shop.'

'I did love her straight away,' I said. 'I wanted to *be* her.'

'I think there was something sneaky going on, in fact,' he said, and I looked up at him. 'I think you introduced us on purpose. My little Cupid. I've never thanked you for that.' He started chopping again.

'Some of the things she's done, though,' I said, pulling the papery skin away from the garlic. 'I just wonder.' I could feel the bottle of morphine in my trouser pocket, digging into the crease of my thigh.

'Things? What things?'

'Like with the stealing. She got us all to write down who we thought it was, and then she named Amy. Right there in class. It was manipulative.'

He frowned. 'I know she was worried sick about the thefts. She blamed herself, in a way – she couldn't bear the fact that something so unpleasant was happening in her classroom. Maybe her method of dealing with it was a bit unusual . . .'

'She said that she wanted to give Amy a chance to put things right. That Amy needed to ask for forgiveness. She rubbed her back.'

'There you are then, you see. She cared about Amy. She really did. I can't tell you how devastated she is about the accident.'

'Suicide.'

'All right, suicide. But where's all this going, love?'

'Amy told me she saw her steal a jar of tea from their shop.'

'Oh, darling. I know it must be hard to hear, but Amy was a troubled girl. Of course she'd say something like that if she'd been exposed as the thief.'

'This was before Mrs Price named her.'

He paused. 'Well, she must have realised it was coming.'

'And she takes pills,' I said. 'Lots of pills.' I rested my hand on the bottle in my pocket. I could pull it out right then and there, show him that the prescription was under someone else's name. But how would that look? If he knew I'd been snooping in her medicine cabinet?

'I know all about that,' he said. 'She hurt her back playing tennis, years ago. It's never come right.'

'She told me it was for her nerves.'

'It's all related – the pain got a lot worse when she lost her husband and daughter. Everyone has their wounds, love. But listen, I know Amy's death—'

'The stealing's started again,' I said. 'It can't be Amy, can it?'

He sighed, looked at me. 'We wondered if this might happen,' he said at last. 'Dr Kothari mentioned we might face some . . . some resistance to the wedding. I know it's a big change for you.'

'What's Dr Kothari got to do with it?'

'Well, we had a chat last time I saw him. He likes to take into account what's going on in his patients' lives.'

I bit my lip. 'We're keeping Mum's clothes,' I said quietly. 'I know we have to shift them out of the armoire, but we're keeping them.' Mrs Price's things hanging there. The fragmentary words inside fading every time she opened the door.

'Of course!' said Dad. 'Of course, love. I don't know what came over me that day.' He turned back to the onions, but his hand slipped and he sliced into his finger. 'Goddamn it!' He threw aside the knife.

Blood was dripping all over the chopping board, trickling down through the mound of onions.

'Here,' I said, taking his finger and holding it under the tap. 'Keep still.'

I made him press a tissue to the cut while I fetched the plasters. It bled right through the first one, so I replaced it with a bigger strip, but it bled through that too.

'Do you think we should go to the hospital?' I said. 'Do you think it needs stitches?'

He shook his head. 'It'll stop in a minute. No need to panic.'

'You look pale.'

'I'm fine.'

I ended up covering it with a dressing from the first-aid kit and then a bandage. We rinsed the onions, and he insisted on cooking the meal. By the time Mrs Price arrived for dinner, pinpricks of blood were showing through again.

'We had a little accident,' he said, waving it at her.

'Oh my goodness! Are you all right?'

'It's nothing serious. Justine looked after me.'

'Good girl,' she said. 'Something smells delicious.'

'Apricot chicken.'

'Aren't you clever.'

Dad poured her some wine, and she sat down on the blue-and-white couch.

'*Santé*,' she said, holding up her glass – and that was when I saw it. Glinting on her wrist, the old gold mellow as butter: the

Georgian DEAREST bracelet Dad had shown me. The one I thought he'd put aside for my Christmas present.

She must have noticed me staring, because she said, 'Isn't it the loveliest thing? Your father gave it to me. An engagement present.'

'It's beautiful,' I said.

'And there's a secret,' she said. 'Shall I tell you?'

'All right.'

'Look at the stones. Diamond, emerald, amethyst, ruby, emerald, sapphire, topaz.'

'I don't get it,' I said.

'Well, what do they spell?'

'Spell?'

'If you take the first letter of each stone, they make a word.' The faintest note of irritation in her voice.

'Do they?'

She gave a tight little laugh. 'Goodness me, who on earth is your teacher?'

'Don't be naughty, Justine,' said Dad.

'I'm not being anything.'

'Dearest,' said Mrs Price, turning the bracelet around her wrist. All the tiny hands with their tiny engagement rings. 'It spells dearest. A message from the lover to the beloved.'

'Hm,' I said, and checked the TV listings.

The apricot chicken was delicious – I have to give Dad that.

'Look at it,' said Mrs Price. 'So tender. Practically falling off the bone.' She wiped a drop of sauce from the corner of her mouth. 'Better than mine. I feel outshone by my own pupil.'

'It's not a competition,' said Dad, laughing.

'Of course it's a competition,' she said, but allowed him to kiss her cheek.

'Are you going to tell her about the secret ingredient?' I said. She smiled. 'What's that?'

'Love,' he said.
'Blood,' I said.

I didn't sleep well that night – noises coming from Dad's bedroom woke me. Muffled voices, laughter, animal grunts and cries. The rhythmic knocking of the antique bedstead against the wall, then the scrape of it across the floor as someone pushed it clear. I swaddled my head under the blankets. All I could think about was the key behind the mirror. The things I knew I would find in the locked room.

Mrs Price looked peaky when I saw her at school. Her cheeks were sallow under her makeup, and she kept licking her lips. She wandered around the activity tables, pretending to show interest in our craft projects – we were making potato-print wrapping paper stamped with blotchy angels, and cellophane Christmas cards meant to look like stained glass. 'What lovely colours,' she said, and, 'Careful with the knives,' but she was barely looking. She didn't even notice when Jason Daly stamped pink angels on the back of Gregory's shirt, nor when Jason Moretti dared Brendon to take a bite of raw potato and then forced it between his teeth because he said no. With just a week left of primary school, we were growing restless, reckless – and still things were going missing, something new every day. The Wise Men pipe-cleaner from Jacqui's nativity, the little folding comb Katrina kept in a zipped purse. The sanitary towels Paula's mother had given her just in case, though I heard only whispers of that; when I tried to sit with the girls on the stormwater pipes one hot lunchtime, Paula told me she was saving the space for another friend and there wasn't room for me.

We walked over to the hall for folk dancing with Sister Marguerite that afternoon. Mrs Price walked with us, making sure we crossed the road safely and telling us she expected perfect behaviour for Sister, who would waste no time in letting her know if anyone played up. Lagging to the back of the group, I grabbed Dom's wrist and waited till we were out of earshot. 'I found the key,' I whispered.

His eyes grew wide. 'What's in there?'

'No time to look. I'll have to wait till she goes out again.'

'Come on, you two,' called Mrs Price. 'Enough secrets.'

As we lined up in rows in the hall and waited for the music to start, she disappeared back in the direction of the school. I saw her through the window, stopping in the carpark to check inside her car for something. She opened the doors and leaned in, first on the driver's side and then on the passenger side, lifting up mats, looking under the seats. Frantic. Then 'The Dashing White Sergeant' started playing, and Sister Marguerite was calling out the steps while we tried not to make a mess of things, forming ourselves into lines and circles, stepping first to the left, then to the right. I joined hands with Dom and turned and turned, then joined hands with Karl. In and out of one another we wove.

I'd hoped Mrs Price would have errands to run after school, but when I arrived at her house to do my cleaning, the Corvette was parked in the driveway. Inside, she was searching the sunken living room, looking under cushions and behind curtains, opening dresser drawers to rifle through their jumbled contents.

'Have you seen them?' she demanded.

'Have I seen what?'

'My pills! I can't find my pills!'

'Are they in the medicine cabinet? Shall I check?'

'Of course they're not in the medicine cabinet! That was the first place I looked!'

'Okay,' I said. 'Sorry.'

She glanced at me then, sweat glinting on her upper lip, and she sighed. 'No, *I'm* sorry. It's just with the wedding so close, and everything I still have to organise – I'm a bit overwrought.'

I smiled, picked up the washing basket of clean clothes. 'I'll get started on the ironing.'

In the laundry I shook out her blouses and skirts, her Brooke Shields jeans. I poured water into the iron and let it heat up, then tested it with my finger: one swift little touch, something I'd seen my mother do. I could hear Mrs Price dialling a number on the phone in the hall and waiting for someone to answer. Tapping something – a pen? – against the Formica telephone table. After a moment she hung up and dialled again. *Taptaptaptaptap.* As the iron puffed and hissed I guided its tip around each button, smoothing down plackets and re-creasing pleats, the pressed fabric almost too hot to hold. In the tub, a bucket of lacy underwear sat soaking, the flimsy gussets poking up through the suds.

'Hello, Mr Buchanan?' she said at last. 'Angela Price here. I'm afraid I'm in a spot of bother with a prescription. No, please don't hang up!'

She must have carried the phone into the living room, pulling the cord around the door jamb; I could no longer make out her words, just her wheedling minor-key cadences – then a snarl. She dialled three or four more numbers, each time failing to get the answer she wanted: her voice turned harsh, and she slammed the receiver down. Something smashed and chimed like a cash register. Then she started crying.

I stood the iron safely on its end and went to the living room. She was holding her head in her hands, slumped on the edge of the conversation pit. The phone lay sprawled on its side, the receiver off its cradle.

'Mrs Price? Um, Angela? Are you okay?'

Mascara smeared her cheeks, the kind of streaky black left behind when you squash a mosquito and wipe it away. Her feet were bare, and she kicked a heel into the carpeted wall of the pit over and over like a child.

'Nobody will help me,' she sobbed. 'Nobody understands. All these people I thought were my friends – you can't trust anyone these days. They're all just in it for what they can get. How much they can squeeze out of you. They don't *care*.'

She was spitting her words. She looked up at me.

'If you make a promise to someone, Justine, what does that mean to you?'

'Oh,' I said. 'Well, you keep your word. You can't go back on a promise.'

'*Correct*,' she said, a hint of triumph in her voice, as if I'd answered a question right in class, as if I'd understood something important she'd taught me. 'Especially when money's changed hands,' she added. 'A *lot* of money. They've basically *stolen* from me, you know. Those chemists.' She dragged an angry hand across her eyes. 'I bet they'd change their tune if I showed up in person and made a bit of noise.'

I picked up the telephone, returned it to the table in the hall.

'Unless you might be able to help out again . . . ?' she said.

'Me?'

'Perhaps you might still have some old pills lying around? Ones you don't need any more.'

'No,' I said. 'They're all gone, sorry.'

'Right.' She nodded. 'Right. The thing is, I'm feeling so awful. I just need a bit of help to get through the next few days. Maybe there are some tucked away that you've forgotten about.'

'Sorry,' I said again.

She let out a long, shuddering sigh and began to pick at the side of a fingernail, opening an old cut.

'You *should* show up in person,' I said. 'Go and see Mr Buchanan.'

'And say what?'

'Well, that he needs to keep his promise.'

She let out a single laugh. 'Like he has any morals.'

'Make a bit of noise, then. He can't turn you away if he sees how upset you are.'

'Money-grubbing bastard,' she said. 'He's an out-and-out thief.'

'So take it up with him. Go and see him.'

She regarded me for a moment. 'You're right,' she said. 'The man owes me, after all. You're right.'

She got to her feet and smoothed down her skirt, buckled on her strappy gold sandals, then went and fixed her makeup. When she emerged from the bathroom, she was almost the old Mrs Price again, glossy and poised. Almost.

I kept ironing as she backed the Corvette down the driveway and disappeared in the direction of the shops. I couldn't shake the feeling that she'd return for some reason – she'd have forgotten her wallet or sunglasses, or just wanted to check up on me. After a few minutes I switched off the iron, left a half-finished blouse trailing its creased sleeve, and went to the hall. In the mirror opposite the spare bedroom my reflection looked back at me. My mother's eyes. *What are you waiting for?* Slipping my hand behind the frame, I felt for the hidden key and pulled it free of its nail. It was cold and hard, the brass teeth sharp against my fingertips. I slipped it into the lock.

The room smelled musty, and with the curtains drawn I couldn't make out much. I stumbled over something on the floor – a cardboard carton that rattled when my toes collided with it. Then I switched on the light.

Objects covered every surface, some in boxes, some arranged in precarious stacks. I couldn't see the carpet for them, nor the bedspread on the single bed, nor the top of the chest of drawers. The first thing I recognised was Rachel's Ronald McDonald doll grinning with its red clown mouth among the mess; it sat wedged into a cluster of Cabbage Patch dolls and teddy bears and Barbies. Then I saw Vanessa's bell-shaped umbrella hanging open like a bowl on the wardrobe door and filled with bits of PE gear. I saw long woollen scarves looped around the bedposts, including the stripy one Leanne had knitted. Inside a box of pebbles and pumice and sea glass and shells, what looked like Jason Moretti's pāua shell. The curtains were familiar too – thickly woven cream fabric, with threads of orange and brown

– and I realised they were the ones missing from the back room of the church. On the crowded shelves above the bed, lined up in a legion of figurines, Paula's Sleepwalker Smurf held out his arms, about to step over the edge. There they all were, our missing things, crammed into Mrs Price's spare room like exhibits in some strange museum. A koala keyring tangled in a pile of keyrings; a harmonica on top of a carton of harmonicas and recorders and whistles; a tower of Rubik's Cubes; a pyramid of Matchbox cars. Erasers and pencils and pens and felts; five bottles of Twink, their brushes dried to white stubs. A dozen little boxes of raisins all in a row like books. Cairns of metal and plastic knucklebones glinting under the electric light; ice-cream containers brimming with marbles. Families of Care Bears with rainbows and four-leafed clovers and shooting stars stitched across their plush bellies. Clutches of Tamagotchis that had long since given up on anyone coming to feed them. And hanging from the glitter ceiling on threads of dental floss, a swarm of cotton-wool bees and butterflies made by the dental nurse, their eyes black ink dots.

It was true, then. Mrs Price was the thief. I thought: I have lost her. I have lost her just the same as I have lost my mother and lost Amy – and yes, it felt like a death. A step into nothing but air; a stone tumbling down a cliffside. I wanted things to be the way they were. I wanted to be her favourite, the person she chose ahead of anyone else, the person she reserved her special smile for. I wanted to be her pet. But hadn't I known for a long time that something was wrong? Hadn't I suspected, ever since I found the pen in her handbag? Ever since she made Karl pick up the scalpel and sever Susan's foot? Amy had tried to tell me: she had seen her steal the jasmine tea. She had *seen* her. And I had even found it in the pantry. Yes, I had known.

I reached up and ran my fingers through the bees and butterflies, set their gauze wings fluttering. And as I watched, the ceiling became a sun-shot sky, and I had been there before, in that jammed room, and all the things were my things, things I had owned and lost, and there I stood in the midst of my own memories of harmonica songs picked out with a gentle mouth that tasted every nickel note, and iridescent shells that held all the shifting seas and skies, and knucklebones that clicked and scattered and hit my own knuckles as they fell, and Rubik's Cubes that twisted and twisted until they came right, and tiny white wings at my temples and throat. And my hand against the sky above me, the mole on my knuckle, the scar on my thumb: these were mine, mine. And my hand was both my hand and a streak of pale birds flying in formation, both my hand and the disjointed legs of broken Barbie dolls, both my hand and a twitching crab.

I'm home, said my mother. *Tails, heads, tails. How hungry are you? Will I know who I am?*

Hollow head, hollow hands. The birds and bees at my temples, my throat, wanting in. Burnt sugar on my tongue, sticking to the backs of my teeth, sticking my mouth shut. I had to get out of there. I had to leave everything as I'd found it, as if I'd never set foot inside that space, backtracking like a detective. I had to lock the door and return the key to the nail on the mirror. I had to get out. Get out.

But the seizure was coming for me and there was no stopping it. The stolen curtains billowed like sails and the floor shifted beneath me and we were away under the glittering sky, the bears and the dolls and I, the clown, the sleepwalker. The key bit into my palm.

2014

CHAPTER 27

I start in 1983 and work my way back, looking for accidents, tragedies. It takes me a while to learn how to handle the dial on the microfilm reader: too much pressure and I speed through days at a time, the black-and-white pages blurring to grey, streaking past like shadows. Then I have to go forwards again, try to find where I've been. And I do come across plenty of possibilities: *tragically taken*; *taken too soon*; *tragically as the result of an accident*. No fathers and daughters, though, in those old deaths – and nobody at all named Price. I think of how Dad used to check the newspapers for leads – circling the death notices of elderly people, then tracking down their surviving relatives. He was always respectful when he contacted them, though he never waited long. Sometimes I used to hear him on the phone in the shop: *I'm so sorry to bother you at this sad time. It can be difficult to know what to do with a loved one's possessions. I'm happy to come to the house, give you a quote on the spot. You'll find I offer a fair price.*

I'm scrolling through early 1983 when I catch sight of it slipping by: *Crieve, Elizabeth Celine.* My chest clenches, and I turn the dial slowly until she floats back into view. *Peacefully at Wellington Hospital after a long battle with cancer. Loved wife of Neil and adored mother of Justine.* I don't know why I'm so shocked to see it – I knew Dad had put a notice in all the major papers. I suppose I wasn't looking for that particular death. And was it peaceful? Towards the end she didn't speak, didn't open her eyes – she just lay silent against the hospital pillows, swollen with the drugs that would make her more comfortable. 'Not much longer now,' the nurses told us. 'You probably don't want to go anywhere.' They brought watery cups of tea for Dad and glasses of orange cordial for me. It was too strong, and it made my tongue feel tight along the edges, but I drank it anyway, just to have something to do. 'She knows you're here,' they said. I wasn't so sure. I kept waiting for my mother to say something, even to squeeze my fingers. How could she leave us so quietly? And then, when it happened, she looked no different. 'I think . . .' said Dad. He had to go and get a nurse so we could be sure; it was so slender, that border between here and not here. *In lieu of flowers, a donation to the Cancer Society may be left.* People had dropped money into a box at the front of the church, as if they were paying to attend the funeral. As if it were some kind of show. And they'd sent flowers anyway – bunches of carnations and lilies and roses that I had to find vases for, and then, when the vases ran out, preserving jars that had held my mother's apricots and pears. I tore open the little sachets of flower food that would keep them alive for longer, and I stirred it into the water like sugar. I cut off the ends of the stems, and I placed the bouquets away from sunlight, heat and draughts. Every two days I changed the water and retrimmed the stems – I did everything right, but they died anyway. Green slime coating the insides of the vases and jars. A rank smell.

Now and then Emma asks me if I'm going to die young the way Nana Crieve died young. Of course not, I say; I'm perfectly well. And in any case, there are all kinds of treatments. All kinds of cures.

'Do you think it's in me too?' she says.

'There are all kinds of cures,' I repeat.

I turn the dial and scroll back through 1982, 1981, 1980, checking the news stories as well as the death notices for any mention of a fatal car accident – but again, I find none involving a father and young daughter. When I get home that evening, Dom says maybe I should just stop looking. Leave it all in the past, where it belongs.

'Leave what in the past?' says Emma.

'Nothing, big ears,' I say.

'*You've* got big ears.'

'No *you've* got big ears.'

She skips out of my reach and puts on some music so she can show us her new dance moves.

'It was folk dancing with the nuns in our day,' says Dom.

Emma laughs: so uncool, she says. But she wants Dom and me to show her the steps, wants us to hum her the tune. Neither of us can quite remember, so I look it up on YouTube – and there it is, with all the other forgotten things, and we do our best.

She wasn't my first pregnancy. I was twenty-five the first time, and I still remember staring at the two little lines on the test: a pale road taking me nowhere I wanted to go. For a week I did nothing, told no one. My body felt no different – did it? No nausea, no tenderness. I went to work as usual, came home as usual. Watched TV with Dom, had Dad round for dinner. Drank a glass or two of wine. I know I should have told Dom, but in my mind it wasn't real. It wasn't a baby, not even the idea of a baby.

We'd talked about children, of course; he wanted a family, and I said I hadn't ruled it out for later on – but privately I knew I was not mother material.

'How many were you thinking?' I said as we lay in bed, the secret knot of cells dividing and dividing in me.

'Ten? A dozen?'

I shoved him with my foot.

'Okay, a couple. I don't know.'

Our cat Blizzard started kneading the duvet, her claws catching in the weave of the cotton, pulling the threads into bumpy little loops.

'We have plenty of time,' I said.

When I took a second pregnancy test I was fully expecting a negative, but there they were, the two little lines, dark as a tongue. I wrapped the stick in toilet paper, then in newspaper, and threw it away at the office. I still felt normal. Not a hint of the thing inside me. The next day I went to my doctor and told him I wanted it taken care of.

Dom's mother rang us the day before my procedure – I remember that. She couldn't possibly know, I told myself, yet all through the conversation I kept listening for clues, giveaways. I imagined she was listening for them too. Hearing something guilty in my voice. Dom was on the phone in the kitchen, and I was on the extension in our bedroom; I stretched out on our bed, the bed she pretended she didn't know we shared.

'And how are *you*, Justine?' she asked, after Dom had finished telling her about the vegetable patch he'd planted, the runner beans that had escaped the trellis and made their own spiralling jungle.

'Really great,' I said. 'Still plodding away at the council – you know. Hoping to move sideways into Compliance or Consents.'

'And your dad?'

'He's the same.'

'Do you know, they've sold the old convent,' she said. 'Cut the building into bits and shifted it out to a lifestyle block. Some of the parishioners went to watch them lift it off the trucks and put it back together again, but I just couldn't.'

'What about the nuns?' I said. 'Sister Bronislava?' I thought she'd always be there, trimming the crusts off club sandwiches with the electric knife, lifting the salt and pepper shakers in the shape of Māori warriors to wipe the oilcloth-covered table. The stained-glass window on the landing casting its coloured light on her as she passed. I saw her in her empty bedroom, looking out over the cypress hedge, keeping an eye on the children in the adventure playground.

'They're living in the community now,' said Dom's mother. 'The couple of them left, that is.'

Then she had to go – it was her turn to do the flowers for church, and she wanted to cut the roses before they bloomed. 'God bless,' she said, which was what she always said instead of goodbye.

I don't think I felt anything during the procedure. Maybe that's normal – I don't know. I remember staring at a poster on the ceiling as they went about their business: a cartoon of a New Zealand landscape with words drawn in the shape of the things they represented. There was the BEACH in big soft sandy letters; there were the WAVES and the CLOUDS. A flattened HORIZON; a CLIFF. Some of them you had to look very hard to make out: DRAGONFLY. SEAGULL. I lay there and listened to the hum of the machine, then the distant whooshing like wind, like waves.

Then someone was touching my shoulder and saying they were all finished, it was all over, and hadn't they told me they wouldn't need long? Some women wanted to see the pregnancy tissue, they said – even take it home with them. No thank you, I said.

That night I acted as if nothing had happened, and Dom never suspected. We were pro-choice by then, and I had made a choice. I have never told him.

I knew I was pregnant with Emma before I took the test, even though I was on the pill. My breasts hurt, and I could hardly keep my eyes open, and the nausea kept welling up in me, a feeling of motion sickness, like lurching around corners in the back of a hot car. Dom guessed, and this time I was too tired and too sick to keep it from him.

'I don't think I can do it,' I sobbed. 'I'm not cut out for it.'

'Of course you are,' he said. 'You're a good person. A kind person. I see how you are with Blizzard.'

'Blizzard's a cat. And I shut her tail in the door.'

'And she was fine.'

I shook my head, unable to stop crying. 'I'm dangerous. I'm not mother material. Some people aren't.'

'Is this about Mrs Price?' He wouldn't let me avoid his gaze. 'Is it?'

Yes. No. Not only. 'I'm not mother material.'

'Let's just see,' he said.

And then Emma was born, and I loved her, and I love her. Fiercely. Hungrily. I would do anything for her.

But I know I won't have any more.

1984

CHAPTER 28

J ustine. Justine. Can you hear me?'

My mother was calling to me across the water, waving a white hand. I tried to answer her, but my lips would not open, and my tongue lay dead behind the rocks of my teeth.

'Justine? Are you there, my darling?'

Her words turning to foam, her white hand turning to foam. The cry of a gull.

My head hurt.

Brown eyes looking into mine. Blond hair. Bits of glitter on the ceiling above. Gold scatter cushions packed around me, the way you barricade a baby to stop it falling from a bed.

A bed, queen size, dark pink.

A pillow that smelled of jasmine, honeysuckle, something rambling and rampant.

'Hello, sleepyhead,' said Mrs Price.

'Hello.'

'How are you feeling?' She sat back, stroked a hand over my hair. I flinched.

'Sorry, my darling. It must have been quite a knock.' Her fingers creeping across my scalp, searching for where I'd hurt myself. Parting my hair, looking for blood.

'Did I fall?'

'Yes, sweetheart. You had a seizure when I was out.'

Late-afternoon sun filled the room, thick and low. I must have lost a couple of hours.

The key. Where was the key? Where had she found me?

'Shall I bring you some water? Do you think you can sit up? Slowly now.'

I was waterlogged, filled with sand. She lifted my feet to the floor, one, two, thud, thud, and I sat on the edge of her bed and tried to remember. I opened my left hand: no key, but perhaps the jagged indentation of a key. She saw me looking – I shouldn't have looked – and said, 'Stay there. I'll bring you some water.'

My head hurt. Had I hit it on the chest of drawers in the spare room? Was that where she had found me, sprawled on the piles of stolen things? But if so, why hadn't she mentioned it? Tried to explain it all away? Perhaps I had locked the room behind me, hung the key on its nail on the back of the mirror. It was possible; often I couldn't recall the moments before a seizure as well as the hours after. Perhaps Mrs Price had found me in the laundry, exactly where I was supposed to be. Or perhaps I'd never even entered the spare room, and my miswired brain had invented it. I knew how I could deceive myself – the phantom taste of burnt sugar; my mother's voice as clear as if she were right beside me. I forced myself to stand up and walk to the bedroom door. I could hear water running in the kitchen. Down at the end of the hall, the door to the spare room was shut, the mirror glimmering. No time to check for the key. I returned to the bed and grabbed the *Australian Women's Weekly* from the bedside table. *Could you survive a P&O cruise?* asked an ad. A moment later Mrs Price was there, offering me a glass of water.

'I'm not thirsty,' I said.

'Come on now, my darling – just a few sips. You'll feel better.'

'I'm *not thirsty*.' I never spoke like that to adults.

Her smile didn't falter. 'All right, I'll just leave it here. Perhaps you'll want it later.'

'I need to go home.'

'You know you're more than welcome to stay and rest.'

'Where's my bag?'

'In the living room, I think – but Justine, you're in no state to go anywhere. You could have an accident.'

And she was right – I couldn't imagine even climbing on my bike, let alone riding it uphill.

'Let me drive you. I'd never forgive myself if something happened.'

She carried my bag to the car for me and buckled me in when I couldn't get my fingers to work properly. 'You see, my darling?' she said. She was humming to herself as she backed down the driveway.

'Did you get your pills?' I said.

'I did. Mr Buchanan was very understanding in the end, so thank you for helping me with that. We need to look out for each other, don't we? You and I.'

We drove past the end of Amy's street, and I craned my neck to see her house. I had the strangest feeling that if I looked hard enough I might see her checking the letterbox or weeding the dahlia beds for pocket money. Lurching down the pavement on her roller skates, trying to jump the cracks.

'I still can't believe she's gone either,' said Mrs Price. 'I keep expecting her to walk into the classroom and sit down at her desk. Ask me some curly question that I can't answer.'

Had Amy asked questions like that? I didn't remember her speaking up much at all in class.

'Everyone thinks it's my fault she killed herself,' I said.

'Oh, sweetheart,' said Mrs Price. But she didn't contradict me.

'Do you think that?'

'I think we shouldn't torture ourselves wondering about the actions of the dead. We can't ask them, can we?'

'She might have said something in the note. If I could just see it—'

'Justine, this isn't healthy.'

'Do *you* think it's my fault?'

The engine strained as the street began to climb, and she changed gear. 'Shall I give you an honest answer?'

'Yes.'

'I think Amy felt abandoned by you. You were growing up, leaving her behind, and then suddenly you were going to Melissa's house on the weekends, spending all your time with her and her friends . . . I could see how upset Amy was. I think she started stealing those things because she wanted to be part of the group, somehow.'

Around the narrow bends she steered the car, the bush dense and dark on the hill above us.

When I didn't reply, she said, 'I'm sorry, my darling. I know it's hard to hear, but you did ask.'

We were almost home. She said, 'I think your dad's going to tell you about the cruise this weekend. Remember to act surprised!'

'Okay.'

'Wait, show me your surprised face.'

I raised my eyebrows, opened my mouth. My jaw felt heavy as stone.

She laughed. 'Well, you can work on it. Try it in front of the mirror till it looks real.'

'Why are things still going missing?' I said.

We sat at the corner of our street. The indicator ticked as we waited for a line of cars to pass.

'That I don't know,' she said. 'Perhaps they've just been mislaid – it happens all the time and most people hardly notice. We're a bit on guard since the business with Amy, I think.'

'Or it never was Amy. It was someone else, and they were quite happy to let her take the blame, only they still can't stop stealing.' I kept my tone conversational, but something seemed to shift and tighten between us.

'I understand you want to defend your friend,' said Mrs Price, watching the traffic for a gap. 'And I commend you for that, of course I do.'

'People think it's me. Me and Dom.'

'I know. You just have to rise above – and anyway, you'll be finished with primary school next week, and everything's different at high school, trust me. You'll be the babies again.'

I wasn't going to let her change the subject. 'Wouldn't Amy's parents have found the stuff?' I said. 'Stashed in her room, or wherever?'

Currents of air from the passing cars buffeted the Corvette. Any one of them might have crashed right into us, waiting there in the middle of the street; the drivers seemed to be veering so close they barely missed us. I told myself it was just the after-effects of the seizure and the strangeness of sitting in an American car – sitting on the wrong side, like my own reflection. I was quite safe.

'Hmm,' said Mrs Price, turning into our street at last. 'I suppose they must have found it. I imagine they think it's hers – you know how children collect things. Swap things. Little magpies, they are.'

'They know about the stealing, though, don't they? The Fongs?'

'Sweetheart, I have no idea of the situation in their household. And really, it's none of our business.'

'Someone should ask for it back. The Fongs would understand, if someone explained.'

I studied her face for any trace of a reaction. She was shaking her head, and one long earring caught in her hair: a tassel of silver chains. 'Justine, no – the situation is very delicate, and imagine how upsetting that would be. We can't put them through it. Anyway, all those things she took – they're of no real value, are they.' She reached up and untangled the earring from her hair, strand by strand, driving one-handed.

And I opened my mouth, and I couldn't stop myself: the

wedding was nine days away, and after that we'd be a family. It would be too late. I said, 'I looked it up.'

'Looked what up, my darling?'

'In the library. I looked up kleptomania.'

Did she jerk the steering wheel just a little? I thought I felt the car twitch for a second. All along our street, the pōhutukawa trees were shedding their flowers, the silky red threads carpeting the pavement. Branches rose up either side of the power lines, the hearts cut out.

'And what did you discover?' she said.

'That it's a disorder. People who have it are sick. They can't resist stealing, even though the things they take aren't worth much.'

'So we can't hold Amy responsible,' she said smoothly. 'She had no control over her actions, just as you have no control over your epilepsy.'

We pulled in behind Dad's car, and she carried my schoolbag up the driveway for me. I stumbled at one point – my body still wasn't working properly – and she held out her arm for me to lean on.

'You know, Justine,' she whispered in my ear, 'they used to think epileptics were possessed by the devil. They used to drill holes in their skulls, and the Victorians locked them up in the madhouse.'

Ever the teacher.

Dad leapt from his chair when she told him I'd had a seizure. 'Did you hurt yourself? Show me your tongue. Are you all right?'

'A bit of a bump on the head,' she said. 'No blood.'

'Thank goodness you were there, Angie. Come on, love, come and sit down.'

He led me to the couch, and I lay with my head in his lap like I always used to. I wanted to sleep right there.

'We'll have to go back to Dr Kothari,' he said. 'Ask him to

increase the dose, or try you on something different. This can't keep happening – it's dangerous.'

'She gave me such a fright,' said Mrs Price. 'Lying there on the floor, out cold. I thought she wasn't breathing.'

On which floor? She didn't elaborate, and I didn't dare ask.

'I wonder if all this with Amy is playing a part,' said Dad. 'Hm? Dr Kothari said intense emotions can trigger a seizure.'

'Maybe,' I said. His belly soft and warm against the back of my head.

'Or was anything else going on?'

Mrs Price sat in the armchair opposite us, her eyes on mine. I couldn't read her face.

'No, nothing else,' I said. 'Just a normal day.'

'She was doing my ironing,' she said.

'God, you could have burned yourself!' said Dad. He lifted my arm, looking for injuries.

'I didn't, though. I *didn't*.'

'Lucky for me you only had the tea towels to go,' said Mrs Price. 'I make such a mess of blouses and skirts and things.'

Dad laughed, but he carried on checking me over.

I thought I remembered a pile of clothes still waiting in the laundry basket. The arm of an unfinished blouse trailing off the edge of the ironing board. Or was that a different time?

'Oh, while I think of it—' She took out her wallet and put ten dollars on the coffee table for me.

'I didn't even finish, though,' I said.

'Now now, I'm almost your mother,' she said, laughing. 'And I think I can live with creased tea towels. Personally, I don't know why you bother with them!'

Dad nudged me. 'What do you say, love?'

'Thank you.' I left the money where it sat on the table. My mother's writing had long since vanished from the underside.

'Goodness me, you do sound gloomy,' said Dad. 'Maybe a bit of a surprise would cheer you up?'

Mrs Price was beaming at him, nodding.

'Angie and I had a chat, and we decided it wouldn't be fair to leave you behind when we go on our honeymoon. We want you to come with us – on a cruise.'

I sat up, widened my eyes. 'Dad! Do you mean it?'

'We'd love to have you there.'

'Oh my gosh! A cruise? Not just Lake Taupō? Thank you so much!' I threw my arms around his neck, kissed him on the cheek. Perfect acting. His laugh travelled through my own cheek and lodged somewhere in my throat.

'And we had a chat, too, about what you might like to call Angie,' he said. 'Did you have any thoughts?'

'Not Mum,' I blurted, and they looked at each other.

'No no, of course not,' she said. 'I can never take her place.'

'No,' Dad agreed, 'but Mrs Price won't do, will it? What about Aunty Angela?'

'Neil, she's practically an adult. Why not just Angela? Or Angie? Even Ange.'

I said, 'I don't know. They all sound weird.'

'It'll take some getting used to,' said Dad. 'You have a think about it.'

But that was the last thing I felt like doing – imagining her as part of our family. Sleeping in our house, showering in our shower. Maybe having a baby. I *had* seen all the stolen things in her spare room – I was sure of it. Fairly sure.

'I have a surprise for you too,' she said. She reached into her bag and handed me a parcel wrapped in silvery tissue.

'What's this?' said Dad. 'What have you been up to?'

'I wanted to get her something for the cruise.'

It slithered onto my lap when I tore away the paper: a candyfloss-pink bikini.

'See, it ties in bows at the hips,' she said.

Just like the one I'd lied about to Karl and Melissa. I knew it was a coincidence, that she'd simply guessed the kind of thing

I'd like, but it felt as if she'd read my thoughts. Listened in on my lies.

'Well, try it on, my darling! See if it fits.'

In the bedroom I shook out my hair, shed my school uniform and my underwear, and pulled on the bikini. The slippery, shimmery lycra clung to me, stretching to fit my new body, the little bows tickling my hips. I turned side on to the mirror to check the silhouette of my stomach, the jut of my ribs. I smiled like the lady in the Speedslimmer ad, exercising in her swimsuit, attacking her troublespots. Was I worried about tummy bulge? Was I feeling flabby? Should I be? I sucked in my breath and held still. And there at my feet, poking out of the pocket of my discarded tunic, something small and white. Something with black ink dots for eyes.

I bent to pick it up, and it lay weightless on my palm: the cotton-wool bee the dental nurse had made me, or one like it. The thin ribbon of floss bound its gauze wings to its body, and I remembered them all hanging from the ceiling in Mrs Price's spare room, the white bees and butterflies, and I thought I remembered reaching up my hand and snatching one clean out of the sky. Slipping it into my pocket while the others spun and careened. A buzzing in my ears, a white swarm. Proof.

'Are we allowed to see?' called Dad.

I returned the bee to my tunic pocket and went to show them.

'Look at you!' said Mrs Price. 'Aren't you gorgeous?'

I stood there beside the coffee table, fiddling with the halter neck of the bikini; it was cutting into me, and I wasn't sure how to make it sit right.

'It's very grown up,' said Dad, a doubtful note in his voice. He kept his eyes on my knees.

'Like a model! Like Miss Universe!' said Mrs Price, clapping her hands. 'You're coming down the stairs in your nude heels, passing in front of the fountain. You're crossing the stage, smiling in the spotlight, posing as the judges score you. Wait for the number at the bottom of the screen . . . and it's a ten for Miss New Zealand! Now give us a twirl.'

I put a hand on one hip and turned for them, and it must have taken a few seconds at most, but by the time I saw Dad again he had covered his face and was shaking.

'I'm sorry, I'm sorry,' he said. 'She's so like Beth.'

Gooseflesh prickled up my legs, stole across my arms and chest.

'I never thought,' said Mrs Price. 'Of course she is. Of course.' She put her arms around him, lacing her fingers together and holding him tight. Then she gestured towards the hall with her head: get out of here.

Back in my bedroom I stripped off the slick pink bikini, left it lying on the floor like a shucked skin. I put on my old track pants and my baggiest T-shirt and tied my hair back in its school ponytail, then listened in the hall – she was talking to him in her gentle voice, though I couldn't make out any words. I fetched the black light, crept to my parents' bedroom and climbed inside my mother's armoire.

'What did I see in her locked room?' I said.

The petals of my father's best Rosa Mundi, she said.

'Is it my fault Amy died?'

Going twice.

I climbed back out and lay on their bed and dialled Dom's number. I wasn't sure which sister answered, but she yelled, 'Hey Condom! It's your girlfriend.'

Another sister grabbed the phone before he could get to it and said, 'You know he has a weird belly button, right? It looks like a nipple.' Shrieks of laughter, then Dom's voice hissing in the background: 'Shut up, Diane! Shut *up*! Give me that!' The receiver clattered as if dropped on a wooden floor.

'Hello?' he said.

'Hi.'

'Oh hi.'

'Who did you think it was?'

'What?'

'Well, how many girlfriends do you have?'

'None. I don't know.'

'You don't know?'

'Uh . . .'

'Can I come round?'

'Now?'

'Yeah.'

'Okay.'

We sat in the warm sunroom and flipped through his album of coins: little suns, little moons. In the bedroom one brother pinned down another and shouted, 'Give yourself to the Dark Side! It is the only way you can save your friends!' Dom handed me his latest coin – a two-krone piece from Denmark – and I looked at it under the magnifying glass. Looked at the marks from handling, the tiny spots of damage made when people had traded it for something they wanted. A scrape across King Christian's ear; pitting in his cheek. The grain of my skin came into sharp focus too, and the ridges in my nails. The secret markings of my own hand exposed. I could still feel the drag of the seizure.

'I got into the locked room,' I said.

'What? When were you going to tell me?' He grabbed the coin and the magnifying glass and fixed me with a look. 'Well? What was in there?'

'Everything. All of it.' I told him about the piles of stuffed animals and toy cars and keyrings and combs, the box of pebbles and shells from the beach, the PE gear, the raisins, the marbles. The cotton-wool bees and butterflies, the bee I'd managed to snatch. The curtains from the church. And as I spoke I felt something slipping away from me. The white cat hunched on the windowsill, twitching her tail, chittering at the birds in the garden. Impatient to hunt.

Dom slumped back in his chair, let out a low whistle. 'That sounds like more than she's taken from us,' he said.

'A lot more.' I bit my lip, then started to cry.

'What's wrong? Justine?'

I couldn't stop the tears; they burst from me like rain, splashing onto the two-krone piece, the magnifying glass, the album full of coins arranged according to face value. At one point I made out the two brothers standing blurry in the sunroom doorway, then silently retreating. Dom slipped his skinny arm around me, and I leaned on him and wept my heart out, and I knew I was weeping for Amy and my mother and for Dad too – and for Mrs Price, beautiful Mrs Price who had chosen me to be her pet.

'It's all right,' he murmured. 'Everything's all right.'

I took a deep, staggering breath and said, 'I had a seizure.' I hated talking about it, hated even the sound of the word, which made me think of invisible hands grabbing my shoulders and shaking me till I forgot my own name. 'I was still in the room – I'm pretty sure.'

'Wait,' said Dom, 'she found you in there?'

'I think so. I can't remember. Right before and right after are always a bit hazy . . . It's possible I got out when I felt it coming, and had time to lock the door and put the key back. But I think she probably found me in the room and led me out and locked the door herself.'

'What's the first thing you do remember?'

'Waking up on her bed.' My mother calling to me across the water. The cry of a gull. 'I wanted to get out of there – go home – but she wouldn't let me bike. She drove me.'

'So she was looking after you?'

'Maybe.'

'Did she say anything?'

'No. I mean, not really.' *You know, Justine, they used to think epileptics were possessed by the devil. They used to drill holes in their skulls, and the Victorians locked them up in the madhouse.*

'You must've got out in time, then. She would have said something.'

'I guess. She gave me a bikini.'

Stupid thing to mention. Stupid, stupid.

'What?'

'A present – they want me to come on their honeymoon cruise.'

'She wouldn't give you a present if she found you snooping,' said Dom. 'Or invite you on a cruise.'

I shook my head as if to dislodge the seizure's dregs, but the pain flared. 'I just have a feeling she knows.'

'Did you tell your dad?'

'He didn't believe me when I told him about the jar of tea. He won't hear a word against her.'

'This is different, though. Now you know for sure.'

'He'd come up with some excuse or other. Even if he saw the room himself.'

'Well, you have to tell someone.'

'I know. I know.'

'What about Father Lynch?'

'He loves her.'

'Sister Bronislava?'

I remembered the way she'd grasped my elbow in the playground that day, telling me that she disapproved of the way I was treating my old friend. That I was making a mistake. My chest tightened with shame.

'She's a hundred years old,' I said.

'Mr Chisholm, then,' said Dom.

'He hasn't been much help so far. And he loves her too.'

'He's the headmaster,' said Dom. 'He's the one you go to.'

'Everything okay?' said a voice at the door. Mrs Foster,

smiling at us, scanning my blotchy face. She must have heard me crying, or Dom's brothers must have told her.

'Just talking about Amy,' said Dom.

'Poor girl,' she tsked, and I didn't know which one of us she meant. 'Are you staying for tea, Justine? It's chop night.'

'I should be getting home,' I said.

'Oh!' She touched her stomach, and I realised she was pregnant. 'He's a busy little bee today.' She laughed. 'Look at your face! Would you like to feel?'

She took my hand and held it to her soft blue sundress – and the baby inside her moved like a cat, as if responding to my touch.

'Sometimes, later on, you can even see shapes,' she said. 'A tiny hand or foot, trying to push its way out.'

'Do you have to, Mum?' said Dom.

'What? It's perfectly natural. Boys can be so squeamish, can't they, Justine?' Her fingers looked swollen, the pink flesh puffing up around her skinny wedding ring.

'When is it due?' I said.

'Early April. An Easter baby! Goodness knows where we'll put him. Maybe in here . . .' She looked around the sunroom.

'No way,' said Dom.

'Oh, he won't take up much space. A little cardboard box in the corner. A little blanket tucked in the desk drawer.'

I wasn't sure if she was joking or not.

'Do you know it's a boy?' I said.

'Just a feeling.' She smiled. 'You're supposed to say it doesn't matter, as long as it's healthy – but I'd love another wee cherub like this one.' She planted a wet kiss on Dom's cheek.

'Ugh, Mum!'

'What if it's a girl?' I said.

'Then that will be a blessing too. At any rate, it's in God's hands.'

'Mum!' called one of the sisters. 'The carrots have boiled dry!'

'So take them off the heat!' she called back. 'Goodness me, where's the common sense? Dominic, will you lay the table, please?'

I tied my sweatshirt around my waist and thanked Mrs Foster for having me.

'You're sure you won't stay?'

'I'm quite tired.'

'You do look peaky. Got to get your beauty sleep for next weekend, I suppose.'

I nodded.

'Try to enjoy it, won't you? Despite everything – despite Amy – it's a happy, happy occasion for you and your dad, and you're going to be the prettiest bridesmaid ever. I told Dominic I'd bring him to the church so he can see you in your dress. We'll—'

'I think Sarah needs your help with the carrots,' said Dom. 'I can smell something burning.'

'All right, all right.' Before she left the room, Mrs Foster touched my arm. 'You're a good girl, Justine. Amy's with the Lord now, but she'll always be looking down on you.'

I was afraid of that.

I couldn't fall asleep that night, despite the exhaustion the seizure had left in me. I'd gone to bed early to avoid talking to Dad about Mrs Price; there was no way I could tell him what I'd found – was there?

I wanted my mother.

When I did begin to nod off, I saw babies shut in boxes, shut in desk drawers, trying to push their way out. Their little gold feet kicking and kicking until they bled.

The next day, after the final bell rang, I knocked on Mr Chisholm's door. He was standing at his office window, watching the children on the adventure playground while they waited for their mothers or the bus to take them home. They flung themselves from the wooden spools and the stormwater pipes, ran at the tractor tyres and ricocheted back off, grabbed the climbing rope and swung on it so hard I thought they would collide with the steel frame.

'Do they *want* to hurt themselves?' he said to me. He took a sip from a plastic shaker and grimaced. 'They think they're bulletproof at that age. They think they're unbreakable. And if they do cut open a knee or snap a bone, someone comes along to scoop them up and make it better.' He sat down at his desk, motioned for me to take a seat too. 'It used to scare the living daylights out of me when I started teaching, I don't mind telling you. Do you know, in America, the parents of a ten-year-old sued her school for a million dollars because she tripped on a hopscotch stone? Madness.' He shook his drink and took another sip, pulled another face. Glanced at the tin of toffees at his elbow.

'Was she all right?' I said.

'Who?'

'The girl who tripped.'

'Well, she landed on her head, so no, not really. But she did get a million dollars.'

I nodded. I'd been rehearsing what to say to him all day, but now, sitting in his office, I couldn't think how to begin. In my tunic pocket my fingers closed around the ferry pen. 'It's Mrs Price,' I said.

'Again?' He drained the plastic shaker, screwing up his face as he swallowed the last of the drink. 'She's the one who put me on to these. Chocolate! Chocolate, they call it! Still, I've lost half a stone, and I don't feel deprived if I don't dwell on it.'

'She's been stealing from us,' I said.

He wiped the corners of his mouth. 'I beg your pardon?'

'She's been stealing from us.'

'Justine—' he began, then stopped. He placed the shaker very precisely on a coaster of the Wellington cable car, removed his glasses and rubbed at the dents on either side of his nose. 'I know you must miss your mother. I understand that. And I expect you blame yourself for Amy's death.'

I wished people would stop saying that.

On the wall above us, the face of the man on the Shroud – his eyes weighted with coins – seemed to float. A snapshot of the resurrection.

'Amy wasn't the thief,' I said. 'It was always Mrs Price.'

He sighed. 'When we feel guilty, we can lash out at others – try to lessen the burden of that guilt. It can make us do terrible things. Think of Judas, hanging himself from a tree.'

I said, 'She has a secret room in her house where she keeps all the things she's stolen. I saw it yesterday.'

'A secret room? A secret room? Hidden behind a swivelling bookcase, is it? Listen to yourself, Justine.' He picked up the shaker and tried to take a sip, realised it was empty and glared at it. Outside the window, Mrs Price was crossing the grounds, heading for her car.

'The stealing hasn't stopped,' I said. 'Since Amy died. Everyone's been accusing Dom and me.'

'Dom and I.'

'Dom and me.'

He blinked. 'Mrs Price came to us from a *very* exclusive Christchurch school. Do you know how lucky we are to have attracted someone of her calibre?'

'She's from Auckland,' I said. 'She told us Auckland. And every single thing stolen from our class is at her house, and a whole lot more, and the church curtains are hanging in her window. The ones that went missing from the back room.'

'Justine,' he said, and drew in a deep breath, 'this is an ugly side of you. What exactly are you trying to achieve?'

'Will you come with me? To her house?'

'Her *house*?'

'Yes.'

He picked up the plastic shaker, put it down again. Hands folded, he regarded me for a moment or two and did not speak.

'Otherwise,' I said, forcing my voice not to tremble, 'I'll have to tell the police.'

'About a few missing pencil sharpeners?' An unpleasant little smile.

I rose from my seat. 'It's up to you.'

'If I come,' he said, 'will that be the end of it?'

'That'll be the end of it.'

We drove there in silence. His car smelled of hot vinyl, and a laminated quote swung from the rear-view mirror: *Never travel faster than your guardian angel can fly*. Mrs Price was just getting out of the Corvette when we arrived, and she looked puzzled to see the two of us pulling into the driveway behind her. Mr Chisholm raised a hand in greeting.

'Sorry to intrude!' he called.

'What's all this?' she said. 'Justine? Is everything all right?'

'Could we have a word inside?' said Mr Chisholm.

'Oh my God, has something happened to Neil?'

'No no, nothing like that. Nothing to worry about.'

She unlocked the front door, and we followed her into the house.

'I'll get right to it,' he said. 'Justine here seems to think you have a whole cache of stolen items hidden away. An entire room of ill-gotten gains.' He laughed. 'I'm really so sorry to bother you with this.'

'Goodness!' she said. 'Teacher by day, cat burglar by night? Where's this coming from, Justine?'

'I saw it,' I said. 'The Rubik's Cubes, the toy cars, the curtains. The bees and butterflies. The raisins.'

'Raisins?'

'I know, I know,' said Mr Chisholm. 'Humour us.'

I licked my lips. 'It's the room at the end of the hall. She keeps it locked.'

'I do keep it locked,' she agreed. 'It's where I store my mementoes – things I don't want to throw out, but also don't want to see every day. You understand.'

'Of course,' said Mr Chisholm. 'I wonder – if it's not too much of an imposition – could we have a quick look? Just to put this to rest.'

She hesitated. 'It's a very private space . . .'

'Of course,' he said again. 'We'd only need to pop our heads round the door.'

Sighing, she motioned for us to follow her down the hall. I thought she would stop at the mirror, but she turned to the spare room and opened it with a key on her keyring. Hadn't I tried them all in the lock?

'Here we are,' she said, and we followed her inside.

The room was almost bare – as bare as Sister Bronislava's convent room. A white bedspread edged with a broderie anglaise flounce covered the narrow bed, and a single ragdoll with woollen hair lay against the pillow. On the chest of drawers, a framed photograph of a dark-haired young man paddling at the beach, holding a little girl by the hand as they squinted into the sun. Next to it, a baby's bottle, the teat chewed by baby teeth. A lock of pale hair tied with a white thread. Nothing on the shelves but a plain gold wedding ring. Nothing hanging from the ceiling. I opened a drawer. Empty. At the window, a wispy net curtain blurred the riotous green of the garden beyond. A blowfly looped crazily behind it, bashing itself against the glass.

'Are you happy now, Justine?' said Mr Chisholm.

I stood in the centre of the room and turned and turned and couldn't get my bearings. 'What have you done with it all?'

Mrs Price spread her hands. 'My darling, I'm sorry, but I don't know what you're talking about.'

When I dropped to my knees to check under the bed, she whispered, 'Is she . . . is she unwell? She's on some pretty powerful medication . . . Oh and she had a seizure yesterday. Banged her head on my laundry floor.'

Mr Chisholm took my elbow and began to steer me towards the hall. 'I think we've seen enough,' he said. 'Thank you – we'll leave you alone now.'

I kept scanning the vacant space; somehow I expected the piles of belongings to reappear out of thin air if only I looked hard enough. Mr Chisholm's fingers were digging into me, and Mrs Price was smoothing the ragdoll's patchwork dress, and I could see the mirror in the hall, could see myself leaving the empty room, white and wild-eyed. My headache crashed against my skull, and I thought it might break open.

'. . . owe her an apology,' Mr Chisholm was saying, but I ignored him, shook off his hand.

'The wardrobe,' I said. 'Let me look.'

He sighed. 'May we, Mrs Price?'

'I suppose so.'

And surely that was where she'd hidden the things; surely she'd crammed them all inside as high as the ceiling – but even as I reached out my hand to open it, I knew it could not possibly contain everything I'd seen. The door swung open, and the wardrobe released its musty breath, and only a handful of garments hung inside: clothes for a little girl. A pinafore with a bee on the front. A party dress, all ribbons and tulle. A white christening gown that trailed from the hanger like a ghost.

'There you are, you see,' said Mr Chisholm, looking at his watch. 'Shall I drop you home now?'

But I ran across the hall to Mrs Price's bedroom and began to search, yanking open the drawers, flinging aside the bedspread. Plunging my arms into the racks of dresses and blouses.

Then I tried her office, then the bathroom, then the kitchen.

'Let her get it out of her system,' I heard Mrs Price say as I passed.

When I found nothing in the house, I ran outside to the garage – but that was empty too. Just her garden tools hanging on the wall, her cactus-proof gloves side by side on the work bench. The green tracks from her lawnmower crisscrossing the concrete.

They were waiting for me in the sunken living room, Mr Chisholm sitting awkwardly on the edge of the carpeted step.

'Well?' he said.

I shook my pounding head.

'Is there anything you'd like to say to Mrs Price?'

'No.'

'No?'

'Can we just let it go, Dennis?' she said.

'I must say, that's very generous of you.'

'We're family now.'

Not quite.

'What about the tea?' I said.

'Sorry?'

'The jar of jasmine-flower tea.'

'What does tea have to do with it?' said Mr Chisholm.

'She stole it from the Fongs' shop. Amy saw her.'

'Ah. Amy,' he said, and exchanged a look with Mrs Price.

'Mm,' she murmured. 'I only wish I'd recognised the signs . . .'

'We mustn't blame ourselves.' He rose to his feet. 'Come on, then – I'll take you home.'

'Her dad won't finish work for a couple of hours,' she said. 'Perhaps she should stay with me.'

'Justine?'

'Home,' I said. 'Take me home.'

As we filed to the front door he glanced in at the kitchen. 'You wouldn't have a toasted sandwich to tide me over, would you? Or a couple of biscuits? I'm ravenous.'

I rang Dom as soon as Mr Chisholm had driven away.

'What do you mean, empty?' he said.

'I mean she'd cleaned it out. Got rid of everything. Or I imagined it all.'

'No. What about the bee?'

I thought of the little weightless scrap of cotton wool and gauze.

'I don't know where I got that. I don't remember.'

'Yes you do. Justine, you *do*.'

Dad and I were eating our Saturday pancakes when she showed up at the house the next morning, letting herself in the front door.

'You're just in time,' he said, kissing her on the lips. 'Butter? Golden syrup?'

'Yes and yes.' She rolled up the pancake he served her, then ate it with her fingers. 'Mmh,' she groaned. 'This needs to become a tradition.'

'It already is,' I said.

'Perfect!' She watched Dad pouring the batter into the hot pan, tilting it so it ran all the way to the edges. The DEAREST bracelet glittered on her wrist. 'You know, when I was in Corsica,' she said, 'I found a stall selling crepes out in the middle of nowhere. It was a greasy little caravan, and I had no idea how to order, and he didn't speak a word of English, so I just pointed at a picture on the wall. And do you know what he did? Once he'd cooked it? He scooped out a blob of cream cheese and wiped it over the crepe with his grubby hand!'

'Ugh, no!' said Dad.

She laughed. 'Best thing I've ever tasted. Oh, and he gave me too much change – far too much – so I went back and tried to return it, and he thought I was complaining about something and started shouting.'

'What did you do?'

'What *could* I do? I kept the money and hot-footed it out of there.'

'Very wise,' said Dad, sitting down at the table with us.

Mrs Price touched my back. 'How are you feeling this morning, sweetheart?'

'Fine.'

'Glad to hear it. No hard feelings.'

'What?' said Dad.

'Nothing,' said Mrs Price.

I stared at my plate. He looked at me, looked at her, looked back at me.

'What's going on? Justine?'

I shrugged.

'Angie?'

'We had a little misunderstanding,' she said. 'I think it was the seizure – and maybe the bump to the head – but somehow Justine got the idea I'd been stealing.'

'Excuse me?'

Mrs Price smiled. 'She thought my spare room was full of ill-gotten gains. Brought Dennis Chisholm round to have a look.'

'I can't believe what I'm hearing,' said Dad. 'Justine, what on earth . . . ?'

'It's all right, Neil – really and truly. I do think it was the seizure, but Justine has probably had some doubts about me too, which is perfectly normal when a parent's seeing someone new. I think it's a good thing she had the courage to put them out in the open so we could clear everything up before the wedding.' She touched my back again. 'We're actually more alike than you realise, my darling.'

'She owes you an apology, at the very least,' said Dad.

'That's not necessary.'

'Yes it is. Justine?'

They were both looking at me, waiting.

'I . . . I made a mistake,' I said. 'I'm sorry.'

Mrs Price waved it away. 'We'll be sailing off into the sunset soon enough. Consider it forgotten.'

After breakfast it seemed clear she intended staying for the day: in the living room she tucked her feet up and started browsing the Property section of the newspaper, asking Dad if he felt like getting out in the garden after lunch. At one point I saw her running her hand over the blue-and-white couch, pressing her fingers into the old-fashioned lady on the swing. Making dents. When she saw me looking she said, 'It's getting a bit tired, isn't it? Perhaps we could freshen it up. You could help me choose some new fabric.'

I shut myself in my room and tried to read, but I could still hear her talking. And I could still hear Dad answering. Agreeing. In one week they'd be married.

She was there all Sunday too, and came straight round after school on the Monday – she even beat me home. It was as if she'd already moved in.

'I'm going to Dom's,' I told her.

'What about dinner?' she said. 'I thought I'd shout us McDonald's.'

'I'll have something at the Fosters'.'

'No French fries? No hot apple pie?'

'I'm okay.'

'Well, wear a hat, at least,' she said. 'The sun's fierce.'

I took my feet off the pedals of my bike and sped down the hill, fallen pōhutukawa flowers spraying up either side of my tyres. Faster and faster I went, and I should have squeezed the brakes, tried to slow myself down: the road had dangerous bends, and Dad was always telling me to be careful because you couldn't see what was coming. I didn't care. I wanted to get away from her as quickly as I could. Between the trees, between the houses, I caught glimpses of the bright blue sea.

The Fosters were piling into their station wagon when I skidded to a stop at the bottom of their driveway.

'Justine!' said Mrs Foster. 'What a nice surprise!'

I noticed that each of them, even the boys, wore a gold badge – the tiny feet.

'Are you coming with us?' she said. 'How lovely!'

'You don't have to,' muttered Dom, but already his sisters were squashing together to make room for me in the back of the car. Sarah shifted a pile of placards, stacking them on her lap: *Life Trumps Death* read the painted slogan on the top one. Peter, sitting on Marie's lap, fiddled with the chin strap on his helmet. 'Too tight?' said Marie. He nodded, and she loosened it for him.

'The witches didn't eat you, then?' I said to him, and he frowned at me. 'They were going to drop you in their cauldron, I thought. With parsley and onions.'

'There's no such thing as witches,' he said.

Claire started to draw with her fingertip on his back.

'A house!' he said.

'Nope.' She drew the pattern again.

'A boat!'

'Nope.'

'A truck?'

'Not even close. Give up?'

'Aren't we lucky with the weather?' said Mrs Foster, peering out the window at the perfect day. 'Toodle-oo!' she called to her husband, who was setting off on a bike with one of the smaller Fosters on the back. Wherever we were going, he must have taken time off work for it.

We drove around the bay to a dead-end street up behind the hospital and parked outside a large old roughcast house. A group of about ten people stood at the entrance, and they greeted us as we joined them, also remarking on our luckiness with the weather. They carried placards too: *No One Dies Here*

Today and *Let God Plan Families* and *I Am A Person NOT A Choice*. The women ran their hands over Mrs Foster's belly and told her how radiant she looked.

'Do you want *Jesus Is Pro-Life* or *We Are Here To Rescue Babies*?' asked Sarah, and I realised she was talking to me.

'Um . . . *We Are Here To Rescue Babies*?'

'It's my turn for that one!' said Marie.

'You had it last time,' said Sarah.

'No I didn't, you did! So it's my turn now!'

'Well, Justine chose it, and she's our guest.'

'She's not our *guest* – she just showed up. And this isn't our house.'

'But she came to our house, and Mum invited her to join us. That makes her our guest. Duh.'

'You're the duh.' Marie tried to grab the placard, but Sarah wouldn't let go.

'You'll tear it!' shouted Sarah. 'Mum! Mum! She's tearing *We Are Here To Rescue Babies*!'

'It's your fault if it tears!'

'That's enough now,' called Mrs Foster. 'You're young ladies, not animals.'

'She started it,' hissed Marie.

'Did not. Did not.' Sarah turned to me. 'Who started it?'

'Ah . . .' I said. 'I wasn't really looking.'

'Does it matter?' said Dom.

'Shut up, Condom,' said Marie.

'I don't mind which one I hold,' I said.

'See? See?' said Marie.

'You're holding this one,' said Sarah, handing me *We Are Here To Rescue Babies*.

'Okay,' I said. Marie glared at me.

Sarah gave Dom *Life Trumps Death*. I thought I could make out a scuffle of shoe-prints across a corner. Maybe they'd fought over that one as well.

Then Father Lynch climbed out of a car, and the women fluttered over to him. One of them offered him a pikelet, while another plucked a leaf out of his lustrous brown hair, handing it to him and laughing. A third thanked him for arranging the fine day, and he said he'd ordered it weeks ago to be on the safe side. He carried his own placard, which showed a photocopied picture of a baby floating in its bean-shaped bubble, eyes closed, arms and legs curled in on itself. *I Believe In Science* it read. *This Child Is Real*. Whoever had done the lettering had run out of room for *Real*, and at first glance it seemed to say *This Child Is Red*.

'Fresh blood,' he said when he saw me. 'Very good, very good.' He rested his hand briefly on my head as if to bless me.

Soon afterwards Mr Foster arrived on his bike. Dom's little brother on the back was screaming fit to burst, so Mrs Foster stuffed a pikelet in his mouth. 'There we are!' she said. 'Good boy! All fixed!'

'What are we doing?' I whispered to Dom. 'Where are the babies we're meant to rescue?'

'Inside the patients,' he said. 'It's the abortion clinic.'

'The what?'

'The abortion clinic?'

I shook my head.

'Sorry,' he said, closing his eyes for a moment. 'You shouldn't have come. Just . . . copy everyone else. Sorry.'

Another car pulled up – a woman with a girl only a few years older than I was. Mother and daughter, by the looks of it.

'Positions, people!' called Mr Foster.

We all linked arms, and for a moment I thought Sister Marguerite might appear to take us for folk dancing. Two of the women in our group jostled to stand next to Father Lynch. Dom's sister Sarah, who was on my left, clenched my arm tightly in hers.

The door at the front of the building opened. 'Hello again, everyone,' said a woman in a weary voice.

'Lovely day for a murder, Nurse,' said Mrs Foster.

What was she talking about? I looked at Dom, but he was picking at a splatter of dried paint on the back of his placard and wouldn't meet my gaze.

'Do you bathe your daughter with those hands?' one of the men asked the nurse. 'Little Jennifer?'

'I'm not taking the bait, Fergal,' she said. 'If you'll step aside . . .'

'Abortion stops a beating heart!' the man began to chant, and the rest of the group joined in, jabbing their placards in time with the slogan. On my right Dom was staring at the ground and repeating the words, so I did too. 'Abortion stops a beating heart! Abortion stops a beating heart!' And though I still didn't understand their meaning, there was a power in them. I felt the air around me pulsing with our voices, twenty or more against one. We were there to save babies.

I looked at the photocopied baby pasted to Father Lynch's placard. *Was* it real? How had they taken the photo?

The mother and daughter climbed out of their car.

'You don't have to do it, love,' called one of our group. 'Is she making you?'

'You're not alone. You have choices,' called another.

'We love you and your baby.'

'You're already a mother.'

Heads down, the two of them hurried towards the entrance, but the group – the human chain – wouldn't let them through.

'You're worthy of love. We value you.'

'Please,' said the girl. 'Please.'

'We have an *appointment*,' said her mother.

Behind us the nurse said, 'You know we'll just call the police again.'

'The police?' I whispered to Dom.

He blushed. 'They've only done that once before.'

'We can offer you proper counselling, love,' Mrs Foster was saying to the girl. 'So you have all the facts.'

'You should at least understand the risks,' said Mr Foster. 'You could bleed out. We've seen ambulances take patients away from here because the doctors can't stop the bleeding.'

'Or you could go into septic shock,' said Father Lynch. 'Are you willing to kill yourself as well as your baby?'

Further down the chain, the woman with the pikelets closed her eyes and said, 'It was you who created my inmost self, and put me together in my mother's womb; for all these mysteries I thank you: for the wonder of myself, for the wonder of your works.'

The mother eyed Dom's little brothers and sisters. 'You should be ashamed of yourselves, bringing children to a thing like this,' she said.

'A thing like what?' said Mr Foster. 'What's so terrible about it?'

'You're exploiting them,' she said. 'How can they possibly know what they believe at that age?'

'At least they didn't murder us,' said Sarah. 'They didn't pull us apart before we were even born.'

Marie reached for the girl's hand. 'Have they told you what actually happens?' she said. 'They yank you open and they hack your baby to pieces. Suck it out of you in bits.'

'Don't listen to them, Joanne,' said her mother. 'It's just scare tactics.'

'I can show you pictures,' said Marie. 'You can see little hands, little feet. Little heads ripped off.'

Scanning the row of people, the girl's mother caught my eye – and then she was coming straight for me. I felt Sarah grasp my arm even more tightly.

'You don't belong here, do you?' the mother said to me. 'Let us through.'

I never have been able to work out what it was about me that looked different.

Perhaps she noticed I wasn't wearing one of the little gold feet badges.

'Let us *through*.' She was shouldering her way between our interlocked arms, putting all her weight behind her.

'Sorry!' called the nurse. 'Sorry, you can't do that!'

'Oh I think I can,' said the mother, shoving at me.

'Assault! Assault!' shouted Sarah.

But I felt myself pulling away from her, my arm slipping free of her grip. The woman and her daughter rushed through the gap, and the nurse bundled them in through the doors.

'Thank you,' the girl mouthed at me as she passed.

And though I denied it later to Mrs Foster, who couldn't hide her disappointment in me, I knew the mother had not pushed me out of the way: I had stepped back.

Everyone lowered their placards, unlinked their arms. Sarah and Marie started to cry. For a few moments, no one spoke.

Then Father Lynch said, 'We'll pray for them,' and he knelt right there on the concrete, so we all knelt with him, and two of the Foster boys started crying too, and even some of the adults. We'd say the rosary together, Father told us, for the little life that would be lost, and saying it would place us in the company of Mary, whose holy name caused a blinding pain to evildoers and banished the devil along with his tricks and his tearings apart. And we'd ask for mercy for all souls, including the souls of the evildoers, because being in need of God's mercy was the greatest poverty.

I'd knelt on a sharp little stone, but I didn't dare reach down to brush it out of the way. There we stayed, repeating the Our Father, the Hail Marys, the Glory Be, while inside the house – the clinic – the nurse washed her hands and readied the instruments. And I felt the tears smart and spill down my cheeks, and at first I wasn't even sure what I was crying for, until I remembered the day we found out about Amy, when the whole school had said the rosary together. Mrs Foster looked over at me and nodded. The stone cut into my knee.

CHAPTER 29

O n Wednesday, the day before the last day of school, Dad and I went to the airport to pick up his brother for the wedding. While we waited he bought me a Fanta that turned my mouth orange, and we sat in the hard plastic seats next to the ashtrays that were filled with sand. He gave me a handful of two-cent pieces for the old flip-ball machine on the wall – Mum had never let me near the games alcove with its scrums of teenage boys – and I fed my coins in one by one, flicking the silver lever at the bottom to send the little silver ball skittering round the tracks. If it disappeared through the right hole, I turned a handle to receive my reward, which was more two-cent coins, and each time I thought I was losing I won enough to keep playing a bit longer. I flicked and turned, listening to the sound of the ball scouring the inside of the machine and dropping out of sight; I didn't want to think about the fact that in a few days we'd be back here, Dad and Mrs Price and I, catching a plane to Auckland so we could set off on the honeymoon. When they announced that Uncle Philip's flight had landed, we went to the arrivals gate and watched for him coming down the ramp. Next to us, a man held up a sign: *The Widow*.

'What do you think that means?' I whispered in Dad's ear.

He glanced at the man. 'It must be a joke, love,' he said.

Because of the slope of the ramp, you couldn't see the passengers properly until they were almost at the swinging doors:

first their feet appeared, then their legs, then their bodies, and finally their faces.

'The white sneakers?' said Dad. 'The grey business shoes?'

I couldn't tell; Uncle Philip lived in Australia, and I didn't know him very well. He'd come over one Christmas and had given me a track suit – you couldn't buy anything like that in New Zealand at the time, and I wore it till the cuffs no longer reached my wrists and ankles. He'd come over for Mum's funeral, too, and had led Dad away from the grave when all the other mourners had gone and the sextant was waiting with his shovel. 'If I leave, it'll be real,' Dad kept saying.

I recognised him as soon as he emerged through the swing doors: a slightly taller, more tanned version of Dad, with the same sandy hair and wide, curling mouth. He stood there for a moment, scanning the crowd, then saw us waving and strode over to clap Dad on the back and give me a stubbly kiss.

'God but you're like your mother,' he said. 'Ah, sorry. Sorry.'

'It's fine,' said Dad. 'There's no getting away from it.'

'Well, better that side of the family, eh?' Uncle Philip punched Dad's shoulder.

'Flight okay?'

'You could do with a few feet more of runway. Thought we were going to hoon right into the sea.'

'You get used to it.'

The man holding the strange sign was still waiting for his passenger as we walked away.

At baggage claim, Uncle Philip leaned on the trolley and said, 'So what do you reckon about all this, Justine? The wedding and everything.'

I cleared my throat. 'It's good,' I said. 'Dad's happy.'

'I can see that,' he said. 'He's like the cat that's got the mouse.'

'Cream,' said Dad.

'Cream, mouse, whatever. She's not getting away now.'

'Not a chance.'

The suitcases began to rattle past us. A grey one with scuffed corners slumped over the edge of the carousel, and Uncle Philip pushed it back into place with his foot. 'Is she good enough for him, though?' he asked me. 'Or is she only after his body?'

'Phil,' warned Dad.

'What? I'm looking out for you.' He lowered his voice. 'It's pretty fast, is all I'm saying. I just want you to be sure.'

'I'm sure.'

'Justine?'

I shrugged. 'He's sure.'

'Well, you're a braver man than I am. Once was enough for me.'

'How is Lara?'

'No idea. She refuses to speak to me when she drops the kids off. It's all, "Mandy, would you please tell your father you need new pyjamas, and don't get the flammable ones this time?" And I'm standing *right there*.'

'Sorry, mate,' said Dad.

'Yeah. My neighbour asked me out for dinner, but . . .'

'You should go! Where's the harm?'

Uncle Philip pulled a face. 'She's a bit of a dog, mate.' He pulled his suitcase off the carousel. 'There's a wombat in there for you,' he said to me. 'Wait, how old are you? Do you still like stuffed toys? Or is it all makeup and boys these days?'

'She's twelve,' said Dad. 'Thirteen next month.'

'Fasten your seatbelt then, mate.'

The crowd had thinned, and I saw the man with the widow sign waiting with his arm around a small, well-dressed woman. She wore pearl earrings and a silk blouse, and her thick grey hair was cut in an asymmetrical bob. I couldn't tell her age; she might have been his mother or sister or even his wife. As I watched, she stood on tiptoes to whisper something in his ear, and he began to nod, then darted away: they'd missed her suitcase, and he pushed past other people, trying to grab it as it sailed on out of reach. She was laughing, and when he returned to her without the case he gave her a single slap on the bottom.

After a quick bite to eat at home, we drove to the church for the wedding rehearsal. Mrs Price made her own way there, so she and Uncle Philip met for the first time in the church foyer. He went to shake her hand, but she said, 'I think we can do better than that, can't we?' and threw her arms around him.

'Steady on, Angie,' said Dad. 'You'll scare him off.'

'He doesn't seem scared,' she said, reaching up to thumb her lipstick off his cheek.

'So this is the famous Angela,' he said, standing back, look-ing her up and down and nodding his approval. 'Neil, you're one lucky man.'

'I told you so,' said Dad.

'What else has he told you?' said Mrs Price.

'Why? Is there something I should know?'

They were all smirking like they were in on some big adult joke. I don't know what I'd thought might happen when Uncle Philip arrived – that he would see right through her, perhaps; convince Dad not to marry her. But he was as charmed as everyone else.

Father Lynch appeared then and opened the doors to the main body of the church.

'Ah! My little warrior,' he said when he saw me. I hadn't told Dad about the protest at the abortion clinic; I knew he wouldn't approve. 'You've raised a good girl here, Neil,' Father went on. 'You should be very proud.'

He went to switch on the lights, and I dipped my fingers into the holy-water font to bless myself, but the sponge inside was dry.

'Warrior?' said Dad.

'Oh yes, she's quite the activist,' said Father. 'Aren't you, Justine?'

'I didn't do anything,' I murmured.

'What are you talking about?' said Dad.

'The vigil on Monday,' said Father. 'At the abortion clinic.'

'Why was my daughter at an *abortion* clinic?'

'Goodness, it's nothing like that! No, she was *outside*, with us. Protesting. Praying. Saving babies.'

'Justine?' said Dad.

'We didn't save any,' I said.

'Why am I only finding out about this now?'

'The Fosters took me.'

'Well, I think it sounds heroic,' said Mrs Price.

'We didn't save any babies,' I said again.

'Yes, but that's not the point, is it?' She was beaming at me. 'The point is, you made yourself heard. Stood up for what you believe in.'

'That's exactly right,' said Father.

'No way your dad would have done that at your age,' said Uncle Philip. 'He was such a mouse.'

'They can turn violent, those protests,' said Dad. 'I saw one on the news. The police were dragging people away.'

And I knew this was true: after we left the clinic Dom told me that one day he'd had to cling to his mother as the officers hauled her off, her heels scraping the concrete. He'd screamed at them that they were arresting the wrong people, that the murderers were inside the building, killing babies right then and there, and why couldn't they see that? It's all right, darling, his mother had called to him. They are persecuting us in His name. We are blessed. Blessed.

'Neil, I can assure you she was quite safe,' said Father. 'I give you my word. We're concerned with the welfare of children, after all, and that extends to the ones already born.'

'Do you ever change their minds?' said Uncle Philip. 'The unmarried mothers?'

'Often,' said Father. He was sounding a bit annoyed by then.

'I don't mean to be rude, but shall we get cracking?' said Mrs Price. 'It's a school day tomorrow.'

'The last one,' I said.

'Yes,' she said. 'The very last one.'

'Right then,' said Father. 'No confetti, because it's a nightmare for Mr Armstrong to clean up. No rice, ditto, but also, if the birds eat it, the grains swell in their stomachs and they die a horrible death. No flowers directly on the altar, but they can be placed around the sanctuary as long as they don't obstruct movement or present a hazard. Any pew bows must be attached with ribbons or rubber bands only, not sticky tape. Have you brought your unity candle and your offering?'

Dad took a cheque from his pocket and handed it over. 'And the candle, Angie?' he said.

'I don't have the candle,' she said.

'But that was your job. The unity candle.'

'I don't think so.'

'Is it in your bag?'

'Neil, I don't have the candle. You were supposed to bring it.'

Father laughed. 'Never mind, never mind – it's not an omen! We don't believe in those.'

'I'll bring it tomorrow,' said Mrs Price.

'Sorry,' said Dad.

'All right,' said Father, 'so Neil and Philip, the two of you arrive half an hour before the wedding and meet me in the sacristy.' He showed them the little room off to the right of the altar, where the parish ladies cleaned the candlesticks and did the flowers. 'Then the guests take their seats, and just before two o'clock the bridal party assembles in the foyer while the bridegroom and best man come out to the altar and stand here.'

'And where do I stand?' I said.

'You're part of the bridal party,' he said. 'In fact, you're the one who kicks it all off. Your father's up here with me, and the guests are waiting in the pews, and you and Angela are in the foyer. Then – lights, camera, action! The music starts, and you enter. Will you be strewing petals?'

'From our garden,' said Mrs Price, as if I couldn't answer for myself.

'Lovely, lovely,' said Father. 'Show me.'

I picked up an imaginary basket, scattered imaginary petals.

'Mm,' he said. 'I would just advise you to keep your movements small. Contained. You're feeding chickens, not throwing a frisbee, all right?'

We didn't do any work in class the next day. Sister Bronislava came and took us for singing – Christmas carols this time – and Mrs Price stayed and sang with us. The classroom was hot and close, and we could hardly sit still. Some of the boys started bawling the words to the carols: *Field and FOUNTAIN, moor and MOUNTAIN*, and *The cattle are LOWING, the BABY AWAKES*, and *Far as the CURSE is FOUND*, until Mrs Price told them that was quite enough. At the end of the hour, Sister Bronislava handed out Polish gingerbread biscuits – heart-shaped, piped with white icing. Her mother had made them for her at Christmas time when she was a girl, she said, and Jason Daly put up his hand and said, 'Won't they be a bit stale by now, Sister?'

And she strode to his desk and whipped the little heart out of his hand and ate it herself in one bite.

After lunch we went over to the church for the break-up Mass. To mark our final day at the school, Father Lynch called our class up to the altar one by one, presenting us with white vinyl Bibles and announcing which particular Fruit of the Holy Spirit each of us demonstrated: Melissa got gentleness, Jason Asofua joy, Paula faithfulness, Rachel patience. I got self-control, which everyone knew was the least desirable Fruit. Melissa smirked at me. We were to keep our Bibles with us always, Father said, and turn to them in difficult times as well as happy times, and he knew that everything we had learned at St Michael's would stand us in good stead as we followed the paths to adulthood that God had chosen for us.

I don't have my Bible any more.

Back in the classroom, we cleared out our desks and took down our artwork from the walls. The pictures seemed childish and embarrassing to us now, and we piled them into a heap for Mr Armstrong to burn. Most of us piled our exercise books there too: we would not need them again. Through the open windows we could already smell the smoke from the incinerator.

'One last thing,' said Mrs Price. 'The autographs!'

We'd been waiting for this – the chance to desecrate our uniforms. Year in, year out, we'd watched each senior class scrawl on their shirts and blouses on their last day, and finally it was our turn, and we fell on the permanent markers that Mrs Price handed out. The girls unbuttoned their tunics at the shoulders and the boys untucked their shirts, and we began to write our messages and sign our names so that we would remember one another. *Good luck*, we wrote, and *Forever friends*, and *Stay in touch*. I drew my initials in an elaborate monogram on Dom's sleeve, like a tattoo, and he wrote something on the back of my collar that I couldn't quite see but that tickled deliciously as he moved the marker. Nobody mentioned the stealing, and I could almost believe that everything was all right: every single person signed my blouse – Mrs Price was the first – and the girls were crying and hugging me and saying they'd never forget me, and I said I'd never forget them either, which was stupid because we were all going to the same high school. Then the final bell rang, and we burst out of the classroom and ran across the grounds towards our marvellous summers while Mrs Price gathered up the things we'd decided to burn.

And then, when I got home, I took off my blouse and read the messages on the back. And I knew I would never forget what they said.

I hate you Justine.
Dirty thief.
I wish you were dead.
Liar.
Why don't you kill yourself?

I screwed the thing into a ball and shoved it to the back of my wardrobe, then curled up on my bed and squeezed my eyes shut, but I could still see the messages flickering across the black of my eyelids. I could still *hear* them, just as I'd heard them at school – whispered to Amy in class, yelled at her across the adventure playground. Hissed into the stormwater pipes, the smooth concrete amplifying every word. Why hadn't I stood up for her? Why, even when I suspected Mrs Price was the thief, had I failed to defend my best friend?

No, not suspected – knew. I knew.

And then, another thought, an old thought that wouldn't leave me be: if I could just see Amy's note. She might name Melissa, Rachel, Karl, Paula and the rest of them, but surely she wouldn't name me. And that would count for something, wouldn't it? That would prove something.

I pulled on a T-shirt and shorts, transferred the ferry pen from my tunic pocket to my shorts pocket. Uncle Philip was clattering around in the kitchen. I waited in my room until I knew Amy's parents would be home from the shop, then I called out a quick goodbye to Uncle Philip and biked down the hill to her house.

The front garden was even more neglected, the lawn overgrown and full of dandelion heads. David, her little brother, answered the front door when I knocked. As soon as he saw me, he launched himself across the threshold, wrapping his arms around my waist.

'Justine! Justine! Do you want to play marbles? Do you want to play Snakes and Ladders?'

'It's nice to see you,' I said. 'How are things?'

'I hurt my leg.' He pointed to a small plaster on his shin.

'That looks sore.'

'Not really. I'll survive.'

'David?' called Mrs Fong, and then she appeared, and I wanted to run to her the way David had run to me.

'What do you want?' she said.

Dirty thief.

Liar.

Why don't you kill yourself?

Hadn't Mrs Price heard those words at school too? Wasn't she just as much to blame?

'I saw all the stolen things,' I found myself saying. 'She'd locked them away, but I saw them. She'd hidden the key behind the mirror.'

'What key? What are you talking about?'

'I'm her cleaner,' I tried again. 'Mrs Price's. There's a locked room at her house and I got inside and I saw all the things she'd stolen. So it wasn't Amy.'

I suppose I thought Mrs Fong would thank me for telling her, but all she said was, 'Of course it wasn't Amy.'

Mr Fong came to the door then too. 'Justine,' he said in a tired voice. 'You need to go home. David, come inside.'

'I found the stolen things at Mrs Price's house,' I said quickly. 'She locked them away in her spare room and then she blamed Amy. It was all her fault.'

Yes, her fault – hers.

Mr Fong was eyeing me now, his hand on the doorknob. 'Have you told anyone else?'

'I told Dom – my friend Dominic Foster. And I told Mr Chisholm.'

'Eric,' said Mrs Fong, shaking her head. 'What difference does it make?'

But Mr Fong ignored her. 'What did Mr Chisholm say?'

'He . . . he didn't believe me. And then we went round to her house, and the room was empty.'

'Empty?'

'She must have realised. I don't know. I had a seizure and my memory's a bit foggy, but I know what I saw in that room.'

'Justine, are you making this up?'

'No!'

Mr Fong tapped the doorknob for a few seconds. Then he invited me inside.

I heard them speaking to each other in Chinese as I took a seat on the couch. David turned on the TV and said, 'What do you want to watch? You can choose.' He nestled into my side and waited for me to answer, but I just sat there, frozen, trying to make out what his parents were saying, staring at the Goddess of Mercy in her white crown.

After a few moments they came and sat down with us.

'David, go and play in your room,' said Mrs Fong.

'But we were going to watch TV!'

'Later. Go and play.'

They waited for him to disappear upstairs. Then Mr Fong said, 'Amy told us she saw Mrs Price steal some tea from the shop. And we should have raised it with the school – with Mr Chisholm – but we decided not to cause trouble. We thought that would be best.'

'But she said she didn't mention it to you,' I said.

'She told us a while after it happened,' said Mrs Fong. 'You weren't really friends any more.'

I bit my lip.

'You knew about it, though?' said Mr Fong.

I wasn't sure what to say. I didn't want to confess that I hadn't believed her – hadn't wanted to believe her.

'We should have gone to Mr Chisholm then,' said Mr Fong. 'And later on, when Amy told us it was more than just the jar of tea, we should have gone to the police. She begged us to. But we thought if she could just see out the year without making waves . . .' His voice started to break.

'I'm sorry, I'm so sorry,' I said. 'I miss her. I wish I could undo it all. I miss her.' I covered my face with my hands, and Mrs Fong rubbed my back. 'Do you think . . .' I said. 'Do you think I could see her note?'

Mrs Fong sighed, and I felt her breath on my cheek. 'All right,' she said.

The two of them went upstairs to fetch it; I could hear them moving around above me, their footfalls setting the chandelier shivering. In the corner of the room the black lacquered chest with all the little drawers glistened as if wet. I squinted at the Chinese characters, tried to decipher their meaning. A mountain? A house? Windows? Water? And I had the strangest thought: that Amy was in there, that her body was in there, and if I opened a drawer at the top I might see the black spill of her hair, and if I opened a drawer in the middle I might see a white hand. And then I was crossing the room and grasping one of the thin brass handles – it was smooth as a coin, cool as a fish – and I peered inside and saw nothing, nothing. I opened another drawer, and another, but every single one was empty. And here came Mr and Mrs Fong, their slippered feet thudding softly on the stairs, and I leapt back to the couch and sat there innocent as you please.

Mr Fong held the note out to me with both hands. White paper, ruled with thin blue lines and a red margin: part of a page from a school exercise book. I took it and unfolded it, and there was Amy's printing, neat and small:

Dear Mum and Dad, I am sorry to be leaving you in this way. I know you will be sad but it is my only choice. Remember me.

'Is that all?' I said, turning the paper over, and even as I spoke I knew something was wrong. I felt it in the soles of my feet, cold and tight, and it crept up my body and lodged in my chest. I recognised those words. And they weren't Amy's: they were mine.

'That's all,' said Mr Fong. 'We've read it so many times, but we still don't understand.'

The writing started to tremble then, and it took me a moment to realise my hands were shaking. I refolded the note along its creases and placed it on the coffee table, but it wouldn't stay folded: the paper moved of its own accord, opening itself again, showing itself, until it lay like a white leaf fallen from a white tree. I remembered Father Lynch showing us the film about the man in Chile who dressed as a clown and printed forbidden leaflets – the brave Catholic they'd thrown in prison, who sang his song even though he knew they'd shoot him. I remembered the firing squad, the blood-stained wall. The buckling body. The other prisoners singing for their dead friend. And I remembered Mrs Price asking us to write a letter in our Religion books – a note from the man to his family, saying goodbye.

'It was on Bonnie's collar,' I said.

'Yes, tied to her collar,' said Mr Fong.

Amy looking over at my book to see what to write. Asking me: *Now what?* Then copying me word for word.

I couldn't make sense of it. How had that note, written in class, ended up on Bonnie's collar the day Amy killed herself? Why on earth would she use it in that way?

Except she hadn't.

'Do you still have her school books?' I said. 'Her exercise books?'

'You brought them round yourself,' said Mr Fong.

'Could I see them? Just . . . just to remember.' I couldn't say what I was thinking. I could barely even think it.

Mr Fong disappeared upstairs again. Mrs Fong stared into the middle distance and then, almost as if to herself, said, 'It's the wedding on Saturday, isn't it.'

'Yes,' I said. 'The day after tomorrow.'

'Your father's happy.'

'Very happy.'

'And you?'

But Mr Fong had returned with the exercise books. He placed them on my lap, and I ran my index finger over their scuffed spines: one, two, three, four, five. I leafed through the Language and Reading book, the Social Studies book, the Maths book, the Science book, stopping every few pages and pretending I'd seen something of interest – until finally I allowed myself to open the Religion book. I knew Father had shown us the film in autumn; I remembered Amy losing her woollen gloves that same day, and Mrs Price lining us up in the chilly corridor to check our bags for them. But when I searched the pages from that time of year I found nothing at all about the film, or about Chile or executions or the three reasons we were lucky to live in New Zealand. Someone had pulled out the whole page, along with the corresponding blank one in the second half of the book. Ripped them clean away from the staples, as if they'd never been there in the first place. Only they had – and I could prove it.

'Thank you,' I said, closing the book, keeping my voice calm, my breathing calm. This was no time for a seizure.

David came running down the stairs as I was leaving.

'Mum, can Justine stay for dinner?' he said, grabbing at the back of my T-shirt.

'I have to go now,' I said, but he was still hanging on, following me to the front door.

'She has to go now,' said Mrs Fong.

'I'll come and see you again,' I said over my shoulder.

'Why?' she said.

I walked down their front steps, wheeled my bike to the end of their driveway. Turned and waved to David, who was seeing me off as if we were friends. Then, when I was out of sight, I jumped on my bike and headed for the school, pedalling as fast as I could.

CHAPTER 30

The Corvette was still in the carpark when I arrived. I slotted my bike into the bike stand without bothering to lock it, then darted past the classroom window, catching a glimpse of Mrs Price carrying a pile of textbooks to the stationery cupboard. I didn't think she'd seen me, but I kept close to the wall. Over by Mr Armstrong's shed, the incinerator blazed, and as I drew nearer the smoke began to sting my eyes and the fire flung its heat against my skin. And there he was, his arms full of papers, and I called to him and ran to stop him before he could throw them into the flames.

'Justine?' he said. 'What's the matter, love?'

'Are those from our class?'

He peered at them. 'Could be. Did you change your mind about something?' He set the papers down and said, 'Help yourself.'

I rummaged through them, shoving aside old cyclostyled tests and photocopies of photocopies, handprints of paint that made hedgehogs and peacocks, drawings of Jesus feeding the five thousand, dead fish piled up at his feet. Nothing I recognised.

'I wanted one of my exercise books back,' I said. I glanced over at the school building. Was that a movement, a shadow, in my classroom window?

'You're welcome to look in the shed,' he said. 'I think Mrs Price did bring over some exercise books, in among all the other stuff.'

I followed him inside and waited for my eyes to adjust to the gloom. It was boiling hot under the low iron roof.

'Let's see . . .' he said, checking the piles of papers. 'No, not those . . . not those . . .'

I looked too, and I knew it was getting late and Dad would wonder where I was, and I knew he wanted to take us all out for dinner that night, Uncle Philip and Mrs Price and me, though I couldn't imagine sitting down to eat with her. Watching her rest her arm around my father's shoulders, caress the small of his back. Then I saw something familiar poking out from underneath a concertina of computer paper. I snatched up the stack of wallpaper-covered exercise books, and yes, there was my Religion book, looking like a remnant of my bedroom. And there, about a third of the way through, the note I'd written:

Dear Mum and Dad, I am sorry to be leaving you in this way. I know you will be sad but it is my only choice. Remember me.

In Mr Armstrong's hot little shed I felt cold as the sea.

'Found it?' he said.

I nodded. Breathed in, breathed out. No time for a seizure.

And then Mrs Price was at the door.

'Justine?' she said. 'What are you doing here so late?'

She'd already seen the book – there was no point trying to hide it – and I could tell she'd seen my face, too. My eyes huge with fright.

'I wanted a souvenir,' I said. 'I'd better get home.'

'I'll give you a lift. You'll be late for dinner.'

'My bike's here.'

She looked at her watch. 'You should get going, then. I'll walk you over.'

Mr Armstrong started to sing to himself as we left – a song I knew from our sessions with Sister Bronislava: *Come now, lively lads and lasses, let us all a-dancing go . . .* I don't know why that has stayed with me. He dumped another armful of papers in the incinerator, and the flames flattened for a moment, then flared back higher and hotter than ever.

'Which one did you choose?' said Mrs Price, gesturing towards the exercise book I was holding close.

'Religion.'

'Why Religion?'

We had entered the adventure playground by now, and the climbing rope cast its long snaky shadow across our path, and the tractor tyres and wooden spools were gigantic, and the mouth of the stormwater pipes opened like a cave. In the distance the late sun filled the walnut tree with bright green light. Beyond that, the carpark and my bike, so far away.

'Why Religion?' she said again. Her voice pleasant, relaxed.

Somewhere behind us, Mr Armstrong kept singing: *Parted hands that once were linking, as each sweetheart says goodbye . . .*

I shrugged. 'It was on top of the pile.' I willed my legs to keep moving, my lungs to keep taking in air.

'Let's see,' she said, lifting the book from my hands.

Perhaps she wouldn't notice. Perhaps she'd skip right past that day's page.

She flicked through my notes on 'How God Calls Us to Serve' and 'Living by the light'; my drawings of Symbols Used by Jesus: keys, lambs, a rock. The hymns we committed to memory, the prayers: *Dear God, please help me to be like your disciples and leave all my possessions to follow you.*

Then she stopped.

And her expression shifted.

And when she looked at me, I knew she'd realised something she hadn't known before: Amy had copied her note from mine.

I grabbed the book and ran for my bike, but she ran after me, her footsteps shaking the tractor tyres, the spools, the rope, the shining walnut tree, so I doubled back, heading for Mr Armstrong's shed. I'd tell him what she'd done, and he'd protect me, he'd have to protect me . . . except I couldn't see him any more, and when I tried to shout to him my breath sputtered in my throat. I changed direction again, sprinting past the classrooms, searching for any sign someone might still be inside – but all the windows were shut, the glass reflecting only the sky back at me.

And she was getting closer.

With nowhere else to go, I dived into the stormwater pipes and squirmed along the smooth concrete floor until I sat in the very middle, trying to catch my breath. Even if she crawled in after me, I'd see her coming and kick her away, then shoot out the other end. I strained my ears but heard nothing. No whistling. Not a single footstep.

Then a soft voice: 'Justine, what's the matter? Hmm?'

I hugged the exercise book to my chest and drew up my knees. Breathed in the powdery smell of the concrete.

'I'm not sure why you're so upset, my darling. Why don't you come out so we can talk about it?'

Her voice seemed to be closer to the walnut-tree end of the pipes, so I began to inch towards the other end. Far off I could see Mr Armstrong's shed, the incinerator a rusty dot now, the flames dying away.

'This is so silly, Justine. We're friends, aren't we? We're *family*.'

About a metre from the opening I turned so my legs would emerge first. Where was she now? I pushed my feet out, quietly, quietly – and she snatched at me, wrapping her fingers around my ankle. I kicked as hard as I could, my free foot slamming into her chest. Her grip loosened and I scuttled back inside the pipes, but she came after me, crawling along on all fours.

'I just want to talk to you,' she said, grabbing hold of my wrist. 'Can we talk? Please?'

'You cut the note out of Amy's book,' I said. 'You tied it to Bonnie's collar.'

Her fingers were digging into my bones. 'Darling, calm down. Why would I do something like that?'

'Amy knew you were stealing. She saw you take the jasmine tea from their shop.'

'Oh my goodness, not the jasmine tea again!'

'And you saw her in the shop mirror and knew she'd tell someone. You knew you'd be caught and it would all come out – the things of ours you'd been stealing for months. The way you turned us against one another. When did you remember those stupid notes we had to write?'

'Justine, listen—'

'I bet you were so pleased with yourself when you thought of the notes. When you checked Amy's and knew you could use it – just pull out the whole page, and nobody would notice. But you didn't check mine. You didn't know she'd copied off me.'

'We'll go back to Dr Kothari,' she said. 'We'll ask him to review your medication, yes?'

I tried to wrench my wrist free, but she was too strong. 'You knew where she walked her dog,' I said. 'You pushed her off the cliffs. Made it look like she'd killed herself.' I waited for her to deny it.

She held my gaze for a second, and something changed in her face. 'Oh, sweetheart. I knew you didn't remember.'

'Remember what?'

'You went up there that day. You wanted some fresh air, your father told me.'

'Yes, but I had a seizure.'

'I saw you, my darling – when I was out for a run. You and Amy, arguing on the track, quite a distance from me. You stormed towards the edge, where you knew she'd never go otherwise, and of course she followed. You grabbed her plait – yanked it hard. Then you pushed her.'

'What?'

'You pushed her.'

'I think I'd remember that.'

'You had the seizure as soon as you'd done it. And you know how foggy you get.'

'You're crazy.' As I tried again to wrench my wrist free, she pinned it to the concrete. I'd dropped the book, but she wasn't interested in that now. I started to shove against her shoulder with all my might.

'You'd fallen out with her,' she went on. 'You hated her.'

'She was my best friend!'

'It didn't look that way.' She shifted her weight so she loomed above me, the tiny gold crucifix swinging free. 'You knew she was going to accuse me of stealing. You knew that, and you wanted to protect me.'

The scent of her perfume hung all around me, too sweet, too close. 'Let me go. Let me *go*.'

She gave a sad little smile. 'I sent you home, then caught the dog and took her back to my car. After that I drove to St Michael's to copy Amy's handwriting – to write a note. That's when I found the one in her Religion book. I did it for you, my darling – to protect you, just as you'd protected me. Because you were always my favourite. My pet.'

I started to scream for help but managed only a single cry before she knocked my head against the wall. I slumped sideways, and then she was on top of me, and no matter how hard I kicked and writhed I could not free myself.

'Stop it,' she hissed. She fixed her hands around my throat and squeezed hard, and my blood jammed up against her grip and my eyes turned hot in their sockets. I could see myself reflected in her pupils, a tiny squirming doll, an insect, a nothing, and above her the roof of the pipe, as smooth and cool as the inside of a shell, and surely I could hear the ocean rushing, and surely it would rush into the pipes and wash us both away. In the distance, someone was singing: *Breathless now, the dancers sighing, back and forth they ebb and flow . . .* I tried to force my fingertips under her hands to prise them away, drove my nails into the fleshy edges of her palms. Scratched at her as hard as I could. Nothing worked. 'Stop it, stop it,' she hissed again. Her breath filled my face, took up all the air, and I let go of her clamped hands and scrabbled around for something, anything I could use against her, but found only the gloss of the concrete. Jesus, help me. Mother Mary, help me. St Michael, help me, help me. Still the tune threaded in through the mouth of the pipes, perhaps just an echo now, a memory conjured by the fading brain. Stop it. Stop it. She tightened her grip, and the black started to creep in from the edges of my vision.

I tried to move, but I was heavy as concrete, I was vanishing into concrete, and where was my father? Where was my mother? Black sky, black water. Amy calling my name, and someone singing . . . and something hard pressing into the crease of my thigh like a strange bone. I rammed my fingers into my pocket, working them between Mrs Price's body and my own, prising us apart millimetre by millimetre. *Breathless now, the dancers sighing* . . . And finally, wedged into the seam, the ferry pen. I dragged it free and gripped it like a spear in my fist, and then with all my strength I thrust it straight up, deep into her eye. Deep into my own tiny reflection. She cried out and let go of me, rearing up, grasping for the pen, and with an open palm I slammed it further in, and she thudded back hard onto the concrete. I heard the sick sound of her skull cracking, and then she lay still. Her good eye stared at me, and blood began to pool around her head, black in the gloom of the pipes, creeping towards my hip. Inside the pen the little white ship sailed down and down, over the waves and into the dark Sounds, until it disappeared inside Mrs Price's eye.

My throat throbbed with the memory of her hands, and I swallowed a few times, drank in as much air as I could. I knew she was dead, and I started to cry – for her, for Amy, for my father. For myself. She was dead, dead, no question. The small hard space sent my every sob ringing and ricocheting back to me, and I held myself and rocked myself and she was dead.

Then, at the end of the pipes, a black shape. A raven, a crow, alighting in the walnut tree. A black swan beating her wings.

'Are you all right?' she said, and she crawled into the pipes, and her voice was Sister Bronislava's voice. 'Justine? What has happened?'

I sat back so she could see Mrs Price, and she drew in a sharp breath, then leaned across me to feel for a pulse. Her rosary beads clattered against the pipe. A silent moment passed.

I started to sob again, and she said, 'Come away. Come out of here.' When I didn't move, she wrapped her arms around me and held me to her black breast. 'Oh my child,' she said. 'Oh my child. Don't look.'

The ambulance came, though she was already dead. They checked me over too, assessing the bump on the back of my head, the red marks around my neck. The blood under my nails. A man held up a finger, and I followed it with my eyes. I knew my name, though I could hardly speak it, and I knew where I was. Straight after that, the police came.

They moved me away to the walnut tree, and one of them stood with me while they cordoned off the scene. I wasn't obliged to say anything unless I wished to do so, he told me, and anything I did say would be written down and might be given in evidence. I looked up into the branches at the walnuts swelling in their cool green husks. The ambulance officers had left their bags by the pipes and weren't allowed back in to retrieve them. I couldn't understand why, because the bags were sitting right there. Then a policewoman arrived to take me to the station, and as we were pulling away a man with a massive camera climbed from a car. I saw the police shaking their heads at him, holding up their hands: *Back. Stay back.* On the way into town we passed a girl walking a spaniel, a girl with black hair pulled into a plait, but as I peered out the back window she turned her face away. The policewoman kept trying to chat to me.

Uncle Philip was waiting at the station, and they told me he would be my support person.

'Where's Dad?' I said.

'You can catch up with him a bit later, love,' said Uncle Philip.

I heard Dad shouting then: 'I need to see my daughter! She's my *daughter*! I need to make sure she's all right!'

But the detective took me into a small stuffy room and sat me down. It can't have been much more than two metres wide, and the only window was in the door; he covered it up with paper. Perhaps he wanted to stop Dad from finding me; I wasn't sure. He brought in a chair for Uncle Philip, and one for the policewoman who smiled at me and asked if I'd like a can of Coke or maybe a pie. I shook my head.

'Mr Crieve,' said the detective, 'would you go over the caution with Justine, and make sure she understands it please?'

I turned to see if Dad was joining us after all, but Mr Crieve was Uncle Philip, and he said, 'Do you understand that you don't have to say anything?'

'Yes,' I said.

'And do you understand that what you do say will be written down, and might be used in court?'

'Yes,' I said.

'Though it's very unlikely this will go to court,' he added. 'Because you've done nothing wrong.' He gestured to the marks on my neck.

Then the detective started to ask me questions, pausing after each answer to jab at the keys of a typewriter. I could smell ink, hot vinyl chairs, carbon paper.

'What time did you wake up today, Justine?' he said.

'Around seven,' I said. 'The same as usual.'

'What did you have for breakfast?'

'Toast with strawberry jam, and a bowl of cornflakes. Oh, with milk.' I glanced at my Uncle Philip, who nodded at me. These were the right answers; I was telling the truth.

'What time did Dad leave for work?'

'At 8.15.'

'And what time did you leave for school?'

'The same time.'

On he went, establishing the course of my day – the final Mass, the signing of my blouse, Mr Fong handing me Amy's note. Every single step. The bike-ride to the playground. Mr Armstrong's shed. Mrs Price at the door. The bit in my Religion book that was exactly the same as Amy's note. Closer and closer we moved to the pipes and then we were inside them and he was asking me what she said, exactly what she said.

'That I was always her favourite. Her pet,' I said.

He typed that.

'And then she said I pushed Amy off the cliff.'

He began to type, then paused. 'You pushed her? Or she did?'

'She said she did.'

He typed what I said. I had the feeling that my body was answering, my mouth forming the responses to his questions – *because she knew I'd found out about the note; because she knew I was going to tell on her* – but my eyes were somewhere else: up by the ceiling with its tiles full of holes, looking down at a robot that resembled me.

'Good girl, good girl,' said Uncle Philip.

I did not know whether to believe him. My voice was beginning to fail me. Pressure on my throat. The windowless room too small and my uncle both like Dad and not Dad, and pale beside me, his tan somehow vanished.

'How about that Coke?' said the female officer.

While she fetched it the detective told me I was doing really well, and was my throat feeling okay? Could I still talk? Then he opened the Coke for me because my hands wouldn't stop shaking.

On we went, and my robot voice kept answering, and the silvery arms of the typewriter kept shooting out and hitting the paper and the carbon paper, recording my story three times over, a little fainter each time.

When we'd finished the detective gave me the typed page to check and sign, and the words were my answers and also not quite what I'd said. *I woke up around seven today, the same time as usual. I had toast with strawberry jam for breakfast, and a bowl of cornflakes with milk . . .* A photographer took pictures of my injuries, and they gave me a white suit to put on – they needed my clothes, they said, and Uncle Philip hadn't thought to bring me any fresh ones, and only then did I notice the blood all over the hip of my shorts, the splatters on my T-shirt. The policewoman stayed with me, and as I removed each item she dropped it into its own plastic bag, separating even my socks. After that someone who said she was a doctor examined me, and she made note of my injuries too, her face expressionless as she took in the bruises at my throat. She scraped under my fingernails and saved what she found, which looked like tiny curled grubs. The suit felt papery and was far too big – a suit for an adult, not a child. I thought I might disappear inside it.

When Dad arrived I couldn't meet his eye, but he gathered me up in his arms and said he was sorry, he was so so sorry.

The story was all over the news, of course, but I was never named. I had to speak to the police twice more, just so they had all the details, they said. Just so they didn't miss anything. They assured me – almost everyone assured me – that it wasn't my fault, I wasn't to blame, and did I understand that? Yes, I said, I understood, because I could see that was the answer they wanted. At home, Dad nodded when Uncle Philip told him what a brave daughter he had. 'I'm very proud of her,' he said. Several times.

Then one Sunday afternoon, without warning, Mr Chisholm and Father Lynch showed up at the house.

'I thought we might have seen you at Mass,' said Father.

'We're keeping to ourselves,' said Dad. 'You can understand.'

'Oh naturally, naturally,' they said.

'So long as you know you're still part of the parish,' said Father.

Dad nodded. 'Yes, thank you.'

'No judgement on our part,' said Father.

'Well, why would there be?'

Father smiled a confused smile. 'As I said, there isn't any.'

'Not our place to judge,' added Mr Chisholm.

'No,' said Dad, and paused. 'You know, she did tell you. Justine did tell you what was going on.'

'It's deeply unfortunate,' said Mr Chisholm. 'The individual concerned was clearly very skilled at hiding her true nature. From everyone.' He rested his eyes on Dad.

'At any rate,' said Father, 'the most important thing is that we put it all behind us. Now is the time for healing. Not for negative publicity.'

Soon after that, Dom told me, the school uprooted the pipes and concreted over the spot, but someone scratched *AP was here* in the wet concrete so they had to do it again. A few of the fathers stood guard while it set overnight – they'd organised a roster, just like cops, and they talked about it like cops too. Someone produced a set of walkie talkies, and they hitched these on their belts, patrolling the perimeter, flashing their torches at hedgehogs and possums. Then, when the concrete had hardened, they painted hopscotch squares on it.

Mrs Knight brought casseroles and soufflés and kept asking me and Dad, 'But how are you *really*?' Melissa came with her the first time, but she didn't speak to me, couldn't look at me; she hung back beside the fridge and twisted her sapphire earrings. No more sitting in her spa pool, then. No more dressing and undressing her Cabbage Patch doll. We haven't kept in touch.

Selena, Rachel and Paula visited one day, too; I heard them giggling on the doorstep before they pressed the bell. 'Mum said I had to come and say sorry,' said Paula. 'So, yeah, sorry.'

'Okay,' I said.

'Um, are you going on holiday this year?' said Rachel.

'What?'

'I don't know. Mum said I should chat normally, like a normal person.'

'Right.'

'Well, are you? Going on holiday?'

'*God*, Rachel,' said Selena, and then, shooting me an apologetic smile, 'I told her not to be embarrassing.'

'We're not going on holiday,' I said.

'We're off to Rotorua,' said Paula. 'The hot pools cook you alive if you fall in.'

I nodded. For a moment no one spoke.

'Are you, like, going out with Dominic Foster?' said Rachel. The others burst into giggles again.

'He's my friend,' I said.

'Melissa and Karl broke up,' said Selena. 'It turns out he doesn't even like horses.'

We fell silent again. Paula elbowed Rachel in the side. Rachel elbowed her back. 'Go on,' hissed Selena.

Rachel cleared her throat. 'Have you been to confession?' she said.

'What for?' I said.

'Well, I mean,' she said, looking at Paula and Selena and then back at me, 'you killed someone.'

'And we were wondering what the penance would be for something like that,' said Paula.

They were staring at me, mouths ajar, waiting for my answer. 'Dad,' I called. 'Dad!'

He came running.

From the living-room window I watched the girls head back down the driveway. They jostled one another, laughing, shrieking. Just before they disappeared from view, Rachel snatched up a stick and pretended to ram it into Selena's eye.

For weeks I found things belonging to Mrs Price in our house – lipsticks and tampons, deodorant, a coffee mug with a polar bear on it, a hair band snarled with a few blond strands. Bits and pieces of jewellery. Once, when I had to eat the last of the dusty rice bubbles for breakfast because I'd finished the cornflakes, a note in her handwriting tipped into my bowl: *You are my snap, crackle and pop xxx*. At first I thought she'd written it to me, but then I realised it must have been for Dad. I threw it in the rubbish along with everything else – though I kept my pink bikini, hiding it at the bottom of a drawer and only ever trying it on when I was alone. When I was alone, too, I checked our house with the black light, searching for the remains of my mother's invisible ink. I found almost nothing – just a few scattered fragments in the darkest corners of the armoire: *Going twice, petals of, more bids, my darling*.

One hot morning Dom came round with his albums of coins, and we lay on our stomachs at the bottom of the garden and slipped the shillings and kroner and centimes out of their protective pockets. Imagine, he said as we studied their strange designs: people overseas use these every day without even thinking about it. I rubbed the soft corners of a hexagonal two-franc piece from the Belgian Congo. My hands smelled like keys. If I ever came across a coin with a mistake on it, said Dom, I should keep it in a very safe place. Error coins were worth lots of money – sometimes hundreds of thousands. There was a John F. Kennedy error coin – a half-dollar that showed the top of his head all mangled. Which was pretty weird, considering.

I told no one what Mrs Price had said that day in the pipes: that I had pushed Amy. That we had argued, that Amy had followed me to the edge. That I didn't remember it because of the seizure, but that she had seen me do it. I allowed the cliffs to take shape in me, the wild sky, the gulls, the scent of fennel and brine and the great fleshy spreads of kelp that moved beneath the surface of the water. Amy threatening to tell on Mrs Price, to ruin everything: *She's a thief and a liar and you know it*. My own voice shouting into the wind: *You better leave her alone. You better back off.* My hands yanking her black plait. My hands at her back, her shoulderblades like bumps of driftwood, her spine like little stones. Bonnie running about in the wind, whining, snuffling at my fingers. I didn't remember any of that, I reminded myself, because it never happened. It never happened.

At home, Dad and I rarely discussed the matter. What was done was done, he told me, and we couldn't change it – but sometimes I thought I saw him staring at my hands with a queasy look on his face. He wouldn't let me cook for him: 'Let me do it,' he insisted. I worried that he might start drinking again, but he refused to touch a drop; he said he wanted to remain in control of himself at all times.

One evening, long after I was supposed to be asleep, I heard him talking to Uncle Philip on the phone. 'Why didn't I see it?' he said. 'It was right in front of me. In my own house.' Whatever comfort his brother offered him made him scoff. 'Can I say that I *miss* her?' he asked in an angry whisper. 'Am I allowed to admit to that?'

He pored over the death notices as usual, circling those of elderly people who might have owned antique snuff boxes and scent bottles, occasional tables and claret jugs, but he never made contact with their families. In January he hung *SALE!*

notices in the front window of Passing Time – notices that looked like bombs, like fire – and he let things go for next to nothing. When I asked if I could help out at the shop he said no, I should stay at home, because people knew who we were, and he didn't want them coming in to gawk at me.

'Please?' I said. 'I'll stay out the back.' In truth, I didn't want to be by myself in the house, where every creak and rustle made me catch my breath, search the shadows for someone who wasn't there.

'All right,' he said at last. 'But you can't show yourself. I mean it.'

I scanned his face. 'Dad,' I said, 'are you ashamed of me?'

'Don't be ridiculous.'

'Are you?'

'Listen,' he said, catching at my hand. 'No, listen. Angela is the only person who should be ashamed. Except she's not here to pay for everything she did.'

After that, he never spoke her name again.

From the back room of the shop I heard a woman ask him what he had in the way of fob chains, sovereign cases, curb-link bracelets. 'Anything of that nature,' she said.

'Are you after a gift?' said Dad. 'Or something for yourself?' A click as he unlocked the jewellery cabinet underneath the counter.

'Just interested to see what you have,' she said.

'Well, there's this – hallmarked Birmingham 1882. A lovely weight to it. And we have a double sovereign case in rose gold, which is quite a rare find – Edwardian, so a bit newer. Or a guard chain, perhaps? This one drapes beautifully around the neck – you can wear it doubled or even tripled. Sweet little repoussé vesta case, if that's your sort of thing – London 1861. Then there's . . .'

'How much for the lot?' she said.

'Excuse me?'

'I'll give you twelve hundred for the whole cabinet.'

'There must be over thirty pieces in there.'

'Well, take it or leave it.'

A pause. 'All right.'

After she'd gone I came out to the counter. 'What are you doing, Dad?' I said.

'It has to go. All of it.' He swept his hand through the air, clearing the shop.

'But that was practically criminal.'

'Highway robbery,' he agreed.

Still, he kept on accepting whatever outrageous offers people made, and soon the place was all but empty of stock. Just a couple of pewter mugs. A candle-snuffer. A chamber pot. A trench-art ashtray made from a shell casing. A daguerreotype of a dead baby laid out in its christening gown.

On one of the last days I heard a woman ask if he still had a Victorian biscuit barrel – one with pink roses and a silver lid, she said.

'I know the piece,' said Dad. 'It does have a chip on the base.'

'That's right,' she said. 'My father knocked it against a tap.'

I peered through the door to see her: a young mother, jiggling the handle of a pram.

'It was yours?' said Dad.

'My mother got rid of everything after he went. I thought I'd better grab it before you close down.' She checked the price tag. 'That's a bit steep,' she said. 'Considering the chip.'

'I'm open to offers,' said Dad.

'Twenty-five?'

He gave a tight little laugh. 'Just take it.'

I must have moved, I suppose, or made a noise, because she looked up then and saw me. Shifted the pram to behind her back. 'Do you keep reliving it?' she asked me. 'I don't know how you could ever forget something like that.'

'I think you'd better leave,' said Dad.

She looked surprised. 'Well, excuse *me*. It was a genuine question.'

'All the same.'

'Okay,' she said, pushing the biscuit barrel towards him, 'but can I get a bit of tissue paper round it?'

When *The Love Boat* started again, Dad and I couldn't get past the opening credits. In my peripheral vision I could sense him shifting uncomfortably on the couch, glancing over at me as Captain Stubing smiled and smiled next to the lifeboats. 'Shall we change channels?' he said.

We moved to Auckland towards the end of summer, and I started at a high school where nobody knew who I was. I pretended I'd gone to a different primary school in Wellington, and that we'd lived in a different part of town; for a while I was nervous that someone would have a cousin at my pretend school or an aunt near my pretend house and would ask me impossible questions, but I seemed to get away with it. When I wrote to Dom I told him about school camp, where a girl had broken her wrist abseiling and then the rest of us weren't allowed to try it, and he wrote back to me about his cat Rice, who brought him a dead sparrow, yowling as she laid it gently inside his shoe – but he loved her anyway, and would always love her. We debated whether Cheezels tasted better than Twisties, and whether the doubloon in *The Goonies* could be real, and he sent me pencil rubbings of his latest coins, which I pinned above my bed: the pale currency of some ghost country. And at night, next to my bed, I kept the Victorian penny the colour of his freckles, the queen all but rubbed away. I was allowed to ring him a few times in those first months, though toll calls cost an arm and a leg. Once, when he answered the phone after his voice had broken, I thought I was talking to his father. 'It's *me*,' he insisted, but I didn't believe him until he said, 'We watched her that day through the ice, remember?'

Once a week I saw a counsellor, who told me I needed to forgive myself.

'That makes it sound like it's my fault,' I said.

'Do you think it's your fault?' She was good at turning the tables like that.

'No,' I said. I couldn't meet her eye.

'This doesn't have to define you, Justine,' she said.

'No,' I said.

'Are you agreeing or disagreeing with me?'

'Mm,' I said.

Plenty of single women and some married ones approached Dad – at the supermarket, the beach, school prizegiving, my netball games. I knew what flirting looked like by then, understood those sidelong glances women make, the sly half-smiles, the brushes of the hand. While Dad was friendly enough, he made it clear he wasn't looking. He found a job with a furniture restorer and spent all his time out in the workshop where he didn't have to talk to people. When he came home smelling of linseed oil and turpentine he asked me about my day, and I told him the French phrases I was learning. *What time is it?* and *How much is this?* and *I love you.*

'We'll go there, eh?' he said. 'You and me. We'll eat snails and wear berets. Or eat berets and wear snails.'

He tried his best to make light.

We never went to France.

It wasn't until years later, when Dad started to lose his memory, in fact, that we broached it. I had just dropped him home from the shops, and he asked if I'd come in for a cup of tea. I was due back at work but could probably stretch my lunch break out a bit longer. Make something up. 'I'll get it,' I said, plugging in the kettle and trying not to imagine all sorts of accidents with boiling water, all sorts of terrible burns. He was no longer safe on his own; we both knew it.

We sat on the blue-and-white couch, and he stared into the blank TV screen.

'We've never really talked about her,' he said. 'Have we.'

I had just taken my first sip of tea, and it was far too hot, but I swallowed it down. 'No,' I said, because I knew he didn't mean Emma or my mother or anyone else.

'I wanted to tell you that I—' he began. 'Before everything goes. Before I forget it all. I wanted to tell you that I'm sorry.'

'You don't have to say that, Dad.'

'Yes I do. I brought her into our home.'

'But I introduced you,' I said. 'At the shop, remember?'

'She admired a Victorian lustre vase. Her grandmother called them earthquake vases because you could see the crystal drops trembling even if you couldn't feel anything.'

'So she did.'

'I should have seen it, Justine. You were a child. And because of me, my need for, for companionship, for love . . . I let that monster in the door.'

'Dad, she fooled everyone,' I said.

Just about everyone.

'You know,' he went on, 'part of me welcomes the prospect of forgetting.'

I nodded, blew on my tea. Tried another sip. Cooler now. 'Did she ever say anything odd to you about Amy?' I asked. 'About her death?'

At first he looked at me as if he didn't remember Amy at all. Then he said, 'What do you mean, odd?'

'When we were in the pipes,' I said, studying his face, 'she came out with all kinds of nonsense about me. About how Amy died.'

'No,' he said quickly. 'Nothing.'

'No strange theories?'

'She said nothing to me.' He paused. 'And who could trust her, anyway?'

I've never asked him again.

And yet.

I am arguing with Amy. The wind snatches at our clothes, our hair. The wild fennel shakes its scent across our path. *You're jealous of me. You've always been jealous. You're going to ruin everything, do you know that?* Bonnie waits for us to play with her, whines for a stick, a ball, but I'm leaving the track, I'm running for the edge of the cliff, though I can feel the wind shoving me back. Then Amy is beside me and she is shouting *Why can't you see?* And I scream and scream and I hate her, and the hate is a stone in my throat and my heart is full of fire like the heart of Mary, and something is burning, something has burned, sweet and brittle and gone, gone. And the waves shatter into nothing, and beneath the water the kelp moves its dark limbs. My hands close around Amy's plait and yank, hard, and I feel the tug at the roots, the give in the scalp. Then, under my fingers, the bumps of her back. Gulls high above, crying and crying. A step, a shove. A stone, falling.

I imagine it so vividly it feels like a memory.

2014

CHAPTER 31

Dad's memory loss seems to accelerate in the months following my first seeing Sonia at the retirement community; we have fewer and fewer good days. The staff still encourage him to take part in the group activities, shepherding him down to the big pastel lounge with its TV playing videos of André Rieu, and its potted palms which I suspect are fake. He no longer speaks up in the weekly Curious Questions quiz; I sit with him and try to hold his hand as one of the caregivers reads from a fat book of trivia called *Did You Know . . . ?*

'The wedding of which member of the royal family was the first to be televised?' she asks, looking around the room.

Dead silence.

'The first royal wedding to be televised?' she says. 'Whose was that? No?'

A woman in brown knee-high stockings nudges Dad and whispers, 'What's she saying?'

'Princess Margaret,' says the caregiver. 'Nineteen sixty. Okay, next question: what is the Italian for pie? The Italian for pie?'

'Risotto,' says a man down the back.

'Not risotto,' says the caregiver. 'The Italian for pie is . . .' She pauses, as if someone might still chime in with the correct answer. 'Pizza! It's pizza. Moving on. What are the three Baltic states?'

'I can't understand her,' says the woman in the knee-high stockings. 'We can't understand you!'

'The three Baltic states?' the caregiver repeats, her voice bright. 'How about just one of them?'

Another woman looks up from her Sudoku and says, 'We live in New Zealand, not *Europe*.'

'Lithuania, Latvia and Estonia,' says the caregiver, flicking through her book.

'We do live in New Zealand,' says Dad.

'Okay, the elderly are more at risk of being deficient in which vitamin?'

No one knows. No one answers.

'Vitamin D. We need our sunshine! Our garden walks!'

Silence.

'Let's see . . . music. Music's good. Who sang "Que Sera, Sera"?'

Again, no one replies, but the woman in the knee-high stockings begins to sing the words to the song, and Dad joins in with a few snatches here and there. *Not ours to see . . .*

One Saturday morning I arrive to find Sonia shifting his breakfast tray from the bed. He's hardly eaten a thing.

'Look at all your lovely porridge, Mr Crieve!' she is saying as I enter the room. 'Are those blueberries? And almonds? Goodness me, it's like a five-star hotel in here! Sign me up!'

He is staring dully at the CD player beside his bed. We bought it for him for his birthday, and I lined up all his CDs on his shelves, but he's never touched it. The stickers I wrote for him in red Sharpie – *PLAY* and *PAUSE* and *VOLUME* and *STOP*, with arrows pointing to the right buttons – are peeling away. One day I saw half an After Eight dinner mint in the CD tray. Dom has told me I have to accept that my father isn't the same person any more. I told him I don't have to accept anything.

'Morning, Dad,' I say, kissing his cheek.

'Who are you?' he says.

'Hello,' says Sonia. 'We're just about to have a shower, but you're welcome to wait.'

I still can't get used to seeing her with Dad. Walking and talking, large as life. My brain keeps telling me: this can't be true. She can't be real. When she squeezes past me to get a fresh shirt and trousers from the wardrobe, though, she brushes against my side – warm, solid. No phantom.

'Show Justine your sun-catcher,' she says over her shoulder. 'We had Craft Time yesterday. Look, there it is.'

Hanging in the window, a handful of glass nuggets glued to a transparent plastic lid. Twirling in the spring breeze.

'So where are you from?' I say.

'From here.' She smiles. 'From Auckland. You're Wellington people originally?'

I must look puzzled.

She says, 'Your father talks about Wellington sometimes.'

'Oh,' I say. 'Yes, of course. But that was a long time ago.'

'The blue shirt today, Mr Crieve, with the grey trousers?' She waggles the clothes on their hangers. Far too cheerful.

I'm no good at such dogged simulation of normal life. My father moves his head in her direction but doesn't respond.

'Good choice,' she says.

My tongue feels dry in my mouth, my throat tight, but I have to ask her. I have to know.

'It's been niggling away at me,' I say. 'You remind me of someone.'

'Scarlett Johansson? Jennifer Lawrence?' She winks at Dad.

'A Mrs Price. Angela Price.'

Sonia freezes for a second. 'No,' she says, shaking her head. 'I don't know who you mean.'

'Are you sure?'

She stares at me.

'I'm sorry if it's painful,' I say.

'No,' she says again. Then her hands sink to her sides, the

shirt and trousers collapsing to the floor. 'How do you know that name?'

'She was my teacher.'

She sits down on the bed. Dad is looking at her now too, really looking. The sun-catcher casts shifting patches of green and blue on the heavy-duty carpet.

'So you *are* related to her?' I say.

'Who's asking?' Almost a whisper.

'Just me.'

She nods, gazes at her hands. 'I'm . . . I'm her daughter.'

'Daughter?' says Dad. 'Daughter? Daughter?' The word starts to lose all meaning.

'She let us think that she'd lost her husband and little girl. That you'd died in a car accident.'

Sonia gives a brief, harsh laugh.

'She was so beautiful. You look just like her.'

'So beautiful,' echoes Dad. He does that sometimes; it doesn't mean anything.

'We're nothing alike,' says Sonia. 'Anyway, I hardly remember her.' Is she going to cry?

'I'm sorry,' I begin. 'I shouldn't have—' I pick up the shirt and trousers and hand them to her.

'That poor girl she pushed off the cliff,' she says, shaking her head. 'You must have known her, too.'

'Not very well.'

'Amy Fong – only twelve years old. No one deserves that.'

'Amy, Amy,' says Dad. 'They sold the juiciest stone fruit in town. Stacked them into pyramids. Oh yes, they were the best of friends, those girls.' He stares out the window at a gazebo threaded with well-trained clematis. 'I used to say, Who are you? What business do you have with my daughter?' He laughs. 'A jewel thief, she said. A kidnapper. A long-lost twin. Justine stayed at their place as often as she could. An only child, you see.'

Sonia is watching me as he speaks. Smoothing the sleeves

of the shirt, the legs of the trousers. 'It was you, wasn't it,' she says slowly.

And hasn't this been coming for decades? The great dark hulk of it always adrift in me – butting against my ribs, pushing my heart into a corner. Dom swooping in to stop me from saying anything when I drink too much. Insisting we keep it from Emma. And I have pretended for her sake: of course, my darling, the world is a good place. It is filled with butterflies and dancing and ice cream and hopscotch, and you are quite safe. But sometimes I think I see Amy. A girl with a short black plait, a girl walking a spaniel, running on ahead of me along a twisting track. A stone, falling.

And did Sonia say 'It was you' or 'It *was* you'? Has she known all along? Tracked us down?

She is waiting for me to respond. I nod, and she holds my gaze for a moment. Those same eyes. Those same cheekbones.

'Someone broke into the shop,' says my father. 'Stole all the Royal Doulton teapots. The Hiawatha. The Bird of Paradise. The Jackdaw of Rheims.'

'Oh God,' says Sonia.

'I know!' says Dad. 'In broad daylight, it was.'

'The police will find them for you, don't worry,' I tell him. 'I've had a word.'

'I should think so,' he says. 'They'll want to take fingerprints, I expect?'

But Sonia is breathing hard now, blinking rapidly, and she mutters, 'Excuse me,' and hurries from the room.

'Has *she* got my Doulton?' says Dad. 'Stop her! Catch her!'

'She hasn't stolen anything,' I say.

'Well, somebody has. I don't trust her.'

'She's perfectly innocent, Dad.'

But I go to look for her anyway.

I find her in the staffroom down by the main entrance. She's holding a folder in her lap and pretends to be busy with it when I come in.

'Sonia?'

'You shouldn't be in here.'

I take a seat opposite her. On a chipped coffee table, a pile of glossy brochures show elderly people playing lawn bowls and swimming. On the wall, a laminated sign: *COVER YOUR FOOD OR CLEAN THE MICROWAVE!!!*

'What do you want?' she says.

'I'm not sure.'

She shrugs, flicks through some Fall Risk charts.

'So there was no car crash?'

'No.'

'Why would she let everyone think you'd died?'

She closes the folder. I can see how tightly she's gripping the edges.

'My mother was an addict and a compulsive liar and goodness knows what else. She couldn't tell the truth about the *weather*.'

'I'm sorry,' I say. 'She was one of those people who just pull you into their orbit, you know?'

'Not really.'

'I mean . . . none of us could say no to her. We all wanted her to love us.'

'So you never noticed anything off? Not the tiniest hint?'

I look straight into her eyes. 'Not the tiniest hint.'

She snorts. 'If you say so.'

'Well, I was only twelve.'

She snorts again.

'Did she really hurt her back playing tennis?' I say. 'Is that how it all started, with the pills?'

'Look,' she says. 'She took pills because she wanted to. She stole because she wanted to.'

'Maybe she couldn't stop,' I say.

'Listen to yourself. After everything.'

I sigh, nod.

'Sometimes I worry that it's in me too,' she says, her voice quieter now. 'That it's genetic.'

'No,' I say. 'No. Don't think that.'

'There are studies, though.' She picks at the label on the folder. 'Did she ever . . . talk about me?'

I can hear the longing in her. 'Often,' I say. 'She was always telling me how much she missed you. How pretty you were. She kept a lock of your hair tucked away, and a photo of you and your dad paddling at the beach.'

'Really?'

'Oh yes. They were her most precious possessions.'

'She left me at home on my own when she went to get pills. I think that's my earliest memory – hammering on the front door after she locked it behind her.'

'I'm sorry,' I say again.

'Dad told me he confronted her when he realised what was going on, and she broke down and said it would never happen again, and she'd get help, and nothing was more important to her than us – and he believed her. And then it kept happening.'

'You were three? Four?'

'Four by the time she lost custody. Dad said he was expecting a battle in court, the full *Kramer vs. Kramer*, but she just signed away her rights and moved to Wellington. Reinvented herself. She didn't even fight for me.'

'Did she keep in touch?'

'She sent me a present when I was nearly five, about to start school. A box of half-used notebooks and marker pens that didn't work very well. A cracked pencil sharpener. All the rejects, I suppose. While she was starting over with you.'

I can't apologise again, so I say nothing.

'I came to Wellington once,' she continues. 'When I was twenty. I went to the place where it happened – the school.

I don't know what I expected to find. I never told Dad. He'd . . . lost his way so badly already.'

'Did you follow us here?' I blurt – but another caregiver enters the staffroom. When she sees me sitting there, she raises her eyebrows at Sonia: *You're breaking the rules.*

Sonia gathers up her folder, brushes imaginary crumbs from her lap. 'Thanks for bringing your concerns to me, Justine,' she says. 'I'll be sure we fix that.'

I want to keep talking to her, keep watching the movement of her mouth, her brow, the warm brown glint in her eyes. Trick myself that Mrs Price is back, that the past never happened. I want to know if she suspected before today. But she won't give me that; she is getting to her feet and saying, 'Now, we should see to your father. He's waiting for his shower.'

Back in the room she helps him to his feet, murmuring to him all the while: 'Here we are now, Mr Crieve. You're fine, I've got you. Good. Up we go. That's it, that's it. Yes, I've got you. Well done. Let's get you to the bathroom. This way, this way. Yes. You'll feel better when you're all nice and clean.'

'You're very kind,' he says. 'I'm very lucky.' And then, looking back at me, 'Who's that?'

'That's your daughter Justine.'

'No. She looks nothing like her.'

'What does your daughter look like?' I say.

'Well . . .' he begins, turning to me with halting movements. 'Well . . . curly blond hair. A small frame. Brown eyes.'

He is describing Sonia.

Or Mrs Price.

'She never comes to see me, though,' he continues. 'I think she's gone overseas.'

'Lots of people do these days,' says Sonia, who will be gone herself next time I visit. We'll never see her again.

'What's that?' says Dad, pointing to my wrist.

'Just a bracelet.'

'Let me see.'

I hold out my arm to show him the thing I took and hid when we cleared the house of Mrs Price; the thing that should have been mine anyway. Without knowing who I am, who I really am, he touches the little gold hands with their gold lace cuffs and their tiny gemstone rings. Too lovely to let go.

'Dearest,' he says as Sonia leads him away. 'Dearest.'

Acknowledgements

Thank you to my publishers Fergus Barrowman (Te Herenga Waka University Press) and Christopher Potter (Europa Editions) and their wonderful teams; my editors Jane Parkin and Sarah Ream; my agent Caroline Dawnay and her colleagues at United Agents; and my colleagues at the University of Waikato.

I am grateful to Tusiata Avia, Calvin Beckford, Tracey Devereux, Maria Galikowski, Inspector Ross Grantham, Sarah Page Heady, Brendon Hurley, Fay Joseph, Renee Liang, Rose Lu, Melody May, former Inspector Richard Middleton, Bhaady Miller and Simon Upton, Angela and Philippa Pidd, Harry Rinker, Katrina Rowe, Dr Carol Shand, Tracey Slaughter, Alison Southby, Jude Spier, Chris and Kathy Tse, Tim Upperton, Jonathan Usher, Dirk vandenBerg, Alison Wong, Helene Wong, Matthew Wood and Rachel Zajac.

Special thanks to my sister Helen Mayall; the late Sandy Henderson, headmaster of my primary school; Kat Aitken and Sue Orr for their feedback on the manuscript; and, of course and always, Alan Bekhuis and Alice Chidgey for their support and love.

ABOUT THE AUTHOR

Catherine Chidgey's novels have been published to international acclaim. *Remote Sympathy* was shortlisted for the DUBLIN Literary Award and the Jann Medlicott Acorn Prize for Fiction, and longlisted for the Women's Prize for Fiction. Her first novel, *In a Fishbone Church*, won the Betty Trask Award and was longlisted for the Orange Prize. It also won Best First Book at the New Zealand Book Awards. Her second novel, *Golden Deeds*, was a Notable Book in the *New York Times* and a Best Book in the *LA Times*. Her many awards include the Prize in Modern Letters, the Katherine Mansfield Award, the Katherine Mansfield Fellowship, the Janet Frame Fiction Prize, and the Acorn Foundation Fiction Prize. She lives in Ngāruawāhia, New Zealand, and lectures in Creative Writing at the University of Waikato.